BLACK MIRROR (ETHAN DRAKE BOOK 4)

N. P. MARTIN

N.P. Martin

Black Mirror

Ethan Drake Series Book 4

Copyright © 2020 by N. P. MARTIN

info@npmarin.com

Cover design by Original Book Cover Designs

FREE BOOK

I awoke to a commotion outside my trailer, thinking for a second that the noise was part of the nightmare I'd been having, until I heard a familiar voice pipe up from outside.

"You're killing me here, you little bastards!"

It was Haedemus' voice, though what the hell he was doing at this hour of the morning, I had no idea. Groggy as hell from the whiskey I'd drank to put myself to sleep what seemed like only a few hours ago, I reached for my cigarettes on the little table next to the bed, lighting one before daring to sit up, the bed sheets damp with sweat as usual, even though it was freezing inside the trailer. I sat for a moment half-heartedly smoking my cigarette, the harsh smoke hurting my dry throat as I tried to clear my head of the images left over from my dark dreams. Then Haedemus' accented voice sounded from outside again, jerking me out of my reverie.

"I can't do this," I heard him say, sounding out of breath. "I think I'm going to die, seriously…"

"You already dead, horsey!" another voice shouted—one of the Hellbastards. Cracka.

"Yes…thanks for reminding me," Haedemus all but gasped. "But I still…need to…stay in shape."

Shaking my head, I swung myself out of bed, doing my best to ignore the pounding in my head. Wearing only boxers and a T-shirt, I trudged to the door to see what was going on, wishing I hadn't when the freezing morning air blasted me.

"What the shit?" I said as soon as I saw what was going on outside.

Haedemus was busy running back and forth across the yard while Cracka and Scroteface ran alongside him. Despite not being alive in the conventional sense, Haedemus looked like he was about to die.

"Move it, you lazy horsey!" Cracka was shouting in his tiny voice.

"Feel the burn!" Scroteface said as he ran alongside the Hellicorn. "Feel it, you big galoot!"

"Oh, I'm fucking feeling it!" Haedemus gasped. "I'm feeling it alright! Oh, god—Ethan." He stopped when he noticed me watching and did his best to straighten up and look like he wasn't about to collapse. "How long have you… been standing there?"

"Long enough," I said, taking a drag of my cigarette. "What the fuck is going on here? Are you…*exercising?*"

"We trying to get him fit, boss," Cracka said.

"Like Rocky," Scroteface said. "Do you know where we can find a chicken?"

"What for?" I said.

"So fat horsey can chase it like Rocky," Cracka said.

"Hey!" Haedemus said. "Watch it! This horsey is not fat, I'll have you know. I'm just big-boned."

"You eat too much human meat," Scroteface said.

"You fat piggy!" Cracka said.

"Fuck you, Crackers," Haedemus said. "If you hadn't

already run me into the ground, I'd chase you around this fucking yard."

"Fat piggy! Fat piggy!" Cracka giggled to himself as he danced around Haedemus.

"Ethan," Haedemus whined. "Please tell him."

"Tell him what?" I asked.

"That I'm not fat," he said. "I may have overindulged my eating habits lately, but I am not fat. Am I?"

"Well," I said. "I didn't think it was possible—"

"Don't you say it, Ethan, don't you fucking say it—"

"—you seemed to have filled out a little...a lot, actually."

"Oh, god!" Haedemus moaned. "I'm fat!"

"You don't seem as decayed as you were," I said. "Has Hannah done something to you?"

"Come to think of it," Haedemus said, "I felt a spark when she touched me a while ago. Do you think she's passed on her celestial energy to me somehow?" He paused for a second, then said, "Oh my god! Do you think I might be...*alive*?"

"You still smell like you're dead," Scroteface drawled.

"Shut up, ball-sack!" Haedemus snapped at him. "No one asked you."

"Smelly horsey," Cracka snickered.

"Oh god, do I really smell?" Haedemus said, looking even more worried now. "Ethan, I may have to borrow your cologne."

"I don't do cologne," I said.

"Then maybe you should," another voice said. It was Hannah, walking towards us as she passed the towers of crushed scrap metal that were stacked everywhere in cubes.

"Ha-ha," I said as I tossed the butt of my cigarette away. "Haedemus is getting fat. He says it's all your fault."

"My fault?" Hannah said as she came to stand by my

trailer, dressed in a dark pantsuit, her hair tied neatly in a ponytail.

"Yes, your fault, woman," Haedemus said. "I was once a thoroughbred and now look at me. I have a gut the size of Ethan's ego."

"*My* ego?" I said.

"I fail to see how your minuscule weight gain is my fault, Haedemus," Hannah said, smiling in bemusement.

"You must have done something to me," Haedemus said. "You must have infected me with your angel energy or something. Sometimes I think I can feel my heart beating. It's not normal, I tell you."

Hannah shook her head. "I don't think I did. Not as far as I know, anyway."

"Who the hell cares?" I said grumpily, only wanting my morning coffee and Mud now. "You're a fucking Hellbeast who isn't in Hell anymore. Changes are inevitable. Deal with it. I'll buy you a Jane Fonda workout DVD or something. Or better yet, a few sessions with a shrink, you neurotic motherfucker."

"Fuck you, Ethan," Haedemus snapped. "I hope your dick falls off."

"In this fucking cold, it just might," I said. "I'm going inside to get ready for work. Keep working those abs, fat boy."

"Keep banging your balls against Hannah's ass, Ethan!" he shouted back as I turned and went inside the trailer, shaking my head at his comment as Hannah followed in behind me, sliding her arms around my waist.

"So what do you say, big boy?" she said. "You wanna bang your balls against my ass or what?" She laughed after she said it, but I knew she was serious.

Turning, I cupped her face in my hands and kissed her on the mouth. "Maybe later. We'll be late for work otherwise, and you know how the new boss feels about tardiness."

"I don't think Director Bradley would mind all that much," she said as she began rubbing my cock through my boxers, a smile on her face as she did so. "He gave us carte blanche to do what we wanted. More or less."

"I haven't even had a coffee yet," I said, turning away from her. "You want one?"

"No thanks." The mild annoyance in her voice made me wish we had just stayed partners. Now I felt obligated to show her affection, which I wasn't good at. If my ex-wife weren't dead, she would whole-heartedly agree. "I'll get one on the way."

"Is Daisy up yet?" I asked her, changing the subject.

"I never checked her trailer. Do you think I should?"

"We'll both check on her before we leave."

"I'm worried about her," Hannah said as she pushed past me, grabbing a cup, spooning instant coffee into it and then filling it with water from the tap. As she held the cup, a faint light glowed in her hand, and a second later, steam rose from the cup.

"Thanks," I said as she passed me the now hot coffee after giving it a quick stir with a stained spoon. "Daisy is still grieving. It's only been a month since she lost her mother."

"She barely comes out of her trailer, and when she does, it's to work in the smithy. I've never seen anyone beat steel with so much conviction."

I shrugged as I sipped my coffee. "It gives her something to focus on. It's what she needs."

"Have you mentioned the adoption to her yet?"

I shook my head. "Not yet. It feels a bit soon, to be honest. For the time being, I think she's just glad she has somewhere safe to be so she can work things out in her head."

"I just want her to be okay."

"Yeah, we all do. And she will be."

"Even with everything that's going on with her?"

5

"The Joan of Arc thing, you mean?"

"Yes."

"She seems to be handling it okay."

Hannah sat down on the couch as I hovered by the door. Outside, Haedemus was continuing with his workout, egged on by the two Hellbastards. "There seems to be many like her around these days," she said. "Going by the one's we've dealt with recently, most of them don't seem that stable. I don't think humans were built to handle such power. It's too much for most of them, and the ones that do handle it, end up corrupted by it. Like that guy Hickman we brought in a couple weeks ago. How corrupted was he by his powers?"

Ajay Hickman was a middle-aged science genius before the concentration of celestial energy here awakened something in him, and he became his own version of Hephaestus, Greek God of blacksmiths, craftsmen, and volcanoes. What Hickman ended up doing was devising traps to ensnare other Mytholites—or Supernormals, as Director Bradley calls them—whom he hated, killing nearly a dozen of them by the time we caught up to him. Upon his arrest, Hickman admitted he had been seeing what he called a "brain mechanic," a psychiatrist by the name of Adrian Tanner. Upon further investigation, Hannah and I discovered that Tanner was working with several other psychiatrists that specialized in "treating" these Supernormals.

"Hickman's behavior was mostly down to what his shrink was telling him," I said. "Before he started seeing Tanner, Hickman didn't exhibit any deviant behavior. The shrink made him fucking crazy."

"If only we could prove that," Hannah said.

"We'll prove it."

"And if we don't?"

I stared at her. "Then we take matters into our hands. It's a dangerous world out there. Accidents happen."

Hannah smiled and shook her head a little. "I'm glad to

see joining the FBI hasn't changed your sense of morality any."

"Sense of justice, you mean. These fucks deserve what's coming to them, you know that. And anyway, it's *your* presence here—along with all the other Fallen—that's created these Supernormals. What does your sense of morality say about *that*?"

She stared at me for a moment before looking away. "I can't help who I am."

"Neither can they, the Mytholites, I mean. And as far as Daisy goes, we're gonna be here to help and guide her through everything, and to make sure she stays on the right path."

"It's dubious whether we're on the right path at all," Hannah said.

"Fuck it," I said, pouring the rest of my coffee down the drain. "It's the path we're meant to be on. Otherwise, we wouldn't be on it, would we?"

"Careful there, Ethan. You're starting to sound like you trust God's plan, or that he even has a plan for you."

After retrieving my cigarettes, I lit one up and stood by the sink for a minute. "When you came back to me that time in Yagami's place, I felt a higher power in the room, a greater presence filtered through you, or at least through your celestial form. It affected me."

"How?"

"It made me feel differently about my life and everything I've experienced. I still hate God for taking Callie away from me, but…" I trailed off, hardly knowing what I wanted to say.

"It's okay," Hannah said, reaching out and taking the rest of the cigarette off of me. "You don't need to explain it. Any relationship with God is complicated and not readily explainable. I think that's how He likes it."

"So we can't question His motives?"

She shrugged. "God is knowable only to Himself. Along with the rest of my kind, I quickly found that out. We learned not to question Him."

"Convenient, don't you think? Sounds like a dictatorship to me."

"Ever the cynic," she said, a smile crossing her face.

"It's what keeps me alive, baby," I said, smiling along with her. "That and good whiskey."

Hannah shook her head at me. "Get dressed. We're going to be late."

I went into the small bedroom and emerged five minutes later dressed in my usual attire of dark slacks, light shirt with black tie, and a brand new tan trench coat. Contrary to popular belief, FBI agents do not dress in black suits all the time. The white-collar crime guys do, but the rest dress according to the environment in which they work. As I'm basically doing the same job as I did as a cop, I continued to dress as I did before. Besides, Hannah and I were not regular agents. We were more like specialists who did our own thing, but we still carried a badge.

In the kitchen, I opened a cupboard and took out a large Mud jar and filled up a dropper bottle with the murky liquid, dropping a dose into my mouth before putting the dropper bottle into my trench pocket. The Mud hit me straight away, and I felt my body relax under its influence. Hannah was staring at me when I turned around. "What?"

"Just as well we don't get drug tested," she said, standing up.

"I wouldn't care if we did or not. Mud doesn't show up on any test."

"I thought you were cutting back on that stuff."

"That was before."

"Before what?"

"Everything."

From a drawer, I took out my gun and holster and

clipped the holster onto my belt. Then I found my ID wallet and slipped it into my trench pocket.

"Are you still having those nightmares?" Hannah asked me as I stood to light a cigarette. "You look like you haven't slept properly in weeks."

I stared at her for a moment before nodding. "I'm still plagued by them every night."

"Are you still dreaming of the same shadow figure?"

"Yeah."

I took a drag of my cigarette, only wanting to get going, but I knew if I didn't indulge her concern now, she would only bring up the nightmares again later. I'd been having the dreams for about a month now, most of them featuring the Shadow Man as I nicknamed the bastard—a dark, featureless figure that seemed to take great delight in orchestrating various nightmare scenarios every night, many of them featuring my dead wife and daughter, others drawing upon long-buried memories for inspiration, twisting them into frightening and grueling ordeals. I was at the stage now where I felt haunted. My gut was telling me it was the Spreak who had had my family killed. I hadn't seen him since that night in the alley, but I was thinking maybe the bastard was infiltrating my dreams, trying to drive me crazy. I had only come to this conclusion recently once I realized it was the same figure showing up in my dreams. I could be wrong. It might not be the Spreak at all. It might just be my messed up mind that has created this Shadow Man—this Nightmare Man. Lord knows, there's enough darkness in me to create such a figure; enough pain and guilt for such a figure to emerge from, come to punish me for my sins.

"I wish you would let me help you," Hannah said. "I think I might be able to look inside your mind and—"

"Forget it," I said. "I told you before, no one gets inside my head, especially not—"

"Me? I don't think you have anything to be ashamed about, Ethan. I wouldn't judge."

"I said no."

"You won't let me look inside your head, but you let Richard Solomon in there when it suits you?"

"Yeah, when it suits me. When I need something from him."

"You don't trust me?"

My eyes closed for a second as I shook my head. "Of course I trust you. Don't bust my balls, Hannah."

"Well, just to point out, someone already is in your head, and I think we both know who it is. You need to get him out of there, Ethan, before he destroys you."

I nodded. "I'll figure something out. Come on, let's go to work."

Hannah didn't seem satisfied by my response as I brushed past her, which I expected. This wasn't the first time she had pulled me about the nightmares, and it wouldn't be last. She was concerned, I understood that. But I would handle things myself.

On the way out, I glanced at the picture of Cal hanging on the wall, and almost heard his voice in my head saying, "You ain't learned shit, have you, son?"

Piss off, Cal.

Outside, Haedemus appeared to be alone now as he stood staring glumly down at the ground.

"You okay, Haedemus?" Hannah asked him.

"Not really," he said. "I think I'm depressed."

"What about?" I said. "Your weight? You look exactly the same. I was just messing with you earlier."

"I know," he said, walking toward us, coming to stand by me. "It's not that."

"Then what is it?" I asked him, frowning, as I'd never seen him so down in the dumps.

Haedemus sighed before answering. "It's this world. I

don't know who to be in it, or even what to do in it. Hell was easy. At least I knew my place there. But here...I don't know who I am here."

Patting him on the side of his thick neck, I said, "Don't worry, buddy. None of us knows who we are here. We're all just floating around aimlessly like motes of dust, waiting to die."

Haedemus blinked as he stared at me. "Was that nugget of wisdom supposed to make me feel better, Ethan? Because I can tell you, it didn't."

"I think what Ethan meant to say was that you are not alone, Haedemus," Hannah said. "Right, Ethan?"

"Yeah, sure," I said. "We're here for you, buddy."

"At least sound like you mean it, Ethan."

"Jesus, I do mean it."

"Then lay of that Mud stuff. It makes you emotionally detached."

"That's kinda the point of it."

"Maybe I should start taking it then. Do you think it would work on me?"

"You don't need any substance, Haedemus," Hannah said. "What you need is a purpose."

"A purpose?" Haedemus' thick, half-rotted lips moved as he appeared to mull this over. "My purpose was once to be your faithful servant, when you were Xaglath. But now Xaglath is gone, so where does that leave me? I can't even say I'm Ethan's sidekick, since he hardly takes me anywhere these days." His nostrils flared as he sniffed. "Oh god, my life is meaningless, joyless, filled with—"

"Oh, for Christ's sake," I exclaimed, interrupting him. "Just get a fucking grip, will ya? You're clearly just going through some shit, like all of us do sometimes. Go take a walk or something, focus on something else besides yourself."

Haedemus glared at me. "Honestly, Ethan, you sorely

lack in the sensitivity department. I spill my guts about my existential crisis, and you tell me to go take a fucking walk? That response was *sooo* lacking in compassion, even for you, Ethan."

"And this is why I became a soldier and not a shrink," I said, walking away now. "Hannah, sort him out."

"Yes, walk away, Ethan," Haedemus called after me. "If it can't be fixed, then fuck it, right?"

"I'll get you some Prozac while I'm out."

"Yeah? Get some for yourself as well. And don't forget the fucking personality transplant, you fucking insensitive prick!"

Shaking my head at Haedemus' angry outburst, I got inside the 1970 Chevrolet Chevelle LS6 that I'd been driving now for the last two weeks, my old Dodge having finally packed in and sitting with the rest of the scrap cars in the east side of the yard. The Chevelle was one that Cal had been restoring, though he died before he got a chance to give it a proper paint job. As it was, the car had patches of primer all over its black exterior. At some point, I would get the car a new paint job, if only because I knew Cal would hate me driving it around in the state it was currently in.

Starting the Chevelle's 450 HP engine, I turned on the radio just as Ministry's "N.W.O." came on, and I sang along as I waited on Hannah. "I'm in love without the tears of regret, Open fire 'cause I love it to death, Sky high with a heartache of stone, You'll never see me 'cause I'm always alone…"

Before I could get to the chorus, though, something up ahead caught my attention. A figure standing between two towers of cubed scrap metal. The figure was too far away to make out any features, but it appeared to be a woman going by the long hair and small build. But there was something else about the figure that disturbed me, like it was familiar somehow. When I blinked, the figure disappeared, leaving me to wonder if I hadn't imagined it. Maybe the Mud or my lack of sleep was causing my mind to play tricks on me, which wouldn't be the first time.

Hannah climbed into the front passenger seat a moment later. "You've upset Haedemus," she said. "He thinks you don't care about him anymore, if, quote, you ever did, unquote."

I couldn't help a slight laugh. "Jesus Christ…"

"I've never seen him this bad. I'm not sure what to do about it."

"Can't you summon him a female Hellicorn or something?"

Hannah stared at me for a second to see if I was serious, which I was. "I don't know, maybe. I've never thought about it."

"Maybe you should. Seems to me, old Haedemus is just lonely. Though, I'm not sure if I could stick listening to another Hellicorn. Are they all as mouthy as him?"

"Some are, some aren't. There aren't that many, actually."

I put the car in gear and drove through the yard toward the main gates. "Let's just see how it goes. In the meantime, let's grab a couple of coffees from that fancy place in Westhurst."

"But we're already late for work."

"Well," I said as I pulled out onto the street, "ten more minutes won't hurt then, will it?"

D irector Raymond Bradley wasn't exactly straight with me when we first met. He told me the FBI was putting together a team to combat the supernatural influences in the city. What Bradley neglected to tell me, and which I later found out, is that the FBI already has such a team in place.

More than a team, the Bureau has a full-scale organization operating in secret behind the veil of the official Bureau. This "second Bureau" as Bradley called it, comprised hundreds of agents and administration staff, with the main headquarters being in Washington, and branches spread out across the country in nearly every state. The organization went by the name of "Special Affairs," and was initially conceived in the eighties as an anti-subversive group, before branching out into all things supernatural. As Director, Bradley oversaw the whole of Special Affairs, and answered only to the FBI's Bureau Chief, who was under pressure not to ask too many questions. As such, Special Affairs retained almost total autonomy.

Bradley walked me through the Special Affairs building in Bankhurst as he explained the whole organization to me, and as he did, my face gradually dropped until I smiled to myself and shook my head as though Bradley was shitting me. The more he explained about Special Affairs, the more it all sounded painfully familiar. Within the organization was different departments, and Bradley insinuated that there were even different factions within each department. He didn't have to tell me that each of these departments and factions had their own agenda and were undoubtedly working more toward advancing their own interests rather than the interests of the organization. I'd seen it all before, and I eventually stopped outside Bradley's plush office and said, "I can't so this. Not again."

Bradley had frowned at me for a second before nodding as if he understood. "Ah," he said. "You think we're just another Blackstar, don't you?"

"I think you're just Blackstar with a badge."

Bradley had smiled, taking no offense. Not that I had cared if he did or not. "You don't want to be a part of what we've built here? You don't wish to use your unique skill set for the betterment of mankind?"

No, I'd told him. I'd done my time as a cog in somebody else's wheel, both with Blackstar, and to a lesser extent, with the FPD. Standing there and looking out at all the people working busily in the massive office space—many of them throwing me suspicious looks—I knew I couldn't be a part of Bradley's organization. Going solo as a PI seemed like a better—like the *only*—option to me.

Telling Bradley thanks, but no thanks, I walked away from him.

But as I did, he said, "What if I offer you complete autonomy?"

I stopped and turned around. "I've heard that before," I told him. "That just means you have the option of tossing me to the wolves when shit inevitably goes belly up."

"Not at all," Bradley had said. "I assure you, Ethan, I

protect all of my agents like they were my own kin. Ask anyone here. I've thrown no one to the wolves. Whatever your past experiences are, that's not what we do here."

"Well, forgive me if I don't take your word for it."

"So don't. You and your partner come work for me, and I will, as I said, give you complete autonomy. You will, of course, answer to me, but I won't stand in your way, and you will have access to the vast resources we have built up here. You can pick and choose which cases you work. You will also be paid handsomely, with as many benefits as you can handle. You will want for nothing here. Try it for a month, and if you don't like it, then you can leave with no hard feelings."

"And what do you get out of the deal?"

"I get the benefit of your extensive experience and your partner's unique perspective and abilities. That's enough for me."

"How would you know what experience I have? Most of it isn't on file."

Bradley smiled. "I don't need to see any file. I can see it in your eyes. That's good enough for me."

Hannah and I joined Special Affairs and got our badges a few days later. I had to admit, it was weird carrying an FBI badge, for it was an organization I thought I'd never be a part of, especially given my history with Blackstar. I also couldn't help wondering if Wendell Knightsbridge had his hooks in Special Affairs as he did with the official FBI. Time would tell on that score.

It was now almost 9.00 a.m. on a Monday morning in late January as Hannah and I entered the Special Affairs Department (SAD) building, going through security, before making our way up to the top floor. Unlike the setup I had going with Commissioner Lewellyn, we weren't relegated to the basement this time, out of sight of everyone as we came and went like rats from their hole. No, this time, we had our own spacious office just down the hall from the Director himself. It was a gesture on Bradley's part, a way for him to assuage any fears I had about being some expendable asset that should hardly ever be seen or heard from, kept hidden like a dirty secret as Lewellyn did with us.

Bradley, to his credit, called together everyone in the building on the first day we started so he could announce that Hannah and I would be joining the team as "special investigators," which I thought all SAD agents were, anyway. But I knew what Bradley was doing. He was highlighting our experience and skill sets, which like it or not, set us apart from most of the other agents, who had a very two-dimensional view of things, as I later found out from speaking with a few of them. It was flattering, being given so much credit, but also uncomfortable because I saw the look on most everyone's face as they stood staring at us, a look I'd seen before on the faces of the cops I worked with, and which said: who the fuck does this guy think he is? I was well used to such animosity, so I didn't let it bother me. I don't think Hannah did either, who smiled at everyone like she was happy to be there.

On the door to our office was a plaque that said SPECIAL INVESTIGATIONS. The office was medium-sized with large windows on two sides that afforded a generous view of the city that stretched all the way to Puritan Bay and the ocean beyond—a stark contrast to the damp walls of the FPD subbasement.

Bradley had also set us up with a desk each, and a computer that gave us access to the FBI database, as well as SAD's own database, which held information on the Occult Underground in Fairview, and in every other city in America too. Much like the CIA, SAD also had offices across the world, so the database contained information on MURK activity in other countries. Not that I paid the various databases much attention. If I needed information, there was only one place I could go where I knew I would get everything I needed and more, and that was Artemis' and Pan Demic's place. And speaking of the Terrible Twosome, I'd be paying them a visit soon. They'd been off on vacation of late, so I hadn't seen them in a few weeks.

Since joining SAD, Hannah and I had been working on cases involving the so-called Supernormals. Director Bradley seemed to be more worried about this new breed of powered beings than the established MURKs in the city. The Supernormals were rapidly increasing in number in Fairview and the surrounding areas, but they were also popping up in other cities across the country, and throughout the world.

For whatever reason, Fairview had a higher concentration of celestial energy, with a more significant number of Fallen than anywhere else. When the Fallen escaped from Hell and tumbled through the Maelstrom surrounding it before falling to Earth, they exited, mostly, here in Fairview. No one knew why, according to Hannah, who explained to both me and Bradley that the exit points from the Maelstrom appeared to be entirely random. The legions of Fallen could just as easily have landed anywhere else in the world. But they didn't. They landed here in Fairview in their droves, bringing their celestial energy with them. I doubt even they could have foreseen the effect their natural energy would have on the human population. Though thinking about it, this is perhaps why God forbid the Elohim from interacting with His creations in the first place, and also maybe why He banished the rebel Elohim, who at the end of the day, desired such interaction with us humans.

In any case, the Supernormals were on the rise, and so was the trouble they brought with them. Many couldn't handle their powers and ended up leaving a trail of self-destructive behavior in their wake that affected the Unawares around them also. SAD had found itself managing many clean-up operations of late as they struggled to keep the existence of these Supernormals under wraps, which was becoming increasingly difficult. Go on YouTube, and you'll find a slew of videos purporting to show footage of people doing stuff that no normal human should be able to do—feats of strength and agility, conjurations, transformations, displays of psychic powers, teleportation and other "magical" tricks. Most of these videos were viewed as no more than entertainment—deep fakes that nobody took seriously.

Only enough people were taking it all seriously that an underground movement was forming. A movement that sought to bring these "superheroes" out into the light by drawing online attention to them. It was a small enough movement at this point not to be too worried about, but soon enough, it would grow the more people came to believe in it.

Luckily for us, there were still more skeptics and cynics out there than believers. And besides, just like with the established Occult Underground, people turned a blind eye to things outside of their sphere of understanding. Even when an Unaware saw the impossible with their own eyes, they inevitably explained it away for the sake of their sanity. And even if they believed, most were too apathetic to even care. They might discuss it, maybe on Facebook or some other sacred online sanctuary, but they wouldn't take proactive action against what they saw. Sheep only care about grazing, not protesting.

Which left organizations like SAD to pay full attention to these new Supernormals, and to do something about them. It's also where Hannah and I came in.

"Good morning," Director Bradley said as he entered the Special Investigations office. "Heavy traffic was there?"

I nodded as I sorted through various folders on my desk. "Something like that."

Bradley stared at the coffee cup on my desk. "More like there was a queue at the bistro down the street."

"Ethan insisted, sir," Hannah said with a slight smirk on her face. "You know how he is about his morning coffee."

I threw Hannah a look as she smiled at me. "Anyone would think you're angling for a promotion, Walker, sucking up to the boss like that."

"I'm off-setting your air of anti-authoritarianism, Drake," she said, shuffling papers. "Lest the Director fire us over you being a rebel and all, coming in late just because you wanted coffee from a certain bistro."

I shook my head at her as she smiled. "Anti-authoritarianism, huh? We're all about the big words today, aren't we? Let's see if you know this one: sycophantic."

"Are you saying I'm a sycophant?" Hannah asked with mock offense. "I can't help it if we have the absolute best boss in the world, can I?"

I laughed to myself as I opened up a case file. "Shut up, Walker."

"Get to work, Drake."

"Alright," Bradley said, hovering between the two desks now. "When you two are finished ribbing each other——"

"I wish, sir," I said.

"Ethan, Jesus…" Hannah said, shaking her head and smiling. "And it's not like I didn't offer earlier."

Bradley mashed his lips together for a second as if we were testing his patience. "Anyway," he said. "I came in to get an update on the psychiatrist ring case, since I've been away in Washington the last few days."

"Well, sir," Hannah said, always eager to get stuck in. "We've identified three different psychiatrists that might be involved. All three have links to Supernormal patients who have gone…off the reservation."

"Off the reservation?" I said. "Four of these Mytholites

have killed people. One of them blew up a goddamn building with people in it."

"I take it you've spoken with these psychiatrists?" Bradley said, looking at me, his blue eyes as keen as always.

"Yeah, we have," I said.

"Our conversations didn't yield much as you might expect," Hannah said. "All three shrinks basically stonewalled us. They feigned innocence, of course, but—"

"It was fucking obvious they knew what they were doing," I said. "These bastards are winding up these Mytholites to near breaking point, before sending them out to cause carnage and take their own lives."

"Are we any closer to finding out who the ringleader of this twisted group is?" Bradley asked.

"Not yet, sir," Hannah said. "The shrinks are obviously not saying much, and of the four Supernormals we linked to the shrinks, three are dead, and the fourth is...unavailable. I'm sure you read the report."

"I didn't, actually. That's why I'm here. What happened to the fourth?"

"Medically speaking, he's comatose," I said. "But we think he may be stuck in some self-inflicted mind-loop."

"A Hell of his own making," Hannah said. "We're pretty sure the shrink he was seeing convinced him he deserved to be punished somehow. It's becoming clear that that's what they do, these shrinks. They convince the Supernormals— who are already at a low ebb—that they are worthless and a scourge on society, and that they should kill themselves."

"Preferably taking other Supernormals with them," I said. "The guy who used his powers to blow up the derelict tenement building did so because several other Supernormals were using the building as a sanctuary of sorts, and as a meeting ground according to one source who escaped the blast."

Bradley frowned as a disturbed look came over his face. "A meeting ground? Are you saying the Supernormals are organizing now?"

"I'd say it was inevitable, sir," I said, about to reach for my cigarettes when I remembered there was no smoking in the building, much to my annoyance. Sometimes I longed for the eighties, when everybody smoked everywhere. "The Supernormals are no different from all the other MURKs. They organize for various reasons, strength in numbers being chief among them."

"I'm not sure I like the idea of so many powered people getting together," Bradley said. "I don't think the President would either."

"It's early days, sir," I said, holding a pen between two fingers as a poor substitute for a cigarette. "Most of these Supernormals are far too messed up in the head to be organizing anything. It would give most of them trouble just organizing their own thoughts. Most would also adhere to secrecy purely out of fear of being found out."

"Well, I hope you're right, Ethan," Bradley said. "In the meantime, don't get too comfortable behind your desks. We just got word of a disturbance in Bricktown, the blue-collar residential district."

"My old neighborhood," I said with little fondness. "What's going on?"

"It's a domestic disturbance," Bradley said.

"And what does that have to do with us?"

"An Ajay Singh lives there with his wife, Kavita," Bradley said. "A few days ago, he called social services for assistance with his wife, who he said was behaving strangely, locking herself away with the couple's six-month-old child, neglecting the child's needs. Social services weren't able to reach Mrs. Singh, so they called the local police. The officers broke down the door to the bedroom where Mrs. Singh had locked herself in. They found the woman to be stable, and social services deemed the child to be safe."

"In other words," I said, "neither the cops nor social services wanted the hassle, so they left."

"Yes," Bradley said. "Though the social worker made an official report, and in it, she remarked about Mrs. Singh's strange behavior."

"Strange how?" Hannah asked, now leaning against the edge of her desk.

"Mrs. Singh was apparently speaking in a language that clearly wasn't native to her," Bradley said. "The social worker also told one of our agents when we followed up that Mrs. Singh's skin had a strange tone to it. A blue tone."

"Blue?" Hannah said. "That is strange. Could she be one of the Fallen?"

"It's possible, I suppose," Bradley said, his eyes lingering on Hannah for a second as if he had just realized she was one of the Fallen herself, a look which appeared to make Hannah uncomfortable as she shifted her weight slightly on the desk.

"What language was she speaking?" I asked.

"We're not sure," Bradley said. "The social worker described it as 'archaic' in her report."

"Archaic, huh?" I said. "Maybe she's possessed by some MURK."

"That's what I want you to find out," Bradley said. "Twenty minutes ago, the FPD received a call from Mr. Singh saying his wife is out of control and threatening to hurt their baby. I expect the police are there now at the apartment. I'd like you and Hannah to check it out. Whatever is going on with Mrs. Singh, I don't think a couple of uniforms from the local PD would be equipped to handle it. They may just make matters worse, in fact, pushing the woman over the edge, forcing her to hurt her baby."

"What do you want us to do, sir?" Hannah asked, standing and ready to go. "Should we bring her in?"

"Yes," Bradley said, "but only if you think she's a Supernormal."

"What if it's something else?" I asked.

"Deal with it as best you can," Bradley said. "Protect the child and make sure Mrs. Singh doesn't hurt anyone, especially herself."

"And what if Mrs. Singh is just crazy?" I said, putting on my trench.

"Then call the relevant authorities and have her picked up," Bradley said as he headed toward the door. "Keep me informed and let me know what happens."

"Yes, sir," I said as Bradley left the room, before turning to Hannah and saying, "Let's go to Bricktown."

3

Most of Bricktown is a warren of tall tenements, and I didn't miss living there. Since taking up residence at the scrap yard, I've come to enjoy the relative peace and quiet, especially at night, when I don't have to listen to sirens and screaming and gunshots constantly. The Hellbastards missed Bricktown because it was a haven of opportunity for them, what with all the dealers and degenerates they could prey upon. The Hellbastards complained that they had to travel to get to good hunting grounds now, as if I cared.

"Pull up here," I told Hannah as we approached a block-wide tenement. Hannah was driving, because frankly, I was having a minor trouble focusing. Weeks of disturbed sleep had taken its toll on me, and what with still grieving over Cal, my head was all over the place, with frequent dizzy spells making it hard for me to even do anything half the time, including driving. The Mud helped a little, but it had its own side-effects, chief among them being hallucinations.

As Hannah pulled up outside the tenement behind a parked patrol car, I swore I saw the same figure that I'd seen in the scrap yard earlier. The figure stood down the street while people moved around her as if she wasn't there. Even though I couldn't make out her face, there was something deeply familiar about her.

"Ethan? Are you alright?"

I turned my head away from the woman in the street to find Hannah staring at me with a look of concern on her face—the same look I'd seen countless times since Cal died.

I nodded as I looked out the window again to find that the woman had gone. Perhaps just a hallucination after all.

"I'm fine," I said, opening the door. "Let's go see what's happening."

The Singh's door was open when Hannah and I went inside the tenement. A slightly built man in his early thirties with black hair stood in the cramped living room along with two uniforms who weren't much older than Mr. Singh. Down the hall, coming from one of the other rooms, I could hear a woman's voice shouting in a language I couldn't make out. It might've been Hindi, or some ancient form of it. The two uniforms stared at us for a second until I flashed my ID at them.

"We can take it from here, boys," I told them.

"Wait," one of them said. "Don't I know you?"

"You fucking should," said the other cop, smiling now as if in the presence of some celebrity. "That's Ethan Drake."

The other cop stared at me. "Holy shit. You're the one who caught the Ripper Tripper and dumped his body on the Chief's desk."

"The Captain's desk," I corrected him.

"Well, Edwards is Chief now, so…"

"Edward's is the new Chief of Police?" I said, shaking my head like I wasn't surprised. "So who's Captain now?"

"Jim Routman, if you can believe that," the smallest of the cops said.

I shook my head again as a smile crossed my face. "Fucking Routman."

"Yeah, fucking Routman. So you're FBI now, huh?"

"Seems that way," I said, putting my ID away. "This is my partner, Agent Walker."

"I didn't call the FBI," Mr. Singh said, frowning now in confusion. "Are you here to take my wife away? What about our baby? You can't take our baby…"

"Relax, Mr. Singh," Hannah said as she stood beside him. "No one is going to take your baby away from you. We're just here to make sure everyone is safe, that's all."

Mr. Singh still looked confused. Much like me, he looked like he hadn't slept properly in months, with dark circles under his tired, bloodshot eyes. "I don't know how much more I can take. My wife, she's…" He trailed off as he shook his head.

"It's okay, Mr. Singh," Hannah said. "Why don't you come and sit down and tell me about your wife?"

As Mr. Singh sat with Hannah, I turned to the two uniforms. "Has the wife made an appearance?" I asked them quietly.

The taller of the two cops shook his head. "She's locked herself in the nursery with the baby. Refuses to come out. She sounds hysterical to me. You know how women get after they have babies. Hormones all over the place."

"Yeah," I said, glancing at Mr. Singh, who didn't appear to have heard the cop's considered, professional opinion on his wife. "Thanks guys. You can go now. We'll take it from here. Tell Routman I said hi."

When the two uniforms left, I made my way down the hall to the nursery, standing by the door for a moment as I listened in. It sounded like Mrs. Singh was pacing the room as she muttered to herself in that Hindi-esque language, which I was thinking now might be Sanskrit. That she appeared to be speaking the language fluently told me there was something up with her. It was looking likely she was another Mytholite. Least that's what my gut told me. It was possible she had been possessed by a demon, and the demon was now freaking out as it struggled to adjust to its new human vessel. To make matters worse, the baby was constantly crying, which was probably elevating Mrs. Singh's stress levels even more. For the sake of the baby, I knew we would have to get in there soon.

"Mrs. Singh?" I said, knocking the door. "My name is Agent Drake. I'm with the FBI. Is there any chance you can open the door so we can talk?"

"Go away!" was the screeched response from inside.

"Mrs. Singh, all we want to do is talk to you and make sure your baby is okay."

"I said, go away and leave me alone! You have no business asking about my baby! My baby is mine! Mine!"

After a moment, I crouched down and looked through the keyhole to see a gloomy nursery room, exposed to the elements blowing through the open window, by billowing, tattered curtains. I could also just make out Mrs. Singh as she sat in the corner, now singing a hushed nursery rhyme, which appeared to settle the baby.

Sighing, I walked away from the door and went back into the living room. "Your wife sounds extremely agitated," I said to Mr. Singh as he sat beside Hannah on the couch. "Do you have any idea what's going on with her?"

"Mr. Singh was just telling me how worried he is for his wife and their baby," Hannah said as the man sat with tears running down his face.

"I don't know what's wrong with her," he said, distraught as hell, and rightly so, given the situation. "She was fine until she gave birth to Felicia. Then a few weeks later, the rage outbursts started. She just couldn't control herself, to the point where—" He stopped and dropped his head as if in shame.

"Did you your wife get violent?" Hannah asked him.

Mr. Singh nodded.

"Did she get violent with *you*?" I asked him.

Again, he nodded, bursting into more tears as he covered his eyes with one hand. "She doesn't mean it," he blubbered. "It's not her fault. There's something…something wrong with her."

"Has she hurt your baby in any way?" Hannah asked.

Mr. Singh shook his head. "No, but I'm afraid she will. She's gotten worse lately, ever since she started seeing that psychiatrist."

Hannah and I looked at each other. "What psychiatrist?" Hannah asked.

Sniffing loudly, Mr. Singh wiped his tears and tried to compose himself, not doing an outstanding job of it. The man was a wreck. I knew how he felt. "After Felicia was born, Kavita went off the rails, so I suggested she see someone. She would fly into the rages, as I said, and her eyes…" Mr. Singh stared hard at the floor for a second as if he was seeing his wife's face in his mind. "I swear I saw fires burning in her eyes. At times, when her rage would peak, I barely recognized her. Her face, her hair, even her skin would seem different. It was like she was—"

"Someone else?" Hannah offered.

"Yes," Mr. Singh said, nodding. "It pains me to say this about my wife, but sometimes she comes across as a…as a monster."

Again, Hannah and I exchanged glances, and I raised my eyebrows at her before addressing Mr. Singh. "So what happened with this psychiatrist your wife went to see?"

"There were two," Mr. Singh said. "The first she only saw a few times before coming home one day saying the doctor was useless, and that he didn't get her condition, or what she was feeling. The first doctor put Kavita's condition down to a bad case of post-natal depression, which Kavita didn't buy. Then one day, while I was researching my wife's condition—if you could call it that—online, I came across a website for a therapist organization called the Mirrorists."

"Seems like an odd name for a therapist organization," I said, wondering if this was the group of degenerate shrinks we'd been after.

"They get their name from the type of therapy they practice," Mr. Singh explained. "It's called mirroring. The technique aims to show the patient their life situation, to reflect it back at them so they can then take steps to fix it. What aroused my interest, though, was the fact that the organization claimed to work mostly with patients who were suffering from a newly emerged condition called "Other Person Syndrome," or OPS for short. I know it sounds vaguely ridiculous, but as soon as I read it, the description struck a chord with me because it almost exactly described what was happening to my wife. Most of the time, it felt like she was some other person, or that she was becoming someone else. So I contacted the organization and arranged an appointment with a local therapist called Dr. Adrian Dunbar."

"And what happened?" I asked.

"Well, Kavita started attending sessions with this therapist," Mr. Singh said, glancing toward the hallway as he spoke as if he expected to hear his wife's voice from the nursery, but all was quiet in there, which unsettled me more than when Mrs. Singh was screaming earlier. If the silence kept up, I would have to break down the door. "After the first two sessions, she appeared to improve. Her mood lifted, and she didn't seem as confused or as angry as she was before. I thought finally she was getting the help she needed, but—" He stopped and stared at the floor for a second.

"I take it your wife only got worse?" I said.

Mr. Singh nodded. "Yes. The outbursts started again, worse this time. She also became despairing, filled with self-hatred. She talked about her condition like it was a disease, and the only way to get rid of it was to…" He stopped, unable to go on as fresh tears welled up in his eyes.

"It's okay," Hannah said, putting a hand on Mr. Singh's leg. "Your wife just needs some proper help."

"Please," Mr. Singh said. "You have to help her, for the sake of our baby…whatever it takes."

Down the hall in the nursery, Kavita's ranting started up again, which was soon followed by the child's crying. Mr. Singh covered his ears like he couldn't stand to listen to it anymore. I motioned to Hannah, and the two of us stepped outside to the hallway for a moment.

"So, what do you think?" Hannah asked me. "Is Mrs. Singh a Supernormal?"

"It's looking likely that's the case, given everything the husband just said."

"How do you want to handle this?"

"Right now, my concern is for that baby," I said. "If the woman is as unhinged as her husband has made her out to be, there's a chance she might hurt the baby or herself. Put the call into HQ and get an Incident Response Team sent here."

"What are you going to do?"

From inside, the baby's screams got louder, sounding like they were caused by pain. "We can't afford to wait any longer. I'm breaking the door down."

"Let me make the call first," Hannah said as she took out her phone. "Then I'll back you up. We don't know what kind of powers Kavita might have."

I nodded and went back into the apartment to find Mr. Singh standing outside the nursery, banging on the door as he pleaded with his wife to let him in. "Please don't hurt our baby, Kavita!" he wailed.

"But what if she's like me?" Kavita shouted back. "What if she's a dirty, ugly monster just like her mother?"

"No, Kavita," Mr. Singh said. "You are not a monster. You are just sick. Our baby is not a monster, either."

"Liar!" Kavita screamed. "Dr. Dunbar showed me what I am! He told me what I have to do!"

"No, Kavita—"

"Stand back, Mr. Singh," I said, moving him aside just as Hannah came down the hall.

"What are you going to do?" Mr. Singh wailed. "Please don't hurt her. She doesn't know what she's doing—"

"No one's hurting anyone," I said, before addressing Kavita. "We're coming in, Kavita. Stand back from the door."

"Don't!" Kavita screamed. "You'll be sorry!"

Yeah? What's new?

The door was flimsy, and one well-placed kick was all it took to send it crashing open. Inside the small room was Kavita, naked and backed into a corner as she clutched her screaming baby close to her bosom as if she were afraid we were about to take the child from her.

Which we were, the first chance we got.

"Kavita," I said as I walked slowly into the room, my hands held up in front of me. "My name is Ethan. I'm here to help."

"No, you're not!" Kavita hissed. "You're here to take me away. To take my baby away!"

"No one wants to take your baby, Kavita," Hannah said as she came into the room behind me. "We just want to help, but you have to let us."

Kavita shook her head, and already I could see her change as she took on a terrifying Visage. Her black hair became long and wild, and her eyes filled with fire as her skin tone turned blue before darkening into black. At the same time, two extra arms appeared under her existing ones. With her long, pointed tongue lolling out of her mouth, she looked like a wild animal as she moved toward the round window, which was half-open. A wind stirred in the room, growing in intensity with each passing second, to where the scant furniture started sliding across the floor.

"Oh my Lord!" Mr. Singh said, perhaps only seeing his wife's full Visage for the first time.

"Look upon my grotesqueness, husband!" Kavita said. "Look upon Shiva—supreme force of destruction!"

As she said it, a crack opened up in the wall and spread right over the ceiling and down the opposite wall as if the building were about to fall apart.

"Kavita, no..." her husband said, his face distraught and full of fear.

"I am an abomination!" Kavita cried. "I do not belong in this world...and neither does my baby. She's like me, I can sense it."

"You are not an abomination, Kavita," Hannah said. "There is a perfectly reasonable explanation for what is happening to you. If you calm down and come with us, we can explain everything, and hopefully, help you and your baby."

"There is no helping a monster like me," Kavita said. "Dr. Dunbar said so. There is no place in this world for me or others like me. None!"

"That's not true," Hannah said as I edged my way closer to Kavita, thinking I could subdue her and take the baby from her. She was holding the child so hard that her long nails were piercing the child's skin. But as I was about to make my move, the wind in the room gathered a fierce strength and encircled me. In seconds, I was trapped within a mini-tornado that lifted me and spun me into the wall, causing me to crash down to the floor a second later.

"Don't tell me what's true and what isn't!" Kavita screamed, barely acknowledging me lying on the floor. "I know there is only one way out of this...for my baby and me."

"No, don't say that, Kavita," Mr. Singh cried. "I love you. I love our baby…"

As I got to my feet, I saw Kavita turn her head to look at her husband, and for just a moment, the fires went out in her eyes, and the no doubt loving woman she once was came to the fore. "I love you too, my darling Ajay. But there is only one way this can end."

Before anyone could react, Kavita, still clutching her screaming baby, threw herself out the window, crashing through the glass before dropping from sight.

"NO!" her husband screamed.

For a second, I thought it was all over, which it should've been. We were on the top floor of a six-story tenement, and the fall would've been enough to kill Kavita and her baby.

There was no saving her.

But Hannah must've thought otherwise, for as soon as Kavita crashed through the glass, Hannah sprinted forward and dived out the window after her.

"Hannah!" I shouted, thinking she had gone crazy.

Rushing to the window, I looked out to see Kavita falling through the air with her baby, mere feet from the ground now. Above them was Hannah, her top half naked as her clothes blew in tatters around her. Hannah now had feathered wings coming out of her back—wings she used to propel herself downward at bullet speed until she could snatch Kavita and her baby in mid-air before swooping upward with them both in her arms.

"Jesus…" I said in response to how close Kavita and the baby had come to splatting off the concrete below, and also at Hannah's aerial display, which I hadn't expected.

A few seconds later, Hannah flew in through the window, still holding a shocked Kavita and her now unconscious baby. Hannah landed with some grace on the floor just as her grayish wings retracted into her back, hardly an ounce of strain on her face as she held Kavita and the child in her arms.

Mr. Singh could only stand staring in shock as Hannah lay his wife down on the floor. Whatever fire was burning in Kavita before she jumped had been put out by the fall, and she now lay docile and unresponsive. She didn't even protest when Hannah gently took the baby from her. The child was still unconscious it seemed, maybe even dead from shock, I realized with some sickness in my belly.

But as Mr. Singh started wailing in shock and panic, Hannah remained calm as she placed two fingers on the baby's forehead. A whitish light glowed from her fingers for a few seconds, before the child opened its eyes, stared at Hannah for a brief second, and then started crying again.

"She should be fine," Hannah said, smiling as she handed the baby over to Mr. Singh, who gratefully received his tiny daughter with tears of relief running down his face.

As I stared at Mr. Singh, and the way he protectively held his daughter, I was reminded of how I used to hold Callie as a baby, and of how small she was, and the strength of her grip as she clenched her tiny fingers around my pinkie. In the end, I had to look away, glancing at Hannah as I did so, her face full of pity as she glimpsed my pain.

It was then that the Incident Response Team came rushing into the room and immediately surrounded Kavita, whose Shiva Visage had now gone, leaving behind a disturbed, naked woman who moaned to herself as she lay in semi-shock on the floor.

A stretcher was brought in, and Kavita was loaded onto it before being strapped in. This wasn't the first Supernormal the IRT had taken away, and they knew the risks. Indeed, before they even put her on the stretcher, one of the team injected Kavita with a sedative that put her out in seconds.

Kavita would soon find herself the newest inmate at a

secret government facility, along with dozens of other Supernormals. According to Director Bradley—and the President—it was the only safe course of action at this point. The more dangerous Supernormals had to be contained until the higher-ups could figure out what to do with them— or how to use them. In which case, the government was no different from Blackstar. I wasn't exactly at ease with the situation, but then it wasn't my job to reason why. I just followed orders.

Before long, the IRT had left, taking a still-in-shock Mr. Singh with them, along with the baby who doubtless would need medical attention after the trauma that Kavita put her through.

Hannah stood with her arms folded over her breasts, her bra, blouse, and jacket probably blowing around on the street outside by now. Taking my trench off, I draped it around her shoulders, and she smiled her thanks.

"That was some move you pulled," I said.

"I didn't think," she said. "I just did it."

"Did you know your wings would open?"

"I hoped they would."

I smiled a little as I shook my head at her. "You're fucking crazy, girl."

"I learned from the best. Besides, I saved Kavita and the baby, didn't I?"

"Yeah, you did," I said. "Though I'm not sure Kavita will be thanking you when she's locked up in a containment cell."

"I'm sure it won't be for long."

"You really think that?" I said, raising my eyebrows at her apparent naivety.

"Well, they can't keep all those people locked up indefinitely. Can they?"

"It's the government. They can do what they like. Anyway," I said, taking out my cigarettes and popping one into my mouth, offering her one as well, "we did our job. What happens next is not our concern."

"At least we got a lead on the therapist organization," she said as we headed out to the hallway.

"I guess there's that," I said.

"Are you okay?"

"I'm fine."

Before I closed the front door, I stared into the empty apartment and sighed at the heavy silence left behind.

Another family destroyed, I thought ruefully.

When would it all end?

As I walked down the hallway with Hannah, I knew it would never end.

For darkness is eternal.

I just thank fuck that I'm not.

4

On the way back to SAD HQ, I stopped at a clothing store and purchased a new bra, blouse, and jacket for Hannah while she waited in the car.

"Not really your style," the young girl who served me in the store said. "I think black would be more your color."

"They aren't for me," I said distractedly, still thinking about Kavita Singh throwing herself out the window with her baby.

"You don't say," the girl said, smiling as she took my money. "We have some nice suits in the men's department. Would you like me to show you them?"

"Do I look like a guy who wears nice suits?"

"No, but you should. First impressions are important."

"So, what's your impressions of me then?"

The girl smiled, showing her perfect teeth. "I wouldn't like to say, sir."

I smiled back. "Wise choice."

Hannah got dressed in the car as I drove toward the office, seemingly oblivious to the looks she was getting from passing pedestrians and other motorists.

"You know," I said, "if you make a habit of going all

airborne, you're gonna go through a lot of clothes. Trust me, it gets tiresome. I'm on my second trench coat this year, and don't even talk to me about shirts."

"Don't worry," she said. "I don't plan on making a habit of going all airborne, as you put it. Only when I have to."

"I couldn't help but notice your wings are gray."

"Gray?"

"Yeah."

She stared for a second and then shrugged. "I hardly noticed."

"Is that normal? I thought brilliant white would be more an angel's color."

"Well, I'm not really an angel, am I?" she said, taking a pack of cigarettes from off the dash and handing me one before lighting one up herself. "Angels are one-dimensional beings. There's more to me than that now. I have different sides to me."

"Don't I know it." I smiled over at her, and she thumped my arm with her fist.

"Fuck you."

"And that's just the kind of language that keeps your wings from being white."

"Screw it. I don't want them white, anyway. I'm my own person now, beholden to no one."

"Not even God?" I asked as I pulled into the SAD parking lot. "I'm sure He'd have something to say about your new independent status. I'm curious—did you connect with Him when you took on your true celestial form that time?"

"I felt His energy flowing through me," she said. "But if you're asking if He spoke to me, the answer is no. The Creator doesn't speak; he just does."

"And everyone is expected to go along with it."

"It's not like we have a choice."

"You do now, though."

"Maybe. Or maybe I just think that."

"Fuck it," I said, cutting the engine off as I sat and smoked the rest of my cigarette. "It's all one big shit show at the end of the day, whether we have a choice or not."

"Exactly, which is why we should make the most of it. We should go on vacation or something."

I snorted. "Vacation? You're starting to sound like Haedemus."

"You don't take vacations?"

"Every morning, with my first dose of Mud."

She shook her head. "You know what I mean. You never went on vacation with your wife?"

"Couple times," I said, preferring not to think about it.

"Everyone needs a break. You more than most. I say we take some time soon, just you and me. What do you think?"

Humoring her, I said, "Where would we go?"

She shrugged. "I don't know. A private island in Fiji sounds nice. Sun, sea, and sand."

"You really are sounding like Haedemus now."

"I'm serious, though. It would do you some good."

"Maybe." I couldn't imagine sitting around on some beach for a fortnight, doing nothing. The thought horrified me.

"I don't care if you hate the idea," she said. "A person can only be wound up so tight before they snap."

"You think I'm gonna snap?"

"I think you've already snapped," she said. "You just don't realize it."

BACK IN THE OFFICE, WE FILLED IN BRADLEY ON WHAT happened at the Singh's apartment, even the part about Hannah jumping out the window to save Kavita and her baby. Despite the fact that Bradley wasn't entirely comfortable with Hannah's MURK status—or "supernatural status" as he would more likely put it—having had little direct experience with MURKs, he was nonetheless impressed by Hannah's heroics, and told her so, much to Hannah's barely concealed delight. After everything, she was happy to be doing some good at last.

After updating Bradley, Hannah and I went into our office so we could do some preliminary research on the Mirrorists group. We started with the information that was freely available on the therapist organization's website. In their mission statement, the organization said it aimed to help those people who had become afflicted with OPS, making sure to mention that such people were a danger to themselves and society. They also said that anyone with OPS was blameless in contracting the condition, but didn't go so far as to say how people contracted the condition in the first place.

"Cases of OPS first came to light two decades ago," the organization wrote, "but things have worsened considerably in the last year or two, with many more cases coming to light. To prevent this condition from becoming a scourge on our great city, we believe that all OPS sufferers should seek help immediately before their delusions of grandeur end in tragedy, as many have already."

The mission statement then goes on to make the Mirrorists out to be saviors—selfless, considerate individuals who only wish to help "the Afflicted" before they come to any harm, or worse, before they harm others.

"The Mirrorists," they wrote, "are a group of seasoned physiatrics professionals dedicated to helping those who can't help themselves."

Yeah, right, I thought dismissively. *The only thing you bastards do is push the "Afflicted" toward suicide.*

I'm not saying Supernormals are all good people who deserve as much care and attention as anyone else. Some of them undoubtedly are good—Daisy, for instance. But it's not really about good or bad, is it? It's about power, and when an individual or group of individuals possess considerable—and in some cases, great—power, they become a threat to the existing power structures. I believe the Supernormals need to be monitored, and when appropriate, contained. In that sense, they are no different from the more established MURKs.

What the Mirrorists are doing, however, is wrong. They are taking dangerous people and making them more dangerous, not just to themselves, but to others as well. Kavita was convinced her baby was like her and thus needed to die. She would never have thought that had she not been brainwashed by a Mirrorist shrink. She may even have found a way to cope with her transformation and to live with it. But these parasitic, manipulative shrinks aren't giving people like Kavita a chance to resolve their problems. Instead, they turn their "patients'" problems against them.

The question is why, though. Why are these Mirrorists doing this? And who is leading them?

If I didn't know better, I would suspect hellot involvement here. Maybe this organization was really a cult, established at the behest of some demon who perhaps has a problem with so many powered humans running around. Powered humans who represent a threat to the demons working so hard to gain dominance and control over the Unaware population. It was a possibility, and one that I didn't dismiss out of hand.

To find out the real truth, we would have to dig deeper into the organization. I thought a good place to start would be to have a conversation with Adrian Dunbar, the shrink who "treated" Kavita. Hannah and I had already spoken to a few different shrinks, but we were unaware at the time they were all part of the same organization. Now we knew what the score was, we could use this knowledge to apply greater pressure to Dunbar than we did with the other shrinks.

Or at least, I could. Rather than have Hannah accompany me to Dunbar's office, I told her to go to the holding cell in the far south corner of the building where Kavita Singh was being held and have a word with the woman. Maybe Hannah could learn something about the Mirrorists group from Kavita.

In the meantime, I left the building and drove to Adrian Dunbar's office south of the river in Old Town.

DUNBAR WAS WITH A PATIENT WHEN I ARRIVED AT HIS OFFICE without an appointment. Flashing my ID at the secretary, I told her I needed to speak with Dr. Dunbar, and after staring at me for a moment over her eye-glasses, she told me to take a seat in the waiting area, which was just a few chairs outside Dunbar's office.

After a fifteen-minute wait, a young guy in his twenties emerged from the office with a dark look on his face, and I wondered straight away if the guy was a Mytholite, and what powers he might have at his disposal. I also wondered if he was off to kill himself or others, acting under the duress of Dunbar.

An angry look came over my face as I watched the guy go, and I decided then not to play nice with the shrink if he tried to give me the runaround, or play mind games. We needed to know who the leader of the Mirrorists was, and Dunbar would tell me whether or not he wanted to.

I wasn't sure if the secretary had informed Dunbar of my presence or not, though he seemed to think I was a new patient when he came out of his office. Until I showed him my ID, that is.

"Ethan Drake, FBI," I told him. "I'd like to talk to you about one of your patients."

Dunbar—a short, squat man in his late forties with a crop of dark curly hair and shifty eyes—glanced at his secretary for a second before smiling and beckoning me into his office.

"I don't have long," Dunbar said as he walked back into his small office and sat down. "But please, take a seat, Agent Drake."

I shuddered when I walked into the shrink's office. Two comfy armchairs facing one another made me visualize clients spilling their guts over a hot beverage. Trauma, betrayal, secrets, unspeakable fantasies—these walls had no doubt heard it all.

What would I tell the therapist if it were me in that chair? I wondered.

Dark thoughts crept up in the back of my mind, reminding me how I'd failed, how I'd come up short, all the time and in every way. I felt what all the clients that came before me must have felt: broken beyond repair.

The difference is I don't talk about it. Some things are better left buried.

Sitting on the chair facing Dunbar, I glanced around the room for a second, trying to get a read on the man. Nothing in his office—the bookshelves, the small desk with a picture of his family on it, the TV in the corner, the certificates on the walls—suggested anything out of the ordinary. Dunbar seemed like a normal small-time shrink. There was nothing untoward in his file either, which I checked before leaving HQ—a couple of unpaid parking tickets, that's all. Nothing to suggest he was some psychopathic manipulator, if indeed, that's what he was. Looking at him in his dark slacks and light cardigan, he seemed astute and intelligently aware, as you would expect a shrink to be. If he had darker inclinations—and I knew he had—he hid them well. I got no

Infernal Itch from him either, so he wasn't a MURK, or a hellot, as far as I could tell. Though he had to have gotten his zealotry from somewhere, meaning he did what he did for personal reasons, or at the behest of the Mirrorist's leader, or both.

"I'm here to talk about Kavita Singh," I said. "I'm sure you know her."

Dunbar nodded. "Yes, of course. A very disturbed young woman. Has she done something bad? Tried to hurt herself or others?" There was a barely perceptible glint in Dunbar's eyes as he spoke, as if inside, he was happy that his plan to turn Kavita against herself had worked. Otherwise, why would an agent from the FBI be at his office?

"She threw herself out a six-story window along with her baby," I said, watching his reaction closely, noticing how the corners of his mouth turned up slightly as if he were about to smile, but caught himself before he did.

"That's tragic," he said, shaking his head. "I'm so sorry to hear that. Kavita was a nice woman, but as I said, highly disturbed. She suffered from delusions."

"She's still alive," I said, taking some pleasure in informing him of this.

"But you said—"

"We managed to save her."

A frown formed on his face. "But how, if she—"

"Doesn't matter how. What matters now is that she's at FBI headquarters giving a statement."

"I see. About what exactly?"

"Her sessions with you, for one."

Dunbar puckered his lips as he nodded, his brown eyes looking hard at me as he perhaps tried to work out what I knew and didn't know. "Are you having some trouble sleeping, Agent Drake?" he asked, throwing me for a second. "I can always tell when someone is suffering from sleep disorders. Perhaps you'd like to talk about it? I have some experience in treating——"

"No thanks," I said. "I'm not here to talk about myself. I'm here because I know you're a part of this Mirrorist organization, and that you go out of your way to treat people like Kavita Singh. Only you don't treat them, do you? You manipulate them into doing terrible things."

Unfazed, Dunbar merely smiled. "When you say people like Kavita, I assume you mean those suffering from OPS?"

"Let's be frank here, Doc," I said. "We both know that OPS, as you call it, is no mental condition as you and your cronies claim it to be, so let's just cut the bullshit here. You know exactly what these people are and what they are capable of. I just don't know why you're so bent on making them hurt themselves and others. What do you and your organization get out of it?"

Dunbar smiled once more. A smile I guessed was supposed to be disarming, but all it did was annoy me. "My patients are often in great pain, Agent Drake. I just try to help them deal with that pain, that's all. I can't be held accountable for someone's actions after they leave here."

Can't you? We'll see about that.

"I beg to differ," I said. "You bring people like Kavita in here under false pretenses, offering them hope and help that you have no intention of following through on. You take already dangerous individuals and make them even more dangerous. Same as the other therapists I've spoken to recently, all of whom, like you, belong to this bullshit Mirrorist organization." I sat forward in my seat and fixed my gaze on him. "So I'm gonna ask you again, Doc. What are you and your cronies getting out of this?"

"Ethan," he said, shifting slightly in his seat. "May I call you Ethan? The Mirrorist organization was started in order to help people, and to protect society from——"

His eyes widened in fear when I shot out of my seat and

lunged at him, grabbing him by the lapels and lifting him clean out of his chair as I held him up, my face mere inches from his. "Maybe you didn't hear me," I said.

"Rita!" he shouted, calling out to the secretary for help, at which point, I head-butted him, my hard forehead slamming into the bridge of his nose, a loud crack filling the room as the cartilage in the bridge of his nose broke, and blood immediately started gushing from his nostrils.

I threw Dunbar back down into his chair just as the door to the office opened and the secretary walked in, a look of shock on her face as she took in her boss sitting with blood running through his fingers as he covered his nose with his hands.

"Oh my god!" Rita exclaimed. "Dr. Dunbar—"

Dunbar tried to say something to her—something about calling the police maybe—but his words were too muffled to make out. And before the secretary could do anything, I crossed quickly over to her with my right hand held out, the tattoo ink already swirling in my palm.

"Look at the hand, Rita," I commanded her, and as always when I did this with people, she couldn't help but look. Soon, she couldn't tear her gaze away, for the swirling, hypnotic pattern of the ink had her attention locked in. "You will forget you ever saw this, Rita. You will go back outside, sit at your desk, and not come back in here until after I leave. Tell me you understand."

Rita, her eyes glassy now, nodded. "I...understand."

"Wita!" Dunbar tried to say through his bloody hands, but the secretary wasn't listening as she turned and left the room, closing the door behind her.

"Now," I said, turning to stare at Dunbar, who had moved to his desk now as he picked up the phone and started dialing, probably 911. "Where were we?"

"Stay the fuck away from me!" Dunbar shouted, his white shirt and cardigan stained crimson now.

"Put the phone down," I told him as I crossed to his desk and snatched the receiver out of his hand, slamming it down in its cradle. "Who the fuck are you gonna call, anyway? I'm fucking FBI, asshole."

"You can't do this!" He was backing into the corner, pointing at me as if that would keep me away. "You aren't allowed to treat people like this, especially——"

"Especially what? Self-important assholes like you?" I snorted. "Treating pricks like you in this way gets me outta bed in the mornings."

"Okay, okay," he said as he now tried to calm the situation, playing the role of shrink once more. "I can see you're in pain, Ethan——a lot of pain. That's why you're doing this, right? That's why you treat people in this way. I can help you with that. I can——"

"Spare me your head-shrinking bullshit," I snarled. "You wanna talk about pain?" I rushed forward and grabbed hold of his bloody nose, squeezing hard as he squealed. "Let's talk about pain, Doc. Tell me about *your* pain." I pressed harder, and he screamed. "Tell me all about it! Does it hurt, huh? Because this is how you make your clients feel. This is the pain you cause them on the inside."

Dunbar squealed some kind of noise that might have been "stop," so I stopped squeezing his busted nose, and he all but fell to the floor, moaning in pain as he covered his face with both hands.

I backed off, giving him a minute to recover as I leaned against his desk and lit a cigarette. He gave me a look when he smelled the smoke, but said nothing. When he finally stood up, he moved around to his desk, giving me a wide berth as he did so, and plucked a few tissues from a small box. He then held the clump of tissues to his nose for a moment, which was greatly swollen by this stage. He'd probably need surgery to fix it. As if I cared.

"What did you do to Rita?" he asked after a few

moments. He sounded genuinely interested and was now looking at me as if I was perhaps 'afflicted' like the others he had as clients.

"Never mind that," I said, stubbing my cigarette out inside a small trash can by the side of his desk. "You just worry about what you're going to say to me next."

The fear was back on his face again as he stared at me. "What do you mean?"

"Tell me what you have against the Supernormals."

"Supernormals?"

"Your clients. Why do you want to hurt them so much?"

"I—I don't—"

I stood to my full height suddenly, towering over him. "I'll ask you again. What do you have against the Supernormals? Why do you hate them so much?"

"I just…want…to help…"

For fuck's sake. I'm beginning to wonder if this guy isn't brainwashed somehow. Does he even know himself why he targets the Mytholites? Or is he just covering for someone else? The person behind the whole Mirrorist organization, perhaps?

Sighing, I shook my head at him as he shrank away from me, probably expecting me to hurt him again. "Alright, Doc," I said. "If you're not gonna give me a reason, then give me a name instead. Who runs the Mirrorist group?"

"It's on the website—"

"That's a bullshit name. We already checked it out. Give me the real name before I rip your nose clean off your face."

Dunbar closed his eyes for a second before answering, as if he knew I wouldn't like what he would say. "The truth is, I don't know. I only know the man who was in charge of our training."

"A name, Doc. Give me a name."

"Franklin," he said. "Joshua Franklin. There was a

group of us last year, and he trained us in the Mirroring Method."

"Where can I find him?"

"Bankhurst. His office is in Bankhurst."

"Write the address down."

Visibly quivering in fear now, Dunbar moved around his desk and found a pen to write on a sticky note before tearing the note off and handing it to me. "Don't tell him it was me who sent you."

"Why not?" I asked. "You afraid of this guy or something? Or afraid he'll stop your paychecks?"

"We all had to sign non-disclosures, me, and the other therapists."

Figures, I thought. *That's obviously how the organization covers its own ass.*

Though, I had a feeling that non-disclosure or not, the organization would "take care" of anyone who tried to harm it.

"Alright, Doc," I said. "You've been very helpful. You might want to get that nose seen to. Quicker you get it set, the less chance you'll have of having a nose like mine."

Dunbar shook his head at me. "You're a violent man, Agent Drake. You need help."

The nerve on this fuck, telling me I need help when he spends his time driving mentally disturbed people toward violence and suicide.

"Oh, and one more thing, Doc," I said.

"What?" he asked nervously.

"Look at my hand…"

5

After I left Dunbar's office, I drove to Little Italy, where I met Hannah for lunch in a restaurant called Valentino's Pizzeria. Hannah was already munching on an anchovy pizza when I got there, looking like she was enjoying it, the corners of her mouth smothered in tomato sauce, making me smile as I sat down.

"You're like a kid eating her first pizza," I said, pouring myself some water from the jug on the table.

"It's my favorite food," she said, polishing off the slice she was eating and immediately picking up another. "I ordered you a calzone."

"Thanks, but I'm not really hungry."

"Tough. You need to eat. And why is there blood on your shirt?"

I looked down at my white shirt and saw the specks of blood there. "Shit."

"Whose blood is that?"

"Dunbar's, the shrink I went to see."

"I take it you didn't like what he had to say?"

"Nope."

Hannah rolled her eyes at me before taking a bite of her

pizza. "You need to be careful. You're FBI now. If Bradley finds out you're getting heavy-handed with people, he won't be happy."

"He won't find out," I said. "I made sure of it."

"You used your tattoo working?"

I nodded. "He won't remember a thing. He'll think he walked into a door."

"I'm guessing it was a heavy door."

"About as heavy as my forehead," I said, looking out the window and across the street to where a black car with tinted windows had pulled up. Three burly men in dark suits got out, stood looking around for a moment as if to assert their dominance over the area, and then walked into a betting shop.

"What's wrong?" Hannah asked, just as a waiter arrived with my pizza, putting the plate in front of me before asking if I wanted anything else. When I shook my head, he nodded and walked away.

"A few mobsters pulled up across the street."

"I doubt they're here for you."

"They aren't," I said, still staring out the window. "But I doubt Don Giordano has forgotten about me."

"If he even knows about you."

"He does. Make no mistake about that. He just hasn't decided what to do about me yet."

"You're being paranoid. If this mobster knew about you, you'd be dead already."

"Maybe."

"You know I'm right. You need to chill out. Eat your pizza."

"Chill out? Is that a joke?"

"No."

I shook my head at her and stared out the window again.

"Maybe we should've gone somewhere else for lunch," she said. "Like Little Tokyo."

"Wow," I said. "You're a regular goddamn comedian today, aren't you? Little Tokyo. We'd be surrounded by Yakuza the minute we set foot in the place."

She smiled as she chewed on her pizza. "I'm actually surprised we haven't heard anything from Susumu Yagami yet. I'm sure he knows it was us who killed his father."

"Me, you mean. I shot him."

"It doesn't matter who pulled the trigger. He'll blame us both equally."

"Maybe we should see if he's back in town," I said. "If he is, we need to be careful."

She smiled and shook her head. "Is there anywhere in this city where you're not a wanted man?"

"Probably not." I stared down at the pizza in front of me, contemplating taking a bite, my curdled stomach having no interest. "So did you learn anything useful in your talk with Kavita Singh? How is she?"

"She seems better," Hannah said, refilling her glass with water. "Though I doubt she'll ever get over almost killing her baby. That's all she talked about. She just wanted her baby back. It was sad, really."

"I'm sure. So did she say much else? Did she mention the Mirrorists?"

"In passing. She spoke more of her sessions with Adrian Dunbar." She took a sip of her water before continuing. "I think she realizes now that Dunbar manipulated her into thinking she was this terrible person who had to kill herself...and her baby."

"He told her to kill the baby as well?"

"Yep. Pretty bad, huh?"

"Fucking prick," I said. "I should've thrown him out the fucking window, see how he liked it."

"Then you would've got done for murder."

I shook my head. "Dunbar is the real danger to society, not his fucking patients. If all these Mirrorist fucks are like him, they all need taken down."

"Arrested, you mean?"

"On what charges? It's hard to prove anything. And even if we proved that these fucks are talking people into violence and suicide, their lawyers would get them off."

"So what are you suggesting?"

"Nothing at this point. If we can get the head of the organization, then the rest should fall too."

"Do we know who that is yet?"

"Dunbar gave me a name and address for one of the higher-ups in the organization. I say we pay this guy a visit and find out who his boss is."

"Will this guy be walking into a door too?"

"That depends on him."

We lapsed into a silence for a moment while I took a bite from my calzone, the pizza like damp cardboard in my mouth as I chewed joylessly. "I can't eat this. I'll grab a burger or something later."

Hannah stared at me but said nothing for a moment. When she spoke, it wasn't about my health or the fact that I looked like shit and wasn't eating properly, it was about Kavita Singh.

"Kavita told me one thing that might be useful," she said, her plate now empty. "She mentioned a woman who came into Dunbar's office one day—barged in during one of Kavita's sessions. Kavita said she felt the temperature drop in the room as soon as the woman entered. She also said she got a sense the woman was different."

"Different?"

"Like Kavita. A Supernormal maybe. Kavita didn't elaborate much."

I nodded as I glanced out the window again, seeing the

mobsters get back into their car and drive away. When they did, my eyes widened as I saw the woman I'd seen earlier standing outside SAD HQ. I knew it was her, not just by how she looked and stood, but because of how she made me feel—sick to my stomach, like I was looking at a ghost. I still couldn't see the woman's face because it seemed to be strangely shadowed, but once again, I was hit with the feeling that I should know the woman from somewhere.

"Ethan?" Hannah said, causing me to look at her. "What's wrong? You look freaked out again."

I looked back out the window, but the woman was gone. *I'm losing my fucking mind here...*

"It's nothing," I said. "I'm just tired. What else did Kavita say about this woman?"

Hannah stared at me for a moment longer, and I held her gaze until she answered me. "She said the woman was tall, late forties. Strikingly beautiful, but with an icy demeanor. Dunbar seemed afraid of the woman, according to Kavita."

"Did Kavita give you a name, or any indication of who this woman was?"

"No," Hannah said. "The woman didn't stay long apparently, and spoke with Dunbar outside the room. When Dunbar returned a few moments later, Kavita said he looked shaken. She was so wrapped up in her own emotions, she thought nothing of it."

Given what Hannah just said, I couldn't help but wonder now if Dunbar had lied to me. Maybe this woman that Kavita talked about was the leader of the Mirrorist group? Or maybe she was just one of the higher-ups? Either way, it was strange that Dunbar didn't mention her. Given the pressure I put him under, his only reason for not mentioning the woman was because he feared the consequences if he did.

When I looked at Hannah again, she was staring down

at the table, her eyes glazed over as if she was somewhere else. "What's wrong?" I asked her.

Mashing her lips together, she shook her head. "Nothing, it's just... I'm feeling bad for Kavita. After I finished talking with her, they took her away to the containment facility. All she wanted was to see her baby again, but they wouldn't let her. The woman's heart has been crushed."

"Where's Mr. Singh? Does he have the baby?"

"Yeah. He's at home, as far as I know, having no idea where his wife is probably."

"They'll tell him eventually once they assess Kavita's threat level."

"Do you think she'll ever be let go?"

I shrugged. "Who knows? Maybe, if she's deemed not to be a threat to anyone."

"She's Shiva, or a version of the goddess, anyway. She'll always be a threat."

"It's a sticky situation. No one knows how to handle these people."

"And what about Daisy? Will she end up locked up as well?"

"That'll never happen," I said firmly. "I'll make sure of it."

"I hope so," she said. "I'd hate for anything to happen to Daisy."

"And nothing will."

She nodded, but her face said I couldn't guarantee anything. And she was right.

"Okay," I said, standing. "I'm gonna go. Thanks for lunch."

"Not that you ate anything," she said. "Where are you going, anyway? I thought we we're going to check out that therapist you told me about?"

"We will. First, I gotta go to the yard and sort some business stuff out with Petey. I also wanna check on Daisy while I'm there."

Hannah nodded. "Okay. I guess I'll meet you back at the office then?"

"Sure. I'll try not to be too long."

"Say hi to Daisy for me."

DURING THE FEW WEEKS THAT I HAD OFF WORK AFTER CAL died, I took some time and did an audit of the scrap business to familiarize myself with it. I'd worked in the yard many years ago when I was Cal's apprentice, but since then, I hadn't paid it much attention. When I looked over the books, I was shocked at how lucrative the scrap business was, or at least Cal's business. With scrap, you're basically playing the stock market, and stock prices can change drastically every day. The trick to making money is knowing when to sell and when to sit tight until the time is right. Going by the books, Cal had a knack for knowing when to sell to maximize profits. The scrap would be loaded onto barges and sold to China or India. In the beginning, Cal sold to the bigger scrap yards before deciding to cut out the middlemen and sell direct.

Now obviously, I didn't know shit about playing the stock market or selling scrap. Luckily, Petey McCallister—Cal's long-time partner—was on hand to take care of that side of things. Petey, as well as having a 40% stake in the business, also handled the day to day running of the yard. But since Cal died, he started focusing more on the business side of things, handling all the transactions, doing the buying and selling. He also employed someone else to take care of managing the workers and ensuring the yard run smoothly.

One of the first things Petey drew to my attention after

he took over the books, was the state of the current machinery being used in the yard. Apparently Cal, tight-ass that he was, hadn't updated any of the machinery in years. Petey said it was always breaking down, and some machines were verging on dangerous. It was only a matter of time before there was an accident, so I agreed with Petey that we needed to replace everything, which we did, at a substantial cost.

As I drove into the yard, I saw the trucks parked every-where, and the men unloading the brand new machinery, including a new crusher. The old one, Petey said, could hardly crush a nut. Stopping and watching the men sort out the new machines, I smiled at the thought of Cal if he were here to see so much money being spent. He'd blow a gasket and I'd've given anything to see him do it, for I missed the hell out of him. His death had left a massive hole in my heart, and after the deaths of my ex-wife and daughter, it wasn't like there was much of my heart left, anyway. The emptiness I felt inside was soul-destroying, and most of the time, it seemed like I was spending every day wandering through a vast, empty wasteland as I tried to resist the temp-tation to put a bullet in my head.

If it weren't for Hannah and Daisy, I probably would.

After parking the car up, I spoke with Petey and some of the other guys for a few minutes, all of whom were happy as shit to see the new machinery, which everyone knew would make their jobs easier.

"I expect to get my 'World's *Best Boss*' mug very soon," I joked. "Or a bottle of Johnnie Walker Blue. Whatever you prefer."

They all laughed, and I went off to my trailer to refill the Mud bottle and get a fresh shirt. On the way out, I smiled at the photo of Cal.

"I spent your money," I said. "But it's okay, because it made all the guys happy."

Well, shit, I could almost hear him say. *As long as the fuckin' guys are all happy…*

Still smiling to myself—in no small part down to the Snake Bite with Mud chaser I just took—I traipsed over to Daisy's trailer to see if she was in there, which she wasn't. I remained inside for a minute, looking around at the piles of books she'd taken from Cal's library. An open book was laid down flat on the couch, and I picked it up to see it was a biography of Joan of Arc. Glancing at the pages, I saw that Daisy had highlighted one line, a quote from Joan herself:

I am not afraid…I was born to do this.

I stared at the highlighted quote for a moment, wondering what to make of it. It was hard to know what Daisy was going through, her mother's death no doubt exacerbating her already fragile state. Though going by the highlighted quote, maybe she wasn't as fragile as we all thought. Maybe she was getting strength from somewhere. From her newfound powers, probably. Regardless, I was still worried about her. Daisy may not have held her mother in the highest of esteem given everything the woman did and the often harsh way she treated Daisy, but she was still Daisy's mother. I knew how it felt to lose your mother under tragic circumstances. How it felt to walk in and see your mother dead…or almost dead.

Daisy walked into her old apartment in Bricktown one day after school to find her mother lying on the living room floor in a pool of her own vomit, having overdosed on a speedball. Daisy tried to save her by calling an ambulance and then giving her mother CPR. But her mother died before the ambulance even got there. Daisy called me at that point, and I rushed over to find her sitting on the floor next to her mother's body. As I stood in the doorway, Daisy looked at me with an expression that was at first blank until she burst into tears and then ran to me, throwing her arms around my waist and saying over and over again, "She's dead …she's dead…"

Once the authorities stepped in, I was able to pull some strings and get social services to agree to let Daisy stay with me at the yard, saving her from the system that gobbled me up and spat me out as a kid.

Shaking my head at the memory, I put the book back down on the couch and went outside to look for Daisy. I tried the Secret Garden first, where Cal's grave was. Often, Daisy could be found there, sitting cross-legged in front of Cal's gravestone, talking as if he were there with her. But upon checking the garden, I saw she wasn't there, which meant she was in the underground bunker, or in the smithy.

The smithy was where I found her. Despite the frigid temperature outside, Daisy was inside the large shed dressed in a sleeveless top and a boiler suit, the arms of which were tied around her waist. She was standing over a massive anvil, banging on a length of blackened iron with a hammer that should've given her trouble to even use, so big and heavy was it. But Daisy, her wiry arms glistening with a sheen of sweat, worked that hammer like it was made of paper mâché. Sparks flew all around her as she hammered the metal, before dropping the hammer and using a pair of tongs to plunge the length of steel into a burning hot forge, where she left the steel to heat up again. When she eventually saw me standing there, she stared for a moment before giving me a smile that I knew was forced.

"How long have you been standing there?" she asked, grabbing a bottle of water. "I thought you were at work."

"I was," I said, walking into the smithy, the hot air burning my lungs. "I just had some stuff to sort out in the yard."

"And you thought you would come and check on me while you're here?"

"Something like that."

"There's no need. I'm fine." She opened the lid on the bottle of water and guzzled half of it down.

Her attitude was disturbingly similar to my own after I lost my mother, even though I was a lot younger at the time. I tried to bury the pain, but no matter how hard I tried, it always came out eventually, most often in ways that weren't exactly healthy. I didn't want that for Daisy, especially with her burgeoning powers complicating matters. Though, as I stood there staring at her, I hardly knew what to do. She was hardening up before my eyes. If she kept on, she'd be as closed off as I was at her age.

"So what's your plans?" I asked her as I walked further into the smithy. A distinct odor hung thick in the air, burning my nostrils with the stench of coal dust and molten iron.

She frowned. "My plans?"

"Yeah. I mean, are you just gonna keep banging on that iron indefinitely? What about school? It might do you some good to go back."

Daisy ran a hand through her short dark hair. "I'm not going back there."

"What?"

"I'm not going back to school. I've decided." She walked to the forge and grabbed the tongs, pulling out the length of iron to check on it before shoving it back into the coals again.

"You don't have a choice, Daisy," I said. "You can't quit school until you're eighteen, you know that."

"I know," she said. "But you know people, don't you? You could pull some strings."

"Pull some strings?" I laughed a little as I shook my head, reaching into my pocket for my cigarettes, taking one out and lighting it. "I don't think it would be that easy, Daisy."

"What about those guys you know? The computer

geeks. They could doctor my records or something, couldn't they?"

"I don't know. Maybe." I took a drag of my cigarette, blowing the smoke out slowly. "I mean, what would you do instead? You're thirteen."

"So?"

"So you can't get a job anywhere, or——"

"I don't need a job," she said, sounding like she had already thought it all through. "I can work here, making blades, taking over from Cal. I have all his designs, and I'm getting good at making them."

"That's what you wanna do with your life? Make weapons?"

She shook her head at me like I didn't understand, traces of anger in her brown eyes. "You're not getting it, Ethan. Don't you see? I'm not normal anymore, if I ever was. I've changed. I'm still changing. I'm a fucking freak, and there's no place out there for me."

Tears welled up in her eyes when she said that last part, and it broke my heart to hear her say it. "Daisy…" I said, tossing my cigarette away and walking over to her, about to put my hands on her shoulders until she stopped me.

"Don't try to tell me different," she said, backing away toward the forge. "We both know what I am."

"You're forgetting one thing, though."

"And what's that?"

"We're all freaks around here. Or haven't you noticed?"

She stared at me for a second and then laughed despite herself. "I may have noticed."

"I mean, come on," I said, raising my hands. "We have Hannah who's part angel, part demon and part human. We have Haedemus the talking Hellicorn, and then the Hellbastards, the biggest freaks of all."

"Don't forget yourself," she said, smiling now.

"Shit, I'm the biggest freak here," I said. "I'm 6' 4, two

hundred and sixty pounds of freak, and don't even get me started on what's up here." I tapped my head with one finger. "It's always a fucking freak show in there."

"You're being ridiculous now."

"Am I?" I walked toward her, and this time she let me hold her. "All I'm saying is, you're not alone. You'll never be alone, Daisy. In fact—"

"What?"

"Hannah and I have been talking, and we were thinking —" I stopped, unsure now of how she would take what I was gonna tell her.

"What?"

"Well, we thought it might be a good idea if we… adopted you, officially like. I mean, you're already family as far as I'm concerned, so it would just be—"

She threw her arms around me and held me tight, saying, "Okay."

"Okay?"

Stepping back, she looked up at me and smiled. "Okay."

"Alright then," I said, smiling back, absurdly pleased that she had said yes. "I'll get things in motion."

"I'm still not going back to school."

Sighing, I shook my head. "So the adoption's not even through yet, and already you're a pain in my ass?"

Daisy's jaw dropped in mock offense before she punched me in the stomach. "I can cause you more pain than that, you know."

"Yeah," I said, holding my stomach. "I can see that."

6

Before I left the yard, I got a phone call from Hannah telling me that Bradley had assigned her to one of the other teams for the rest of the day. Apparently, SAD was getting ready to swoop on some vampire that had gone on one too many killing sprees lately. With so much going on in the city at the moment, Special Affairs was stretched thin, so Bradley was forced to fill the gaps however he could. It didn't help that a virulent strain of flu virus was sweeping through the city at the moment, rendering people sick and bed-ridden, which included many SAD and FBI employees.

It only goes to show that it's not the supernatural element that's the biggest threat, but nature. It doesn't matter how many monsters are in the world—Mother Nature was still the biggest monster of all when she wanted to be.

I didn't mind being alone for the rest of the day. As much as I enjoyed being partners with Hannah, I was still a lone wolf at heart, and preferred to do my own thing from time to time. Besides, I had some non-work related stuff I wanted to take care of.

First, I wanted to go and see Victoria Belford. With

everything that went on after the whole Ripper Tripper incident, I never got to speak with Vic after she was admitted into the hospital. I went to see her a day after, but she was out of it when I got there. Vic was a friend, and I wanted to make sure she was alright, which knowing Vic, I was sure she was. It would take more than a crazy serial killer to bring Vic down.

The other thing I needed to do was visit Artemis and Pan Demic. Pan Demic's mother had died just the other day, and I wanted to pay my respects to the kid.

On the way out of my trailer, I bumped into Haedemus hanging around outside, looking forlorn as usual.

"What's up, buddy?" I asked him. "Still fretting about getting fat?"

Haedemus snorted agitatedly. "Funny guy," he said. "I'll be sure to show you the same sympathy when middle-age spread renders you a fat bastard."

I couldn't help but laugh as I took out a cigarette and lit it. "I was just kidding. You aren't getting fat, Haedemus. It's all in your damn head. You just have too much time on your hands."

"Yes, exactly!" he exclaimed. "There's only so much a Hellicorn like me can do in this world, you know."

"What about the Hellbastards? Can't you hang around with those delinquents? They're always going on adventures."

"Don't talk to me about those little twerps," he said.

"Why? What have they done?"

"Oh, apparently, I slow them down, and I'm just too big to be hanging around with them. In fact, to quote that little shit Cracka, 'Horsey too fat to be hanging around with us.'"

I stifled a snigger. "Cracka is just winding you up. You know how he is—how they all are. Anyway, Hannah and I were discussing the possibility of getting you some company, maybe."

"Company?" he said suspiciously. "What kind of company?"

"You're own kind."

"Another Hellicorn?"

"If Hannah can swing it. Sure."

"Hmm," Haedemus said. "I'm not sure how I feel about that."

"Why?"

"You've never met any other Hellicorns, have you?"

"No, just you." *Thank God.*

"Well, not all Hellicorns have my winning personality, I'll have you know. Most of them are bitter, sarcastic assholes."

"Like you, you mean?"

"Ha-ha—you big meanie. I like to think I've smoothed out my rough edges since coming here."

"That's debatable," I said, blowing smoke in his direction, making him turn his head like the smell offended him.

"Don't be a jerk, Ethan," he said. "Given the company I'm forced to keep, I think I'm doing okay in this place."

"So you're saying you'd be happier on your own? If so, that can be arranged."

"No, that's not—" He stopped when he saw me smiling. "Screw you, Ethan. You never take anything seriously, do you?"

"I take lots of things seriously."

"Just not me."

"You can be hard to take seriously sometimes, Haedemus."

Haedemus sighed and turned his head away, lapsing into a forlorn silence, and after a moment, I realized I'd offended him. Walking over, I placed a hand on his thick neck, being careful to avoid the fleshy holes there.

"Why am I even here, Ethan?" he asked quietly.

"Because Hannah brought you here."

"That's not what I mean." He turned his head a little so he could look at me with one of his bulging red eyes, and for the first time since I'd known him, I saw a vulnerability in him that was almost child-like, making me feel sorry for him. "I mean, why do I exist? I was born a simple animal, and I should've died as one. But instead, I end up as this decrepit beast that you see before you. Why would God do that to me, Ethan? Why would He make me suffer like I do?"

"Just a guess, but maybe because you had sex with a dying man, and animals aren't supposed to consort with humans in such a way?"

Haedemus blinked twice as he stared at me. "So I bring comfort to a dying man, and God punishes me for it?"

"Given the size of your cock, Haedemus, I doubt you brought that much comfort to the guy," I said. "I mean, he probably thought he was being impaled or something."

"Impaled? That's such a nasty way of putting it. I don't remember him objecting much."

"Maybe because he was dying…"

He sighed audibly. "I should've known better than to discuss my existential crisis with you, Ethan. I'm succumbing to ennui and despair here, and you don't even care."

I shook my head as I tossed away my cigarette. "Alright," I said. "Enough of this shit. How about we go for a ride?"

"Oh, yes please."

CONSIDERING THE AMOUNT OF TIMES I'D ALMOST FALLEN OFF Haedemus while riding him bareback with not even any reins, I took the liberty a while ago to purchase a bridle and saddle. As I hadn't ridden the Hellicorn in a while, I forgot to mention to him I'd bought the equipment. When I told him, he balked at the idea of being restrained.

"Piss off, Ethan," he said, staring at the leather saddle on the ground, and the bridle I was holding. "What are you, a child? You don't need those stupid things, and neither do I want them on me."

"Well, I don't want to fall off you and break my damn neck either, so you're wearing this stuff."

Haedemus turned away in a huff. "I refuse."

"Fine," I said, throwing the bridle on the ground next to the saddle. "I'll just take the car then."

"Fine. You do that."

"Enjoy your ennui."

As I neared the car, Haedemus shouted, "Wait!"

Smiling, I turned around. "What?"

"You win," he said grudgingly. "I'll wear your damn stuff, but just the bridle. I won't have that saddle on me."

"But it might save your rotting spine."

"Listen, Xaglath rode me bareback for more time than you can conceive, and my rotted spine held out just fine, although admittedly, your ass is much fatter, Ethan." He snorted like this was funny. "Still, I'd rather your fat ass on me than the saddle, as long as you don't fart. You fart quite a lot, Ethan, you know that? It's disgusting."

"Says the creature that eats dead human flesh and smells like a fucking open grave afterward."

"Yes, well, that can't be helped."

"What do you have against saddles, anyway?" I said as I picked up the bridle and put it over his head before securing it.

"I just never liked them, that's all."

"Uh-huh. I think maybe you just like the feel of my balls on your back."

"Ethan!"

I laughed as I hoisted myself up onto him and took hold of the reins, grinding my pelvis into him. "You feel those, Big Boy, huh?"

"I swear, I will buck you off me."

Still laughing, I kicked my legs against him and shouted, "Ya!" and we took off like a bat out of Hell.

BY THE TIME I'D RIDDEN HAEDEMUS TO THE EDGE OF Crown Point just before we galloped onto the bridge that spanned the river, I realized I had missed riding him. There's a certain sense of freedom you get from riding a horse that you never get with a motorized vehicle like a car or even a motorbike.

Riding atop Haedemus, it felt like I was sitting at an impressive height, towering over people and vehicles, the wind streaming over me as the pulse of the city beat through me. It was even better because no one could see us, at least not the Unawares, who made up most of the population. The only heads we turned were those belonging to the MURKs. The Fallen especially always seemed astounded that a Hellicorn—a creature they last saw in Hell—was galloping through the streets of the city. Some of them even seemed envious that I was riding a Hellicorn, as if they like, "sooo wanted one as well."

I didn't blame them. Despite Haedemus' somewhat decayed, fresh-from-the-grave appearance, he was still a magnificent creature to behold. I was proud to be riding around on him, perhaps more so because I'd never had a pet—a faithful companion—before, and despite the lip he often gave me, Haedemus was that: a companion who would lay down his life for me in an instant, if he weren't technically dead already, that is. I didn't know many who would lay down their life for me, human, creature, or other, so I felt a deep connection to the mouthy beast, perhaps even more so than the Hellbastards. If Haedemus was a dog, then the Hellbastards were definitely cats—loyal to a point, but more concerned about themselves and doing their own thing.

Gripping the reins tightly as we galloped onto the bridge, I said to Haedemus, "Alright, big guy. Let's see what you got. Ya!"

As I applied more pressure with my legs to Haedemus' sides, the Hellicorn increased his speed until it became almost scary how fast he was going. We barreled across the long bridge, mostly going up through the middle of the lines of traffic. I had to concentrate hard, for sometimes a car would swerve out in front of us, and I would yank the reins to the side to avoid the vehicle. Failing that, Haedemus would leap over the car and land without breaking pace.

"This fast enough for you?" he asked halfway across, enjoying himself as much as I was.

"Plenty," I said as the wind cut into my face, causing tears to stream from my eyes.

"I can go faster, but you know, crashes are inevitable in a place this crowded."

When we reached Bankhurst, I pulled back on the reins to slow our pace. Traffic was heavy here, and all the sidewalks were bustling with people, most of them moneyed and professional—the movers and shakers of the city, blind to everything but their wealth and status.

"You know," Haedemus said, "there's a city in Hell like this one, where all the Big Wigs congregate. It's called Pandemonium."

"I've heard of it," I said as I steered him north toward Artemis' and Pan Demic's penthouse.

"Xaglath used to frequent Pandemonium a lot."

"Was she a big deal in Hell then?"

"She was definitely one of the higher-ups, yes. Many of the other demons feared her."

"I can imagine," I said, remembering the last time I saw her, and how ruthless and utterly fearless she was. Hannah still had her demon side, though she had assured me that the Xaglath I knew was gone now, dissolved and melded with the newer version of Hannah, which comprised everything she has ever been—angel, demon, human and all forms in between. I don't think even Hannah knew what she was anymore. She had succeeded in her aim of becoming her own person—her own being. There probably wasn't a being on the planet like her, one capable of great good and great evil, but beholden to neither the way her demon and Elohim kin are. She was human, in other words, but a new breed of human. You might even say a Supernormal.

I doubt even God saw Hannah coming, or the Supernormals.

An icy rain had begun to fall by the time we pulled up outside the curvilinear building—clearly based on an architect's wet dream with its voids within the structure, looking more like it belonged in Dubai than in grim Fairview—where the two delinquent technomancers lived.

"Wait here," I told Haedemus after dismounting him. "I shan't be long."

"You always say that," Haedemus said. "And I always end up standing around for hours while you do god knows what. Who lives here anyway?"

"Just a couple guys I know. There's been a death in the family. I'm here to pay my respects."

"Oh, well, pass along my condolences."

I nodded, unsure if I should tell the guys that "my Hellicorn said to pass on his condolences." Knowing Artemis and Pan Demic, they'd want to see Haedemus if they knew he was here. "I will. Try not to—"

"Eat anybody when you're gone," Haedemus finished in a droll voice. "Yes, yes. As if I would. Anyway, I'm on a diet now."

"Oh yeah, coz you're getting fat. I forgot."

"Piss off before you give me a complex."

"Too late for that, wouldn't you say?"

"Just piss off then."

A STRANGER OPENED THE DOOR OF THE PENTHOUSE AFTER I knocked it—a Goth girl in her late twenties with a deathly pale face, dark makeup, and a look that said she didn't much like the look of my official appearance, as if she knew straight away I was law enforcement. "Yeah?" she said caustically, her dark painted lips curling into a sneer.

"I'm here to pay my respects." I looked past her to see that the penthouse was crowded with people, as many as I'd ever seen in the place. Some of them even looked normal. "Artemis around? Or Pan Demic?"

Goth Girl just stared at me for a moment, her eyes glassy as if she was on something, which given where she was, it was likely that she was loaded on something or other. Before the girl could answer—if she was even going to answer at all —I saw Artemis come up behind her.

"Drakester," he said as he stood beside the Goth girl. His usual cyberpunk/metal attire was absent as he wore a dark suit that seemed a little big on him. Given the money he had available to him, I thought he would've at least got a tailored suit instead of one that was clearly off the rack. Still, it's not like I was the height of style either, shabby bastard that I am. "Nice of you to come."

"Of course," I said.

"I see you've met my sister, Danika," he said.

"Your sister?" I didn't see the resemblance.

"You a cop or something?" Danika asked. "You smell like a pig."

Nice.

"FBI actually," I said.

"Shit, yeah," Artemis said. "I forgot you were a Fed now.

I guess we have to watch out now, huh?" He laughed, his eyes like saucers as usual from whatever substance he was on.

"Not really," I said. "Where's Pan Demic? I'd like to offer my condolences."

Danika rolled her eyes and then walked away as if I warranted no more of her time. "He's here," Artemis said. "Can I get you a drink? Something stronger, perhaps?"

I shook my head as I walked inside. "No, thanks. Who are all these people?"

"Family and friends, Drakester. We buried Gina this morning at Cave Hill Cemetery."

"What happened?" I asked him. "I thought you had a cure for the cancer?"

"Oh, we did," he said, adjusting his eyeglasses. "Gina's cancer went into remission."

"So how'd she die?"

"She fell down the stairs at her home and broke her neck. Fucking tragic, man…"

"Shit."

"Drakester!" Pan Demic, dressed in a slightly better fitting suit, came staggering up to me, wired and drunk, his eyes wet like he'd been crying. "You came."

Before I could stop him, his arms were around me, his head only reaching my chest. As I embarrassedly hugged him back, I noticed the stares I was getting from most of the people in the room. Clearly, Danika had spread the word that a Fed had infiltrated the party. I didn't know much about Artemis' or Pan Demic's family, but going by their faces and the way most of them were dressed, I figured they all strayed on the wrong side of the law as the two techno-mancers did. I could understand their suspicion—and outright animosity in some cases—of me, but I was used to it, so I didn't let it get to me.

"My condolences, Pan Demic," I said as he stood back

from me, his overlong hair worn down, unlike Artemis', which was tied back in a ponytail.

"Thanks, Drakester," Pan Demic. "Fucking tragic accident. Did you know her cancer was in remission? She was getting better, man."

"Yeah, Artemis told me. I'm sorry, man."

Fresh tears ran down Pan Demic's face. "She was my mom, man. I'm gonna miss her…"

"I'm sorry," I said again. "If there's anything I can do—"

"Actually, there is," he said. "I want a ride on your Hellicorn."

"What?"

"I saw you ride it here while I was on the roof getting some air. *Please, Drakester*…it would mean a lot."

I sighed inwardly.

Haedemus will not like this.

"Sure, Pan Demic," I said. "Maybe just a quick ride around the block."

Pan Demic clenched his fist while gritting his teeth, too full of coke for his own good. "Fuck yeah!"

"Can I ride shotgun?" Artemis asked.

Jesus…

"Sure," I said. "I don't see why not."

"Alright!" Pan Demic said. "Let's fucking do this!"

"For Gina!" Artemis said, wired to the moon now as well.

"For Gina!" Pan Demic said, turning heads as he turned around and did some crazy salute to the others before shouting, "The best mom to ever grace this shitty fucking world!"

The crowd raised their drink and mumbled their agreement, most of their stares still on me.

"Alright," Pan Demic said as he turned around again. "Let's go ride a fucking Hellicorn!"

"Hell yeah!" Artemis said.

Hell no, more like, I thought.

But what was I going to say?

～

"No way! No way am I letting these two wired-up dweebs ride on my back. I'm not doing it, I tell you!"

Despite Haedemus' resistance to Pan Demic and Artemis riding him—and his total disdain for the two of them—they both stood looking up at Haedemus in pure awe as if they had never seen a creature like him before, which they hadn't.

"Oh my god," Artemis breathed. "He even talks."

"He talks alright," I said.

Haedemus fixed his red eyes on me. "What is this, Ethan? I said to offer my condolences, not pimp me out like some fucking beach donkey. I am not a beach donkey!"

"I didn't say you were," I said. "But the boys are obviously in grief, and you can help ease their pain by riding them around the block."

Haedemus' eyes narrowed as he continued to stare at me. "I bet you did this sort of thing as a kid, didn't you? Offering other kids a ride on your bike."

"I didn't have a bike as a kid."

"Whatever. Your new car when you were older."

"The only cars I had where the ones I stole. Are you gonna give the boys a ride or not?"

"That depends. What do I get in return?"

"You like coke?" Pan Demic asked, producing a baggie from his pocket and holding it up.

"Put that away," I said. "My Hellicorn doesn't need coke."

"Hold on there now," Haedemus said, turning to face Pan Demic. "I speak for myself here."

Puffing my cheeks out, I shook my head, thinking I

should've just sent a condolences card in the post. "You're not seriously considering snorting coke, are you?"

"Some souls in Hell used to speak fondly of the stuff," he said. "I heard one—Crowley was his name—say that happiness lies within one's self, and the way to dig it out is cocaine."

"Never a truer word spoken," Pan Demic said, now digging into the bag of Bolivian marching powder, scooping out a large pile on the end of his forefinger.

"Haedemus, I'm telling you—"

"Silence, Ethan," the Hellicorn said. "You're not the boss of me."

"Fine then," I said. "Go ahead. Snort that fucking shit till your heart's content."

Ignoring me, Haedemus said to Pan Demic, "I hear this stuff is also good for weight loss. Is that right?"

"Dude," Artemis cut in, "I used to be a fat fuck before I started on the blow, and look at me now."

"Yes," Haedemus said, nodding. "A stiff breeze could indeed blow you over."

"You used to be fat?" I said to Artemis. "When was this?"

"When I was like, twelve or something."

"Twelve? So you started doing cocaine when you were twelve?"

Artemis nodded. "I know, man. It's been a lifeline."

I shook my head, but I could hardly judge. At twelve years old, I was doing whatever drugs I could get my hands on.

"Alright, I've decided," Haedemus announced. "Boy with the drugs—Peter Pan, or whatever your name is—hit me with that shit."

"You got it," Pan Demic said, and he put his finger loaded with cocaine near Haedemus' snout. Haedemus then snorted the mound of coke up his left nostril, his head flying back as he did so.

"Wooah!" Haedemus said, his massive head shaking with the instant buzz of the blow.

"Here," Pan Demic said, moving his finger toward the Hellicorn's mouth. "Let me rub the rest around your gums."

Haedemus pulled his lips back grotesquely and allowed Pan Demic to rub more coke around his rotten gums, causing the Hellicorn to once again shake his head, now as wired as the two technomancers. "Holy shit!" he exclaimed. "This shit is amazing!"

Pan Demic and Artemis high-fived each other. "Greatest day ever," they both said in unison.

"You buried your fucking mother this morning," I pointed out.

"Yeah, apart from that obviously," Pan Demic said.

Jesus Christ...

"Alright, boys," Haedemus said. "Hop on up here and get ready for the ride of your young lives!"

I STOOD AROUND OUTSIDE, WAITING IN VAIN FOR OVER HALF an hour before going up to the penthouse again and getting myself a drink, standing there while everyone stared at me like I was dirt on their shoe. Then Artemis' sister Danika came over and said, "I'm sorry about earlier. I didn't know you were the cop who helped my brother with that gang that tried to kill him and Pan Demic."

"Forget about it," I said. "I've been called a pig so many times over the years, I'm surprised I don't go oink." She smiled at that. "So are you a technomancer too?"

"Yeah, it sort of runs in the family. So you're FBI? Why would you work for the government? I'm sure there are better ways you could help people."

"Oh yeah? Like how?"

"Well." She looked around for a second as if to make sure no one was listening. "I'm actually trying to put a crew together at the moment. I had guys, but they're all dead now."

"What happened?"

"They tried to fuck me over."

"And you killed them?"

She smiled, letting me know there was more to her than the Goth/Cyber girl outer appearance. "They killed themselves."

"I see. Maybe you shouldn't be telling me this."

"You might carry a badge, but I can see you're not like most lawmen."

"That's very presumptuous of you to say so."

She shrugged. "You telling me it's not true?"

I said nothing as I drank from the whiskey glass.

"Anyway," Danika said, carrying on. "I need capable, experienced guys for a job, and you look more than capable."

"I think you've got me confused with someone who wants to get killed or go to jail."

She stared at me for a long moment. "Maybe I was wrong about you then."

"Maybe you were."

"Well, on the off chance that I wasn't, feel free to get in touch. It's a big score. Could set you up for life."

"Like I said, I'm not that guy."

Her eyes narrowed as she stared at me once more. "We're all that guy under the right circumstances...Agent Drake. Let me know if your circumstances change."

Before she walked away, she handed me a card with a phone number on it, and I went back outside. Haedemus still hadn't returned, and it had been over an hour.

Should've just took my fucking car.

Sighing, I jacked a cigarette into my mouth. Taking out a Zippo lighter, I was about to light the cigarette when a voice made me stop and look up. The voice was familiar enough that my blood froze when I heard it.

It can't be. I must be hearing things. Fucking Mud again…

But across the street, I spotted a familiar figure. The same figure I'd already seen three times today. Too many times for me to think I was just hallucinating.

But again, I couldn't make out the woman's face because it was bathed in shadow. The woman was also dressed differently this time. The previous times, she had been wearing a black dress. Now she wore slacks and a white doctor's coat that was filthy and bloodstained.

"Ethan …it's me, Ethan…"

It sounded like she was right beside me.

That voice, though.

I recognized it.

And the woman wore a doctor's coat.

It can't be a coincidence…

Stepping out onto the road, I went to cross the street to go to the woman, but as I did, a loud, "Yeehaw!" made me stop in my tracks, and I saw Haedemus galloping down the street toward me, the two technomancers barely holding on as they sat atop him.

I looked back at the woman, but she was gone.

"…AND THEN DO YOU KNOW WHAT THAT COLD-HEARTED bitch said? She said if you don't like it, you can spend the rest of eternity grazing the Fields of Excrement with the rest of the Hellicorn has-beens, and I just thought to myself, you ungrateful fucking bitch. I mean, there I was, trudging through all manner of shit day in, day out, so she didn't have to get her fucking boots dirty! I mean, it's different with you, Ethan, because I don't mind riding you around, although, that doesn't mean I like you or anything, so don't go getting that idea. Let's be honest, Ethan, no one could like you if they tried, what with your cold heart and gruff attitude, but you do sometimes surprise me with moments of tenderness and understanding, unlike those little Hellbastard fucks who hate me and won't even let me hang around with them while they go off on their adventures I mean why don't I get to go on adventures no all I do is ride Ethan around the city while he visits his friends I like that Peter Pan boy he gave me more coke you have to get me more of this stuff Ethan I think I'm addicted already and I can feel my cock getting hard as we speak when can we get more coke Ethan...oh goodness... I'm out of breath...I can feel the fat melting off me here...I need more of this stuff... Ethan, get me more coke..."

Haedemus had been talking non-stop since he dropped Pan Demic and Artemis off from their ride, which wasn't around the block, but around half the goddamn city. Evidently, they had given him more coke while they were riding around. It was now difficult for me to control the massive beast, so off his head was he.

"Jesus, Haedemus," I protested as he nearly ran into an oncoming truck. "You're erratic to the point of being a fucking danger now."

"I can't help it," he gasped. "I just want to go in every direction at once."

"Well, don't!"

"It's because I'm horny. I need sex, Ethan, right this instant."

"That's not happening," I said as I pulled hard on the reins to get him to turn down a street instead of galloping on.

"Why not? Just look at all these people here begging for it."

"I don't think any of these people are begging to be molested by a goddamn beast like you, Haedemus. Keep your eyes on the road."

"Are you saying I'm too beastly to be attractive? Have you looked in the mirror lately, Ethan? You look like you've been dragged through a bush backward. Several bushes actually—"

I yanked on the reins as hard as I could, forcing him to stop so suddenly that he reared up on his back legs and gave a great whiney as I almost slid off him. "I'm getting off," I said.

"What the hell, Ethan!" he exclaimed.

I jumped down off him. "I can't listen to you anymore, Haedemus. Just go do what you have to do and get that shit out of your system. I'll get a cab home."

"Honestly, Ethan, you're being—"

"Bye, Haedemus."

I walked away, continuing to head to the home of Victoria Belford on foot, still thinking about the woman in the doctor's coat, her familiar voice, wondering if I was going crazy, or if someone was trying to drive me crazy. If they were, they were doing a good fucking job of it.

It's the fucking Spreak. It has to be.

Or just your deranged mind playing tricks, another voice inside me said.

"Ethan!" Haedemus called from behind me. "Ethan, come back!"

But I kept walking, not stopping until I reached Vic's place downtown, which took me over an hour to get there. Vic lived in a loft apartment near the center of Bankhurst, overlooking the park. She seemed surprised to see me when she opened the door.

"Ethan," she said, a smile forming on her face straight away. Without saying another word, she stepped forward and put her arms around me, hugging me tight, and I hugged her back, glad of her warmth and her still familiar touch. When she drew back, she kept her face close to mine as she stared deep into my eyes. She then caressed my face with her slender fingers before leaning in and brushing her soft lips against mine for a second, and as she did, I remembered the desire I used to have for, and the pleasure she used to give me.

"Vic..."

She put a finger on my lips and held it there. "I know what you need, Ethan..."

Her dark eyes full of seduction, she drew me into the apartment, and I kicked the door closed behind me.

7

D arkness had fallen outside by the time I strolled out of Vic's massive bedroom and into the fifty-foot "Great" room that featured a luxurious kitchen, Botticino marble, Mafi hardwood flooring, and deftly placed recessed lighting. It was also dressed with eight oversized windows that faced south; the view now obscured by the darkness outside.

Situated as it was in mid-town Bankhurst, I dreaded to think how much Vic had paid for the luxury loft apartment. Whatever she paid, she could afford it, thanks to the shrewd real estate investments she'd made over the years. Initially, she had purchased a few apartment buildings downtown and turned them into brothels—all legal—to give the working girls she protected somewhere to ply their trade in safety, without having to deal with vicious pimps and greedy landlords. From there, she built an empire, amassing a minor fortune in real estate holdings and shares in thriving tech companies. If Vic wasn't so well known as a Madam throughout the city, she would no doubt be lauded as one of the city's most successful businesswomen. As it was, the mainstream media largely ignored her success, and the rest of the business community treated her with suspicion, and most times, outright contempt. Even the men hated her as much as they wanted to fuck her, especially knowing she wasn't averse to using blackmail to get what she wanted.

I took little notice of Vic the Businesswoman, however. To me, Vic was just a friend—a best friend—who I enjoyed spending time with, even though this visit amounted to the longest time I'd spent with her in some years.

"I gotta say, Vic," I said as I walked over to the kitchen where she stood in a black satin robe making coffee, "you still know how to relax a guy."

She half-smiled as she looked up from pouring the coffee. "I hope I did more than that. Otherwise, that would mean I'm losing my touch."

"Come on, Vic. We all know that's impossible."

Vic smiled again, more fully this time, her dark brown eyes beautiful as they fell upon me, making me remember the intensity in them earlier as she did wicked things to me. "You flatter me so, Ethan. However—" She slid a coffee cup toward me. "—I fear age is taking its toll on me, just as it is you. I remember you having more stamina last time we did this. I didn't get the impression we could carry on until the morning."

"You're a cruel bitch," I said, smiling before sipping on the expensive coffee she made me. "But you're also right. I'm not the man I once was. None of us are."

"Well, if it means anything, you're still in my top ten."

"Wow, thanks," I said with more than a little sarcasm. "Who's number one?"

"A man I met in Brazil thirty years ago. His stamina, and the heights of ecstasy he brought me to, are unmatched to this day. He taught me a lot about male desire."

"What happened to him? Did you eat him after?"

She shook her head at me. "He's dead, but not from me. He ended up dabbling in things he shouldn't, and paid the price."

"The occult?"

"Voodoo."

"Yup, that'll do it, alright."

"Still, you have something no other man has, Ethan."

"Which is?"

"My trust."

"You'll always have that, Vic."

The satin robe barely covered her large breasts as she stood holding her coffee. "I have yet to thank you for saving my life." She took one long-fingered hand off her cup and stroked the scar across her neck.

"I think you've thanked me plenty," I said, smiling. "Don't you?"

"I mean formally." She stared at me for a second, her eyes filling with sincerity. "Thank you for saving my life, Ethan."

I nodded. "Your welcome. Besides, if weren't for you, that crazy fuck would still be running around killing girls."

"I'm glad you killed him."

"He tried to kill *me*."

"Would you have still killed him if he hadn't?"

"Yes," I said without hesitation.

Vic smiled. "That's one thing I've always liked about you, Ethan. You aren't afraid to do what has to be done, no matter the cost. You know what that makes you?"

"An idiot?"

She shook her head. "No, Ethan, it makes you a hero. This city would be much worse off without you."

"And you, Vic. Or the Rook, I should say."

"The Rook is dead," she said, looking away for a second. "She died when the Ripper Tripper cut her throat."

I frowned. "What?"

"I've done my time. It's time for someone else to take over."

"Like who?"

Vic paused for a moment before saying, "For the last year, I've been training six specially selected girls, teaching them everything I know, as well as bringing in outside instruction. By the time I'm finished with them, they will be a formidable force, and will do more to stop the scumbags in this town than I ever did."

"Shit," I said after a moment. "You're still full of surprises, Vic, I'll give you that."

"I thought we already established that in the bedroom."

"We did. I just mean you're always ahead of the curve."

"I know what you meant." She came around and sat on the stool next to me, crossing her long legs, her dark hair spilling behind her as she leaned back against the marble worktop.

"So, what are you gonna do instead?" I asked her, intoxicated by her scent once more, unable to take my eyes off her. "Once your new girls have been trained up."

"I'm considering moving away," she said. "Moving on."

"What about all the girls you watch over? Will you be leaving them in the capable hands of your new vigilante force?"

"They are called the Valkyries, and yes, they will take over all protection duties. They have their own ideas and plans."

"Such as?"

"They wish to train up all the working girls in the city, make it a prerequisite of the job. Every girl should be able to protect themselves from the predators out there."

"Admirable," I said. "Though I'm not sure if a few self-defense classes will cut it."

"It will be more than that. Training will be intensive and ongoing."

"Careful. You might end up creating an army. Besides, guys wanna fuck prostitutes, not soldiers."

Vic looked away and said nothing for a moment, then turned and said, "I was sorry to hear about your friend."

I stared at her for a second, wondering if she was trying to hurt me because I criticized her plans. "Yeah. I miss him."

"It's not easy when people close to us die," she said. "I discovered that when my father died when I was young."

"Is that why you never get close to people?"

"You don't think I'm close to you, Ethan?"

"I think you don't want to be, despite how much I wanted you to be at one point."

"You don't want that anymore?" she asked.

"I'm like you, Vic. I've learned my lesson—too many times."

"And yet you are partners with the Fallen woman."

"Partners, yeah."

"Nothing more? I remember her from that night you found me. I could tell she cared for you. More than cared."

I looked away for a second as I sipped my coffee, wishing I had my cigarettes, which were in the bedroom. Not that Vic would let me smoke in here, anyway. "Hannah and I have an unconventional relationship."

Vic laughed a little. "Unconventional. Seriously, Ethan. You either love her, or you don't."

"It's not like that."

"It's always like that."

"Do *you* love *me*?" I don't know why I said it. Maybe just to stop her talking about Hannah. Maybe just to see her reaction.

As she stared at me, I'd never seen so many emotions cross her normally implacable face, until eventually she looked away and shook her head. "What a ridiculous question," she said, though we both knew she didn't consider it so.

"I'm sorry," I said. "I don't know why—"

"Yes," she said suddenly. "If you want the truth, there it is. I've always loved you, Ethan. Most times, you were just too dumb to see it."

"Or you just hid it well."

"That too."

"Why have you never said anything?"

"I just did."

"Before now."

"For many reasons, one of which is that you were married, don't forget."

I breathed in deep and exhaled slowly before sipping at my coffee, really wishing I had those cigarettes now.

Vic cradled her coffee in both hands. "Would it be asking too much if I asked you to come away with me?"

It was tempting just to up and leave this place for good, especially with Vic. We understood each other, and if I would run away with anyone, it would probably be her. But we both knew it would never happen outside of a fantasy.

"It's okay," she said, taking my silence for turndown, which it was. "I'll save you the embarrassment of saying no. The embarrassment is on me." She stood up then, placing her coffee cup on the counter, tightening her robe around her. "You should probably go, Ethan. I'm sure your 'partner' is wondering where you are."

"Come on, Vic," I said, standing now. "Don't be like that. You know if there was any way—"

"I understand," she said, folding her arms. "You care about this city too much to ever leave it. I can't expect a hero to just walk away."

"There're things I gotta do, Vic—"

"I said it's fine." She came forward and placed her warm hands on my cheeks before kissing me for what felt like the last ever time. "Take care of yourself, Ethan."

A sadness welled up in me as I stared into her large, dark eyes. In a different life, there was no way I'd be getting ready to walk away from her. In a different life, I'd be staying. "You too, Vic."

She gave me a last lingering look as if to burn my face into her memory, then turned and walked around the other side of the kitchen where she rinsed the cups we were using, coming across as if I'd already left.

Nodding to myself, I went to the bedroom to collect the rest of my things before walking to the front door.

"Ethan?" Vic said as I was about to walk out.

I stopped and turned to look at her. "Yeah, Vic?"

"Take a shower," she said. "My scent lingers."

Don't I know it.

"Goodbye, Vic."

WHEN I GOT BACK TO THE YARD VIA A CAB RIDE, I discovered the place to be empty. All the workers had gone home for the day, having installed all the new machinery, the cold moonlight reflecting off the machines' untarnished surfaces.

Hannah hadn't yet returned, and Daisy was gone too, a note in her trailer saying she had gone for a walk and would be back later. There was no sign of Haedemus either (fuck knows where he was, considering the state he was in when I left him earlier), or the Hellbastards.

Least I thought there wasn't until I came out of my trailer to smoke a cigarette, finding Cracka sitting on the bottom step like a little demonic garden gnome.

"Hey, Cracka," I said, frowning down at him, wondering why he appeared to be alone, not to mention forlorn, which Cracka never was. "What ya doing there? Where's the rest of the hellions at?"

Cracka shrugged his small shoulders. "Dunno," he said, sounding depressed.

I sat down beside him on the step as I smoked my cigarette, the night still and silent, the air so cold it was hard to tell what was smoke and what was breath.

"What's bothering you, little guy? Is the crushing weight of existence getting too much for you? Is ennui and dread becoming *your* dominant emotions these days as well? Is the anguish of freedom getting too much for you, and are you realizing that we are all condemned to be free, as Sartre put it?"

Cracka stared at me for a second with his bug eyes and then said, "Waa?"

"Why are you sad, Cracka?"

"I sad because I want to join Muppets, and I can't because Muppets not really real."

I stared at him for a moment, hardly knowing how to react. "And you've just found this out? That the Muppets aren't real?"

"Yes."

"All these years of watching them, you never knew they were just puppets?" I snorted. "Come on, Cracka—"

"But Miss Piggy, she so beautiful."

"Yeah, a beautiful puppet. I can't believe you thought they were real. Seriously. Who told you?"

"Reggie."

"And this just came up in the conversation, did it?"

"Cracka say he going to find Miss Piggy, to declare love to her, and then Reggie tell me she just—" He stopped, the emotion getting to him.

"A puppet?"

"Yes! It not fair! I wanted to live with Muppets!"

"Are you not happy here, Cracka?" *Not that you can leave, anyway.*

"The others, they pick on Cracka all the time. Make me like baby!"

"They make you *feel* like a baby, you mean?"

"Yes!"

"Well, you have to stand up to those guys, and don't let them push you around."

"They bigger than me. Stronger."

"Try ignoring them. They taunt you so much because they know they'll always get you to react, which you do, Cracka, hilariously so most of the time."

"They laugh at me!"

"Well, you're a funny little guy at times, Cracka."

"You think I funny? Like Muppet funny?"

"I think, Cracka, you would make a fine addition to *The Muppet Show*. People would love you. And Miss Piggy?"

"Yeah?" he said, eager for me to go on.

"Well, she wouldn't be able to resist you, would she? After every show, she'd take you into your dressing room— which would be bigger than all the others because you'd be the star of the show—"

"Bigger than Kermit even?"

"Shit yeah. You'd leave that ribbety has-been for dust."

"So what Miss Piggy do to me?"

"Well, she'd take you into your big dressing room, which would have a king-sized bed, and she'd throw you down on that bed and—"

I didn't get any further because a massive explosion erupted in the north end of the yard, an enormous ball of flame lighting up the night, the force of the explosion sending metal flying everywhere.

Both Cracka and I shot to our feet at the same time.

"What the fuck?" I said, wondering what could've caused such an explosion, especially since it happened where the brand new crusher was located.

But before I could reach any conclusions, another explosion happened near the center of the yard, and I saw the new material handler get blown to pieces, followed a second later by another explosion that decimated a brand new fork-lift truck not a hundred yards from my trailer.

As I stood gazing at the devastation in shock, I caught sight of a figure perched atop a stack of cubed scrap metal, a dark figure silhouetted by the flames in the background. Whoever it was, they were dressed all in black, including a black mask. Without thinking, I whipped out my sidearm, about to fire at the person until they back-flipped off the tower of scrap and disappeared from sight.

"What the fuck?" I breathed, still in shock at the devastation all around me.

"What going on, boss?" Cracka asked, his large eyes reflecting the fires in the yard.

"I don't fucking know," I said. "Search the yard for intruders. If you find anyone, take them down and hold them until I get there."

"Yes, boss," Cracka said and leaped off the step before scurrying off and disappearing.

I advanced into the yard myself, my gun out as I looked for the person I'd seen a moment ago, but there was so much smoke around the place, it was almost impossible to see anything. I did find Ace and Apollo, though, cowering underneath an old Buick as the flames continued to rage around them. I managed to coax the two dogs out and lead them to my trailer, where I put them inside and closed the door.

From far away, the sound of sirens carried over. The cops and fire department would likely be here soon, and I would have to try to explain why half the fucking yard had been blown up, even though I had no idea what happened.

One thing I did know, though, was that the explosions were no accident. Even if I hadn't seen the intruder earlier, I still would've known plastic explosives caused the damage. I knew C-4 when I heard it, for I'd used it enough times myself over the years.

But the question remained: Who would go to the trouble of blowing up my fucking yard, along with hundreds of thousands of dollar's worth of equipment?

I continued to search the place until I met up with Cracka as he came strolling out of a patch of fire, his skin unaffected by the flames.

"No sign, boss," he said.

I shook my head, my frustration soon turning to anger as Cal's legacy blew around me in the form of black smoke.

"Fuck! I swear to fuck whoever did this is fucking *dead!*"

"Fucking dead, boss!" Cracka echoed, seeming as pissed off as I was.

Turning, I made my way through the mounds of smoldering scrap on the way back to the trailer, nothing left to do now but wait on the authorities showing up. Whatever investigation there was, I'd get it dropped. I'd do my own investigating, and I wouldn't stop until I'd found the culprit or culprits.

But as it turned out, I didn't have to look too far to know who had done this.

When I reached my trailer again, I stopped and stared in horror as I saw Ace and Apollo lying in the dirt, unmoving, their blood all over the ground.

"No, no…"

I rushed over to the two dogs, but they were both dead.

To add insult to injury, their blood had been used to write a message on the side of my trailer, though I didn't understand what it said because the characters were Japanese.

The very fact that the message was in Japanese told me enough, though.

Suddenly, it all made sense.

This was Yagami's son—Susumu.

Motherfucker.

I turned when I heard a car behind me, thinking it was

the cops. But it turned out to be Hannah. She got out of the car, her face full of urgent concern, which turned to horror when she saw the bodies of Ace and Apollo, and then the message in blood written on the side of the trailer.

"What does it mean?" I half-snarled when she came to stand beside me.

Hannah let out a breath. "It means you are marked for death, Ethan."

8

The cops and the fire department showed up sometime later. While the firefighters doused the flames still burning in the yard, I dealt with the cops, showing the uniforms my FBI ID before giving them a brief statement that said I didn't have a clue what happened. Before they arrived, Hannah and I wiped the message in blood from the trailer and hid the bodies of the dogs in the Secret Garden. The uniforms wanted to get some plainclothes investigators out. But I soon put a stop to that by calling Director Bradley, telling him I'd been the victim of reprisal from an old foe, and that I thought it would be best if the regular authorities stayed out of it, given how sensitive the situation was. Bradley agreed to get the cops to back off, just as long as I explained everything to him at the office the next day. An hour later, the cops were gone. So were the firefighters, having doused the flames in the yard.

When everyone had left, I walked around the yard, inspecting the damage. Every single piece of machinery had been blown to pieces. The business was fucked, and there was no way it could continue to operate unless all the machinery was replaced. The problem was, none of it was insured. We had spent all of our money on buying the machines, intending to sort out the insurance further down the line once our capital had built up again. That also meant there was no money to buy new machinery, and without the machinery, we could make no more money.

Rage boiled in me as I took in the destroyed machinery; rage exacerbated by guilt because it felt like I had allowed Cal's legacy to be destroyed, and his name dishonored. Not to mention Ace and Apollo, both now dead.

"Fuck!" I growled as I walked back to the trailer.

I knew Yagami's degenerate son would want vengeance. I should've taken him out before he got the chance to do anything. Instead, I'd given the bastard time to prepare his revenge, and he now had the upper hand.

What was next? Attacks on me? On Hannah? On Daisy?

I couldn't allow that to happen.

Susumu had done enough damage already.

I had to take the bastard out before he killed somebody.

DAISY HAD RETURNED BY THE TIME I GOT BACK. SHE STOOD along with Hannah outside the trailer, her face full of anger and dismay. As soon as I approached, she turned on me.

"Why did you allow this to happen?" she asked angrily.

I took a deep breath before answering. "You're upset over the dogs—"

"Over all of it! You allowed this Yagami person to destroy our home, Ethan!"

She wasn't wrong.

"I'll take care of it," I said, trying to keep my anger in check.

Daisy snorted. "Oh, you'll take care of it? Like you took care of those fucking werewolves that killed Cal? If Cal was here, he'd be disgusted in you, Ethan. You allowed his place to be destroyed!"

"Daisy—" Hannah went to put a hand on Daisy's shoulder, but Daisy—tears streaming down her face now—shoved Hannah away, and for a just a second, I saw Hannah's eyes turn amber as anger stirred in her. Her Visage, all but invisible these days, turned dark as it loomed over her.

"Everyone needs to calm down," I said.

"No," Daisy said. "We need to go out and kill the person who did this before he kills all of us."

"I won't let that happen," I said.

"Oh yeah?" Daisy said, her voice cold now. "Tell that to Cal."

She glared at me for a few seconds before stomping away toward her trailer.

When Daisy had gone, I turned to look at Hannah, who seemed to be struggling to keep herself in check. "You alright?" I asked her.

She nodded, but said nothing as the dark Visage hovered over her for a few seconds more before fading from view. Her hand shook slightly as she took out a pack of cigarettes and lit one, taking a few drags before looking at me, but still saying nothing.

"Hannah? Talk to me. What's going on?"

She shook her head. "Nothing, I just…lost control there for a second. It felt like…" She trailed off, but I knew what she was going to say. She just couldn't say it.

"That Xaglath was coming out? I saw your Visage. It was dark."

"Too much emotion, that's all. I'm fine."

"You sure?"

She nodded. "Daisy's right. We allowed this to happen, Ethan."

I dug for my own cigarettes and pulled them out, jacking one into my mouth before lighting it. "We fucked up. I know that. We should've taken Susumu out before now. But still, there's not much we can do about it now. We just can't give him a chance to come at us again."

"We're going after him?"

"He hasn't left us much choice."

"What about Bradley?"

"What about him?"

"He'll want to know what's going on. What are you going to tell him?"

"The truth, I suppose."

"And you think he will let us just go after Susumu?"

"He will if he wants us to keep working for him."

Hannah took a drag of her cigarette as she stood in silence for a few seconds before saying, "What about Daisy? She seems upset."

"You think?"

"You know what I mean. One of us should talk to her before she does something foolish."

I nodded. "I'll go talk to her."

Hannah ground the remains of her cigarette underfoot. "I'm going to take a shower," she said. "I stink of vampire filth."

"How'd it go today?"

"Fine. We secured the target. He's locked away in a holding facility."

"You should've just killed the fucker. What do they intend to do with all these fucking MURKs they're collecting like trophies?"

Hannah shrugged. "It's the government. They can't just kill them, MURKs or not."

"Yeah, well, having all those fuckers in one place is just a disaster waiting to happen."

"Let's hope not," Hannah said, lingering by me a second before walking away and saying over her shoulder, "You should take a shower as well."

Anxiety stabbed at my stomach as I looked back at her, my eyes meeting hers for a second, seeing the look in them. *She knows.*

I WAS ALMOST AFRAID TO GO INTO DAISY'S TRAILER, knowing how angry she was at me, and how Supernormal powers could end up out of control in such states. The last thing I needed was for Daisy to attack me with some hitherto undiscovered superpower brought on by her rage.

When I entered the trailer, however, I found Daisy in the bedroom, sitting on the bed with her legs drawn to her chest, her arms wrapped tightly around her knees as she rocked back and forth, tears still streaming from her eyes.

"Daisy?" I said softly as I stood by the door. "Can I come in?"

Daisy nodded after a second but said nothing as she continued to gaze down at the bed as if it had all the answers.

I sat on the edge of the bed for a moment, wondering what to say to her. Even when Callie was alive, I was never very good at talking to her when she got into emotional states. "I'm sorry, Daisy. This is all my fault."

Daisy sniffed and shook her head. "I shouldn't have said what I said. About Cal, especially. I know that wasn't your fault."

"I brought the wolves to the door," I said, swallowing. "That's something I'll always have to live with."

Wiping her tears, Daisy sat in silence for a moment, and then said, "I went to see my mother today. Her grave, I mean."

"Oh," I said, nodding. Now I understood her rage. I'd felt the same rage myself often enough after visiting the graves of Angela and Callie.

Still rocking back and forth, Daisy said, "I thought she was a horrible person when she was alive. I was horrible *to* her. She had problems, and I didn't even try to understand—" She had to stop as she choked on her tears.

Moving closer, I put my arm around her and pulled her into me. "It's okay," I said. "It's not your fault she's dead. You did your best, Daisy."

"No! I hated her! I hated her so much! I—I *wanted* her to die!"

All I could do was hold her as uncontrollable sobbing wracked her. "Shhhh…it's okay…"

"*I miss her*," she choked out. "*I miss her so much…I want her back…I want her back…*"

I mashed my lips together to stop my own tears from coming, knowing how she felt, remembering the times I spent sobbing in some dark corner, wishing my mother was still alive, wishing I had been nicer to her when she *was* alive, reprimanding myself for not doing enough to steer her away from the life she chose.

But what good is regret?

Not that I would pose such a rhetorical question to Daisy. She would find out for herself at some point.

I held her for another while until she calmed down. Until the numbness overtook her.

"What about the dogs?" she asked, eventually.

"I'll bury them next to Cal in the garden," I said. "It's what he would want."

"I'll help you. Just let me freshen up first."

IT WASN'T A PLEASANT EXPERIENCE BURYING THE TWO DOGS. I'd known them since they were pups and felt responsible for them since Cal died. Not only that, but I felt tremendous guilt as I dug the grave next to Cal's, feeling like I'd let him down in so many ways. He had trusted me to look after things in his absence, and I'd failed miserably. If he were here now, he'd probably punch me. And I'd deserve it.

LATER, AS I SAT IN MY TRAILER WORKING MY WAY THROUGH a bottle of Johnnie Walker with Delta blues playing low in the background, I kept glancing at the photo of Cal on the wall, almost feeling his eyes on me as they burned with recrimination.

"You've really made a fucking mess of things, haven't you? I'm gone for two fucking minutes and what happens? My yard is blown to pieces, and my two dogs are dead. What the fuck, Ethan? I thought I could rely on you. Maybe I was wrong. Maybe you're a bigger fuck-up than I thought you were. Those fucking wolves shoulda killed you, not me. At least then, my dogs would be alive, and my yard would still be intact. You're a goddamn liability—you always were. Mommy dying fucked you up good and proper. I don't know why I ever thought I could fix you. You can't be fixed, Ethan. Everything you touch falls to shit. People die around you. I was the wrong person to mentor you. Richard Solomon should've mentored you instead. You both share the same link with Death. Go to him and give everyone else around you a chance to live. As long as you're around, they won't get that chance—not Daisy, not your demon partner...not even you, Ethan..."

Cal's voice sounded clear as day in my head, and despite drinking more whiskey, I couldn't drown it out. Cal just went on talking until I finally fell into a drunken sleep.

And that's when the real nightmare began.

9

I awoke with a start, knowing something wasn't right.

And something wasn't, for I was no longer in my trailer.

I was lying on the floor inside a room that I recognized immediately—the living room of the house I used to share with Angela in Crown Point. Lying on my back, I noticed the pictures on the walls in the dimmed light, even the water stain on the corner of the ceiling, caused by Callie letting the bath overflow once.

"What the fuck?" I mumbled, freaked out, my mouth dry from the whiskey, my throat hoarse from too many cigarettes.

I must still be dreaming.

Sitting up, Angela's prone body confronted me lying on the wood floor, surrounded by blood.

"No," I breathed as I took in my ex-wife's body. "Wake the fuck up, Ethan…"

But I *was* awake. Somehow I knew I wasn't sleeping. This was too real to be any dream. I was here, in the room with Angela on the night she died.

But how?

I stared at Angela's unmoving body for long seconds, half expecting her to get up. I could smell the death in the room, the coppery scent of blood, the stench of loosened bowels. In the silence, the house creaked as if in anticipation.

But in anticipation of what? Why was I here? *How* was I here?

Shutting my eyes, I kept them closed for a moment, telling myself that when I opened them again, I'd be out of this nightmare and back in my trailer.

But when I opened my eyes, I was still in the living room.

And Angela was sitting up, her large, dark eyes fixed on me, her hair matted with blood, half her throat torn away, deep claw marks across her chest, one breast almost shredded.

"Jesus Christ!" I shouted as I slid back away from her, not stopping until my back hit the wall. "You're not real... you're not fucking real...*none* of this is real."

Angela stared at me for another few seconds before turning her attention to the pool of blood she sat in, running her fingers through the crimson mess before bringing her fingers to her mouth and tasting it.

"You know how it tastes, Ethan?" she said, her eyes full of recrimination. "It tastes bitter because when that monster was killing me, all I felt was hatred and betrayal. You promised to keep us safe, Callie and I, but you brought the monster to our door. You led it here so it could kill us."

"No..." I said, shaking my head. "I didn't—"

"Didn't what?" she said, getting to her feet now. "You didn't mean for this to happen? Of course you didn't. You never do, Ethan. But trouble always finds you anyway. If I'd known what a prick you really were, I'd never have married you. I'd never have allowed you to get me pregnant, and then Callie would've been saved from all of this."

There was no sadness in her voice, only bitterness and hatred.

Desperately, I looked around for a second, hoping the room would fade from view, and I'd end up back in my trailer. I was still hoping this was a dream, a very vivid, disturbing dream—but still a dream.

"You think this is all a dream, don't you?" Angela said and then laughed coldly as she came closer to me. "This is no dream, Ethan. This is as real as it gets." As if to back up her words, she walked toward me and crouched down, putting her cold, bloody fingers on my face, which I half flinched away from. "You see. I'm really here, Ethan."

"But if *you're* here…" I looked toward the stairs. "Callie…"

"She's up there," Angela said. "Our little girl, lying in her blood-soaked bed, asking herself why her daddy allowed a monster to kill her."

Almost like I was being controlled by an outside force, I got to my feet and went to move toward the stairs. My little girl was up there, and I had to see her.

"Uh-uh," Angela said, causing me to turn around at the foot of the stairs. "You don't get to see her."

Angela clicked her fingers, and in an instant, we were standing inside my trailer.

"What…" I said, my head spinning as I wondered what the hell was happening.

"It's just you and me, Ethan," Angela said, and I saw she now wore her white doctor's coat. It even had her doctor's ID badge clipped to it, and her stethoscope was in the breast pocket. Underneath, she wore dark slacks and a white blouse. When I looked at her face, I saw her wounds had disappeared, but strange, black blotches were moving around under her skin and around her neck, sometimes causing her face to become enveloped in shadow, so it was like looking at a blank mask.

"It was you," I breathed. "It's you I've been seeing all this time."

She smiled dispassionately, her face lacking the warmth she once had in abundance. "I've been keeping an eye on you for a while now, watching you fuck your life up as you've always done."

"No, this is—you can't be here. You're dead, Angela."

"Don't tell me you don't believe in ghosts, Ethan, when we both know you do."

"You're no ghost."

"Then, what am I?"

"I don't know what you are, if you're even here at all. Maybe my mind has cracked, and I've finally gone insane. Or maybe—"

"What?"

"Maybe you're the motherfucker who had my wife and daughter killed."

Her face never wavered. "And who might that be?"

My eyes narrowed. "You don't even speak like Angela."

"Poor Ethan. You think so much, but know so little."

"Fuck you, whoever you are."

Angela gave a slight laugh as if she found my dismay amusing. "I'll leave it up to you to decide if I'm really here or not, and who I really am, if anyone. Either way, I'm not going anywhere, Ethan. Kinda like that time I caught you fucking that girl from that shithole club you used to drink in. What was it called? The Brokedown Palace?" She shook her head a little in disdain. "You thought I'd still be at that conference in Denver, and Callie was still with my sister. Thought you still had the whole house to yourself, didn't you, Ethan?"

"Stop…"

"I thought I'd surprise my husband by getting an early flight home so I could spend some time with him. But only one of us was surprised. Isn't that right, Ethan? And I can tell you, it wasn't me."

She was speaking of the lowest point in our marriage. It was all over after that.

"You really were a bastard to me, Ethan," she said. "I hope you treat your partner with more respect. I'm guessing you've fucked her already? Yes, of course you have. I'll even hazard another guess and say that you've fucked someone else behind her back." She nodded when she saw the look on my face. "That whore, Vic, was it?"

"You've been following me…"

"I've been watching you, yes. Couldn't help yourself, could you, Ethan?"

A sigh left me as I looked away for a second. "What do you want?"

She shrugged as she looked around the trailer for a moment, her face saying she found it all very distasteful. She always was a snob. "I don't know yet."

"You don't know? What the fuck does that mean? You must want *something*. What's the point of all this otherwise?"

The darkness moved around her face as she came closer. "Maybe I just want to drive you mad, Ethan, to steal from you the last vestiges of your crumbling sanity. For what you did to Callie and me, you deserve a lot worse…and maybe you'll get worse."

"Stop pretending to be her. You're not her. You're not even here…"

Angela rolled her eyes and tutted. "Of course I'm here, you big stupid oaf. The question you should be asking yourself is *why*. Why am I here?"

"You just said, to drive me mad."

"Maybe there's more to it than that."

"Like what?"

"That's what you have to figure out, Ethan. The question is, can you do so before your sanity runs out?"

Turning, I marched to the bedroom and got my gun from off the bedside table before stomping back and pointing it at her. "I should just blow your fucking head off right now."

"Go on," she said, darkness moving around her eyes as she stepped closer. "Shoot your dead wife in the head, Ethan. See what that does to your sanity. It's your answer to everything anyway, isn't it? Violence. It's all you know how to do, Ethan. You're nothing but a one-dimensional character from a comic book. Besides, you want to see Callie again, don't you?"

I shook my head. "Callie's gone."

"Like I'm gone?" She stepped closer to the gun, so it was almost touching her head. "I'm right here, Ethan, in case you haven't noticed."

"Shut up."

"I can bring her to you, our daughter. She so desperately wants to see her daddy again."

"I said, shut up!"

A smile crossed her face just as the door knocked, and a voice said, "Ethan? Can I come in?"

It was Daisy.

"Eh, not right now," I stammered.

"Go on, Ethan," Angela said. "Let her in—your surrogate daughter."

"Shut up!"

"Ethan?" Daisy said, concern in her voice now, probably knowing something was up. Before I could stop her, she opened the door and stepped inside, pausing to stare at me. "Why are you holding your gun out?"

I looked at her and then at Angela, expecting Daisy to look at her as well, but she didn't.

Angela turned and walked toward Daisy and stood to examine her, her face saying she wasn't impressed. "So, this is your replacement for Callie?"

"No," I said.

Daisy, thinking I was talking to her, said, "What? Are you alright, Ethan?"

She can't see her. She can't see my dead wife.

"Another wounded soul for the fold," Angela said. "You're amassing quite the collection here, Ethan."

"Now's not a good time," I said to Daisy, doing my best to ignore Angela, who was still staring at Daisy like she was contemplating doing something terrible to her.

"Why?" Daisy asked. "What's wrong with you, Ethan? You look like you've seen a ghost."

"Is that what I am, Ethan?" Angela asked, coming toward me again. "A ghost?"

"I'm fine," I told Daisy as I put the gun next to the kitchen sink, hardly knowing what to do with my hands afterward.

"You should see your face, Ethan," Angela said, smiling in amusement. "It's like that time I arranged a surprise birthday party for you, and you showed up and didn't know what to do when you saw all those people."

"You don't look fine," Daisy said, coming further into the trailer after closing the door.

"It's just been a tough day," I said, glancing at Angela. "What is it, Daisy?"

"I thought we could talk about putting some security measures around this place," Daisy said. "The yard, I mean. In case the Yakuza guy comes back."

"Security?" I said. "What kind of security?"

"Well," Daisy said, taking a notebook from out of her jeans pocket. "I've come up with some measures. A plan of protection."

"A plan of protection, Ethan," Angela said almost mockingly. "You chose well in her, didn't you? She's a chip off the old block already."

My jaw clenched as I resisted the urge to tell Angela to

shut the fuck up. Not Angela. I was convinced by this stage that this was someone else, or some*thing* else, maybe even a figment of my imagination. But not Angela, the woman I knew and loved.

Unless her soul had become twisted in death, turning her into this.

Jesus, I don't know what to think…

"Don't you think it's a bit late to be discussing plans, Daisy," I said as gently as possible so I wouldn't offend her. "Maybe tomorrow would be a better time to discuss it."

"Well, I just thought because I couldn't sleep, and because you said you weren't sleeping much either—"

"Ahh," Angela cooed, reaching out and touching my face with her cold hands, making me flinch enough that Daisy noticed. "Is my ex-husband having trouble sleeping these days? I wonder why." She laughed.

"—I thought maybe we could—" Daisy stopped and stared at me. "Seriously, Ethan, are you high or something? You look freaked out."

"I just overdid the whiskey…and maybe some other stuff as well," I said. "Can we do this tomorrow? I really want to hear what you've come up with, and I agree, we need security measures put in place, but—"

Daisy sighed as she put the notebook back in her pocket. "Tomorrow. Yeah, I get it." She turned and headed for the door.

"Thanks," I said weakly.

"Get some damn sleep, Ethan," Daisy said. "You're no good to anyone like this."

She slammed the door shut behind her, and I closed my eyes for a second and sighed.

"Get some damn sleep, Ethan," Angela mimicked. "She's a bossy little thing, isn't she? Do you think Callie would've turned out that way? I mean she was—"

"Don't fucking talk about her," I snarled, turning on her,

grabbing her by the throat and pushing her against the wall as she smiled, showing no fear. "Whoever or whatever the fuck you are, I want you gone, you hear me?"

"I hear you," she said. "But as I said, I'm not going anywhere, at least not until *I* decide to go, and not when *you* tell me."

I let her go and stepped back. "Then maybe you should just *decide* to go *now*."

She stared at me for a moment and then nodded. "Okay, I will, just to give you a little time to adjust to your new circumstances. And Ethan?"

"What?" I growled.

My dead ex-wife smiled. "Welcome to Hell, babe."

Then just like that, she vanished, leaving me to wonder if I'd hallucinated the whole encounter.

Dawn broke the next morning, and I still hadn't slept a wink. Not only was I avoiding the nightmares, but I was thinking about my encounter with Angela, if it was even her, which I didn't believe it was, despite some things she said. She was no ghost either, being of flesh and blood.

So if it wasn't Angela, then who was it?

Not a figment of my imagination either. I may be fucked up, but I'm not that fucked up. At least, I don't think I am.

Which only leaves one other possibility in my mind: someone was fucking with me.

It had to be the Spreak I was after. The last time I saw him was a few weeks ago when I was talking to Bradley outside the FPD precinct. I chased the fucker into an alley, but he vanished. I knew I hadn't seen the last of him, and that he'd be out to get me now that I was on to him. Hell, he'd been out to get me since he sent that fucking werewolf merc to kill my family.

The nightmares started shortly after that night in the alley, and I knew deep down that the mysterious Spreak had something to do with it. Now I'm realizing that the figure I keep seeing in my dreams is him. He'd just been building up to making a physical appearance, which he chose to do as my dead ex-wife because he knew that would unsettle me the most, and he was right. The bastard was, or still is, inside my head somehow, which is how he knew so many personal details about my relationship with Angela.

So assuming I was right, what the hell was I going to do about this guy?

The bastard was out to get me, but I didn't know what his endgame was.

Was he planning on driving me insane? Killing me eventually, the way he had Angela and Callie killed?

Why the fuck was he doing this?

AFTER TAKING SOME COFFEE AND A DOSE OF MUD TO CALM myself down—the Mud doing little to take the edge off—I visited Daisy in her trailer and apologized to her for last night. She shrugged it off and said it was fine, still eager to show me the plans she had drawn up to secure the yard against future attacks.

As I read over her notes and viewed the diagrams she had drawn, I was astounded at the level of detail in her plans. This was professional level planning, and no stone had been left unturned. Every major and minor hole in the yard's security had been painstakingly identified, which given the vast size of the yard, was impressive in itself. Daisy had also gone to great lengths to come up with ways to plug the holes, so to speak, which included measures like razor wire around the entire perimeter fence, the setting up of microwave barriers, electrostatic field disturbance sensors, seismic sensors, and a full CCTV system. It was all highly impressive, but unfortunately, completely unviable.

"It's amazing that you came up with all this," I said to

her. "But what you're talking about here would cost a lot of money to set up. Money we don't have."

Daisy stared at me for a moment, her eyes still full of sleep, and then sighed. "Okay."

"Seriously, though. The system you designed here is excellent."

"But pointless."

"Look," I said. "I will try to arrange a meeting with Susumu Yagami and see if we can't sort this shit out without the need for further destruction or violence."

Daisy frowned at me like I was mad. "And you think he'll listen? He blew up near the whole damn yard. He killed the dogs and wrote in their blood that you are marked for death. And you want to talk things out with him?"

She had a point. But conflict resolution was an option I had to exhaust before I could think of other more direct and brutal responses.

The last thing I wanted was a war.

"If things get violent, there's more chance of people getting hurt," I said. "Or killed."

"Wake up, Ethan," Daisy said, wrapping a blanket around herself as she turned on the TV to watch the news. "Things have already gotten violent. They got violent the second you shot that guy's father in the head. You know there's only one way to end this now."

THE HELLBASTARDS HAD THEIR OWN TRAILER. I THOUGHT IT a good idea to give them their own space, so they weren't annoying me and fucking up my place all the time. The trailer is at the back of the yard, near the Secret Garden. As Haedemus still hadn't returned, I went to see the Hellbastards in case they had heard from him. Not that I was worried about the Hellicorn. He could take care of himself.

But I was worried about what shit he might cause while he was running around coked off his head.

When I went inside the Hellbastards' trailer, I stopped and stared in shock when I found them all on the floor, their hands and feet bound with what looked like wire.

All except Cracka that is.

The little demon was walking around with a cattle prod in his hand as the other demons lay moaning on the floor, muttering strange things to themselves as if their minds' were somewhere else entirely.

"Cracka," I said, staring at him. "What the fuck are you doing?"

"Just what you said, boss," Cracka replied with a satisfied grin on his face. "I taking back the power!"

"What?"

"I showing these assholes whose boss so they don't pick on me anymore."

"Cracka, that's not really what I meant…"

"Boss," Scroteface said in a faraway voice that made him sound like he was off his head on drugs. "I didn't know you had wings."

"I don't, Scroteface." I looked at Cracka. "What did you give them?"

"LSD, boss. A lot of LSD. Put it in beer." He grinned, pleased with himself that he'd thought up such a fiendish scheme.

"Boss…help," Toast said in a small voice. "I'm about to fall through the floor…"

"I'm brainwashing them," Cracka said. "Like CIA do. I see it on TV."

Puffing my cheeks out, I shook my head. "Jesus Christ…"

"Ow!" Snotskull cried when Cracka hit him with the cattle prod.

"Tell Cracka you never disrespect him again!" Cracka said. "Say it!"

"Fuck you, you little twerp," Reggie said, his eyes rolling around in their sockets. God knows how much LSD Cracka had given them all.

"You're …dead…Cracka," Scroteface said as though he were struggling to get the words out.

Cracka made a show of tutting and shaking his head. "You still a lot to learn, Scrotey," he said and hit him with the cattle prod, eliciting a scream from Scroteface.

"Cracka!" I ripped the cattle prod from his hands. "Stop this!"

"But boss, you said—"

"I didn't say fucking drug them and torture them, Cracka. Untie them, for Christ's sake."

"I will," Cracka said. "When they tell me I'm the man."

"What?"

"The man, boss. Like the song."

"What song?"

"The song. It goes like, *'I'm on your case, I'm in your face, I kick you and your father back in place…'*"

"Anthrax…boss," Reggie helpfully pointed out, so fucked up he could barely get the words out.

"Cracka?" I said, trying to keep my temper as well as my sanity.

"Yeah, boss?"

"Just untie them and then hope they don't kill you for doing this."

"I think they know who boss is now anyway," Cracka said. "I been doing this for six hours."

"Good lord…"

"I haven't even waterboarded them yet."

"Surf's up…" Snot Skull muttered.

"I'm going to work now," I said. "I expect everybody

back to normal and getting along when I get back later, or—"

"Or what, boss?" Cracka asked.

"You know what," I said to him, before addressing them all. "You all know what. Get along, or it's back to Hell."

"Peace and love," Reggie said. "Sure thing, boss. Nice trunk, by the way. It suits you."

~

WHEN I GOT BACK TO MY TRAILER, HANNAH WAS THERE waiting for me, dressed in a black pantsuit, all ready for work, even if her face wasn't exactly full of her usual enthusiasm.

"You okay?" I asked her.

"I'm not sure," she said. "You slept with Vic, didn't you?"

I paused at the door and stared at her for a second. "Let me get my keys."

Going inside the trailer, I shook my head as I grabbed the car keys from the living room and then went back outside, barely looking at Hannah as we walked to the car.

Once inside, I put the keys in the ignition but didn't start the engine. Instead, I lit a cigarette and stared out the window for a second, hating the situation I was—the situation I'd put myself in. I thought back to the few times that Angela had confronted me about the same thing years ago. Outside, I half expected to see her standing somewhere, but didn't.

"I don't want this to be awkward," Hannah said.

"Too late."

"I'm just not sure how to feel."

"Try pissed off."

"Is that what you want me to be?"

I shrugged. "Maybe."

Hannah frowned as she stared at me. "I've never been in this situation before. I feel like I should hate you, but…"

"But what?"

"I don't."

"Why not? You'd have every right."

"Maybe, if we were…I don't know, married or something. But we're not, are we? We're just partners. Right?"

I nodded. "Right."

She was still staring at me. "Something tells me you don't believe that."

"Believe what? That we're just partners?"

"Yes. You thought there was more to it?"

"Didn't you?"

"I just know that I love you, Ethan."

I stared back at her. "You do?"

"Of course. I'm just not sure what form that love should take. As I said, love has always been just a feeling to me, a given among my kind. But humans—"

"We complicate shit."

"Yes. So I don't know how I should feel about you sleeping with Vic. Should I slap you? Would that be a natural reaction? Even the old Hannah had little experience in this sort of thing. I have nothing to draw upon."

"What does your heart tell you?"

"That you're a fucking asshole."

I snorted and shook my head. "Right on the money, then."

"You feel bad, don't you? Your guilt is like a beacon."

"It just happened. I didn't—"

"I don't want to know. It's done now. Let's just move on."

"Sure," I said as she folded her arms and stared out the window. "Okay."

$\approx$

DIRECTOR BRADLEY BECKONED US IMMEDIATELY INTO HIS office as soon as we arrived. He seemed agitated as he sat behind his desk and looked up at us over his eyeglasses.

"So," he said. "You wanna tell me what the hell is going on? Why did I have to go to great lengths to keep the FPD off your case, Ethan? Chief Edwards wanted a full investigation. He has a stick up his ass when it comes to you."

"Tell me about it," I said.

"So what the hell happened?"

"It's as I said, sir. An old foe has come back to haunt us."

"Old foe? What foe?"

"Ethan saved me from a Yakuza boss," Hannah said. "My father, actually."

"Your father?" Bradley said, frowning. "You mean your *vessel's* father?"

She nodded. "Yes, sir. Kazuo Yagami."

Bradley looked at me. "And I take it you killed him, Ethan?"

I nodded. "Yes, sir."

"And who is trying to avenge this man now?"

"His son, Susumu."

"God damn it," Bradley said, tossing the pen he was holding onto his desk. "We can't afford this distraction. I'm down men because of this fucking virus afflicting the whole damn city now. The government is about to put us all on lockdown to contain it."

"But not us, sir?" I said.

"No, of course not, as long as we don't get sick as well."

"It's just a flu virus, sir."

"It's making people very sick," Bradley said. "Or haven't you heard?"

"I haven't seen the news in a while."

"Honestly, Ethan, anyone would think you live in a cave, and that goes for your appearance as well. Try shaving once in a while. You're an FBI agent now, not some scruffy PI."

I nodded. "How many are out with this thing going around?"

"I've lost a third of my staff so far," he said. "Cases are piling up. Not only that, Supernormal activity is increasing across the city, and last night, the Menesis Clan hit one of our holding facilities, presumably in retaliation for the clan member we took off the streets yesterday."

"That was quick," Hannah said.

"Yes, it was."

"Did they manage to get in?" I asked.

"Thankfully not. There were only a few of them, and security fought them off. I don't think their plan was very well thought out. Probably more of a knee-jerk reaction than anything else."

"How'd they even find the facility?" I asked. "I thought they were all top secret."

"They are," Bradley said. "That's what worries me. The vampires, or at least the Menesis Clan, know where one facility is. How long before they find the others? Or how long before they tell the other clans? I've had to increase security by directing manpower from this place, and because of the virus—which has now been classed as a pandemic—the President is refusing to grant me any more resources."

"I would've thought a facility full of super-powered beings topped everything else," I said. "What if the facilities get overrun, and the inmates escape? We'll be looking at something much worse than just a city-wide pandemic."

"Well, let's hope that doesn't happen, Ethan," Bradley said, turning in his chair. "Jesus. I remember things used to be a lot less complicated than this. Fucking Supernormals and viruses and fucking vampires that don't know their place. The world is going to shit."

"So, where does that leave *us*, sir?" Hannah asked.

"Stay on the Mirrorist case," he said. "I want this group

taken down, and the leader locked up. But before that can happen, you two have to sort out this man who's after you."

I raised my eyebrows a little. "Sort out?"

"I can't have this vendetta putting people at risk. If this person blew up your damn scrap yard, what else is he prepared to do? He obviously wants you both dead. Can't you just talk to him?"

I glanced at Hannah. "We'll try, though something tells me he won't listen."

Bradley fixed his steely gray eyes on us both. "Just get it sorted. I don't care how you do it."

"Do we keep working in the meantime, sir?" Hannah asked.

"Under normal circumstances, I'd say no, but these aren't normal circumstances. Keep working the Mirrorist case. I want it closed as soon as possible."

Hannah nodded. "Yes, sir."

We both went to leave when Bradley called me back, telling Hannah to excuse us. "There's something I want to talk to you about, Ethan," he said, as Hannah walked out, closing the door behind her.

"What is it, sir?"

"Take a seat."

I sat down, wondering what this was about. "Everything okay, sir?"

Bradley sighed and shook his head. "We have another problem, one that is perhaps bigger than all the rest. A Blackstar problem."

The name made me freeze and stare at him for a second. "What about Blackstar?"

"Knightsbridge, that Mephistophelian prick, has been meeting with the President lately."

"About what?"

"According to my source in the Whitehouse, he's pitching for Blackstar to replace Special Affairs."

"What? He can't do that."

"Well, my source says the President is considering it."

"The President would put a private company in charge of keeping the country safe? Seriously?"

The director shook his head at me as though I knew nothing. "Are you sure you know how this world works, Ethan?" he said. "Besides, you know how persuasive Knightsbridge can be. I've been at this game for a long time, and I've never met a player as ruthless or as cunning as him. The man scares me, and he always has. A man like that should not be put in charge of the safety of the people of this country."

I agreed.

"You have to stop him," I said. "Knightsbridge follows only one agenda, and that's his own. He doesn't give a fuck about the security of this country, or keeping the people safe. He'll let anybody die if it furthers his agenda. He already has too much of a foothold. If he takes over from Special Affairs and gains the confidence of the President, he'll have the whole fucking country in his grasp and at his disposal, if he hasn't already."

"What is his agenda? Do you know?"

I shook my head, suddenly needing a cigarette. "That's the thing. No one knows. But I'll tell you this much. I spent ten years working for Knightsbridge, and during that time, I witnessed shit you wouldn't believe, sir. Knightsbridge is the darkest motherfucker I've ever met. If he's planning something—and I have no doubt that he is—it will be bad for everyone."

Bradley stared at me for a long moment as though assuring himself that I was telling the truth. Then he looked away and said, "We can't let this happen, Ethan. Knightsbridge is enacting nothing less than a coup here."

"So, what do you suggest we do, sir?"

"I don't know yet," Bradley said. "But whatever we decide, it will not be easy. That much I know."

I nodded. "It never is, sir."

My phone rang as I was walking to the office I shared with Hannah.

"Drakester, it's Pan Demic."

"What is it?" I asked.

"Just a head's up. Your Hellicorn showed up here this morning. Screamed the place down to get our attention."

"Christ…"

"He was pretty fucked up, man. There was fresh blood dripping from his horn and everything."

"What did he want?"

"More coke."

"Did you give it to him?"

"Yeah."

"For fuck's sake. Why would you do that?"

"Because he had Artemis pinned to the wall and said he would impale him if I didn't get him some coke. A lot of coke, actually."

"How much is a lot?"

"Half an ounce. He made me put it on the ground, and he snorted the lot."

"And then what? Where is he?"

"Well, he just bolted after that."

"He didn't say where he was going?"

"No, man. He's Ctrl-Alt-Gone, I'm afraid."

I shook my head. "That's just great."

"Sorry, man. Oh, and by the way. My sister says to call her. Something about a job? She said the timeline has been moved up. If you want in, you have to call her soon, she says."

I hung up on Pan Demic and went into the office to find Hannah staring out the window. She turned away from the glass when she heard me come in.

"Everything alright?" she asked.

"Not really," I said. "Haedemus is missing."

"Missing? What do you mean missing?"

"I mean he's out there coked out of his fucking mind with somebody's blood dripping from his horn. We need to find him and take him home before he does something bad if he hasn't already."

Hannah frowned and shook her head at me. "Why is my Hellicorn on coke?"

"Don't look at me like that," I said. "I couldn't stop him."

"Jesus, Ethan."

"Hey, he has a mind of his own, you know that. Let's just go and find him." I turned to head out the door when she told me to wait. "What?"

She came walking toward me with a focused look in her eyes, and then out of nowhere, punched me square in the face, her knuckles connecting with my top lip, busting it open.

"Fuck!" I shouted. "What the fuck, Hannah?"

She took a deep breath as she stared at me. "There," she said, wiping the blood from her knuckles. "I feel slightly better now. Let's go and find Haedemus."

As I sat in the car staring at my busted top lip in the rearview mirror, Hannah sat next to me in the front passenger seat with her eyes closed as she tried to get a bead on where Haedemus was, using whatever abilities she had to locate him, wherever the hell he was. After a moment, she opened her eyes and said, "I found him. He's on a ranch a few miles past Redditch Village."

"What?" I said. "What's he doing there? Wait, don't tell me. It's a horse ranch, isn't it?"

Hannah nodded. "I think so."

"You saw him?"

"I did something akin to remote viewing, but the images were fuzzy. I saw the sign for the ranch, though, and remembered passing it a while back."

"That's all you saw?"

"I also glimpsed some dead horses."

I shook my head as I started the engine. "Christ, are we heading to a fucking massacre?"

"I don't know. If we are, you're to blame."

"Me?" I said as I drove away from the SAD building.

"How the hell am I to blame? I didn't force the coke up his fucking nose."

"No, but you stood by and watched him do it."

I sighed heavily as I turned the radio on, the dark tones of Gary Numan's *Jagged* album filling the car. "You're really out to get me today, aren't you?"

Hannah threw me a look before staring out the window, the first drops of sleet beginning to splatter the glass. "You deserve worse."

"A busted lip isn't enough?"

She tutted and shook her head. "Anyone would think you've never been punched before. Don't be a baby."

"You hit hard, you know that?"

"Probably not hard enough."

"You wanna hit me again?"

"Maybe." A crease of a smile appeared on her face.

"You liked it, didn't you?"

"Hitting you? I can't deny it felt good."

I nodded as we headed north out of the city, the streets abnormally empty because most people were inside, trying not to catch the virus going around. "I guess I deserved it."

"You always think you deserve to feel pain, Ethan. It gets a little old sometimes." She rummaged in her pockets for her cigarettes, taking out the packet, sticking a cancer stick between her red lips. "I didn't hit you to add to your pain. I hit you to alleviate my own."

"Your own pain?"

She glanced at me after lighting her cigarette. "You didn't think I was upset?"

"I…I don't know. If you were, you never showed it much."

"Well, I was. I still am. Despite what I said before about us just being partners, I thought we had something—something more than just being partners."

"We do…"

"Do we?"

I frowned at her for a second before turning my attention back to the road. "Look, I'm sorry, alright? I went to see Vic to see how she was doing and—"

"You ended up fucking her instead?"

Yeah.

"You bad boy, Ethan." It wasn't Hannah who said it. My eyes shot to the rearview mirror to see the face of Angela staring at me from the back seat, smiling, her face covered in blood. "You never could keep it in your pants, could you?"

Swallowing, I averted my gaze from the mirror and stared hard out the window, doing my best to pretend that the haunter of my dreams—and now reality—hadn't just returned to torment me.

I glanced quickly at Hannah, but she was staring out the side window as she smoked her cigarette, unaware that anyone else was in the car with us. Surely she should be able to sense Angela's presence, given all her celestial power?

Or maybe her not sensing anything only proved that Angela was all in my head.

"You were hoping I was gone?" Angela said. "No such luck, my dear Ethan. I'm here to stay, at least until you die or kill yourself, whichever comes first."

I glared at her in the mirror as if to tell her to fuck off.

"You know you almost drove me to suicide, Ethan?" she said. "I never told you that, did I? You were so hard to live with, so moody and angry all the time, so messed up on drugs and alcohol, and by the pressure of your job as a cop, that I just couldn't take it anymore. One night, I filled the bathtub intending to slit my wrists and let myself bleed out in the water. But then I decided I could never do that to Callie. I could never leave her alone. More precisely, I could never leave her alone with *you*, Ethan. You would've fucked her up as much as you fucked yourself up. God knows what would've become of her. In some ways, I'm glad she's dead, because now she will never get the chance to become like her useless father. That's why I started gambling online. I needed something to take my mind off the shit you kept pouring upon us, Ethan. And then, of course, you came sweeping in and cleared the debt that I accrued. The big hero, saving me from the debt collectors. Too little, too late. Where were you before that, Ethan? Where were you when I really needed you? You only had to be there, but you couldn't even do that, could you? Your job was always more important."

I gritted my teeth as I gripped the steering wheel, wanting to shout out she was just as bad, that she put her job over our daughter just as much as me, that she abused alcohol as much as me, that she was even inebriated during surgery sometimes, that the gambling was just an excuse to check out from her responsibilities to Callie, that she was just as much of a bad influence on our daughter as I was...

But I couldn't say anything because Hannah was sitting right beside me, and I didn't want to tell her I was going crazy and losing my mind, even though I suspected she knew, anyway. Not about Angela, but about my crumbling sanity.

"Here's the thing, Ethan," Hannah said, suddenly turning to me. "Whether you know it or not, we only have each other. Without each other, we'd be alone and susceptible to our dark side. We'd probably spin out, causing chaos all around us. As far as I'm concerned, we were lucky to find each other at this uncertain time in our lives. Something has brought us together, and I think we need to accept that. We've already established that we would die for each other if it came to it. A little loyalty—a little fidelity—on top isn't too much to ask, is it?"

"Oh honey," Angela said from the back. "You know not what you ask."

"No," I said in a near whisper. "It isn't."

Hannah put her hand on top of mine and squeezed, smiling at me as she did so.

"And there she is," Angela said, more than a note of bitterness in her voice. "The angel you've always wanted, Ethan, come to save you at last."

My gaze went to the mirror and bored into my dead ex-wife's eyes as I willed her to leave. But she continued to sit there, glaring back at me, and didn't leave until we reached the ranch.

HANNAH NEVER REMARKED ON MY SILENCE FOR THE REST OF the journey, probably thinking I was acting no weirder than usual. Before we even reached the ranch and Angela was still sitting behind, I had decided to rid myself of the vindictive bitch, and the only person who would know how to do that would be Richard Solomon. As much as I disliked the man, he knew more about death and its offspring than anyone else. At least he'd be able to tell me if Angela was real or not, and if she was real, whether she was just an extension of the Spreak who was out to get me. Being a Spreak of the highest order himself, Solomon would put me right, and perhaps even tell me how to get this fucking guy.

For a price, of course. There was always a price with Solomon.

In the meantime, I was about to find out precisely what Haedemus had been getting up to while on his coke-fueled adventure.

As I drove the Chevelle up a dirt road between two sprawling paddocks, I knew it wouldn't be good.

"Have you been able to contact him somehow?" I asked Hannah. "Does he know we're coming?"

Hannah shook her head. "I tried to get a psychic

connection, but I couldn't get through. I'm assuming the drugs have addled his brain."

"His brain was addled before the drugs."

"Same as yours, then."

"Thanks."

"I'm kidding. Take a left here. The stables are over there. I have a feeling that's where Haedemus is."

I drove down another road and pulled up at a massive horse barn, the white doors of which were half open and covered in bloody handprints.

"Christ," I said as I stopped the car outside the barn and stared at the blood on the door. "What the fuck has he done?"

Hannah said nothing as she got out of the car first. I got out a second later, dreading what I was going to find. Outside, the earlier strong winds had calmed, and the sleet had stopped falling. An eerie silence hung over the entire ranch, with no sign of anyone anywhere, despite the various vehicles parked around the yard. The main house nearby seemed devoid of life as well, as if everyone had simply vacated or—

"Haedemus?" Hannah called out, not too loudly, as if she felt awkward breaking the silence.

"No answer," I said after a moment. "Maybe he's inside."

Walking to the barn doors, I touched the blood with my fingers. It was still wet.

What the fuck have you done, Haedemus?

Sighing, I pulled one of the barn doors open and stood by the entrance so I could look inside for a moment, almost recoiling at the smell of death that wafted out when I did. "Jesus…"

"Oh my god…" Hannah seemed shocked as she looked into the barn.

The walkway between the stables was covered in blood,

looking like various bodies had been dragged across the floor, veering off into several of the stables.

"Haedemus?" Hannah called out again, but she still got no answer.

"You think he's gone?" I asked.

"No. He's here. I can feel his presence."

We walked into the barn, and I followed one of the blood trails toward the first stable. The stable door was ajar, and inside was the body of a man, half-eaten by the looks of it, his stomach open, his innards gone.

"Looks like Haedemus had himself a snack," I said in mild disgust.

"He had more than a snack," Hannah said from across the way as she stood looking into a different stable. "Come look."

I walked over to see what she was talking about, soon seeing a dead mare lying on the stable floor. The horse's eyes were still open in shock, and blood had pooled around its rear end, soaking into the straw on the floor. "It's not hard to guess what happened here, is it?"

"No," Hannah said, shaking her head.

In the rest of the stables, it was the same story. The bodies of people—three Caucasians and four Hispanic—lay on the floor, looking like Haedemus had speared them with his horn and then ate most of them. Same with at least ten horses that I counted. All dead, the steeds mutilated, the mares raped until they died from shock.

"This is fucking carnage," I said, my horror topped only by my rising anger at Haedemus for doing such deplorable acts. "Total fucking carnage."

"Maybe you'll think twice about giving him coke next time," Hannah said, as horrified by it all as I was.

"I told you—"

I was interrupted by a loud moan coming from one of the far stables. I looked at Hannah, and we both hurried to the end of the barn, stopping and staring in horror as we looked into the stable where the moan had come from.

Inside the stable was another mare, but this one was still alive, even though parts of its neck had been bitten off. Its light coat was soaked with blood, as was its rear end. When the mare noticed we were there, its one visible eye widened and stared at us as if willing us to put it out of its misery.

Next to the mare lay Haedemus, almost twice the mare's size, his massive black body covered from head to toe in blood and gore. His belly was massively distended, as though he had eaten far more than he could even digest. His eyes were closed, and he appeared to be sleeping.

Hannah stood, shaking her head with her hand over her mouth as if the entire thing was too much for her. And I didn't blame her. What Haedemus had done here was nothing short of a massacre, and despite my earlier protests to Hannah, I felt partly responsible for it. I should never have allowed him to take that coke.

While the mare continued to make pathetic groaning noises, I took out my sidearm and held it over the mare's head before squeezing the trigger, putting the animal out of its misery.

The sound of the gunshot was loud within the confines of the stable. Loud enough to wake Haedemus up with a frightened start. His head shot up, and he scrambled to his feet, neighing wildly as he spun around to confront whoever was in the stable with him. When he realized it was us, he just stared, saying nothing.

"Sorry to interrupt your nap," I said disgustedly as I put my gun away. "You must be tired after everything you've done here."

"Ethan—"

"Save it," I said, cutting him off. "Nothing you can say can excuse what you've done here. You've turned this place into...*Hell*."

"But the coke——"

"I fucking warned you not to take it!" I shouted. "Didn't I?"

Haedemus dropped his head and muttered, "Yes."

"But you didn't fucking listen as usual."

"I—I got carried away."

"Carried away?" I shook my head in astonishment. "This isn't getting carried away, Haedemus. This is beyond the fucking pale. This is…completely fucking *insane*."

Haedemus looked at me, his red eyes full of sorrow and regret. "What are you saying, Ethan?"

"What am I saying? I'm saying we're done, Haedemus. I don't want you around me anymore. As far as I'm concerned, you can fuck off back to Hell, because clearly, that's where you belong."

I walked away from him, needing fresh air before the stench of death made me sick.

"Ethan." Hannah caught up with me. "Where are you going?"

"I told you, I'm done with that fucking beast of yours," I said. "And so should you be."

"You're being hard on him," she said.

I couldn't help but laugh bitterly. "Hard on him? Are you fucking kidding? Take a look around, for Christ's sake. Who does this shit? I mean, really?"

"I know it's bad, but he wasn't himself. You know how much drugs he had in him——"

"Save it, Hannah. I don't want to hear it."

Hannah nodded, knowing there was nothing she could say. "Okay. Go then. I'll stay to clean this place up. Someone has to."

Closing my eyes for a second, I sighed and shook my head. "You can't clean all this on your own. I'll stay to help."

"No," she said. "I brought Haedemus into this world.

It's my mess as much as his. You should go and find Susumu and talk to him. I think that's more pressing, don't you?"

"More pressing than this?"

As I said it, Angela appeared beside me. "My my. What a mess we have here."

"Fuck off," I snarled.

"What?" Hannah said, frowning.

"Nothing—I wasn't talking to—" I stopped and shook my head, feeling like the walls were closing in on me. "I'm gonna go now."

I could feel Hannah's eyes on me as I walked away from her, Angela walking alongside me in her bloodstained doctor's coat. When I got outside, I leaned against the wall as I dry heaved, only fluid coming up as I did so.

"Fuck..." I said as I wiped my mouth with my sleeve.

Angela laughed as if it was all funny. "What a day you are having, Ethan."

"Fuck off and leave me alone," I said, not looking at her as I headed to the car.

She was in the front passenger seat before I even got inside. "I'll accompany you back," she said, smiling like we were about to embark on a pleasant Sunday drive. "And by the way, she's too good for you, that one. Just like I was. No one should exist in your orbit, Ethan. No one but you, if your orbit should even exist at all. You should really think about killing yourself. You want to play the hero and help the world? That's how you do it. Take yourself out of the equation, Ethan. This world would be better off without you." Her lips turned into something like a sneer as darkness moved beneath the skin on her face. "Only, we both know you'd never kill yourself. Isn't that right, Ethan? You are much too narcissistic for that. You think the world needs you? You are a cockroach, Ethan. A cockroach that refuses to die, even after it's been stamped on."

I stared straight ahead as I started the engine and pulled

away from the barn, refusing to look at the monster in the front seat pretending to be my ex-wife. She remained beside me for the entire journey back to the city, talking and talking, insinuating and insulting, like a devil on my shoulder with no angel on the other side to offer a different viewpoint.

1 2

By the time I drove back to the city, I was sure of one thing, if I wasn't sure of it already:

Trying to talk to Susumu Yagami would be a waste of time.

If this was about something other than me putting a bullet in his father's head, maybe we could've negotiated a truce.

But this was about revenge, and I knew better than anyone that there would be no talking him out of it.

Which only left me with one choice:

I had to kill him before he killed me.

And speaking of killing, I turned to Angela as I stopped the car outside my trailer in the scrap yard. She hadn't stopped talking the entire journey home, bringing up painful memories, talking about Callie as if my daughter hated me, as if her very soul despised me. I listened to it all without reacting, staring straight ahead like I was alone in the car, even turning the music up to drown her out.

"I know who you are," I said to her as her expression changed. "You can keep showing up in whatever guise you feel like, but it will not change the fact that I'm coming for you. My wife and daughter are dead because of you, and I'll do whatever it takes to avenge their deaths. Even if it kills me."

Angela smiled, but for the first time, I saw someone else behind her eyes—the actual person behind the mask.

"I encourage you to do so," she said, only she didn't sound like Angela anymore. She spoke in a man's deep voice, a voice full of cold menace that sent a chill through me. "The truth is not what you think. If you wish to know the truth, there is only one way to discover it."

"The truth about what?"

The Spreak's face changed, becoming a mass of shifting shadow until another face formed within it—a man's face, but barely recognizable it was shifting so much, only one eye visible, the other a black hole. "About everything."

"Everything? What the hell—"

A freakish grin crossed the Spreak's face before he disappeared, leaving me hanging.

"Fuck..." I growled, sitting in the car for another minute as I wondered what the Spreak was getting at. What truth was he referring to? Was this just more lies to trap me further?

Before I could think any more about it, my phone rang. Digging the phone out of my pocket, I saw it was Petey calling. When I answered, Petey told me he had been going through the books for the scrap business, telling me if we didn't get a cash injection soon, the business would go under. If we didn't resume business in the next few weeks, all the contracts we had with the buyers here and overseas would fall through, and we'd get pushed out by some other company. I told Petey to give me a little time to try to sort something out, but I could tell from his tone that he didn't hold out much hope. Petey was getting on in years, and his desire to fight for anything—never mind a business on the brink of destruction—had lessened enough that he probably would've been happy to walk away, especially after the dramatic and violent destruction of the new machinery, for which he blamed me. He never said so out loud, but I could tell he was thinking it.

After hanging up, I lit a cigarette and stared out the window for a few moments as I thought things over. I couldn't let the business go under. I owed it to Cal to keep it afloat, no matter what I had to do to keep it going. Money was needed, and a lot of it.

Sighing, I reached into my trench pocket and rummaged until I found what I was looking for. The card that Pan Demic's sister had given me. Staring at the number on the card, I keyed it into the phone and put the phone on speaker.

"Hello?" said a voice after several rings.

"Is this Danika?" I asked.

"Who's this?"

"Ethan Drake."

She went silent for a few seconds. "I'm surprised you called."

"Is the job still on?"

"It is."

"I want in."

Another pause. "Tomorrow night. 8 p.m. Kennedy Subway Station. I'm sure I don't have to tell you to come alone."

"I'll be there."

I hung up the phone and sat for another minute, wondering if taking part in a heist with Pan Demic's sister was really a good idea. I was a Special Agent, for Christ's sake. If anything went wrong, Bradley would lock me up and throw away the key just for disrespecting the badge.

But what choice did I have? Let the scrap business go under? Lose everything Cal had spent his life building?

I didn't think so. Enough damage had been done already.

It was time to put things right.

And that included taking out Susumu Yagami.

IN THE UNDERGROUND BUNKER BEHIND THE TRAILER, I WENT to the gun racks and found the sniper rifle there. It was a SAKO TRG 42 Finnish sniper rifle, and one of the best in the world. Cal used to use nothing else on the rare occasion he had to take out a target from long distance. I took the rifle from the rack and pulled out the empty magazine, filling it with .300 Winchester Magnum cartridges before attaching it to the rifle again, after which I screwed in a suppressor.

I'd considered a few different ways to take Susumu out, including sending the Hellbastards after him, but after some deliberation, I thought sniping the fucker would be the cleanest option. Besides, I wanted to make sure Yagami's son went down and stayed down.

Carrying the rifle wrapped in a black cotton sheet, I went out to the car and put the gun in the trunk. If my instinct was right, Susumu would've taken over his father's office in Little Tokyo. Thanks to the enormous windows in that place, he would be exposed. All I had to do was find a suitable sniping point opposite the Yakuza building and then take him out.

As I drove out of the yard and started heading for Little Tokyo, I called Artemis.

"Drakester, what can I do for you?" he asked. "Is this about your Hellicorn, because I—"

"It's not about the Hellicorn," I said, unwelcome images of the barn massacre popping into my head. "I need a cell phone number."

"Name?"

"Susumu Yagami."

"The Yakuza guy's son?"

"Yeah."

"You going after him now too? Did he have something to do with what happened at your yard?"

"What do you think?"

"Alright, gimme a minute. I'll text you the number."

"Send me a recent photo as well."

"How do you want me? Naked? Semi-naked? I do a good philosopher pose—"

"What? I don't want a photo of you, I want—"

Artemis laughed. "Relax, Drakester, I know. I was just kidding."

"Just send me the text."

A few minutes later, as I hit downtown, the text came through from Artemis. In the text was Susumu Yagami's cell number and a picture of the man himself. Driving through the near-empty streets, I held the phone up and looked at the photo. It was a headshot of Susumu, professionally done, for corporate reasons, I imagine. He appeared to be in his late thirties, inky hair and cold eyes like his father, but more handsome than Kazuo was, with a light beard that didn't go past his jawline. With a face like that, I guessed he was a big hit with the girls.

Though not for much longer.

With Yagami's face now burned into my memory, I tossed the phone on the front seat and continued toward Little Tokyo.

Finding a suitable sniping spot in Serenity Square wasn't straightforward. Most of the buildings opposite the Yakuza building were much shorter, making for a hard elevation angle. I could probably work with the steep upward angle, but I thought it best not to chance it. If I missed the shot, Susumu would know it was me trying to kill him, and he would likely react immediately, perhaps attacking the yard again, and I couldn't have that.

The building directly opposite the Yakuza headquarters housed the Japanese American Museum, which was one story less than the Yakuza HQ. The museum was closed because of the virus, so I took the still-wrapped sniper rifle around the back of the building and called Artemis, asking him to shut off the building's security system. Once I got the okay from Artemis, I picked the lock on the back entrance and let myself inside the building. According to Artemis, there were two security guards inside, but they were at the front of the building. As long as I took the back stairs to the roof, the security guards wouldn't even know I was there. To be sure, Artemis disabled all security cameras until I made it up to the roof. He said he would monitor the guards via the cameras while I did what I had to do.

It was approaching late afternoon by the time I stepped onto the roof. Daylight was fading, and I figured I had about an hour before a lack of light made things too difficult. I had my night vision, of course, but I hoped I wouldn't have to use it. Sniping was hard enough without attempting to do it with night vision.

I stood on the roof for a minute, looking around for the best position to set up, finally deciding to use the wooden table that sat near the center of the rooftop. Four chairs were placed around the small table, and an ashtray filled with old cigarette butts sat on top. Clearly, the staff used the rooftop to take their smoke breaks. Lucky for me.

Yakuza HQ was about five hundred yards away across the square, Yagami's office almost directly opposite my position. Cover was obviously an issue. If Susumu looked out the office window, I wouldn't be hard to spot down here, but it was a chance I had to take. At this point, I wasn't even sure if the Yakuza boss was in the office.

Unwrapping the sniper rifle, I unfolded the tripod and rested it on the table as I crouched behind the table itself. Then I looked through the scope, focusing it on Yagami's office window. The lights were on inside, and I could see Yagami's chair behind the massive desk, though no one was sitting in it.

"Shit…"

Too much to expect Susumu to be sitting in that chair, I guess.

"You're a little late, don't you think?" said a voice from behind, making me let go of the rifle and spin around, immediately drawing my sidearm and pointing it at the figure standing over by the door.

"What the fuck?" I breathed, shocked when I saw who was standing there.

It was Cal, wearing the same jeans and T-shirt he had on the night he died. Not only that, he was soaked in blood, his face torn so much it was barely recognizable, yet I still knew it was him. What Cal looked like that night after the werewolves were done with him would forever be burned into my brain.

"Surprised to see me?" Cal said as he came sauntering toward me. "You got a cigarette? I'm all out."

I stared aghast at him before shaking my head. "Stop this. Go away."

"What's the matter, Ethan?" Cal asked. "I thought you'd be pleased to see me. I mean shit, after getting me killed by fucking werewolves and then causing my yard to be destroyed, I thought you'd be jumping for joy to see me, your old buddy."

I closed my eyes for a second, hoping when I opened them again, Cal would be gone.

I don't need this right now…

But when I opened my eyes again, Cal was still there, his face a horrific mask of shredded skin and exposed bone.

Stay calm. You know this isn't Cal. It's the Spreak, trying to get to you again. Don't fucking let him...

"You're not Cal," I said in a level voice, before turning away from him.

Pretend like he isn't there. It's just me, alone on this rooftop.

Taking hold of the sniper rifle again, I sighted through the scope at the Yakuza building, my heart skipping a beat when I saw someone pacing around by the desk.

"You think killing this guy will make up for allowing my yard to be blown to shit?" Cal said from behind me. "The damage is done. You fucked up, Ethan. Again. I'm dead because of you."

I couldn't help it. I turned my head slightly and snapped, "You were dead anyway."

Even though it wasn't really Cal, I still regretted saying it, and I closed my eyes in shame for a few seconds before looking through the scope again.

"Now that's not a very nice thing to say, is it?" He was standing right behind me, his breathing loud in my ears. "After all I did for you? Shit, boy, you still got a lot to learn about manners."

"Stop it," I growled. "Stop trying to be him. You're not him!"

Susumu Yagami was still pacing the room, on the phone, it looked like.

"You're the biggest disappointment of my life, son," Cal went on behind me. "I gave you everything. I housed you, trained you, taught you everything I knew. But it still wasn't enough, was it? You're still the same fuckup as you were when I first met you. I knew you were broken, but I thought I could fix you. More fool me. You're damaged beyond repair. God himself couldn't fix you. God's abortion, that's what you are, Ethan. Slop in a bucket that should've been disposed of long ago. Poor little Ethan whose mommy died and left him all alone, whose daddy didn't even want to know him, whose wife and kid hated him because he didn't have the balls to be a proper husband, a proper father—"

"ENOUGH!" I bawled, letting go of the rifle and lunging at Cal, but before I could reach him, he vanished, and I fell forward as I grasped at thin air.

Laughter echoed all around me as I stood looking for him, but he was gone.

"Leave me the fuck alone!" I shouted.

As the laughter faded, I stood for another minute, half expecting the Spreak to appear again, even though I knew he wouldn't. He'd done what he set out to do, which was to rattle me once more.

And he'd done a damn good job of it. My composure was shot, and my hands shook with all the rage and emotion boiling in me.

Closing my eyes, I took several deep breaths until I felt my composure return, and the rage die down.

This can't go on. I have to stop this fucker before he drives me insane...

Focus. Just focus. We still got a job to do here...

I crouched by the table once more and took hold of the rifle. Sighted. Susumu was still there, sitting at the desk this time.

Slipping my hand into my pocket, I took out my phone and rang the number Artemis had sent me. Through the rifle scope, I watched Susumu lift his phone off the desk, stare at it for a moment, and then answer.

"Yes?" he said, sounding as arrogant as I expected.

"You killed my dogs."

Through the scope, I watched him straighten up in his chair. "I'm going to guess and say this is Ethan Drake."

"Why'd you kill the dogs? You didn't have to kill the dogs."

"I was sending a message. In blood."

"You need to back off before someone dies."

Susumu went silent for a moment as I watched him stand up and walk around to the front of the desk where he paused and stood. "If you are calling to beg for your life, Mr. Drake, you are wasting your time. I saw what you and that bitch did to my father. It's all on tape."

"Your father left me with no choice."

"Didn't he? He was broken, and yet you still walked right over and—" I watched him take the phone from his ear and hold it by his side as he raised his head to the ceiling for a second before putting the phone back to his ear. "You know what you did, and you will pay for your actions. Not only am I going to kill you, Drake, I will kill anyone who knows you. By the time I've finished, it will be like you never existed, for I will erase every trace of you from this world."

"I'm sorry to hear you say that," I said. "I was hoping we could call a truce."

Susumu laughed bitterly. "A truce? Never!"

"In that case, you will suffer the same fate as your father."

"You think you can kill me?" He walked around the desk and stood by the window to look out. "I am not my father, Drake. You should know that before you go threatening me. I am more powerful than he ever was. More powerful than you can imagine."

"Oh yeah? How's that?"

Through the scope, I watched him smile. "You will find out soon enough."

"Yeah," I said before hanging up on him. "I don't think I will."

Dropping the phone into my pocket again, I quickly positioned myself to take the shot, acquiring a good cheek weld, and controlling my breathing.

I was almost centered when my phone rang, making me lose my concentration.

"Damn it…"

It wasn't Susumu. I could still see him standing by the window, looking out as he no doubt mulled over the conversation he just had with me. A second later, he walked away from the window and disappeared into the room somewhere.

"Fuck…" I said, relaxing my grip on the rifle as I reached into my pocket for the phone. "Hello?"

"Ethan, it's Director Bradley. Why do you sound so angry? Is this a bad time? I don't care if it is or not. Where are you?"

"I'm trying to sort out that problem we discussed," I said, trying to keep my anger and frustration in check as I kept looking through the scope, hoping Susumu would return to the window.

"Oh, right," Bradley said. "Well, that will have to wait. Is Hannah with you? She isn't answering her phone."

"She's…beside me, yeah."

"Right, well, the two of you need to get downtown."

"Why?"

"I just got word that a Supernormal is tearing up a grocery store on Kent Avenue. Whoever it is, they appear to have transformed into some kind of golem creature. I'm watching it right now on the store's security feed. He's doing a lot of damage."

"Is there no one else?"

"What?" he retorted, perhaps the first time I'd ever heard him be angry. "Didn't you hear a word I said this morning? I'm running a skeleton crew here. Do your goddamn job, Special Agent, and get your ass to that store. Now!"

"Yes, sir," I said, but he had already hung up.

Fuck this. Talk about bad timing.

145

After pocketing the phone, I looked through the scope and was almost surprised to see Susumu Yagami standing by the window once more, this time with a drink in his hand.

I thought I'd lost my chance, but maybe not.

For the second time, I pressed my cheek against the stock of the rifle and adjusted my grip. As I was in a hurry now, and because I could feel it start to rain—and also because I hadn't fired a sniper rifle in over ten years—I decided not to go for a headshot. Center mass would have to do. Less chance of missing that way.

As I positioned the reticle over the target, I allowed my mouth and throat to open, exhaling most of the air from my lungs as my body gradually became still, and my finger rested gently on the trigger. Soon, the reticle bounced between my heartbeats, and it felt like nothing else existed except what I could see through the scope.

Susumu lifted his drink, and as he poured it down, I waited on my next heartbeat and then fired between beats.

Through the scope, I saw Susumu go reeling back as the bullet penetrated the center of his chest, and then he fell to the floor.

For several seconds, I didn't move as I kept looking through the scope and the bullet hole in the office window.

Not that I expected him to, but the Yakuza boss didn't appear again.

He was down. No one could survive a shot like that.

"*Sayōnara*, asshole."

13

Once I left Serenity Square, I drove for another few blocks before pulling over in a near-empty street. Most of the businesses appeared to be closed, except for those that offered essentials like groceries, and of course, alcohol. I went into a liquor store and tried to give the store worker cash for a fifth of Jack Daniels, but he refused. Card only. Shaking my head, I used my nearly maxed-out credit card to pay for the booze and went back out to the car, opening the bottle and taking a few slugs from it. I would've added Mud to the mix, but I'd already used up the bottle in my pocket.

My nerves were shot to shit. Seeing Cal like that, his face all fucked up, and the horrible shit he said to me, had left me rattled. I knew it was the Spreak fucking with me, that Cal would never say anything like that, but the words still hit home, exacerbated by my existing guilt over my friend's death and the fact that I'd put his business—his legacy—in dire jeopardy.

Still, there wasn't much I could do right now as I had other shit to take care of first, namely the Supernormal causing havoc downtown. At least Susumu Yagami was out of the way, though. Hopefully, there wouldn't be any retaliation from the Yakuza. They might figure out it was me who killed their boss, or they might not. If they did, I would deal with it, but I wasn't worried about that yet.

Taking out my phone, I called Hannah. I couldn't show up to that grocery store alone, or Bradley would demand to know where Hannah was. And as I couldn't exactly tell him she was cleaning up a massacre after the Hellicorn she summoned from Hell went crazy on a coke binge, I thought it best if I picked her up before going anywhere.

"Ethan, hey," Hannah said after answering her phone. "I was just about to call you. It's taken care of."

"You got rid of all the bodies?" I asked. "That was quick."

"There's a lake behind the ranch. I weighted the bodies and then flew them over the lake, dropping them into the water."

"And the horses?"

"I left the horses in the barn before setting fire to the lot."

"You burned the barn?"

"It seemed the quickest way to clean up."

I nodded. "Okay. Where are you now?"

"Riding Haedemus home. We're just coming into the city now. Place seems weird, like a ghost town."

"Everyone is on lockdown. Start making your way toward downtown. I'll pick you up."

"What's going on?"

"There's something we have to take care of. Another Supernormal incident. Time is of the essence here, so get moving. And by the way…"

"What?"

"Susumu Yagami is dead."

She went silent for a second. "You killed him?"

"He made it clear he would not stop hunting us. He left me no choice."

"Are you alright?"

"I'm fine. Just get going."

As soon as I hung up, a text came through from Bradley:

WHERE THE HELL ARE YOU?

Sighing, I texted back:

ALMOST THERE

Tossing the phone in the front seat, I started the engine and peeled off, the tires screeching as I did.

As there was little traffic on the roads, I met up with Hannah in good time. She was just hitting Main Street as I slammed the brakes on next to her and Haedemus. The Hellicorn barely looked at me at first, and I him.

"Hello, Ethan," he said, his voice and entire demeanor subdued.

"Haedemus," I grunted as Hannah climbed down off him and came around the passenger side.

"Listen, Ethan—" Haedemus started to say until I cut him off.

"Save it," I said. "I don't want to hear your excuses. Just get back to the yard and stay there. We'll figure out what to do with you later."

He went to say something else, then closed his mouth, knowing from my expression that it was pointless. His head down, he walked away like a creature who had it all until they lost everything in one moment of stupidity.

"Take it easy on him," Hannah said, now beside me inside the car. "He's sorry for what he did."

I snorted. "He's sorry? He killed a bunch of innocent people, and fuck knows how many horses. Sorry won't cut it. He's a liability, Hannah. I want him gone."

"Does that apply to the Hellbastards as well?"

"What?"

"The Hellbastards. How many innocent people have they killed since they've been here?"

"That's—they don't kill innocents."

"Really? Homeless bums aren't innocent? Or the people they've literally scared to death while out running around fucking shit up?"

I stared at her for a moment before looking away. "We'll talk about this later. We got shit to do now."

As I pulled off, Hannah said, "I'm not saying you shouldn't be mad at Haedemus. But you must remember he's a Hellbeast. He can't help his nature. Plus," she added, "he behaved just fine before you allowed him to take that coke."

I rolled my eyes. "Sure. I forgot. It's all my fault. Fuck…"

"I'm just saying he was your responsibility."

Shaking my head in anger, I stared straight ahead as I drove at speed toward the grocery store, knowing Hannah was right. Haedemus *was* my responsibility, and I should never have allowed him to take that fucking cocaine. "As I said, we'll talk about it later."

Hannah looked out the window and said nothing.

A PANICKED FLUX OF BODIES SCUTTLED OUT OF THE FRONT doors of the convenience store, screaming. Many of them, especially those in the back, were covered with a thick layer of gray-brown mud. As they cleared the entrance, I spotted a crawling puddle of mud flowing down the aisles inside, knocking goods off shelves that sank into the floor like it was quicksand. Over the commotion, I heard the building screech and moan, and noticed several cracks along the gable that were slowly expanding. I wondered for a second what the hell could cause such devastation until another scream from inside caught my attention.

"What the hell is happening here?" Hannah asked as we stood outside the store while more people poured out in terror.

"Bradley said the Supernormal is some sort of golem," I said, staring at the thick flow of mud oozing out of the store entrance. "Looks like he's burst a pipe to me."

Hannah gave me a look. "Was that supposed to be a joke or something?"

"Not really. I was just saying."

"Where's it all coming from?" a woman wailed outside the store.

"Pipes must've burst," some guy said, and I looked at Hannah and smirked.

Despite the citywide lockdown, people could still go out for essential items, which is why the grocery store was full. Though I'll bet most of the customers had wished they had stayed at home now.

"Is anyone else inside?" I asked a man near me, still clutching his groceries, despite being covered in mud.

"I don't know," he said, shaking his head. "Maybe one or two."

"The security guard is in the toilet where all this mud stuff is coming from," another man said. "I saw him go in."

"Security guard?" I said.

"Yeah," the man said. "I guess the store didn't want no trouble during the lockdown or whatever. I'd say they weren't expecting this."

There was a scream from inside—a woman shouting for help.

"What do we do?" Hannah asked. "Is Bradley sending anyone else?"

"It's just us," I said. "I guess we wade in."

Tramping through the thick mud, I entered the store to see a woman sinking into the floor, the mud pulling her down almost to her shoulders. It seemed the more she struggled, the more stuck she became.

"Stop struggling," I told the woman as Hannah stood beside me. "We'll get you out."

The pulsating mud was everywhere now, covering the entire floor. In places, it seemed to be bubbling up from *beneath* the floor, creating pools of sticky mud that resembled quicksand, one of which the woman was stuck in.

"Be careful where you walk," I told Hannah as I made my way toward the still struggling woman, who was sinking at an alarming rate, the sucking mud almost up to her neck now. Her hands were still free, though, and Hannah and I grabbed each of them and hauled the poor woman out to safety.

"Take her outside," I said to Hannah. "I'm going to find the security guard. He's probably the cause of this fucking mud bath."

As Hannah went to walk away with the woman, there was a loud screech from above, and a second later, part of the ceiling collapsed, concrete from the floor above crashing down into the mud near where Hannah and the woman were standing, splashing the two of them with the thick, gray substance.

The woman screamed, and Hannah said, "Shit!" as mud ran down her face, her clothes now ruined if they weren't already.

"That's a good look on you," I said, unable to help myself. "Muddy gray-brown might just be your color."

Hannah shook her head agitatedly. "I hope you fall in."

"Charming."

"I'm all outta charm at this point. I'll be back."

Hannah waded outside with the woman, and I trudged to the back of the store, being careful to avoid the bubbling pools of quicksand all around. Just ahead, there was an open door that led into a narrow hallway, which I guessed is where the toilet was located. The flow of mud seemed to be greater there as it poured out the door like so much shit.

"Hello?" I shouted. "Anyone there? Security guy? This is Special Agent Drake with the FBI. Can you come out?"

"Go away!" a deep voice shouted. "This whole building is coming down, and you don't want to be around when it collapses."

"Thanks for the tip," I said, wading further through the mud, which was past my knees now it was so deep. "But I'm not going anywhere until you come out with me."

"Then you're gonna die as well."

Fuck's sake. Another suicidal Supernormal.

As I waded closer to the doorway, the wall nearest to me cracked, a huge fissure splitting the concrete as the foundations turned to mud, and one side of the building dropped. Realizing I didn't have long before the whole damn building collapsed in on itself, I shouted, "What's your name?" to the security guy.

"Doesn't matter," he shouted back over the noise of the bubbling mud, his voice sounding like it was bubbling as well. I'd never seen a golem before, and I wondered if the security guy resembled a mud man.

"Why not?"

"Coz it'll all be over soon."

"Bullshit. Are you in therapy, by any chance?"

"What?"

"Are you seeing a shrink?"

"I—yeah. How'd you know?"

"Lucky guess. Listen, buddy, why don't you come out so we can talk? There's a very good chance your therapist hasn't been straight with you, and that's why you're feeling like this. I bet you think you're a monster, don't you? That you don't belong here, and that you're a danger to others?"

"I *am* a danger. Take a look around."

"Your powers have just been triggered by your feelings," I said. "Feelings put there by your therapist. Is your therapist a Mirrorist?"

"Yeah," he said. "How would you know that?"

"You're not the only one who's done something like this. Your therapist has manipulated you into doing this."

As the security guy went silent, the entire building shook, and then parts of the ceiling came down, lumps of concrete crashing down onto the shelves, crushing them. Nearby, a steel girder came down, splashing hot mud everywhere as it hit, covering me in the shit.

"Ethan?" Hannah was wading toward me as once-shelved goods floated past her, swept up by the mud. "Are you alright?"

"I hear this is good for the skin," I said, wiping the stuff from my eyes. "Not that it feels like it. It's actually kinda gross, knowing this stuff is coming from that guy in there."

"Is he coming out?"

"No. He wants to sit in there and die. He's not in a good mood, thanks to his therapist."

"His therapist? Another one?"

"Yup."

"So what do we do?" she asked as she finally reached me.

"I'm not sure," I said. "But we would need to decide quick. This whole building is about to collapse."

Hannah thought for a moment. "I have an idea."

"What is it?" I asked as more of the ceiling came down, and the mud swallowed up the shelves next to me.

"Just get out of here," she said. "I'll bring the guy out."

"What are you going to do?" I said, but she never answered because she was already wading through the mud in the doorway and turning into the bathroom.

Shaking my head, I decided to trust her and headed

back through the store again, the patches of quicksand making the brief journey treacherous as hell, not to mention the falling debris. By the time I made it out to the street, I was like a mud man myself, and the few people that had hung around in the street gasped as I trudged out onto the road.

From outside, I could see just how close the building was to collapsing. Fissures ran all over the gable, and the entire building was leaning to the left as the mud continued to eat at the foundations, somehow turning bricks and mortar, even steel, into pure mud.

"Come on, Hannah," I said as I stared into the store, seeing no sign of her or the security guard.

Then I heard a high-pitched scream.

A moment later, a large naked man, the bottom half of his body formed from mud, came wading out as his legs gradually turned to normal again. The look of pure fear on his face was unmistakable, as was the look of astonishment on the few people who had hung around to watch.

The security guard fell to his hands and knees beside me, breathing hard.

"Where is she?" I asked him.

"She's—she's the devil…" he gasped.

I frowned, then nodded, understanding. "Uh-huh."

Clearly, Hannah had given this guy a good scare. But where the hell was she?

Just as I contemplated going back in to get her, the entire building suddenly did what it had been threatening to do for the last five minutes, which was collapse. The gable gave way, enormous slabs of concrete falling out, followed by the roof and then the rest of the building.

But just as I thought, *Oh my god, she's dead*, Hannah came flying out of the building with barely a second to spare as the whole thing collapsed behind her, the mud already turning the rest of the building into yet more mud, swallowing it up.

Hannah swooped out and up like a graceful bird before coming down to land elegantly beside me. "Phew," she said like some comic book superhero, now topless and covered in gray-brown mud. "That was close."

"What the hell kept you?" I asked her.

"I got stuck in the mud." She laughed like it was funny.

"I always said you were a stick in the mud."

She punched my arm, and then someone behind us said, "She's...an angel!"

I shook my head at Hannah. "You see what you've done with your little aerial display? Detain the mud man. I'll take care of the gawkers." I turned to the nearest bystander. "Excuse me, sir? Could you come here a minute, please?"

"She flew! She has wings!"

"I know, awesome, right? You know what else is awesome? This lovely swirling pattern here on my hand..."

14

There were no Incident Response Teams available to come clean up the mess or take the security guard away, so we had to put the man in the back of my car, despite his feet still being formed from his magical mud. Still highly stressed, the man was having a minor trouble returning himself to normal. Consequently, there was mud all over the car. And as Hannah and I were covered in the damn stuff, the car was a total mess by the time we drove to the Special Affairs building.

"Bradley is getting a cleaning bill after this," I said, disgusted at the state of my car.

"Not to mention our clothes," Hannah said, wearing my trench to cover herself, her wings having destroyed her blouse and jacket. "I like this trench, though. I might get one. We could walk around like secret agents, then. What do you think?"

"I think you've inhaled too much mud is what I think."

Hannah laughed. "Seriously, though. We should hit the showers. Maybe the director will send someone out for new clothes."

"Who do you think you're working for, Goldman Sachs?

This is the government, not some private firm. We'll be lucky to get a bar of soap."

Hannah laughed again, strangely elated by this whole situation, as if she got a dopamine rush when she went into angel mode. She'd be demanding sex in the restroom next. "I guess soap will have to do until we get home."

"Who are you guys?" the security guard asked. He was a man-mountain in his late forties, sitting naked and hand-cuffed with a glum expression on his moon-like face. "You don't seem like FBI to me. The FBI doesn't have devils working for them," he added, looking at Hannah, his face saying he was still afraid of her.

"We're special FBI," I said. "Special in the sense that we're mad enough to go after people like you, Mr.—"

"Jacobson," the guy said. "Arnie Jacobson. What are you gonna do with me? Are you gonna lock me up?"

Hannah and I looked at each other for a second. She was clearly thinking the same as me—that Arnie wasn't a bad guy and probably didn't deserve to end up where he was going. But his fate was out of our hands.

"That probably depends on you," I lied to him. "On how much information you can give us."

"About what?" he asked.

"The therapist you are seeing. Or were seeing."

"Doctor Jamal? Are you after him or something?"

"We are now."

"What did he do?"

"Take a look in the mirror, Arnie," I said, and he sighed and looked away.

~

HANNAH AND I GOT QUEER LOOKS FROM THE MINIMAL STAFF inside the SAD building as we trudged in with the naked Arnie Jacobson in tow, who didn't appear to care much that he was buck naked. A few people tutted at the muddy footprints we trekked the entire way through the building.

"What's the matter?" I asked a female member of staff as we walked by. "You never seen a naked man before?"

Arnie, bless him, was actually saying hello to people as he walked by them. "Hi," he would say, a model of politeness in the face of a dire and somewhat compromising situation.

And it *was* dire for him. Even if he gave us information, I doubted Bradley would allow Arnie back on the street again, not after he nearly killed a store full of people with his powers. Powers he clearly had little control over.

We put Arnie in the holding room and told him not to go all mud man again until we got back. Nodding, he seemed happy enough to comply, even asking for coffee, which someone fetched for him.

"You think his magic mud could melt the holding room?" Hannah asked, probably more out of curiosity than anything else.

"Not sure," I said as we made our way to the restrooms. "It's reinforced and magically sealed. Let's hope he doesn't try."

"I wonder why his magic mud didn't melt *us*. I mean, it melted steel and concrete."

"No idea. I'm just glad it didn't. I happen to like my legs."

There were showers in the restroom, so I jumped under one and quickly washed the mud from my body. After I was clean, I put on the black combat fatigues, FBI T-shirt, and boots that Bradley helpfully got someone to provide for me. My own clothes I stuffed in a trash can, for all the good they were now.

When I met up with Hannah in Bradley's office, she was dressed in the same black clothing as I was, and for a second, it felt like I was back in Blackstar again, since this was the kind of clothing I lived in while working there.

"Good job, you two," Bradley said from behind his desk. "The building came down, but at least there was no loss of life, which is something. You took your time getting there, though."

"I told you why," I said. "We were taking care of our problem."

"Yes, the Yakuza," Bradley said. "And how exactly did you take care of things?"

"It's probably better if you don't know, sir," I said. "Plausible deniability and all that."

Bradley stared at me for a moment and then nodded. "I suppose so. As long the situation has been handled, that's all that matters."

"It has, sir."

"Hannah," Bradley said, turning his attention to her. "You seem to be making a habit of spreading your wings, so to speak."

"I did what I had to, sir," she said. "Just like before."

He nodded. "I suppose so. Try to be discreet, won't you?"

"Yes, sir."

"I took care of the witnesses," I said. "No one will remember anything they saw."

"I suppose Blackstar was good for something," he said. "This magic tattoo of yours—can it be replicated?"

"I'm not sure, sir. Maybe if someone knew what they were doing. You'd need a Spreak to do it."

"Spreaks, as you call them, are not on the payroll here. It seems they have no interest in serving for the greater good."

"That's because they're all selfish assholes, sir," I said. "They'd never demean themselves by working for the government. And the concept of the greater good doesn't compute with them. Everything they do is out of self-interest."

"But yet, Knightsbridge got many on board at Blackstar."

"He gave them what they wanted in return."

"Which is?"

"Power, prestige, resources, and the ability to do their own thing. Knightsbridge is one of them, anyway."

"Yes, I'm well aware," Bradley said, lifting a coffee mug and drinking from it. "Anyway, what's going on with this latest Supernormal? Why did he try to bring a building down on himself?"

"Well, sir," Hannah said. "It turns out he's a patient of a Mirrorist therapist."

"Jesus, another one?" Bradley said. "This group has really got their hooks into the Supernormal brigade, haven't they?"

"It seems so, sir," Hannah said.

"Which is why we need to put an end to this group. We can't have any more incidents like this."

"I agree, sir," Hannah said, causing me to smile, for she sounded like an eager rookie out to impress her boss. Myself, I never had that kind of eagerness. My natural distrust of authority never allowed it. Still, it was heartening to see Hannah making an effort and grasping her latest role with both hands.

"Alright," Bradley said. "You two get in there and see what this man has to say about his dealings with the Mirrorists and then follow up on whatever he has to say."

"Will do, sir," Hannah said, and we both headed for the door.

When I reached the door, I stopped and turned around again. "By the way, sir," I said. "Who do I give the cleaning bill to?"

Bradley frowned. "Cleaning bill?"

"For my car, sir."

The director shook his head at me. "I'm sure you have a hosepipe at that yard of yours, Special Agent. Now, go do your goddamn job before I decide to look deeper into your Yakuza situation."

A small sigh left me. "Yes, sir."

SOMEONE HAD FOUND ARNIE A PAIR OF FORENSIC OVERALLS to cover himself by the time Hannah and I entered the holding room. He sat with a Styrofoam cup of coffee cradled between his two massive hands, staring at us with brown eyes that seemed too small for his round face.

As Hannah switched on the recording equipment, I sat down and stated my name for the recording, followed by Arnie's name. Hannah added her own name as she sat next to me.

"You doing okay there, Arnie?" Hannah asked him. "Can I get you more coffee?"

Arnie shook his head. "No, thanks. When can I get out of here?"

We both stared at him. "Arnie," I said. "You brought down an entire building. You endangered lives."

"So, I'm under arrest?"

I was beginning to think Arnie was a little slow. "Yeah, Arnie. You're in our custody."

"Am I going to jail?"

"Why don't we have a conversation first?" Hannah said, smiling. "Then we can talk about what will happen next."

"I want to know now," Arnie said.

"Alright, Arnie," I said. "Have it your way. After we're done talking here, you'll be taken away to a holding facility for people similar to yourself."

"Like a black site?" he asked. "I heard of them on TV."

"Something like that. It'll probably just be temporary until the government can decide what to do with you."

"Doctor Jamal said there were others like me," he said. "How many?"

"People like you? A lot."

Arnie nodded. "I thought I was the only one for a long time. I thought I'd been cursed. Doctor Jamal told me I'd been cursed."

"Did he now?" I said. "You got a full name and address for Dr. Jamal?"

Arnie rhymed off the name—Dr. Azeem Jamal—and the downtown address of the practice. "Dr. Jamal is nice. He only wanted to help me, but I think I'm too broken to help."

"I don't think your broken, Arnie," Hannah said, a note of sympathy in her voice. "No more than the rest of us," she added, glancing at me.

"So, when did you start seeing this therapist?" I asked him.

"Around three months ago," he said. "My wife died last year, and I haven't been doing so good since then."

"I'm sorry for your loss. How'd she die?"

"Pancreatic cancer." He averted his eyes to the table as if reliving a memory of his wife. "She was a beautiful woman. Too good for me, I always said."

"Like someone else I could mention," another voice said from behind me, causing my blood to freeze for a second.

Don't turn around. Just ignore the bitch. Ignore her...

"When did you realize you had these powers?" Hannah asked.

"Maybe a year ago," Arnie said. "It was during a difficult time. Mira, my wife, she was very sick in the hospital. I got depressed, you know? One day I was sitting out the backyard, and I thought about killing myself—" He stopped and pinched the bridge of his nose as tears came to his eyes. "I'm sorry. It was a terrible time."

"It's okay," Hannah said. "Take your time."

"My god," Angela said from behind me. "How do you listen to all this misery day in, day out? Is it any wonder you've been such a miserable bastard all these years, Ethan? And I thought the hospital was bad. I actually feel sorry for you now."

Shut the fuck up...

"So anyway," Arnie said after wiping away his tears. "I'm in the backyard, drinking beer and thinking about gassing myself in the garage. You know, with the car exhaust? I hear it's painless. God help me, I even thought about killing Mira too, to put her out of her misery. She wouldn't have had to endure any more pain then. Neither of us would. We coulda left this world together, you know?"

"There's an idea for you, Ethan," Angela said. "Carbon monoxide poisoning. Better than eating your gun, eh?" She laughed to herself.

"I get it," Hannah said. "So, your powers manifested at this point?"

Arnie nodded. "Yeah. I was sitting, thinking how unfair it was that Mira was dying in the hospital, and the next thing, all this...*stuff* flowed outta me. Like mud. And then it all just...covered me, from head to toe, and it flowed everywhere, covering the whole backyard." He stopped and shook his head. "I was petrified, but I felt...strong. Powerful, you know? Like a freakin' superhero." His laugh was almost childlike.

"Pathetic," Angela scorned. "This man-child thinks he's a superhero because he can turn things into mud? Almost as bad as you, Ethan, thinking you're a hero just because you destroy everything in your path."

Bitch.

"How'd you get it to stop?" I asked him.

"There was a chair out in the yard that my wife used to sit in all the time," he said. "My mud melted the chair, and that made me sad because I thought to myself that Mira will never get to sit in that chair again. Once I thought that, I turned back to normal again. The mud, it just seemed to peel off me."

"Did you tell all this to Dr. Jamal?"

"Yeah, I did. That's why I went to see him in the first place. I saw an ad for the Mirrorist Group in a newspaper, saying they can help people afflicted with strange powers."

"They advertise in the newspaper as well?" I said, more to myself than anyone else. "You'd think they'd be a bit more discreet."

"It is often better to hide in plain sight," Angela said, her voice manly now, as if the Spreak himself was now there, though I didn't turn around to see. "The herd is too stupid and self-absorbed to notice what's around them. That's why organizations like the Mirrorists can do what they do and get away with it. No one notices, and if they did, no one would care because they are so brainwashed by the elite that runs this world. It's people's apathy that allows those like me —and the supernatural underground—not just to exist, but to *thrive*. But you know all this already, don't you, Ethan? I mean, just look at everything you've gotten away with over the years. Even your new boss doesn't know the half of it, does he? If he did, do you think he would still employ you? I think not."

"So," Hannah said as I sat gritting my teeth, trying to suppress my rage at the Spreak standing behind me. "How often did you see Dr. Jamal?"

"Once a week for three months," Arnie said. "Our last session was this morning."

"And what did you talk about?"

"Lots of things, but mostly about the fact that I was afflicted. That's what Dr. Jamal calls people like me—the Afflicted."

"The Afflicted," the Spreak said. "*They* are the afflicted ones, spouting their nonsense."

At least we can agree on that.

"Did Dr. Jamal make you feel bad about being afflicted?" Hannah asked.

Arnie thought for a moment. "Well, I thought he was just showing me who I really was. He kept saying I needed to be honest with myself and take a long, hard look in the mirror. So that's what I did. Dr. Jamal even held a mirror up to my face so I could see…could see what a bad person I was…"

"Did he tell you that?" I asked him. "Did you tell you were a bad person?"

Arnie thought again. "Maybe not in so many words, but…yes, he did. I certainly felt bad after every session. But Dr. Jamal, he told me this was normal, and that all my bad feelings were just coming to the surface, and that he would soon show me how to deal with those."

"And did he?"

"Did he what?"

"Show you how to deal with your bad feelings?"

"I don't know. Dr. Jamal would just talk. Half the time, I wouldn't even understand what he was talking about. I just know that I felt worse after every session."

"So why'd you keep going back?" I asked.

"Because he is dumb, Ethan," the Spreak said. "I would've thought that was obvious."

"I had nowhere else to turn," Arnie said. "I couldn't tell no one else about my affliction. If I did, Dr. Jamal said people would hate me, maybe even try to kill me. Meanwhile, the mud kept bubbling up in me, especially when I thought about Mira. I was all alone. Dr. Jamal was the only person who seemed to care."

"Except he didn't, did he?" I said.

Arnie frowned. "What do you mean?"

"Did Dr. Jamal tell you to do anything?" Hannah asked.

"Like what?"

"Did he tell you to kill yourself?" I asked him.

Arnie shook his head. "No, he never said that."

"He didn't need to," the Spreak said. "All he had to do was plant the seeds and dumb-dumb here would take care of the rest."

"So why did you try to bring that building down on yourself?" I asked.

Arnie seemed confused now as she sat and thought. "I...I'm not sure."

"What else did Dr. Jamal tell you? About yourself, I mean."

"Well, he told me that there are others like me and that we were all a danger to society. He said many people had already died because of the Afflicted and the things they did with their powers, which he called evil."

"He said your powers were evil?" Hannah said.

Arnie nodded almost in shame. "Dr. Jamal said we were the Devil's creations, and that if we believed in God, we all had to—" He stopped as if realizing something.

"You all had to what?" Hannah said.

"We all had to atone for our sins," Arnie finished quietly.

"Did he tell you how?" I asked him.

"He just said I would know how soon enough. That the answer would come if I let it."

"And I'm guessing it came to you this morning?"

"Before that actually," Arnie said. "I mentioned to Dr. Jamal that I was having thoughts about hurting myself, about just going away."

"And what did Dr. Jamal say to that?" Hannah asked.

"He said...he said if I was having those thoughts, then that meant God was sending me a message, telling me what to do, and if God was sending me a message, then I had to listen and do as God said."

"So, God was telling you to kill yourself?" I said, disgusted with everything that was being said now.

Arnie nodded. "It seemed that way."

"Arnie," Hannah said. "Can you not see how this Dr. Jamal manipulated you into thinking this way? God wasn't telling you to kill yourself. God would never tell you to kill yourself."

Tears returned to Arnie's eyes. "Not even if I'm afflicted?"

"No, Arnie," Hannah said. "Not even if you are afflicted. There's nothing wrong with you, Arnie. You're just different, that's all. You aren't a bad person, either. You're just in pain because you lost your wife."

"You know how that feels, don't you, Ethan?" the Spreak whispered, causing my rage to spike once more. Unable to help myself, I spun around in my chair to confront the bastard, but he was gone, only his cold laughter lingering in his place.

"Ethan?" Hannah said, frowning at me. "What's wrong?"

"Nothing," I mumbled, turning around again. "Carry on."

Hannah stared at me for a second longer. I was sure she knew something was up, and I wondered how much longer I would leave it before telling her, if I told her at all.

Arnie was in floods of tears by this point, seemingly oblivious to my distractedness. He had just realized he'd been played this whole time by the unscrupulous Dr. Jamal. I felt sorry for the guy. Arnie, I mean, not Dr. Jamal. Even more so since I knew Arnie would be put away soon, locked up like a stray dog that no one wanted, and perhaps even put down at some point. It wasn't right, and the situation only added to my existing anger and frustration.

"Interview over," I said, before turning to Hannah. "Let's go see this Dr. Jamal fuck."

Hannah nodded, as angry as I was now at the way these Supernormals had been treated by the Mirrorists.

On the way out, Hannah put a hand on Arnie's shoulder. "I'm sorry for your loss, Arnie. No matter what happens, please remember that you are not afflicted by evil. God still loves you."

Does He? I thought. *I'm not so sure about that.*

I'm not so sure he loves any of us anymore.

15

After bringing Bradley up to speed on what Arnie said about the Mirrorist therapist, Hannah and I left the building and went to the car. When we got inside, Hannah turned to me, reminding me of a Blackstar recruit in her black military fatigues and T-shirt.

"So," she said. "You wanna tell me what's going on?"

Anxiety bit at me as I paused, about to turn the ignition. "What do you mean?" I asked dismissively. "There's nothing going on."

Hannah sighed and shook her head. "Seriously. Don't treat me like a fool, Ethan. I'm not blind. You haven't been yourself for days now. You're like a man slowly going insane. Have you looked in the mirror lately? The look in your eyes says it all. You know who you're beginning to remind me of?"

"Who?" I asked, settling back in my seat now, knowing there'd be no escaping her questioning this time.

"The damned souls in Hell," she said. "Most of them have gone mad because they see and hear things all day long, things that no one else sees or hears. Only they do. It's part of the torture, and it never ends. Every damned soul gets tormented by their guilty conscience. They are trapped in a hell of their own making. People think Hell is all about getting tortured by demons, but it isn't. Least not all the time. Most of the time, the torture comes from within. Every damned soul ends up with the same haunted look in their tired eyes, because they can never escape their torment. That's the look I'm seeing in your eyes now, Ethan. So why don't you cut the bullshit and just for fucking once, be honest and tell me what the fuck is going on? If you don't, we're done. I mean it. I'll get out of this car, and you'll never see me again."

I stared at her in near shock. "You'd really do that?"

She nodded, her eyes never leaving mine. "I wouldn't like it, but I'd do it. I spent more time than you can imagine in Hell, a place where everyone told lies all the time, where no one was honest about anything, not even with themselves. I will not repeat the experience here. I'd rather be on my own as being with people who weren't honest with themselves or me. I've been nothing but honest with you since we met, Ethan. You owe it to me to be the same."

I couldn't argue with her there. So far, I'd convinced myself that by keeping my torment to myself, I was doing Hannah a favor by not getting her involved, when really, I was being the same selfish asshole that I always am. Like it or not, the Spreak's torment wasn't just affecting me, it was affecting Hannah and my relationship with her.

"Okay," I sighed, reaching across to the glove compartment and taking out the bottle of Jack there. "You're right. There's shit going on with me I haven't told you about, not because I wanted to hide it from you necessarily, but more because I didn't want you to think I was going mad or something."

Hannah snorted and grabbed the bottle from me. "Are you fucking serious? I already think you're mad." She put the bottle to her lips and took a mouthful of the whiskey before handing it back to me.

"Thanks. Not for the bottle, but for thinking I'm mad."

"I was kidding, mostly. You can't do what you do without being a little mad, right?"

"I guess not."

"So out with it. What's got you crazier than usual?"

"It's the Spreak," I said, glad to be finally telling someone about it. "The motherfucker is in my head, haunting me, trying to drive me mad, I think."

"How?"

"He keeps showing up as my dead wife to torment me. He knows everything that ever happened between Angela and me. Somehow, he's been able to plunder my mind, my memories."

"Is he here now?" she asked, her eyes darting around the car as if she expected to see who I was talking about.

I checked the back seat just to be sure. "No."

"Does he show up as anyone else?"

"He appeared as Cal earlier when I was on the roof about to shoot Susumu Yagami. He said some hurtful shit, I can tell you that."

Hannah nodded. "He's trying to break you, Ethan. But why?"

I shrugged. "I haven't worked that out yet. First, he has Angela and Callie killed, making it look like it was you who did it. Now, he's haunting me, trying to drive me insane by using the people I loved against me."

"And he's given you no indication of why he might be doing all this?"

"Nope. He just said I'd find out the truth eventually."

Hannah took the bottle from me and brought it to her lips once more, swallowing before staring out the window at the rain that had just started to fall, the sky overheard now a murky gray. "We can't let this go on," she said after a moment. "We have to do something about this guy."

"No shit," I said, suddenly struck by the thought that the Spreak might be listening right now, even though I couldn't see him. Was he in the back seat, invisible, smirking to himself in amusement as he listened to us futilely plot against him? "Like what?"

"We kill him, of course. You know where he lives, right?"

"Yeah, but it's not that easy. This guy, whoever the fuck he is, is powerful. There's no way he's gonna let us just waltz into his sanctum and kill him."

"Why not? It sounds to me like he has you beaten already."

I sighed. She was right. The Spreak had worn away at my resolve not just to stop him, but to get to the bottom of why he was doing all this to me. On some level, I had accepted defeat without even realizing it.

"This guy is no ordinary foe," I said after swigging from the Jack bottle. "I'm gonna need outside help to stop him, someone who knows how these Spreak motherfuckers operate."

"You have someone in mind, I take it?"

"Yeah, unfortunately, I do."

"Solomon?"

I nodded. "Yeah, and that's if he even agrees to help me. Spreaks aren't known for going up against each other. There are so few of them that they help more than hinder each other. The Spreaks at Blackstar were a tight-knit group. If you fucked with one, you fucked with them all."

"That was Blackstar," Hannah said. "You're not in Blackstar now, and neither is this guy. Is he?"

"Not as far as I know."

Hannah took the bottle from me. "You need to go and see Solomon, and you need to lay off this stuff. I'm sure it's not helping. If you want to defeat this guy, your mind has to be clear."

"Maybe."

"There's no maybe about it. You should lay off the Mud as well. That stuff probably makes it easy for the Spreak to manipulate your mind."

"You want me to get strung out? How's that going to help?"

"I don't know. Just go see Solomon. Like, now. I'll check out this Dr. Jamal on my own."

"You sure?"

"I can handle it."

I nodded. "Okay. Make sure you he tells you who's running this shitshow. Get a name. Do whatever you have to."

Hannah smiled. "I will, don't worry."

"And be discreet. No flying the guy out the damn window or anything."

"Discretion. Got it."

"Take the car. I can walk from here. I need to clear my head, anyway."

"Are you sure? Where does Solomon live?"

"The European Borough."

"That's miles away."

"I know. I'll get a cab when I get sick of walking."

Hannah took my hand and squeezed, staring at me for a second before leaning over and kissing me softly on the lips. "When all this is over," she said, "you and I are going away somewhere. Just the two of us."

I refrained from rolling my eyes at the mention of a vacation again. This time, a vacation from everything didn't sound so bad.

"Sounds good."

Her eyes lit up. "Really?"

Nodding, I kissed her. "Really. Now go do your job, Special Agent Walker."

"You too, Special Agent Drake."

I KEPT A SPARE TRENCH COAT IN THE TRUNK OF THE CAR, which I grabbed before Hannah drove away. At the rate I was going through coats these days, I was considering buying in bulk next time. Maybe, if this job with Pan Demic's sister panned out, I'd walk into a shop and buy an entire rack of trench coats.

In the meantime, I put the spare one on and trudged down the street in the rain, my hands dug deep into the pockets as I took in the nearly empty city surrounding me. I rarely watch the news or bother with any kind of mainstream media, so I knew very little about this virus going around. The MSM is pure fiction anyway, controlled by the CIA and the global elite (google Operation Mockingbird). Whatever the MSM was saying about the virus, it was probably bullshit. Working at Blackstar for so long—an integral part of the global elite—I knew how things worked. The real story was never made public, and the herd was always led to believe whatever narrative the GE wanted the herd to believe. So if there was a virus going around, it was going around for a reason. It didn't just happen.

Who knew what the psychopathic rulers were up to, and what agenda they had going?

Knightsbridge was up to something if he was cozying up to the President, trying to get his claws into Special Affairs. What was his game, anyway? As far as I knew, he'd never shown much interest in government affairs before. So why was he showing an interest now?

I didn't know, but something told me I might find out eventually, or Bradley might if he kept pushing.

In any case, I had my own problems to worry about. My only concern now was stopping the Spreak, and before that, finding out why he was doing what he was doing.

As the rain continued to fall, I was soon soaked by the time I'd walked one block, though I didn't care. I'd never minded the rain the way some people do. It was cleansing, and it helped wash the filth off the streets.

Still, I realized I had been a bit optimistic when I said I would walk to Solomon's place. Given how much farther I had to walk, it would be well past dark by the time I arrived there, so I looked for transport.

After ten minutes, I was able to flag down a cab, surprised that any cabs were running at all, given the current situation. When I got inside, the driver told me that many cabs were still running to get essential workers to where they needed to be, like myself, I suppose. The driver wore a mask and wasn't going to let me inside the cab because I wasn't wearing one as well. He only relented when I flashed my ID at him, though he scowled at me the entire journey, and probably couldn't wait to get me out of his cab, in case I had the virus.

The cabbie dropped me on the outskirts of the European Borough, which seemed just as deserted as the rest of the city, perhaps because it wasn't as densely populated as many other districts. As I walked down the rain-slicked, Romanesque streets, I couldn't help but marvel at the surrounding architecture, which was a mishmash of Gothic, Renaissance, Baroque, and Rocco, all interweaved with Historicism, creating a dark backdrop of weathered stone buildings, spires that stabbed the sky, and hundreds of gargoyles that watched from above like sentries. It was a dark, eerie place, infused with European superstition and old magic. The Derkas vampire clan was based in this borough. They were a scholarly lot, relatively peaceful compared to some of the other clans in the city, though still not to be messed with. Romanian gypsies had a large presence here too, heading up the largest crime syndicate, having a special interest in magical relics, which they sourced and sold on to the highest bidder.

The population in the European Borough was, unsurprisingly, made up mostly of immigrant families, many of whom had been settled for generations now. Solomon's family was of German descent, which is why he lived here. In fact, while I was at Blackstar, I found out that Solomon's grandfather was a high-ranking Nazi, heading up the SS Paranormal Division along with Heinrich Himmler. It was no surprise then, that Solomon ended up like a Nazi himself, carrying on his family's obsession with the occult. While at Blackstar, Solomon was head of PYSOP, which to many—myself included—resembled a branch of the SS anyway, with all of its secrecy and dark doings.

Which I guess also made Knightsbridge like Hitler, only worse in his own way.

At least Hitler was dead.

The deeper into the European Borough I walked, the narrower the streets became, and the denser the architecture became, every building seeming to display occult symbols on doors and windows, even engraved into the stone itself.

As the light faded and night fell, shadows moved in alleyways, and more than once, I got the impression I was being watched. The few people on the streets wore hoods, perhaps against the rain, but more likely to hide themselves for whatever reason.

This place was fucking Spooksville, no doubt about it.

And it was soon to get a lot worse.

16

Navigating my way through the narrow, winding streets of the inner European Borough, I soon found myself having company in the form of Cal. He appeared alongside me out of nowhere, causing me to stop in fright for a second before I realized who it was.

"What the fuck do you want?" I said as I resumed walking, trying to see the street names so I could find where Solomon lived. I'd never been to the necromancer's address before, and it was proving difficult to find my way around this maze of darkness, which was probably why Solomon lived here.

"Where are you going?" Cal rasped, a lit cigarette hanging from his torn lips. "You're not going to see that fucking freak Solomon, are you? Didn't I tell you before that he was bad news?"

"Fuck off." I kept walking, refusing to look at him. "You're not Cal."

"You shouldn't be in this place," he persisted. "It's dangerous. Remember that time we tracked that Strigoi here? We ended up stumbling upon a nest of the fuckers. There were so many, we had to run. You remember how they chased us through these streets, and the locals tried to grab us so they could hold us for the Strigoi? We barely made it out alive. Everyone in this place is a fucking monster of some sort. You might not make it out of here again."

I shook my head, remembering well the incident he was talking about, annoyed that he seemed to know everything that ever fucking happened to me.

"You really don't want me here, do you?" I said as I turned down another narrow street, having little idea of where I was even going at this point. "I wonder why that is."

"I'm warning you, Ethan." It was the Spreak's voice now, and he had stopped behind me.

Turning around, I saw a tall, grim figure standing in the middle of the cobbled street, his face shrouded in shadow like the rest of him. "What are you going to do? Talk me to death? Go fuck yourself."

"Have it your way," the Spreak said as I stomped off again.

And that's when things changed, slowly at first, and then at a rate so rapid, it felt like I had fallen down a rabbit hole into another world entirely.

It started with the walls of the surrounding buildings, which became covered by a slick, black substance that resembled bubbling tar. It ran disgustingly down the stonework, giving birth to shapeless creatures that crawled along the cobbled streets, limbs stretching out blindly to grab whatever was around, including me.

"What the fuck?" I said, stamping on one of the deformed black creatures before it could grab me, hearing it scream as I crushed it under my boot.

I ran down the rest of the street after that, emerging into a large square where every building was covered in the same ectoplasmic substance, with bigger and badder creatures forming out of it.

The surrounding light had also changed, from the flat

black of night to a muted red. Deep crimson clouds formed overhead at an astonishing rate, and then burst, showering everything with blood.

As the blood rained down, I was soaked by it in seconds, the sharp, coppery taste filling my mouth, the fetid stench of the stuff assailing my nostrils.

The falling blood also seemed to be feeding the black, ectoplasmic creatures forming everywhere, giving them further life, allowing them to grow into bigger, more horrifying forms that now had eyes and mouths and fingers to scratch and grab and tear with, which they didn't mind using against each other.

In no time at all, the square was an orgy of bloody violence as the creatures turned on each other, ripping each other apart, screeching and squealing as they did so.

And then they all stopped at once, and an eerie silence descended for an extended moment as the creatures seemed to turn and stare at me.

Then the screaming started again, and all the creatures headed for me as if they could see nothing else.

Without thinking, I drew my sidearm and fired at the nearest abominations, their deformed heads and bodies exploding in showers of blood as the bullets hit them, which I didn't expect. It was almost cartoony the way the creatures exploded so dramatically, though I didn't stop to think about it.

Instead, I ran through the path I had cleared, down dark streets as I tried to run toward Solomon's place, which I knew couldn't be far away now because his house wasn't far from the square I'd just been in. He told me himself not that long ago, "Left at the square, follow Church Street until you get to the fountain. Turn right at the fountain onto Dorfstraße. Look for the gothic mansion at the end of the street. I look forward to your visit someday."

"Not fucking likely," I had told him, thinking I'd have no need to visit Solomon ever.

But here I was, running through streets that now resembled a version of Hell, with Solomon's house being the only sanctuary.

The layout of the place seemed to have changed, and I hadn't a clue where I was going.

I emerged out of a winding street into another square, this one massive, and which shouldn't have been there. In the center of the square was an obsidian obelisk that stretched far into the blood-red sky. Surrounding the obelisk was a crowd of people, dozens upon dozens of them, many of them seeming to be in various states of deadness.

And not just people, but creatures as well—vampires, demons, werewolves, and every creature in between.

"Behold Ethan," a booming voice said as the tall figure of the Spreak emerged from the crowd. "Every person and every creature you have ever killed, all here to greet you once again."

"What…no…"

I shook my head in disbelief as I soon recognized many of the faces, most of which I hadn't seen in a very long time, though there were still more that I'd seen only recently. The hellots sent by Astaroth to kill me, for instance, and the massive security guard I'd killed at Robert Webb's mountain lair. Even Gretchen Carmichael, the cult leader, stood at the front of the crowd, blood running from the bullet hole I'd put in her head.

They were all there, every person I'd ever killed, even Bryan Bentley, the boys' home pedophile and child killer, the first man I'd ever killed.

My stomach turned over as I stared at them all, their dead eyes still managing to be accusatory and full of hatred.

Have I really killed this many?

It was hard to believe, but it seemed I had.

"So much blood on your hands, Ethan," the Spreak boomed again over the angry noise of the crowd. "Would you like to see just how *much* blood?"

Before I could even say anything, the Spreak raised his arms out, and the next thing, every single person in the crowd exploded at once, their blood coming together to create a tidal wave of crimson that rolled across the square, reaching me in seconds.

The enormous wall of blood loomed over me for a drawn-out moment as I backed away, and then came crashing down all at once, swallowing me up so I couldn't breathe as I tumbled around in it.

The combined blood of all the people I had killed.

And I was drowning in it.

Then, just as I could hold my breath no longer, the blood wave dropped me to the ground and rushed over me as it washed away all over the square, leaving me on my hands and knees as I coughed and spluttered, vomiting up the blood that I'd been forced to swallow.

"How does it taste, Ethan?" the Spreak said, still standing by the obelisk like some dark Demigod. "Does it taste bitter?"

The Spreak's laughter echoed all around me as I got to my feet, soaked to the skin in blood, tasting and smelling nothing else.

"Fuck you! You think you can break me?" I laughed maniacally. "You can't break an already broken man, asshole!"

The Spreak said nothing as he backed away, seeming to merge into the obelisk as he disappeared.

A heavy silence descended as I stood looking around, wiping blood from my eyes as I struggled to see in the gloomy red light.

What the fuck is going on? Where did he go?

There was no movement around me. No shapeless black

creatures. No people. The only sound was the dripping of the blood.

Until I heard a voice.

A voice that was faint at first, but as it got louder, my blood froze when I realized who the voice belonged to.

"Daddy! Help me, Daddy!"

"No…" I said, shaking my head. "Not her. Please not her…"

"Daddy! Please help me, Daddy…"

"Stop this!" I shouted, looking around for the Spreak, but he was nowhere to be found.

"Over here, Daddy!" Callie's voice had changed, going from distressed to almost playful now. "Come find me, Daddy! Let's play."

Her childish laughter echoed around the square, and even though I knew it wasn't real—that it *couldn't* be real—I shouted, "Callie? Where are you?"

Don't. Don't do it. She's not real…

I wanted to heed my own warning, but I couldn't. Her voice was just too real, which meant she had to be real as well, and…and I had to see her. She was my baby girl, and I had to see her…

"Callie?" I called again.

"Over here, Daddy!"

Unable to help myself, I followed her innocent laughter, which led me up a side street that emerged into a small park area comprising two swings, a roundabout, and a small sandpit, all surrounded by a low metal fence.

Approaching the gate, I stopped and nearly dropped to my knees when I saw Callie playing in the sandpit. Tears spilled from my eyes as I stared at her, my little girl, wearing a flowery summer dress that I remembered her wearing the last time I ever took her to the park.

Callie…

I didn't care that she wasn't real. The fact that she wasn't didn't even enter my mind at that point. I just knew she was there, in front of me, and intact, looking as beautiful as I remembered her to be.

Callie finished building a small mound of sand before leaving the sandpit and sitting on a swing, gently moving back and forth as she finally made eye contact with me.

"Are you just going to stand there, Daddy?" she said in her sweet little voice. "Come join me."

I smiled and nodded as I opened the gate and stepped into the park before walking over and sitting on the swing next to her, feeling like I was inside a dream as she turned her head and smiled at me. Whatever kind of reality this was, I didn't dare question it in case it crumbled from beneath me, taking my daughter away from me again.

"Hey, sweetheart," I said, my voice so full of emotion I could hardly speak. "What you doing?"

"Just playing," she said, still swinging back and forth. "I've missed you, Daddy."

My face crumpled, and I bit my bottom lip till it bled as I tried unsuccessfully to hold back my tears. "I—I've missed you," I said in a hoarse whisper.

"Don't cry, Daddy." Callie hopped off the swing and came to stand in front of me for a second before coming forward and hugging me.

It was almost a shock to feel how real she was, as if I'd thought this whole time that she was nothing more than an illusion. But I felt her soft body against mine, felt her warmth, and the silkiness of her hair as I held her head against me. Closing my eyes, I allowed myself to get lost in the moment, in the joy of having my little girl back in my arms again, savoring every second until she finally let go and looked up at me.

"Why did you let the monster get us, Daddy?" she asked. "Why did you let the monster kill Mommy and me?"

"Sweetheart, I—"

I didn't know what to say to her, but even if I'd had, I was interrupted by a monstrous roar nearby, followed by a booming voice demanding, "Where are you, you little bitch?"

"Oh no," Callie said, suddenly afraid. "He's back."

"Who's back, sweetheart?" I said, about to stand up when Callie suddenly got yanked away from me. It all happened so fast, I couldn't comprehend it until I looked across and saw a monstrous demon standing on the other side of the fence, one massive hand wrapped around Callie as he clutched her tight.

"Daddy!" Callie squealed. "Help me!"

"Let her go!" I shouted at the demon as I ran forward.

"Fuck off, human scum," the horned demon snarled, and then, to my absolute horror, lifted Callie to his mouth and used his enormous sharp teeth to bite her head clean off, crushing her skull as he chewed for a second or two before swallowing.

"NOOOOO!" I screamed.

The demon laughed as he continued to grip Callie's lifeless body in his clawed hand. Then two giant wings emerged from the demon's back, and he pushed off the ground and shot into the air like a bullet, disappearing into the blood-red sky.

In the middle of the park, I sank to my knees, gripping my hair and pulling as I rocked back and forth, my mind now shattered into a thousand pieces until it felt like I was drifting on a sea of madness with no way back to shore.

"It's not real…" I whispered over and over again as I tried desperately to convince myself. "It's not real, it's not real…none of this is really happening…"

"Keep telling yourself that. Maybe you might believe it."

I looked up to see Cal standing there on the other side of the fence.

"You enjoying the show, kid?" Cal said, a smile on his face.

"Fuck you," I said without conviction.

"Beaten already?" he mocked. "I thought I taught you to be stronger than that."

Somehow, I got to my feet, my legs unsteady as I struggled to stay upright. "You didn't teach me anything, asshole," I said, most of my emotion gone now as if the demon took it all, along with Callie. There was just numbness now, which I welcomed.

"Maybe not." It was the Spreak standing there now, nothing but a tall shadow with glowing red eyes. "But perhaps I will now. Perhaps I will teach you the meaning of pain."

"Go ahead," I said. "Do your worst."

"You think because you don't care anymore that I can't hurt you?"

"Whatever."

"Let's see, shall we?"

Within seconds I was surrounded by screeching black shapes—wraiths—that flew madly around me for a second before attacking me one by one, each wraith flying right through me, every dark penetration like getting stabbed by the sharpest of swords. The pain was so great, I thought the wraiths were slicing me to pieces as I screamed in agony, but they weren't. My body was still intact, all the better to feel the pain inflicted upon me.

Over my screams, the Spreak laughed. "Perhaps you should run, Ethan," he said. "Before my wraiths *really* get their claws out."

As if to give me incentive, the next wraith that penetrated me did physical damage this time, leaving a hole in my left shoulder akin to a stab wound.

Not knowing what else to do, I bolted out of the park,

leaping over the fence and running as fast as I could into the nearest street as the wraiths screeched after me.

I ran fast, but not fast enough, for the wraiths could still penetrate me as I ran, flying right through me like sharp shadows until the pain became so great that I stopped running and all but collapsed to my knees, surrounded now by the wraiths as they circled overhead, coming together to create a dark vortex that threatened to suck me in and churn me up like a meat grinder.

I was almost resigned to my fate when a familiar voice reached me through the wind created by the swirling wraiths.

"Ethan!"

Looking up, I saw a massive black shape coming toward me, and for a second, I thought it was another creation of the Spreak's, come to finish me.

But it wasn't. To my complete surprise, it was Haedemus.

Or was it? I couldn't be sure what was real and what wasn't anymore.

"Ethan, get up!" Haedemus shouted as he used his horn to disperse the wraiths enough for me to stand up.

"You're not even real," I said flatly.

"What? Of course I'm real, Ethan," Haedemus said urgently. "Now get on so I can get you the hell out of here."

Whatever. Real or not, it had to be better than sitting here waiting to be torn apart by wraiths.

"Get out of here you stinking wraiths!" Haedemus said as he dispersed more of them with his horn. "Hurry, Ethan!"

With what little strength I had left, I grabbed Haedemus' mane and hauled myself onto him, loosely grabbing the reins as he immediately turned and galloped off, the screeching wraiths chasing after us.

"What are you doing here?" I asked him as we turned

down a narrow street. "Is it even you?"

"Yes, Ethan," he said. "It's me, Haedemus Sassoon, poodle groomer extraordinaire. Remember?"

I snorted once as my mind settled back into its dream state again. "I remember."

"Do you? It doesn't sound like it. What the hell is happening here?"

"I'm going mad, that's what happening."

"No, you're not." Haedemus took a sharp right, almost making me fall off of him, the reins the only thing stopping me. "You're being fucked with, that's all. Where are we going? Home?"

"No. Solomon's. I have to go to Solomon's…"

"Where is that?"

"Keep going."

As Haedemus galloped onward, I turned around to see that the wraiths had gone. Not only that, so had the ecto-plasmic substance that previously covered every surface. Just like that, everything seemed normal again. Even the wounds on my body caused by the wraiths were gone.

"What the fuck just happened?" I said.

"I don't know," Haedemus said. "But it seemed to me like your nightmares came true."

"Worse than any nightmare," I said hoarsely, thinking of Callie. "Far worse…"

∾

RICHARD SOLOMON'S HOME WAS AN EARLY VICTORIAN Gothic Revival house built of stone that suggested the cathedrals of medieval Europe with its pinnacles and parapets. In short, it was creepy as fuck and exactly the kind of house I would expect someone like Solomon to live in. The house had probably been in his family for generations, maybe even built by his grandfather when he was undoubtedly secreted here by Operation Paperclip along with hundreds of other Nazi brainiacs.

"Who lives here?" Haedemus said when we pulled up outside the house. "*The Munsters?*" He guffawed at his own joke, then stopped when he realized I wasn't laughing. "You're still mad at me, aren't you?"

I got down off of him, noticing as if for the first time that I was covered head to toe in blood still. "To be honest, Haedemus, I got a lot more on my mind right now than your murderous indiscretions."

"I see," Haedemus said, as if he was hoping for some kind of reconciliation. "So, should I wait for you?"

"No. You can go."

Haedemus, nodding his big head, started to walk away. As he did, I sighed and turned around. "Haedemus?"

"Yes, Ethan?" he said, stopping to look back at me.

"I appreciate the save."

"That's quite alright."

"How'd you even know I was here?"

"I asked Hannah where you were after she arrived back at the yard."

"She's back already?"

"She came back hours ago. It's almost midnight, Ethan, if that tower clock over there is anything to go by."

"Shit…"

"Are you sure you don't want me to wait? I really don't mind. In fact, I insist. It's the least I can do after…you know."

"Yeah."

"I disgraced myself, I know that now. I disgraced you as well, Ethan. I wish I could take it all back."

I looked away for a second, on some level, knowing how he felt. "I know."

"You do?"

"It doesn't mean I forgive you. You got a lot of making

up to do."

"Yes, of course. So shall I stay and wait for you?"

I nodded. "Alright. I might be a while."

"That's fine," he said, walking toward me. "No problem. Take your time. I'll be waiting."

"Okay, Haedemus."

Turning, I headed toward Solomon's house, opening the creaky metal gate and walking up to the front door, which opened before I even had time to knock it. Standing in the doorway was the tall figure of Richard Solomon, dressed, as usual, like an undertaker, his face deathly white, his pale blue eyes like two chips of ice.

"Ethan," Solomon said in his hissing voice. "I'd say I'm surprised to see you, but I'm not. I've been watching with interest your entire ordeal since you arrived here in the borough."

I stared at him in near astonishment. "You were watching? And you never thought to help me?"

Solomon allowed himself a slight smile. "I wanted to see how things played out." As if that was all the explanation needed, he looked past me at Haedemus. "I see your Hellbeast is with you."

"Hey there," Haedemus called. "Lovely evening, isn't it?"

Ignoring Haedemus, Solomon looked at me. "He speaks."

"Yeah. Too fucking much."

"I heard that," Haedemus called, making me to shake my head.

"Well," Solomon said, "I suppose you had better come in, Ethan." He looked at me like he had a bad taste in his mouth as I stepped inside the house. "Maybe you'd like to get cleaned up a little before we discuss your problem."

"And what problem would that be?" I asked.

Solomon's cold eyes narrowed. "Your warlock problem."

The interior of Solomon's house was mostly wood floors and paneling, with much in the way of opulent furnishings, most of which looked old to the point of being antique. Many of the walls held huge paintings by artists such as Hieronymus Bosch, William Blake, and several others I didn't recognize, but which delved even further into the dark side of the human psyche.

As well as paintings, the walls held many old photos in ornate frames, most featuring tall, distinguished gentlemen and ladies. There was even one of a man shaking hands with Hitler, which I presumed to be Solomon's grandfather.

"So the rumors are true," I said, looking at the picture.

"Yes," Solomon said. "My grandfather was high up in the SS before he settled in this country."

"What did he do when he came here?"

"He did much, none of which I can discuss."

"Classified, huh?"

"Something like that," he said. "Come. I'll direct you to the bathroom."

I followed him out of the reception room, noticing the

strangely exotic scents in the house for the first time, which surprised me. Before, when I thought of Solomon's abode (which admittedly wasn't often), I pictured a gloomy place filled with the smell of rot and death. The scents emanating through the house now were downright pleasant in comparison, making me wonder what other surprises Solomon had hidden about himself. Was I soon to find out he was actually a renowned collector of china dolls? Or that he enjoyed cross-stitch?

On the way to the bathroom, I thought about asking him if there was a lady of the house, making a joke of it because I knew there would be no lady. But I never mentioned it. I wasn't of a mind to be making jokes, not when all I could think about was Callie.

"I'll arrange some fresh clothing for you," Solomon said as he showed me into the large bathroom, which I was glad to see had a modern shower installed.

I thought his choice of wording odd, but didn't question him on it as he left, closing the door behind him. Standing in the bathroom, I looked around for a moment, still weirded out that I was even in necromancer's house. For a bathroom, it held very little in the way of toiletries beyond a bar of soap and a washcloth, making me wonder if Solomon even bathed. Maybe in his quest to become like Death, bathing didn't come into it.

I stripped off and stepped into the shower, staying under the hot water for a good twenty minutes as I washed the blood from my hair and body, vacantly watching it swirl down the drain as I arranged things in my mind to lessen the trauma of my recent experience. At Blackstar, all recruits are taught ways to handle trauma. If they didn't teach us how to cope psychologically, we would never have lasted beyond the first few missions before our minds would've fallen apart, and we became walking examples of extreme PTSD.

So while the hot water washed the filth from my body, I used visualization and repeated phrases to wash away the filth from my mind, or at least to lock away the memories of Callie and that demon, hiding them from my conscious mind so they wouldn't drive me crazy. To be sure, I also used a working taught to me at Blackstar that allowed me to disassociate myself from the memories until it became almost like they happened to someone else.

By the time I had finished the workings, I felt better. The feelings were still there, but they were less potent without the accompanying memories. I swear, I had locked away so much trauma and terrible memories over the years, my mind probably resembled a labyrinth by now, with locked doors everywhere, behind which monsters lurked. If they ever broke free all at once, they'd turn my mind to mush.

Just as I turned the water off, I heard the bathroom door open. Stepping out of the shower, I was about to ask Solomon if he knew the meaning of privacy when I saw someone else standing in the doorway—someone whose appearance made me freeze for a moment and stare.

It was a person, but a profoundly ugly person, since their face seemed to have been stitched together using parts from different people. The eyes were two different colors—blue and green—and each was shaped differently. The nose was too large for the face, and the mouth was too small. Rows of stitches crisscrossed the person's entire face, continuing on down the neck. This short, composite of a person wore something resembling a priest's smock that was too short on the arms, revealing where their hands had been stitched at the wrist, hands that were not the same in size or shape, the fingers on the left hand being longer than those on the right. The person also had no hair and different sized ears, and stood there holding a pile of folded clothes.

"For you, thir," the patchwork human said, speaking

with a lisp as he offered me the clothes. "From Mathter Tholomon."

"And who are you?" I asked, almost afraid to find out.

"My name ith Thtitth. I am at your thervithe."

"Thtitth? Are you trying to say Stitch?"

Stitch nodded. "Yes, thir."

"Okay, well you can just leave the clothes here, Stitch. Tell Master Solomon I'll be along shortly and to have my drink ready."

"Drink? Whith drink, thir?"

"Whiskey will be fine. And cigarettes as well, please."

"Cigaretteth and whithkey. Yeth, thir. Very good, thir."

Stitch continued to stand in the doorway even after he had laid the clothes carefully on the floor. He appeared to be staring at my dick.

"That'll be all, Stitch. Thank you."

Stitch raised his eyes to mine. "Yeth, thir." Bowing slightly, he withdrew from the doorway and disappeared down the hallway.

Puffing my cheeks, I shook my head. Solomon had been playing Dr. Frankenstein and had created his own manservant. Jesus. It made me wonder what other sick shit he got up to in this house. Not that I wanted to know. The only thing I wanted from Solomon was to know how to take down the Spreak, though I dreaded to think what Solomon would want in return for such a big ask. I would be asking him to betray one of his own. If he helped me at all, fuck knows what he'd ask of me in return. Though, whatever the price, I would pay it. Anything was preferable to having the Spreak on my back for much longer.

The clothes that Stitch brought me must have been borrowed from Solomon's wardrobe, comprising black slacks, a black shirt, and a red tie of all things. There was also a black suit jacket and a pair of black leather shoes.

Shaking my head at the outfit, I didn't have much choice but to put it on, minus the red tie, which I think would've made me look like Marilyn Manson, so I left it by the sink.

When I was dressed, I checked my appearance in the mirror above the sink and shook my head again. "I look like a fucking alcoholic preacher," I muttered, the conservative style of the suit being far from fashionable. It also made my skin crawl that I was wearing Solomon's clothes, something else that would've been unthinkable before now.

My own clothes still lay on the floor. Lifting my blood-soaked trench, I retrieved my phone from it. The phone was covered in blood as well, but it still seemed to be working. After wiping it over, I discovered several missed calls from Hannah. I considered calling her back, but then decided against it as I was unwilling to explain everything to her, at least not yet. I texted her instead:

AT SOLOMON'S. SORRY I MISSED YOUR CALLS. SEE YOU IN THE MORNING X

Slipping the phone into the pocket of my slacks, I gathered up the rest of my bloody clothes and left the bathroom, finally finding my way back to the reception room where Solomon sat on a red velvet Victorian couch. He smiled when I walked into the room.

"It's like looking in the mirror," he said, remarking on my appearance.

"Ha-ha," I said. "You got a bag or something for these?"

"You can give your clothes to Stitch. He will make sure they are laundered before you leave here."

Stitch was standing by the side of the couch. He came forward and wordlessly took the clothes from me before leaving the room with them. I watched him go before turning to Solomon. "You never told me you had a pet."

"Stitch is not my pet, he's my servant," Solomon said. He gestured to the table in front of him, on which sat a decanter of whiskey and, I was glad to see, a pack of cigarettes.

"You created him?" I asked as I went to the table and poured whiskey from the decanter into a glass tumbler. I didn't offer Solomon any as he already held a glass of red wine. Taking the glass and the cigarettes, I sat next to him on the couch, which I found hard and uncomfortable.

"Stitch is made from the body parts of corpses," Solomon said. "I sewed them all together and used workings to animate the new creation."

"Who you named Stitch."

"It seemed appropriate."

"Was the lisp intentional? Added for comic effect?"

"No, it was not."

"Lucky break then. I bet every kid would love a Stitch."

"Don't be ridiculous, Ethan."

I smiled as I opened the pack of cigarettes and jammed one between my lips, realizing there was no lighter. "You got a light?" Solomon held one long finger out, and a small flame ignited from the tip, which I used to light the cigarette, looking at him as I did. "Handy."

"A simple parlor trick. Nothing more."

"Not like creating your own person from dead people, right? I'm surprised you're allowing me to smoke in here."

"It's just smoke."

"I admire your progressive attitude, Solomon. I wish everyone thought the same way."

Solomon stared at me for a moment. "You seem more yourself."

"Yes, well...I did what Blackstar taught us to do and disassociated myself from what happened."

"A protocol I helped design."

"Really? I guess I should thank you for saving me from being a blubbering wreck then."

Solomon said nothing for a while as he sipped on his

wine, and I sat drinking my whiskey and puffing gratefully on my cigarette, staring around the room at the same time. I still felt weird being inside Solomon's sanctum, like being inside his head, a place I always had no wish to go. Yet here I was, now privy to his personal life and family history, neither of which made him seem much more human to me. If anything, his family home and lineage made him seem even more unlike the rest of us.

Despite this, I couldn't deny his willingness to help me, not just now, but all the times in the past I had called upon his expertize. Sure, he always wanted something in return. But didn't everybody?

"So," I said after stubbing out my cigarette in a glass ashtray. "Did you really see what happened to me out there?"

"Most of it," he said, crossing his long, thin legs. "I was able to remote view it from here. The person who did it altered your reality."

"No shit."

"Most of it was an illusion. Much of it was in your mind."

"I saw my little girl," I said, still haunted by the memory, despite having dissociated myself from it. "She was taken by a demon."

"Yes, I saw."

"It wasn't…real, was it?"

"It was real to you. That's all that matters."

"Did you happen to see the director of that fucking horror movie?"

Solomon stared at me for a moment before nodding. "Yes."

"So, who is he? Someone as powerful as that, you must know him. The motherfucker had my wife and daughter killed and then tried to make me think it was my partner who did it. Who the fuck would do that?"

"Someone I used to work with at Blackstar a long time ago," Solomon said. "Someone powerful."

My jaw dropped slightly. "Are you kidding me? This fuck used to work for Knightsbridge? Who is he? Does he still work for Blackstar?"

"I don't know if he still works for Blackstar, but his name is Heinrick Cane."

"Heinrick Cane?" I mulled the name over for a moment, finally glad to be able to put a name to the shadow face. "How well do you know this fucking monster? Are you friends?"

Solomon rolled his eyes and snorted at what appeared to be my naiveté. "Really, Ethan? You'd think after all this time, you would know how I worked. People like me don't have friends, and the same goes for Cane. We walk very particular paths, paths that have room only for one."

"When is the last time you spoke to this Cane?"

"You're interrogating me now?"

"I'm just asking."

"The last time we worked together was when we retrieved the God Machine. You remember that, don't you?"

"Yes. It was my last mission for Blackstar. I remember you entering the room with the other Spreaks. You were an asshole to me that day. Was Cane part of your team?"

"He was. Cane was a very gifted illusionist, among other things."

"You're telling me," I said. "The bastard has been tormenting me for weeks now, appearing as my dead wife, and as my dead friend, Cal. And then all this shit tonight. I don't know what his game is. He stepped things up tonight."

"Because he knew where you were headed to."

"To see you."

Solomon nodded. "Yes."

"You think he was trying to stop me from coming here?"

"Probably. If Cane has raped and pillaged your mind, which he undoubtedly has, then he knows about our…relationship. He knows that if anyone can help you, it is I."

"And are you?"

"Am I what?"

"Don't fuck with me, Solomon. Just answer the question."

"I wouldn't have let you in here if I wasn't planning on helping you."

A sense of relief went through me. Finally, I wasn't alone in this shit.

"Okay," I said, lighting another cigarette. "Let's get this out of the way before we discuss how to stop this guy."

"Get what out of the way?"

"What do you want in return for helping me?"

Solomon gazed at me with a creepy smile on his face. "It's not so much what I want, Ethan. It's more what you must do."

"And what's that?"

"What I've been trying to get you to do for so long now." He paused, savoring the moment. "You must step into my world, Ethan, and make a friend of Death."

Christ…here we go.

"So, when you say Death, do you mean death in a general sense, or death as in *Death*?"

"Death is an entity all its own, Ethan. This is what I've been trying to put across to you all this time."

"So Death is like a person?"

"Much more than that, but yes. If you want the power to stop Cane, you must give Death what He wants."

"Which is?"

Solomon focused his ice-blue eyes on me. "Your soul."

I stared at him. "My soul?"

"The reason Cane can torment you as he does is because he piggybacks on your soul energy," Solomon explained as he poured himself more wine. "Over time, he has evidently established that connection, probably by invading your dreams first, which would've then given him access to your whole mind, and then your soul. Once this connection has been established, there is no breaking it. Only Cane himself can break it, which he isn't likely to do. So the only option you have at this point is to take away his means of getting to you. Without your soul energy, Cane will have no access to your mind."

"And then what?"

"Then you must draw him out and get him to confront you physically."

"And once he does…"

"Then you must stop him, though that might prove difficult. Cane, through his power, is immortal. He cannot be killed by conventional means."

"Then how do I stop him?"

Solomon sipped on his wine and then smiled. "This is where it gets exciting, Ethan. Having given Death your soul, He will grant you certain powers. Death's Touch—the ability to kill whoever you please. In effect, you will be an extension of Death Himself. It is the only way to kill a warlock like Cane."

"And what about my soul? Will I be giving it up for good?"

"Giving Death your soul is a show of commitment. As long as you provide Him with another soul, He will return yours to you."

"And if I don't…"

"Your soul will belong to Death, and you will become His Disciple."

"Like you, you mean?"

Solomon nodded. "It is a great honor."

"I'm sure it is," I said, shaking my head. "But I have no

desire to become one of Death's disciples, thank you very much."

"Well, that's a shame, Ethan, because you have such potential."

"Look, I just wanna get this Cane guy off my back for good. After that, I wanna get back to my normal life again."

"So be it, though you may change your mind when you feel Death's power flowing through you."

"Let's hope not. So when do we do this?"

"It will take me a day or two to prepare the ritual. A lot goes into it. On doesn't just call up Death and ask for a favor. There are protocols."

"So what do I do about Cane in the meantime? He's probably gonna be pissed that I've been talking to you about this."

"I have something that will help you avoid him temporarily until we can do the ritual."

"What is it?"

"In a moment," he said, placing his wineglass on the table before staring at me. "First, I haven't heard you ask about why Cane might be targeting you."

I frowned. "You sound like you know."

"I have some idea. I want to know if you do."

My frown deepened as I thought about it. "Well, you say Cane worked for Blackstar. Does he still work there?"

"Not officially."

"But unofficially…"

"He may still do on occasion."

I suddenly felt sick to my stomach. "Do you think someone at Blackstar sent Cane after me?"

Solomon said nothing as he continued staring at me.

"Fuck," I said. "What if this is Knightsbridge? What if Knightsbridge contracted Cane to kill my wife and daughter?"

"What if, indeed."

The idea didn't seem all that far-fetched, but I could think of no reason Knightsbridge would want me destroyed in such a brutal manner. Killing my wife and daughter? He certainly had the capacity to do it, but—

Long runs the fox, Ethan...

"Jesus Christ..."

"What?" Solomon asked, enjoying watching me put the pieces together.

"Something Knightsbridge said to me on the day I left the Company. He said, 'Long runs the fox, Ethan.' I hardly registered it at the time, but now..." I shook my head. "This can't all be about revenge, can it? All I did was leave the fucking Company..."

"You did more than that," Solomon said. "You twisted Wendell's arm, forced him into letting you go."

"But to kill my wife and daughter? That's..."

"Not beyond him at all."

"Fucking hell..." I leaned forward and put my head in my hands.

"As an investigator," Solomon said, "I'm sure you know this is all speculation at this point. What you need is proof. Perhaps you could start with Cane once you have him where you want him."

I sat back in my seat and lapsed into intense silence as I thought everything over, feeling like someone had hit me in the gut with a sledgehammer. If Knightsbridge really was behind the deaths of Angela and Callie, then I should've seen it long ago. Despite me thinking I was clever to get out from under Blackstar all those years ago, a part of me thought it was still too easy. A part of me always thought it wasn't over, and there would be reprisals. But I was out from under the thumb of the Company finally, and so I didn't want to think there would ever be further consequences to my departure. Any thoughts of reprisals were pushed to the back of my mind because I so desperately wanted to believe that I had beaten the great Magician.

But now I knew.

Now I knew I hadn't beaten him at all, and he had just been playing me this whole time.

Long runs the fox, Ethan.

Yeah, it ran alright. For over ten fucking years.

"Despite what your gut tells you," Solomon said eventually, "you still need proof. It would be unwise to go after someone as powerful as Knightsbridge without proof, and even then, it would be suicide."

I flashed him an angry look. "So I'm supposed to just forget about it? If this is Knightsbridge, he won't stop till I'm dead, anyway."

"Perhaps, but rushing off half-cocked won't help matters. You need to exercise caution."

Staring at Solomon, I asked him, "How long have you suspected this was all Knightsbridge?"

"A while."

"A fucking while? And you never thought to mention it until now?"

"It's not my place to interfere."

"So what are you doing now then?"

"This is different. You came to me."

I shifted forward in my seat, on edge now, as if I wasn't before. "No offense, Solomon, but how do I know you're not a part of this whole fucking thing? I mean, you're asking me to give up my soul now, for Christ's sake."

"Temporarily, to help you," he said. "And I thought you knew me better than that, Ethan. Have I not been straight with you all these years? Have I not given you my help every time you've asked for it? And yes, I may ask for minor things in return for that help, but I am not playing you, as you seem to think. No offense, Ethan, but playing you wouldn't present too much of a challenge for me."

I shook my head at him. "Fuck it, you're right. I'm just wracked with paranoia now."

"Understandably."

Letting out a lengthy sigh, I sat back and lit another cigarette as I stared forward at nothing for a while, trying to wrap my head around everything. In one sense, Solomon was right. I had no proof of anything at the moment. To stop myself getting too caught up in the emotion of it all, I had to think like an investigator, which meant following the evidence until I had proof, even if following the evidence meant I had to temporarily give up my soul to defeat Cane and find out why he was targeting me.

With my mind calm again, I turned to Solomon. "You said you had something for me?"

Solomon nodded and then called Stitch's name, who came ambling into the reception room a moment later, his posture hunched as if his spine was crooked.

"Yeth, Mathter?" Stitch said, coming to stand in front of Solomon.

"Get the amulet from the workroom," Solomon said. "Bring it here."

Stitch bowed his head slightly. "Of courthe, Mathter."

When Stitch ambled off again, I asked Solomon how Stitch knew which amulet he had to get.

"He assisted me in making it earlier," Solomon said. "I knew you would have need of it."

"Thanks, Solomon. As much as I don't show it sometimes, I appreciate your help."

"I'm not doing this out of the goodness of my barely beating heart, you know."

Here we go…

"Of course not. What do you want from me this time?"

Solomon smiled. "It's not so much what I want from *you*, Ethan. It's more what I want from your celestial partner."

"Hannah? What the hell do you want from her?"

"I need to borrow her power for a while."

"What for?"

"It doesn't matter."

"Like fuck it doesn't matter," I said. "You're asking me to pimp out my fucking partner, I wanna know what for."

Solomon sighed. "I need her to open a portal to Hell for me."

"What the fuck for?"

"That's my business. I just need her to open a gateway. Nothing more."

"That's it?"

He nodded. "I've asked worse of you."

"I'm not sure Hannah would agree."

"If you want the amulet, you had better make sure she does."

"God damn it Solomon. Is there nothing else you want? I have plenty of dark secrets I can tell you."

"Save them for another time. I need the Hellgate opened."

"When?"

"Soon. I'll let you know."

Stitch arrived back a moment later, handing Solomon the amulet, who then handed it to me. It appeared to be a bird skull, etched with blood-red symbols, with a length of leather threaded through it. "Just what I always wanted," I said, tying the leather and looping it over my head, so it hung around my neck.

"Don't forget our deal," Solomon said.

A knot of anxiety twisted in my stomach at the thought of asking Hannah to work with Solomon, who I knew she hated. "What about my clothes?"

"One moment, pleathe," Stitch said before shuffling out of the room again, returning a few moments later with my clothes, perfectly folded in his arms.

"Wow," I said, looking at the pristine clothes. "Great job there, Stitch."

"Thank you, thir."

I reached out and patted him on the head. "Everyone should have a Stitch."

Solomon tutted and shook his head as Stitch smiled bashfully. "You are too kind, thir."

18

Glad to be back in regular clothes again—even if it was just military fatigues and T-shirt with a trench over the top—I left Solomon's house at after 6 a.m. to find Haedemus still waiting outside.

"You're still here," I said, stopping beside him.

"Yes," he said. "Despite a ridiculously long wait."

"You deserve worse."

Haedemus sighed. "I was rather hoping we were past all this."

I snorted. "Yeah, right."

"Come on, Ethan. I said I was sorry, didn't I?"

"What you did was despicable and disgusting. I hope you know that." I shook my head. "Those poor people. Those poor *horses*."

Haedemus looked away. "You should never have let me—"

"Don't even fucking say it. I tried to stop you."

"Not hard enough. Didn't you see I was suffering? That I just needed something to numb the pain?"

"Fuck off, Haedemus. Go see a fucking shrink next time."

"A shrink," he said. "Yes, that might be——"

"I wasn't serious about that, you idiot."

"Still, it might be——"

"No, it wouldn't. I don't have time for this." I climbed up onto him and took hold of the reins. "Let's go. Back to the yard."

"You seem stressed, Ethan," Haedemus said as he trotted away before breaking into a gallop. "Maybe we should both see a shrink, hmm? I'd like a professional opinion on some of my behavior. I think I might have deep-seated trauma, possibly caused by——"

"Too much bullshit."

"Your sensitivity sucks, Ethan."

"So does your breath."

"I said sucks, not stinks."

"Whatever."

WHEN I RETURNED TO THE YARD, I WENT STRAIGHT TO Hannah's trailer and knocked on the door. She was already dressed as she opened the door, her hair tied back in a neat ponytail. "Hey," she said. "You just back or something?"

"Just back from saving his ass," Haedemus said, as if Hannah was talking to him. "He was deep in the shit before I pulled him out."

As Hannah frowned, I tutted and shook my head. "What's he talking about?" Hannah asked.

"Ethan had a run-in with some wraiths," Haedemus said. "I helped him escape."

"Wraiths?" Hannah said. "Is that true?"

I nodded. "Unfortunately. I'll fill you in over coffee."

"I just made some. Come in."

"So, we're all friends again?" Haedemus said as I stepped inside Hannah's trailer. "Great. I'm so blessed to have such forgiving friends. From now on, I promise to be on my best behavior. No more cocaine for me. I'm done with *that* stuff."

I said nothing as I carried on inside the trailer to the living room where I sat down. At the door, Hannah said to Haedemus, "That's a start, I guess. You still have a lot of making up to do, though."

"Sure," Haedemus said. "I'm just glad you two realize you can't do without me. It's splendiferous that we're all on the same page now."

"I don't think anyone said—"

"Chat later. Things to do, people to see. Bye now."

Hannah closed the door as I watched Haedemus trot off up the yard to do God knows what. "Crazy fucking Hellicorn," I muttered, taking out my cigarettes and lighting one before looking at Hannah. "That conversation we had about getting some company for him? Forget we ever had it. I couldn't cope with two Hellicorns."

"But you can cope with one?" Hannah asked, smiling.

"We'll see. I haven't decided anything yet."

Hannah went into the kitchen and poured two mugs of coffee before handing one to me. "What was he talking about out there? You were attacked by wraiths?"

"I was attacked by the Spreak," I said. "The bastard dragged me into a living nightmare in the European Borough."

Hannah came and sat beside me. "Living nightmare? What do you mean?"

"Some kind of illusion, but everything still felt real. The blood was real anyway, and—"

"What?"

"I saw Callie. It was...nice before it turned horrible."

"You saw what the Spreak wanted you to see. He's inside your mind, Ethan."

"Not anymore," I said, holding up the amulet.

"Solomon gave me this. It should keep the Spreak away until I can work a more permanent solution."

"What permanent solution?"

"Solomon is going summon Death—*the* Death—to give me the power to kill the Spreak."

Hannah stared at me for a second. "Really? That sounds—"

"Dangerous as fuck? I know. I mean, what can go wrong, right? It's only Death incarnate."

"But you'll be able to kill this guy, though?"

"Supposedly. Solomon said the Spreak's name is Heinrick Cane. Surprise-surprise, Solomon used to work with this asshole…at Blackstar."

"*Blackstar?*"

"Yep."

"So you think Blackstar has something to do with all this?"

I shrugged. "I'm not sure yet, but I intend to find out."

"What if your old boss is behind everything? What if he had your family killed, Ethan?"

"Then I'll kill *him*."

Hannah reached out and took my hand. "I'm sorry, Ethan. This must be hard for you, finding all this out."

"It hasn't been easy, I'll say that much." I paused as I sucked on my cigarette. "I know nothing without proof, though."

"Then you have to get some."

"I intend to."

"How?"

"I'll start with Pike. He might know something."

"He had the shit beat out of you last time you spoke with him."

"He did what he had to do. I forced his hand. He'll talk to me. Anyway," I said. "How'd you get on yesterday with the Mirrorist shrink?"

"I got a name," Hannah said. "Of the person in charge of the entire Mirrorist organization."

"What? The shrink gave you a name? Just like that?"

"Of course not," Hannah said, smiling now. "I had to force it out of him. Or rather, his secretary."

"You threatened the secretary?"

"Not exactly. I was hanging the not-so-good doctor out the third-story window when the secretary walked in."

"You hung the guy out of a window?" I shook my head. "You've been hanging with me too long, girl."

"You said to do what I had to."

"I know. So what happened?"

"Well, the secretary, she walks in after Dr. Jamal starts screaming because he thought I was going to drop him."

"Would you have?"

"Drop him?"

"Yeah."

"I was going to if he didn't cough up a name."

I raised my eyebrows. "You were really gonna drop the guy from a third-story window?"

"Yeah, but I was going to fly out and catch him before he hit the ground. Then I would fly him around for a bit, maybe drop him once or twice to get him to talk."

I laughed. "The fucking guy woulda died from a heart attack."

Hannah shrugged, smiling. "Maybe."

"Try explaining that one to Bradley."

"Well, luckily, it didn't go that far. The secretary was so freaked out, she told me the name as soon as I threatened to drop her boss."

"Then what?"

"Then I dragged the guy back inside, dumped him on his ass, and left."

"Awesome. You make me proud."

Hannah smiled and shook her head. "Stop it."

"You do, seriously."

"Anyway, turns out the head honcho of the Mirrorists is a woman called Evelyn Mathers. Not only does she run the therapist organization, but she also runs Danvers Asylum."

"That's fitting, I guess."

"Yeah, it gets weirder, though. I did a background check on Mathers, and according to her record, the woman is one hundred and five years old."

"What? That can't be right, can it?"

"According to her record, it is."

"At that age, the woman probably couldn't run the bath, never mind an asylum and an underground therapists organization."

"Unless she's a Supernormal, which wouldn't make much sense, since the organization is dedicated to wiping Supernormals out."

"Hellot, maybe?"

Hannah nodded. "That's what I was thinking. Or even a vampire. Who knows? We would need to meet her ourselves. I was planning on going to the asylum today."

"Have you filled Bradley in yet?"

"Not yet."

"Okay," I said, standing. "Let me get more appropriate clothes on, and then we'll go see Bradley before hitting Danvers."

Hannah grabbed my hand and pulled me back down again, her strength unnerving. "What's the hurry?" she said, climbing on top of me before kissing me on the lips. "I think you need relaxing. I think we both do."

To be honest, my mind was still whirling with thoughts of Callie and everything else that was going on. Sex wasn't high on my list of things to do. But I didn't want to offend Hannah by pushing her away, so I made myself forget about everything else for the time being.

"I think you're right," I said, standing up as she

continued to cling to me while I headed for the bedroom. She giggled like a schoolgirl when I tossed her down on the bed. "Let's work off some of that tension…"

"He wants me to do *what*?"

I had just told Hannah what Solomon wanted in return for helping me. The two of us were still in bed, naked now as we shared a cigarette between us.

"I know it's fucked up," I said. "But all dealings with Solomon are fucked up. You don't have to do it if you don't want to."

Hannah took the cigarette from me and took a drag, blowing a stream of smoke toward the yellowed ceiling. "I didn't say I wouldn't do it. I just didn't expect to have to, that's all. Do you know what it will mean if I do?"

"Yeah," I said. "It means you'll have to bring Xaglath back."

"Only demons can open portals to Hell. In my current in-between state, I wouldn't be able to." She shook her head a little. "I'd have to give that bitch control again."

"You're right," I said, sitting up. "It's too much to ask. Too dangerous, especially with Solomon being there. Fuck knows what he'd do—or get you to do—as Xaglath."

Hannah sat up as well. "No," she said. "It's fine. We don't have a choice. Without Solomon's help, you'll never get this guy Cane off your back and out of your mind. He'll end up killing you."

"I wish there was another way."

"There isn't." She put her warm hand on my lower back. "Don't sweat it. I'm stronger now. I'll be able to handle Xaglath. She knows who's in charge now."

"Maybe, but I doubt that'll stop her from making a play. She's a demon. It's what they do."

"After what happened at Yagami's, I think she's afraid of me now, anyway. She experienced my full celestial self and the power I hold. I could probably destroy her totally if I wanted to."

"Why don't you? What use is she?"

"Would you destroy *your* dark side if you could?"

I shrugged. "I guess I wouldn't get far without it."

"Exactly. Xaglath is my dark side personified. I still draw on her power when I need to. Like most people, my life is about trying to balance light and dark."

I put my hand on her cheek and then kissed her. "Just don't let the dark win."

Hannah smiled. "I won't."

ABOUT AN HOUR LATER, I WAS SITTING IN AN EMPTY PARKING lot behind a closed-down shopping center on the edge of downtown. I told Hannah to go see Bradley without me, and that I would meet up with her soon at Danvers Asylum.

In the meantime, I sent a text to Eric Pike's phone and asked him to meet me, unsure of whether he would or not. Our last meeting at the old school used by the cult didn't go well, resulting in me shooting the cult leader dead, pissing Pike off to the point where he asked his men to beat the shit out of me, which they did. But as I said to Hannah, I didn't hold any grudges. If I was in Pike's position, I would've done the same thing.

Besides, Pike and I had known each other for a long time, and despite everything, I still considered him a friend. We knew each other as well as anyone did, and the bond we forged through serving together would never be broken, no matter what happened between us. We may hate each other's guts at times, but that didn't mean we wouldn't come if the other called. Even though Pike still worked for the enemy—as I viewed Blackstar now—I would still help him out if he asked me to.

Luckily, Pike must've felt the same way, for he texted me back a few moments later with a time and location to meet. I had been sitting in the parking lot for five minutes before Pike showed up in a black SUV clearly borrowed from the Blackstar facility outside the city. Pulling up alongside me, he got out and got into the Chevelle, closing the door behind him. Dressed in black military fatigues, he looked like he had just come off the range.

"I have recruits to get back to," he said. "Make this quick, whatever it is."

"You're not still pissed about the cult leader, are you?" I asked him, handing him coffee in a Styrofoam cup. "I got you one of your faggot lattes to make up for it."

Pike shook his head as he nonetheless took the cup from me. "Knightsbridge gave me hell after that little stunt you pulled, I hope you know that."

"What did he do? Spank you?"

"Fuck you. He used his fucking freaky mind power on me. I thought he was gonna fucking kill me."

I shook my head. "Well, I keep saying it. You should've left a long time ago."

"Fuck you. You know it's not that easy. We can't all blackmail our way out."

"Did I, though? That's the question."

"What?"

I dug out my cigarettes, handing one to Pike before lighting his and my own up. "I'm beginning to think Wendell didn't let me go at all."

Pike stared at me with his large blue eyes. "What are you talking about? You've been out for over ten years now. Are you still taking that Mud shit?"

"Yeah, but that's got nothing to do with it."

"Why'd you ask me here, Ethan?" Pike said, before taking a draw of his cigarette. "What do you want?"

"I want you to be straight with me."

Pike frowned. "What about?"

I turned in my seat, so I could stare straight into his face. "Did Knightsbridge have my wife and daughter killed? Tell me the fucking truth."

After staring hard at me for a few seconds, Pike looked away and shook his head. "What the hell, Ethan?" he said like I was losing my mind or something. "Why would you ask me that?"

"Why the fuck you think?"

"You think *I* had something to do with killing your family?"

"Maybe not directly. But Blackstar did."

"Why would you even think that?"

"You're saying it's not true?"

"Fuck, what do you want from me, Ethan? I can say with a hundred percent certainty that I had nothing to do with your wife and little girl getting killed. It was a goddamn tragedy what happened. Fuck, I shed tears for you when I heard, man."

I looked deep into his eyes as he stared at me, knowing he was telling the truth. "I wasn't accusing you," I said, turning back around in my seat.

"I fucking hope not. Jesus…"

"I just learned some information recently that might implicate Blackstar in Angela and Callie's murder."

"What information?"

I paused before answering, hoping I could still trust him. "Heinrick Cane. You heard of him?"

"Heinrick Cane?" Pike nodded. "He used to be PSYOP. He left years ago. What about him?"

"*Did* he leave, though? Or does Wendell still have him on the payroll?"

Pike frowned. "You wanna tell me what the hell is going on?"

Deciding I could still trust him, I told Pike everything about Cane and what he was doing, and about what Solomon told me. I also described my last meeting with Knightsbridge and what he said to me.

Taking a last drag of his cigarette, Pike tossed the butt out the window before turning to me. "So let me get this straight. You think Wendell contracted Heinrick Cane to arrange the murders of your wife and daughter, and then to what? Drive you crazy? And all because of something he said to you when you last spoke?"

"Don't make things out to be far fetched, Pike. You know the lengths Knightsbridge goes to, and the kind of game he plays. It would be just like him to wait this long before getting his own back, waiting until I had the most to lose."

"Yeah, but to kill your wife and daughter, Ethan? And to do it fucking ten years later? Why wait *that* long?"

"Long runs the fox, he said. He allowed me to think I was getting away, when really, he was just allowing me to set myself up for the consequences of trying to outplay him. No one outplays Knightsbridge. I fucking knew that, but…I was desperate to leave, and my desperation created a blindspot that Knightsbridge took full advantage of."

"Sorry, bro," Pike said. "That still seems like a stretch to me."

"Then you don't know Knightsbridge as well as I thought you did."

Pike sighed and shook his head. "So what do you want me to do here, Ethan? Ask Wendell if he had your fucking family killed?"

"Of course not," I said. "He'd probably kill you for asking."

"What then?"

"We both know he keeps a record of everything he does. He has a hidden room in his office where he keeps his ledgers, which document all the off-book contracts."

"No—"

"If you can get access to the ledgers, you can check to see if Cane's name is in there—"

"No," Pike said, more emphatically this time. "Have you any idea what you're asking?"

"You're the only one with access to his office. Wait until he's not around, and then go in and check."

"So, hypothetically, if I did this, how would I access the hidden room? It has a fucking biometric lock."

"You're a smart guy, Pike. You'll figure it out."

"Fuck you. Don't try to flatter me into doing this bullshit. It's fucking suicide."

"Only if you get caught."

"Only if I get caught? This is fucking Knightsbridge we're talking about here. He's like Sauron, the all-seeing fucking eye. He misses nothing. Or has that fucking Mud fogged your brain that much that you've forgotten that?"

"We're talking about my wife and little girl," I said through gritted teeth. "They're both dead. Brutally fucking murdered. Or have *you* forgotten *that*?"

Pike shook his head. "Come on, Ethan," he said. "Don't fucking hit me with that. Course I haven't forgotten. But, what you're asking me to do, it's crazy. If Knightsbridge found out I was snooping through his ledgers, he'd turn my fucking brain to mush in seconds with just a thought."

"So that's it? You're not going to help me?"

"I'm sorry about your wife and daughter, man, I really am," Pike said. "But I can't help you with this. And if you want my advice—"

"I don't."

"Well, I'm gonna give it to you anyway. Drop this before it gets you killed. Move on, get on with your life."

"And what if I can't, huh?" I said angrily. "What if it's me that's gonna get hit next? What then?"

Pike shook his head sadly. "I feel for you, brother, I really do. But as I said, I can't help you."

I stared hard at him for a second before looking away. "Fine. Get the fuck out then."

With a sigh, Pike opened the door and got out of the car. When he was outside, he paused with his hand on the door. "Thanks for the coffee, Ethan," he said before shutting the door, leaving me to stew in anger and frustration as he got inside his SUV and drove away.

"Fuck!" I said, slamming the steering wheel before starting the car, the tires screeching as I drove off to meet Hannah at the Asylum.

19

Danvers Institute for the Criminally Insane is a three-story red brick building set on an isolated, wooded hill on the outskirts of the city, overlooking a peaceful suburb. As I ascended up the hill toward the asylum, the weather took a turn for the worse. Clouds huddled together like black sheep, and it got cold quick. Soon, the rain turned to slush, and then to snowflakes, softly piling on the hood of the Chevelle. Up above, between the ever-greens, I could see a menacing old manor, buried under the snow. As I approached the asylum, lightning crackled behind it, lighting it up like a fairytale ice castle.

As the snow came down heavier, the car suddenly hit a patch of black ice and started skidding off to the left. I tried to wrestle back control by turning out of the skid, but the car snaked out of control before finally crashing into a tall fir tree.

"Fuck!" I said, sitting with my hands on the steering wheel as the engine kept running. Luckily, I wasn't going that fast, so the damage seemed to be minimal. At most, I thought I had a broken headlight. Reversing as I cursed my luck, I turned the car and drove the rest of the way up the hill, parking at the front of the asylum next to Hannah's car. The car was empty, so I figured she was already inside, waiting for me.

Getting out, unable to believe how quickly the snow had started—and how heavy it was coming down—I walked to the front of the car to inspect the damage. As I suspected, the headlamp was broken, the surrounding metal a little dented. Nothing I couldn't fix myself at the yard. Removing a piece of still hanging glass, I cut my finger, and blood dripped down onto the snow, the crimson drops stark against all that white.

"Well, that's not a good fucking sign," I muttered as I stared at the blood and then sucked my finger. It was just a tiny nick and had already stopped bleeding, mostly.

The front entrance had a sally port—a double door airlock—and I was buzzed in from the guard room after a minute of standing in the snow. By the time I stepped through into the reception room, I was covered in large flakes of snow, which I brushed off while the receptionist scowled at me for messing up the floor.

The receptionist was a middle-aged, stern-looking woman with scraped back blonde hair and dark brown eyes that were altogether too pretty to be on the face of someone so serious and clearly uptight. "Can I help you?" she asked as if visitors to the place were strictly forbidden, and I had no right to be here, even though I had every right.

"Yeah," I said, showing her my ID. "I'm meeting my partner here. Where is she?"

The receptionist stared at me for a second. "She's in the administrative offices down the hall. I'll take you to her if you follow me."

"Thanks," I said as I brushed the last of the snow from my hair. "You wouldn't have a Band-Aid, would you?"

"Sorry, no," the receptionist said without looking at me. "This way, please."

"Seriously? You don't have Band-Aids? This is a hospital."

"It's an asylum for the criminally insane, not a hospital."

"Oh, okay. I guess you just let them bleed here, huh?"

The receptionist threw me a look over her shoulder but said nothing as she opened a heavy door in dire need of a paint job. The entire place, from what I'd seen of it anyway, seemed to be in various states of dilapidation, as if they had done nothing to the place in decades. The overall feel was of a forgotten prison, built to house now forgotten inmates, and the minimal staff were just here to keep the place barely ticking over. It was also freezing, colder than it was outside if that was possible, to the point where my breath plumed in front of me as I walked.

Brushing past the receptionist, I went through the doorway and into a large office filled with filing cabinets, with three other doors leading away to other parts of the building. Inside the office was Hannah, who was sitting behind an old desk with a sour look on her face.

"Hey," I said. "Sorry I'm late."

"Don't worry about it," Hannah said before glaring at the receptionist for a second. "People around here aren't being accommodating, anyway."

"As I explained to your partner," the receptionist said. "You are welcome to look around the building and speak with whatever patients are willing to speak to you, which won't be many, believe me. All files and such are off-limits. If you want to look at files, you'll have to come back with a warrant."

"And Dr. Mathers?" I said. "Where is she? We'd like to speak with her if possible."

"Dr. Mathers is a busy woman," the receptionist said. "I'll have to see if she's available."

"Busy doing what?" I asked. "This place seems pretty dead."

"Don't bother," Hannah said to me. "It's clear they don't want us here. We should head back and get a warrant."

"Let's take a look around first," I said, and then smiled at the receptionist. "I'm sure you won't mind. In the meantime, maybe you can locate Dr. Mathers and tell her the FBI wants to speak to her."

"What is this about?" the receptionist asked, her eyes full of suspicion.

"That's for us to discuss with Dr. Mathers," Hannah said. "Not her receptionist."

The receptionist glared at Hannah, who glared right back. "Very well. I'll see if I can find her for you."

"Thanks," Hannah said, her voice dripping with sarcasm.

When the receptionist left, I turned to Hannah. "What was that about?"

"She's a total bitch, that's what it's about," Hannah said, standing up. "Do you know she wasn't even going to let me inside the building when I got here? She demanded a warrant."

"So how'd you get her to let you in?"

"I told her I'd have her arrested for obstruction if I had to come back with a warrant."

"Which technically, you couldn't."

"I know, but she didn't know that."

"I don't think information will be easy to come by here," I said, looking around at the file cabinets. "If the receptionist is cagey, what's everyone else going to be like? I doubt we'll get to speak to Dr. Mathers at all today."

"Then we come back with a warrant and a search team. She'll soon make an appearance."

I nodded, smiling at her. "I love it when you get all FBI."

"Shut up," she said, smiling back as she shook her head at me. "How'd it go with your friend, Pike?"

"I'd rather not talk about it."

"That bad, huh?"

"He can't help me."

"Can't or won't?"

"Both, I guess."

Hannah rubbed my arm for a second. "I'm sorry. I'm sure we'll find another way."

"Yeah," I said. "You wanna take a look around this place since we're here? We might get something from the patients."

"What like? A fucking disease? Have you seen the state of this place? It's filthy."

"I noticed. Still, let's look around, anyway. Maybe we'll even get to speak to Mathers."

"I doubt it," Hannah said. "That shrink I hung out the window has probably told Mathers we're coming. She'll be hiding from us."

"Let her hide. We'll find her eventually."

Speaking of Mathers, I noticed a picture of her on the wall of the file room, along with pictures of half a dozen others, most seeming to be therapists here at the asylum, and no doubt Mirrorists as well. Mather's picture was in the middle, with her name printed on the inside border of the frame. The woman in the picture was physically beautiful in a classic sort of way, with a perfect bone structure and ice-blue eyes that didn't give off much warmth even though she was smiling.

"Check this out," I said to Hannah as she walked over. "Dr. Mathers looks pretty spritely for someone who's supposed to be over a hundred years old, don't you think?"

Hannah stared at the photograph and then nodded. "She also matches the description of the woman that Kavita mentioned."

"Well," I said. "Either Mathers' file is wrong, or—"

"That's someone else," Hannah finished.

The asylum was a U-shaped building with a smaller main building at the center and two wings stretching inward along the sides of the perimeter.

The main building held the reception, administrative offices, guard barracks, and the guard room. The security guards monitored the perimeter of the asylum, and only dealt with the patients in case one of them tried to escape, according to one guard we spoke to. The guard also explained that the asylum was surrounded by a tall brick wall topped with barbed wire with a single wrought-iron gate at the front and a small locked door in the back by the woods. There were security cameras on the perimeter wall. Behind it stretched a barren yard of brown, wilted grass, covered in frost and snow. Staring at it out the grimy window, it looked like no one had been out there in a long time.

The South Wing held most of the miserable patients who called this place home, many of whom were far from criminally-minded, suffering as they were from mental health conditions far worse than they had when they first arrived. Patients were kept in rooms that were probably once white, clean, and pretty, designed not to look like the prison cells they essentially were. The lock to each room's door was electrically controlled via the wing's nurses' room. Otherwise, movement within this particular ward was less restricted than elsewhere, but there were watchful nurses everywhere, almost all of whom refused to talk to us.

Someone who did talk to us was a patient—an old woman who sat in a chair staring at the TV on the wall, even though the TV wasn't on.

"You're never gonna find who you're looking for," the old woman croaked without looking at us as we came by her.

"And who do you think we are looking for?" I asked, stopping by her.

"The time traveler," the old woman said, still staring at the blank TV screen.

"The time traveler?" I said, looking at Hannah, who shook her head dismissively as if this were just the ravings of an old lunatic.

"Dr. Mathers," the woman said. "She can travel through time. That's why she appears so young, you see."

I frowned at the old crone, wondering why she would say that. "How old is Dr. Mathers?" I asked her.

"I been in this place most of my life," she said. "Dr. Mathers was young when I got here, and she's still young now. Hence, she's a time traveler. She travels here from the past, but under a different name, so no one knows it's her."

"And what name is that?"

"McQueen. Krystal McQueen."

I glanced at Hannah again, who was hardly listening, having dismissed the old woman as crazy. But there was something to her story that rang true for me. Sometimes it can seem like people are talking crazy, but really they are just explaining things crazily or in a way that makes sense to them.

"So Dr. Mathers still looks young?" I asked her.

The old woman nodded. "Still a looker. Still a cold-hearted bitch."

"That's enough now, Vera," a nurse said as she approached the old woman with a tray full of meds. "Time for your medication."

"The Ice Queen is gonna kill us all," Vera remarked nonchalantly. "That's why she keeps traveling here from the past. She wants to kill everybody."

The nurse laughed, a little nervously, I thought. "Stop with your fantasy now, Vera. A bit less TV for you, I think."

"The TV isn't on," I pointed out.

"Could you please excuse us?" the nurse said, her smile gone. "Vera needs her medication. She gets confused, otherwise."

Hannah and I walked away, leaving the nurse to feed Vera her pills.

"That was weird," Hannah said. "Crazy old woman."

"Yeah," I said. "Crazy."

Many of the nurses we tried to stop ignored us as if we weren't there, though in most cases, not out of arrogance. After a while, it became clear from the nurses' faces and furtive looks that they were too afraid to speak to us, as if someone had warned them not to.

The one nurse who spoke to us did so in hushed tones from a shadowy section of corridor blind to the security cameras. The nurse was young and looked like she hadn't long started working here, which she confirmed when she told us she couldn't get a job anywhere else.

"I hate it here," the nurse whispered. "The patients are treated like cattle, and the staff are terrorized into keeping quiet about everything that goes on in this place."

"Terrorized by who?" I asked her.

"By Dr. Mathers and her therapists. It's like a cult, the way they run things."

"So why don't you leave?" Hannah asked her.

"I have a sick kid at home. I need this job to pay for his medical bills. The only good thing about this job is the pay. Plus—" The young nurse stopped talking when another nurse up the corridor gave her a stern look.

"What?" Hannah said.

The nurse shook her head like she didn't want to talk anymore. "I shouldn't be speaking to you. I'll get punished if they find out."

"If who finds out?" I said.

"The therapists. You don't understand what goes on here. This place…it turns people dark and hateful…"

"You seem okay."

"I haven't long started, but I see what the other nurses are like. There's a strange power here—"

"Melina," said a loud, stern voice from up the corridor, and we all turned to see a burly nurse standing. "You're needed in the North Wing. Now."

Melina nodded, her face full of fear as if she had been caught doing something she shouldn't. "I have to go," she said and rushed away, stopping by the other nurse for a few seconds, the larger nurse grabbing Melina by the arm, saying something to her before letting her go. As Melina walked away up the corridor out of sight, the other nurse stared down at us for a moment before going inside one of the patient rooms.

"Melina is right about one thing," I said. "This is place is weird as fuck. Something sinister is definitely going on."

Hannah and I headed up the corridor toward the North Wing of the asylum, but didn't get very far because of the locked security door. A guard stood nearby, and I asked him what the North Wing was for.

"That's where the patients go for therapy," he said, hardly looking at me.

"What kind of therapy?"

The guard looked around before answering. "The experimental kind."

"What about the basement?" Hannah asked.

"That's solitary confinement, where we put the more problematic cases."

"Can you show us?"

The guard snorted as if the idea was ridiculous. "I gotta go," he said and walked off down the corridor.

"They're a helpful bunch, aren't they?" I said. "Come on. Let's head back to see if the receptionist has found Dr. Mathers."

"Ten bucks says she hasn't," Hannah said.

"Ten bucks says Mathers isn't even in the building."

When we reached the reception room, the receptionist smiled across her desk at us. "I'm sorry," she said, "but it appears Dr. Mathers is not in the building, I'm afraid."

Hannah and I looked at each other before I turned back to the receptionist, handing her my card. "We'll be back with a warrant to search your files," I said. "In the meantime, have Dr. Mathers call me, and then perhaps we won't have to come here with a warrant at all."

"Of course," the receptionist said, holding the card without looking at it, which I knew would end up in the trash as soon as we left. "What shall I tell Dr. Mathers when I see her?"

"Tell her we intend to shatter the mirror," I said. "I'm sure she'll know what that means."

20

As all the restaurants and food joints were closed in town, Hannah and I headed back to the yard to grab something to eat. When we reached the yard, the large metal gates were closed, and the locks had been changed. Security cameras had also been installed on either side of the gates.

"What the hell?" I said as I got out of the car and inspected the keypad and new lock on the gates, which appeared to be an electromagnetic locking system.

"When was this done?" Hannah asked. "More to the point, who did it? Did you pay for this?"

I shook my head. "No, I didn't, but I have an idea who did this."

A second later, a text came through on my phone from Daisy containing a six-digit number, which I punched into the keypad. When I did, the lock activated, and the gates opened.

"Daisy did this?" Hannah said, sounding surprised.

"Yup," I said. "She mentioned her plans for additional security to me the other day. I told her we couldn't afford it."

"So how was she able to install the new security lock? And the cameras?"

"That's what I'd like to know."

We got back in the car and drove through the gates into the yard, the gates closing behind us again after. When we reached my trailer, Daisy was standing there looking pleased with herself.

"Hey," she said, smiling, wearing ripped black jeans and a black Punisher T-shirt despite the cold temp and carpeting of snow on the ground. Looking at the T-shirt with its menacing skull made me nostalgic because I used to have one myself many years ago when I was a kid, only I made my own with white paint.

"Hey yourself," I said, noticing how much happier she looked compared to the last time I saw her. "You wanna explain the cameras and new lock on the front gates?"

"Sure," Daisy said. "I went ahead and installed the security system I designed. There are cameras all over now, as well as microwave barriers, electrostatic field disturbance sensors, and seismic sensors. No one can enter this yard now without us being alerted. I've sent a link to an app on your phone. Download the app and use the credentials I sent you. If anyone or anything triggers the sensors around the perimeter, you'll get an immediate alert on your phone."

Hannah and I looked at each other and then at Daisy. "Where did you get the money to do all this?" I asked.

"Don't worry," Daisy said. "It didn't cost anything."

"And how is that?" Hannah asked, probably thinking the same thing I was now.

"Well," Daisy said. "I found other means to get what we needed."

"Other means, Daisy?" I said.

"Yeah," she said, nodding, looking like she was hoping we wouldn't delve any further into the matter, which of course, wasn't going to happen.

231

"I think you'd better explain yourself, Missy," I said. "Like, right now."

Daisy sighed. "You're not gonna get mad, are you? I mean, I got it all done. That's all that matters, right?" she added hopefully.

"Not really," I said, shaking my head. "You still need to explain yourself."

"Yeah," Hannah added almost comically, like she was having a go at playing parent. "You'd better explain your-self...Missy."

"Okay, well," Daisy began, "I sort of took advantage of the city-wide lockdown by, um...breaking into a few places, and um, you know, getting what we needed."

"I didn't say we needed *any* of this stuff," I said.

"You didn't have to," Daisy said. "You know as well as I do that the damage done here could've been prevented if we'd been alerted to the intruder before they got a chance to plant any explosives."

It was difficult to disagree with her, but nonetheless, I was still annoyed. "So how did you manage to steal all this stuff? I'm assuming you had help?"

"Scrotey and the gang helped me."

"Of course they did."

"We took one of the old cars from the yard here and went out last night after dark and got what we needed."

"You took an old car? Who drove it?"

"I did."

"Since when can you drive?"

Daisy shrugged. "I've been teaching myself for a while now, just driving around the yard here while you guys are out. It's not that hard."

I looked at Hannah, who was now covering her smile with one hand. "You believe this?" I said.

"Yeah," Hannah said. "I sort of can."

"So," I said, looking at Daisy again, who still seemed pleased with herself. "You stole a car from the yard—"

"Borrowed," Daisy said.

"You stole a car from the yard," I went on, "and then you drove out into the city and burgled how many places?"

"Three altogether," Daisy said. "The seismic sensors were hard to come by."

"How'd you get past the security systems?"

"I called your friends, Artemis and Pan Demic. Those guys are crazy. You know what they said when I called and told them who I was? They said it's Baby Wick on the phone. I didn't know what they meant until they explained it to me. I watched the movies. They're pretty good."

I stared at her in disbelief. "Wait a minute. You called those two crazy-heads? How did you even know about them?"

"I heard you mention them a few times, like they're your go-to tech wizards or whatever."

"How'd you get their number?"

"Oh, that was easy. I downloaded an app from the Dark Web to hack your phone. You should really think about changing your passcode, Ethan. I mean, your birthday. Seriously?"

Hannah sniggered at this, and I turned to her. "I'm glad you're finding this funny."

"I'm not," Hannah said, trying her best to stop from grinning. "This is…unacceptable, Daisy."

"Yeah, you really sound like you believe that," I said.

"So anyway," Daisy said. "Artemis and Pan Demic, they told me the best stores to hit, and they also disabled all the security systems for me. So all we had to do was break in and take what we needed. It was easy, actually. And so much fun. It felt like I was in *Grand Theft Auto* or something, it was awesome."

"Sure was, boss." Scroteface had just appeared from

around the corner of the trailer. "Daisy knows how to have a good time, you know what I mean?"

"No, I don't, you little shit," I said to him. "What the hell are you playing at, going along with this?"

"Relax, boss," Scroteface said, his long ears twitching. "We protected Daisy good."

"I'm sure you did," I said. "Jesus."

"You're mad at me, aren't you?" Daisy said.

"Jesus, what do you think?" I said, needing a cigarette as I took the pack out of my trench pocket. "What if you'd been caught? You coulda got yourself arrested."

"But we didn't get caught," Daisy said, shrugging like it didn't matter.

"If the cops hadda came," Scroteface said, "we woulda took care of them."

"Yeah, by fucking killing them probably," I said.

Scroteface stared at me. "Of course. How else?"

"Get outta here before I kick you back to Hell," I told him.

"Sure, boss. See ya, Daisy."

"See ya, Scrotey," Daisy said.

"Oh, and me and the guys," Scroteface said, "we'll be around if you need us for anymore—" He tapped his bulbous nose with his finger. "—you know what."

I made as if to run at the Hellbastard, and he scampered away, leaving small footprints in the snow. "Little shit…"

"You should really be impressed," Hannah said to me. "That Daisy pulled all this off without getting caught." She looked at Daisy. "Did you install all of this on your own?"

"Yeah," she said, smiling proudly. "Artemis helped me with some stuff, explaining over the phone. He says he can't wait to meet me in person, and that I should come visit him at his penthouse. He says it's a cool place, and that I'll love it."

"Eh, no fucking way," I said. "You are not going anywhere near that place."

"Why not?" Daisy asked, not understanding.

"Because those guys are a bad influence."

"Why?" Daisy asked.

"They just are. Trust me on that. I don't want you going near them, or calling them again."

"But they're your friends," Daisy said. "What's the problem? Do they do bad things or something?"

"Bad things?" I said. "Yeah, they do."

"Pot kettle," Hannah coughed.

"What does that mean?" Daisy asked.

"Nothing," I said, giving Hannah a look.

"Well," Daisy said. "Unless you're gonna ground me or something, I think we're done here. I got some further adjustments to do to the new security system, so I'm just gonna like, go to my trailer now. Ethan, make sure you download the app, and you too, Hannah."

"Sure thing," Hannah said, still amused by everything.

Before I could say anything else, Daisy hurried off, disappearing among the scrap metal as she headed to her trailer. When she was gone, I turned to Hannah. "Seriously?"

"What?" Hannah asked, all innocence.

"You could've backed me up a little. We're supposed to be her guardians."

"And we are," Hannah said. "But you can't expect Daisy to be a normal kid, Ethan, not with who she is and who we are. There's no such thing as normal around here."

I sighed and shook my head as I finally lit my cigarette. "You got that right."

"Come on." She linked her arm with mine. "Let's go to my trailer, and I'll make us some dinner."

"You can cook?"

"A little."

"I guess we'll see."

"Shut up."

I smiled. "There's something I want to talk to you about, anyway."

"What is it?"

"It concerns the future of this yard. If I'm still alive after eating your food, I'll fill you in."

Hannah jammed her elbow into my ribs. "I ought to poison you for real for saying that."

"Then who would be around to tell you how beautiful you are?" I stopped and kissed her.

"So you do have charm. I was beginning to worry you hadn't."

"I got charm for days, baby."

Hannah laughed. "Hit me with it then."

"Sure, once I get a drink…"

* * *

Over a dinner of pasta and meatballs, I discussed with Hannah the job I agreed to do with Pan Demic's sister. I considered keeping it from her at first, but then thought that's not what partners do, so in the interests of transparency, I told her everything. At first, she shook her head at me for planning to do exactly what I had given off to Daisy for doing.

"You're a hypocrite," Hannah said. "That's what Daisy would say if she knew about this."

"Yeah, I know, but this is for the future of the business," I said. "I don't have a choice."

"I'm sure Daisy thought exactly the same thing."

"I'm sure she did, but that doesn't mean we're gonna turn into a family of criminals. This will be a one-off to get us out of trouble. That's it."

Hannah smiled as she sipped on red wine. "You think we're a family."

"Well, don't you? What else would you call it?"

"You're right. We are a family. Maybe a dysfunctional one, but still a family."

"Name me one family that isn't dysfunctional."

"I don't think there are any," she said. "So what about this job? What does it entail?"

"I'm not sure yet," I said. "I just know there's money at the end of it."

"Can you trust this woman?"

"She's Pan Demic's sister, and I trust Pan Demic."

"Even though he helped Daisy go on a crime spree?"

"Yeah, I'll be having a word with him about that. And Artemis."

Hannah smiled. "So, when's the job?"

"I have to meet Danika tonight. I'll find out then."

"You want me to come with?"

I shook my head. "She said to come alone."

"I'd like to help."

"We'll see after I speak with her and find out the plan. In the meantime, you should see about getting that warrant for the asylum."

"That place freaked me today," she said. "It reminded me too much of Hell, all those patients trapped in their own heads, their own nightmares."

I nodded. "I know the feeling. It's such a relief not to have that sadist Cane tormenting me."

"Let's hope he doesn't approach you before you get a chance to do that ritual with Solomon. He might kill you."

"Something tells me he won't. His goal was to drive me crazy, to break me. He can't break me if I'm dead."

"And you still think he's doing it for your former boss?"

I shrugged. "That's what my gut tells me. I'll find out, don't worry."

I helped her clear the dishes, drying as she washed. "Look at us," she said, smiling at me. "All domesticated and shit."

"Yeah," I said, the very idea of it appalling to me up until recently. But now, not so much. There were much worse positions to be in.

Once the dishes were done, we sat back down to finish our drinks.

"So what do you think about this Evelyn Mathers person?" she asked. "My gut tells me something weird is going on. I mean, besides the whole creepy Mirrorist thing. Did you see how afraid everyone looked in that place today, the nurses, especially? And that young nurse didn't paint a pretty picture either."

"Yeah," I said. "Something tells me Mathers isn't who she appears to be. I haven't even met the woman yet, but I already think something is up with her. The warrant won't help much. We'll be able to check their files, but so what? If Mathers knows we're on to her, she's probably removed any incriminating files by now. And even if we found files on the Mirrorist patients, it wouldn't matter. No one has broken the law. They're very careful not to. All they do is influence, which isn't a crime."

"But what about the asylum? There has to be bad shit going on in there. The guard we spoke to mentioned the experimental therapies. That doesn't sound good to me."

"Probably not, but it's Mathers herself we need to dig into." I poured more whiskey into my glass and lit a cigarette, giving one to Hannah. "She's the key to this entire case. If we can find out what secret she's hiding, we can take her down."

"You think she's hiding a secret?"

"Let's just say, I don't think she is who she says she is."

"You think she's a time traveler like the old woman said?" Hannah balked at the idea.

"Maybe not a time traveler. Something else, though. We would need to look into her history to find out. Tomorrow, we should go and see Artemis and Pan Demic, get them to dig up whatever dirt there is on Dr. Mathers."

"Cool," Hannah said. "I'll finally get to meet those two."

"Believe me," I said, "the pleasure will be all theirs."

Hannah laughed. "I guess we'll see."

I drained my glass. "You'll see alright."

21

I arrived at the disused Kennedy Subway Station at 7:45 p.m. and stood inside the dank tunnel, waiting on the platform for Danika to appear. As enormous rats scurried around nearby and bats screeched overhead, I wondered why Danika would want to meet in such an oddly inconvenient place.

Five minutes later, I was surprised to hear a train coming up the tracks. This was followed a moment later by a bright light that lit the tunnel until a single train car finally emerged and stopped at the platform.

Staring through the window, I saw Danika emerge from the engine room just as the door to the train opened. She had dyed her hair since I last saw her. Her long locks were now streaked with bright pink and purple, the left side shaved close, the rest swept to the right side of her head. Her pale face contained various piercings that weren't present when we first met. She also wore a leather outfit that included a jacket with pink and blue neon strips going down the sleeves and pants that clung tightly to her shapely lower half.

In short, she rocked the whole cyberpunk aesthetic,

though I'm sure if I'd mentioned it, she would've disagreed. Cyberpunk probably wasn't even a thing with kids these days, and William Gibson had probably been replaced by some underground tech guru like the Mole, who had been making waves and gathering a large following after publishing his tech philosophy book online a few years ago. Whatever street subculture aesthetic Danika was sporting, it made me feel old because I knew I would never "get it." I don't "get" a lot of things these days. It's like the older I get, the more detached from modern culture I become, preferring instead to live within my little bubble of outdated mores. When you get to a certain age, you stop giving a shit what's trending in the world and what isn't. The only trends I follow now are the ones that usually lead me into trouble, though I was hoping Danika wouldn't be one of them.

"Hop in," she said after scanning the platform for a second as if she expected to see someone else standing.

"Seriously?" I said, walking inside the train. "Where are we going?"

Danika smiled, the first time I'd seen her do so. It suited her face and made her seem less dark and serious. It also helped put me at ease. "To my secret hideout. Take a seat and enjoy the ride."

I have to say, I was impressed that she had her own subway train, and also apparently, an underground hideout. She wasn't the only one. The tunnel system spanned the entire city and beyond, and much of it was disused, at least by Unawares. Parts of the tunnel system went three to four levels deep, home to all sorts of MURKs, including colonies of goblins, orcs, at least one vampire clan, and a race of sub-humans originally created as slaves for the elite, but escaped underground when the elite tried to eliminate them all.

The Catacombs, as the central part of the abandoned subway tunnels was known, was used by all sorts of shady criminal types, including Mafia gangs, cults, and drug push-ers. There was also the Flea Market, located at a once grand station terminal far below the streets of the Warehouse District, comprising illegal arms merchants, assassins' guilds, counterfeiters, fences, dealers in stolen art, and other providers of illicit goods. The Underground was a hive of activity and commerce, and the Unawares above ground had no idea about any of it.

Clearly, Danika was a part of this vast underground network, a fact that became obvious once the train stopped about ten minutes later at another abandoned subway station. Unlike the Kennedy Subway Station, this one was painted black, on to which dozens of neon murals were painted.

"This your place?" I asked Danika as we exited the train.

"Sure is," Danika said, her voice husky, her confident walk full of youthful vigor. If I had to guess, I'd say she was in her late twenties, making her Pan Demic's slightly older sister.

"Nice artwork." Looking closer, I could see the level of detail in the murals, most of which appeared to be street scenes populated by figures not unlike Danika herself. "Who are all these people?"

"Some are real people, others I just made up."

"You're very talented."

"Thanks. I get it from my mom. She was an artist."

"I'm sorry she died. You must miss her."

"Not really. We didn't get along."

Cold. Okay.

Danika led me toward a section of wall where she removed a tile to reveal a retinal scanner that she looked into for a second before there was a beeping noise and then an electronic door came out of the wall and slid to the right, revealing a dark entrance. Danika waited for me to step through the entrance before hitting a button inside that closed the door and lit up the hallway we were standing in. I followed her down the hallway to another door that was also electronically locked. Danika punched some numbers into a keypad on the wall, and the door clicked open.

"You like your security," I said as I followed her through the door into a sizeable room.

"You can't be too careful down here in the Underground," she said, flicking a switch that threw on the ceiling strip lights, illuminating the entire room with white light. "There are many who want what I have."

"And what *do* you have?"

"Lots of things. Information—the most valuable commodity these days." She threw me an almost defiant smile. "Big Data ain't got nothing on me."

Compared to the outside, the room we were in was basic, with white cinderblock walls and a high ceiling, the floor scuffed concrete. The equipment in the room was far from basic, though, with electronics spread across one entire wall, including half a dozen large screens with terminals underneath, as well as a few other strangely constructed machines that appeared to be a mess of wiring, flashing lights, and neon cool tubes. When I asked Danika what the machines were, she gave me an enigmatic smile.

"My own builds," she said. "I won't even try to explain them to you. You don't look the tech type."

"I'm not."

"Let's just say they help me get what I need. Remember I said information is the most valuable commodity?"

"Yeah."

"It's not. Knowledge is. Those machines help me turn raw information into useable knowledge."

"Sounds useful," I said. "You must show me how they work sometime."

Danika said nothing as I crossed the room to a stack of

crates, which upon closer inspection, contained not only guns but also bottles of pills, hi-tech computer equipment, and a crate of absinthe of all things.

"Why don't you grab one of those bottles and we can talk," Danika said as she sat in front of a computer terminal and started tapping away on a back-lit keyboard. "There are glasses off to the side there. I'll just be a few minutes."

"It's been a while since I've had absinthe," I said, grabbing a bottle of the green liquid and two shot glasses, bringing them over to where Danika sat, pulling up a chair next to her. As I opened the bottle and poured two shots of the absinthe, I asked her what she was doing.

"Checking my bitcoin account," she said, taking the shot I offered and downing it in one before handing me the glass back. "I'm making sure that someone has paid up."

"And if they haven't?" I asked out of interest.

"Then they're in for a nasty surprise."

Watching Danika, she seemed to be more clear-headed than Pan Demic (which admittedly, wasn't hard), with a more professional approach to things than her younger brother. I also got the impression that if you messed with her, she wouldn't hesitate to fuck you up, not just electronically, but physically as well.

In the far corner of the room, I saw a BOB punching bag, and a few sets of Kali sticks hanging on the wall. Looking at the sticks, I wondered if she was any good with them. Going by her tight forearms now that she had her jacket off, and firm biceps, I could see she was in good shape. She had that quiet confidence I often looked for in a person that signified they could handle themselves physically.

So far, I was impressed by Danika and liked her more than her brother after spending only twenty minutes with her. Don't tell Pan Demic that, though. He has a sensitive disposition and would probably take it badly that I liked his sister more than him. At least Danika wasn't an inveterate coke head obsessed with conspiracy theories and sexual deviancy. Not that I knew of, anyway.

"Alright," Danika said after she had finished on the keyboard. "Now we can talk."

I handed her another shot. "This stuff is good."

"It should be. It was made in Prague by a private distiller and goes for a thousand dollars a bottle."

I whistled at the price. "Expensive shit. You have any sugar cubes?"

"I'm all out. Last time my brother was here, he gorged himself on them. He gobbled a pound of sugar cubes."

"Seriously?"

"You know how Aaron is. Anything for a hit. I used to be the same."

"It sounds weird hearing you call him by his real name. I've always known him as Pan Demic."

Danika rolled her eyes. "He loves the mystique. Same with Brian."

"Artemis, you mean?"

"Yeah. Tools that they are."

"They *are* tools, but I'm still fond of them. They're my go-to tech guys, and funny in their own way. They've always had my back. I can't take that away from them."

"Yeah, they told me. Those two worship the ground you walk on, you know that, right?"

I smiled and nodded. "Yeah. They just don't know any better."

Danika stared at me for a moment, her green eyes seeming to search for something. "You're not like any lawman I've ever met. Why is that?"

"Maybe because I spent a long time on the other side of the law, like you. I also used to work for Blackstar, but I'm sure you know that already. No doubt, you've done a full background check on me."

She nodded. "Of course. I like to know who I'm working with. Blackstar are scum. Why'd you work for them?"

I shrugged. "I didn't know any better, I guess."

"You know better now?"

"What do you think?"

"You're not still secretly working for them, are you?"

"Do you think I'd tell you if I was?"

"No, but I'd find out."

"Well, I'm not. Why you so afraid of Blackstar, anyway?"

"I've cracked their system a few times, leaked some stuff."

"That was ill-advised. I hope you like looking over your shoulder constantly."

"I'm used to that. I'm careful. I spend most of my time down here in the Underground. Blackstar doesn't venture down here much."

"It's the one place the Company could never get a foothold," I said, refilling my glass, and then hers. "It's too big and too wild."

"And that's why I hang out here. It's outlaw heaven down here."

Taking out my smokes, I offered her one, but she declined. Lighting up, I said, "I can't help noticing it's just us in here. Is anyone else coming?"

"No."

"So it'll just be us two on this job, whatever it is?"

"That depends."

"On what?"

"On whether you want to go it alone or not," she said. "My brother said you're some kind of super-soldier."

I snorted and shook my head. "I know my shit, but despite what your brother told you, I'm not fucking Rambo. I can die like everybody else."

"Well, the thing is, I don't *have* anybody else I can trust with this job. So if you want backup, you'll have to provide your own."

"You trust me enough to bring in other people?"

"I don't completely trust anyone," she said before downing another shot of absinthe. "But if you try to screw me over on this job, I'll ruin you and everyone you know. Trust *me* on *that*."

"Don't worry," I said. "I'm not going to screw you over."

"Good, because if you do, I'll make sure little Daisy ends up in the hands of a Satanic pedophile ring that will probably sacrifice her before you can even bless yourself."

I stared hard at her, and she stared right back. "Be very careful what you say to me," I half-growled, moving toward her, but as I did, she pulled a flick knife from somewhere and pressed the point of the blade into my throat.

"You're the one that needs to be careful," she said, her stare stone cold.

"Alright." I moved my head back slowly away from the knife. "I think we understand each other."

"Good." She lowered the knife, retracting the blade, but leaving the knife on her seat.

Well, that escalated quickly, I thought as I refilled our glasses. *It looks like I'll have to be careful around this one.*

"So," I said, handing her the absinthe. "Getting back on track. What's the job?"

"It's simple," she said, seeming to relax again.

"No job is ever simple, but go on."

"Well, this one is, relatively speaking. You'll be breaking into a factory in the Industrial Zone in order to steal something."

"What kind of factory? And what will I be stealing?"

"It's a factory run by the Furer vampire clan."

"The Furer Clan? A bunch of fucking savages. Why would you fuck with them?"

Danika sighed as if I was testing her patience. "I didn't bring you here to question my motives. I brought you here to discuss carrying out my carefully laid plans."

"I'm just saying, the Furers are raging psychopaths."

"Aren't all vampires? There won't be many of them there, anyway."

"Why not?"

"They're moving their operation to a different location outside of town. They've already ceased production."

"Production of what?"

"Soul Energy. And Adrenochrome."

I knew of both substances. Soul Energy is exactly how it sounds—pure soul energy that is sold in small amounts for an exorbitant price. It is favored mostly by the rich because it's the closest thing to an immortality drug you can get. It keeps a person looking youthful and extends life by decades as long as you keep taking it. Last I checked, a small vial of Soul Energy sold on the black market for half a million dollars. It was a lucrative trade.

Same with Adrenochrome. Adrenochrome, in case you don't know, is a substance extracted from the adrenal glands of humans. More specifically, from children. And not just any children, but from children who are scared and pumping out fear. The more scared the child, the more potent the Adrenochrome. Again, the vile substance is favored by the rich and global elite who take the stuff to get high. Like Soul Energy, Adrenochrome is also known to keep a person looking youthful.

"I'm not sure how I feel about stealing that shit," I said. "What are you planning on doing with it? Are you gonna sell it?"

"The Soul Energy will be sold on, yes."

"And the Adrenochrome?"

"I plan on destroying that."

"Why?"

"That doesn't matter right now."

"You know how all this stuff is obtained, don't you?"

"I'm well aware."

"And you're okay with profiting from it?"

Danika sighed as if she'd heard the same argument before. "You know as well as I do, this is the world we live in. I know your business is in deep trouble. You need the money. Just focus on that instead of the moral implications."

"Maybe I do need the money, but profiting from other people's misery and death?" I shook my head. "I dunno…"

"I know it's hard to stomach," Danika said. "But there's more to this job than just profit."

"Really?" I said skeptically. "Like what?"

"This is personal for me. I want to take the Adrenochrome off the market."

"Why?"

"I don't feel like talking about it now."

"You're not making this easy for me, Danika."

"Look," she said. "We both know you need the money, and this job is the quickest way to get it. What you earn will put you well into the black again."

I sat back in my seat and thought for a few moments as I sucked on a cancer stick. There was no doubt, this job would be dirty and morally reprehensible. But then, morals rarely stopped me from doing what I had to do. The bottom line was that I needed the money the job would net me, and I'd be helping to put a dent in a sickening underground industry.

"Alright," I said. "What's the plan? Talk me through it."

"Okay," Danika said. "The merchandise has already been loaded into the back of a security truck, along with several million dollars in cash."

"How do you know this? Do you have someone on the inside?"

Danika nodded. "The Furer has ghouls to do their dirty

work. The ghouls kidnap the children and adults, who they then process at the factory."

"Jesus…"

"They also have ordinary humans working for them, men and women working to prove themselves so they can become ghouls, and if they're lucky, vampires. I'm blackmailing one of these people."

"How?"

"It doesn't matter how. I just am."

"Okay. So I just go into the factory with all guns blazing and steal the truck, is that it?"

"More or less," Danika said. "You'll have support, though. First, my man on the inside has planted an EMP device, which I will activate before you go in, knocking out all the electronics, meaning all security systems and doors will be down, as well as all lights. Basically everything. Second, I'll be manning drones from here. If anyone tries to follow the truck, I can take them out. I can also clear you a path to the drop off point by manipulating the stop lights."

"Where's the drop off point?"

"Right above us," she said. "There's a tunnel leading right to the platform outside this room."

I nodded, impressed by her professionalism and planning. "It seems you've thought of everything."

"That's my job. I leave nothing to chance."

"So how many vampires and ghouls are going be inside the factory?"

"According to my inside man, most of the workers have moved to the new factory already, leaving around a dozen people to protect the truck and finish dismantling the rest of the machines."

"And how many vampires?"

"Two or three at most."

"You're sure about that? You can trust this guy on the inside?"

"The lives of his family and all of his finances depend on his cooperation, so yeah, I can trust him."

I shook my head. "You don't fuck around, do you?"

"Fucking around and leaving things to chance is how you get killed. Am I right?"

"You're right."

"The question now is, can you handle all the threats, or do you need backup going in?"

"As I said, I'm not fucking Rambo, so I'll need backup."

"Do you have anyone in mind?"

"My partner. She's the only one I trust."

"Isn't she a demon?"

"She used to be."

Danika frowned. "Used to be?"

"It's complicated. It doesn't matter, anyway. Point is, I can trust her, and so can you."

Danika nodded. "I have plenty of guns here, as you've already seen, and ammunition. You're familiar with Dragon's Breath rounds?"

I nodded. "I've used them in the past."

"You know how hard vamps are to kill. Setting them on fire is your best option, in my opinion, unless you want to do things differently."

"Fire is good. I'll also take one of the Smith and Wesson .500 Magnums you have over there. Something tells me I'll need the stopping power."

"I'll have the weapons ready for you."

Pouring two more shots of absinthe, I handed one to Danika and said, "So, when are you looking to do this?"

"Tomorrow night. The truck is due to move at midnight."

"What? That's not much time to prepare."

"Prepare for what? Everything has been planned. You just need to show up, steal the truck, and get the merchandise here. I'm sure you've worked on shorter timelines."

I had, though I still would've preferred a longer lead time. But beggars can't be choosers, can they?

"Okay." We clinked glasses and downed the absinthe. "I guess Operation Nightwing is a go then."

Danika raised her eyebrows. "Operation Nightwing? Seriously?"

"What? You don't name your ops?"

"No, I don't. I'm not some General who read too many comic books as a kid."

I laughed as I raised my glass. "To Operation Nightwing."

Danika tutted and rolled her eyes, but raised her glass. "To Operation Nightwing."

The next day, Hannah and I went into work and spent the morning helping on a cult case being run by a few of the other agents. We also caught up on some paperwork, which Bradley was a stickler for. When it came to reports, he expected all *I*'s dotted and *T*'s crossed.

Around midday, I told Bradley we were heading out to run down a lead, and that we probably wouldn't be back in until tomorrow. Bradley nodded, distracted as he sat at his desk.

"Everything okay, sir?" I asked him.

The Director sighed. "Not really, Ethan. I just got a call from Washington telling me that Special Affairs has now been put under review."

Frowning, I walked into his office and stood in front of his desk. "Why?"

Bradley took his glasses off and pinched the bridge of his nose between thumb and forefinger. He looked like he hadn't slept properly in days. "The powers that be in the White House are discussing whether SAD has run its course. They're talking about retiring SAD altogether, and me along with it, no doubt."

"They can't do that," I said. "Who else will do this job?"

"You *know* who, Ethan."

"Blackstar?"

He nodded. "I already told you this might be coming. Knightsbridge has pushed his take-over proposal into the Oval Office. According to the Chief of Staff, the President is seriously considering it."

"The President would allow a private company like Blackstar to replace Special Affairs? That's just fucking madness."

"Private companies run everything else, so what difference would it make? It's how things are now, Ethan. The corporations run everything."

"And there's nothing you can do?"

"I don't know. I'm already doing all I can, but I'm not sure it'll be enough." He looked up at me. "I'm sorry to say our days might be numbered here, which is a shame because you've only just got here."

Fucking Knightsbridge!

Anger stirred in me as it seemed like Knightsbridge was doing everything he could to ruin my fucking life. Not that I thought Blackstar's hostile takeover of SAD was anything to do with me, but it sure *felt* like it was.

"I'm sorry too, sir," I said. "I know how much this job means to you."

"And to you, Ethan."

"Yes, sir."

He shook his head and sighed. "Go on. Run down your lead. I'll keep working to save us. There's still some people I can call."

He didn't sound very hopeful, and I didn't blame him. This was Knightsbridge we were up against, a man who always got what he wanted. Both Bradley and I knew Blackstar's takeover was a foregone conclusion, and it was just a matter of time before Knightsbridge had full control of the infrastructure put in place by Bradley and the government to combat the supernatural—and Supernormal—threat. And speaking of Supernormals, Knightsbridge would also end up with full access to all the Supernormals being held in the holding facilities around the country. Fuck knows what he would do with all that untapped talent. It was too much power for one person to have, and I knew it wouldn't end well.

I left Bradley's office dejected and angry, wishing there was something I could do, not just for Bradley and Special Affairs, but also for myself. I was now more convinced than ever that Knightsbridge had something to do with the murder of my wife and daughter. Once I got the proof I needed, nothing would stop me from going after the Magician and his shady fucking organization.

I would bring it all down, even if meant bringing it down on top of me.

I was sullen on the drive to Artemis and Pan Demic's. Hannah asked me what was wrong, but I told her it was nothing, and that I was still a little shaken up by everything that had happened recently.

Which I was. Seeing Callie again, even if she was just some illusion, had deeply unsettled me. Every time I closed my eyes, I saw her face, and then I saw that demon do what it did. No father should ever have to witness his daughter die in such a way, illusion or not.

When we got to the penthouse, Artemis opened the door and predictably started fawning all over Hannah. He was quickly joined by Pan Demic—the two of them now out of their funeral suits and back into their normal black clothing and death metal T-shirts—and they bombarded an overwhelmed Hannah with questions about being a demon, asking her what Hell was like, how many souls she had tortured, what the fall from Heaven was like, and on and on.

"Did you get to meet the Big Man up there?" Artemis asked as Hannah looked at me for help.

"What kind of dude is He?" Pan Demic asked.

"Do you think He listens to death metal?"

"Is there porn in Heaven?"

"Is there porn in Hell?"

"Is it torture porn?"

"Is the Devil a Morbid Angel fan?"

"Do you want some coke?"

"Can you show us your wings?"

"What drugs do they do in Hell?"

"All right, guys," I all but shouted. "Enough, for fuck's sake. Give her a friggin' break, will ya? She didn't come here to listen to your stupid fucking questions."

They all stopped and stared at me, including Hannah. "What's eating you today, Drakester?" Artemis asked. "You on your period or something?"

I gritted my teeth and resisted the urge to grab him by the throat and throttle the life out of him. Not that he was doing anything wrong by being his usual self, but I was annoyed, and I wanted to take it out on someone.

"You have any weed?" I asked Pan Demic.

"Shit, yeah, course we do," he said. "Indica or sativa?"

"I just need to relax a little," I said as Hannah looked at me strangely.

"Indica it is then," Pan Demic said.

"Nothing too heavy. I still have shit to do."

"Oh yeah, that's right" Pan Demic said as he went to the coffee table in the living room and opened a drawer. "You're doing that job with Danika later."

"We both are," Hannah said.

"Cool," Pan Demic said, now handing me a joint and a plastic lighter. "Danika will keep you right. No worries."

"It's hard to believe she's your sister," I said before sparking up the joint.

"What do you mean?" he said.

"I mean she's a pro."

"Are you saying we're not pros?" Artemis said, looking offended as he turned in his seat. "Drakester, you hurt us so."

"I don't care," I said, coming to sit by him as I inhaled on the joint.

"My sister thinks she's better than everyone else," Pan Demic said, flicking his long hair over his shoulder with some annoyance, hinting at a possibly fraught relationship with his sister. "Like she never did drugs or anything."

"Or got pregnant at nineteen," Artemis added, but looked like he instantly regretted saying it when he saw the look on Pan Demic's face.

"Dude," Pan Demic said, serious for a change. "We don't mention that. Like ever."

"My bad," Artemis said, holding his hand up. "I'm sorry."

"Danika has a child?" I asked.

"She did have," Pan Demic said. "She doesn't anymore."

"What happened to it?" Hannah asked, coming to stand beside me.

"We don't talk about that," Pan Demic said. "You wanna know what happened, you'll have to ask her yourself."

An awkward silence descended in the room, and Artemis turned the death metal music up via his computer. As I sat puffing on the joint, I figured something bad must've happened to Danika's child, though I didn't dwell on it too much because I was trying to improve my mental state, and dwelling on dead children wasn't the way to do it.

"So what you got playing?" I asked Artemis to change

the subject. "Sounds like Obituary's *Cause of Death* album to me."

Artemis stared at me for a second in surprise and then shook his head and smiled. "Drakester, you old dog, you. I knew you knew your shit. All this time, you've been pretending to hate the death metal."

"I don't hate it," I said. "I just don't listen to it anymore. I did as a kid, though."

"Who was your favorite band?" Pan Demic asked, taking a seat at his computer, stretching his fingers out for me to give him the joint.

"I listened to lots of bands," I said. "My favorite death metal band was Death."

"Chuck Schuldiner was a fucking god, man," Artemis said. "Favorite album?"

"*Human*," I said. "No question."

"Goddamn it, Drakester," Artemis said, holding his hand for me to high-five him, which I did with a shake of my head. "My respect for you grows every time you come here."

I looked up at Hannah, who was standing with a wry smile on her face. "So, *Drakester*," she said to me. "Are you going to tell Artemis and Pan Demic why we're here? Don't forget, we have to prepare for later."

"What can we do for you today?" Artemis asked, flexing his fingers as he prepared to hit the keyboard.

"We need you to run a name," I said, feeling more relaxed now that the weed had done its job. "Evelyn Mathers."

"*Doctor* Evelyn Mathers," Hannah said, looking at Artemis as if she were about to witness something special.

"Evelyn Mathers," Artemis said, fixing his eyeglasses before typing the name into his computer. "Let's see now… Director of Danvers Institute for the Criminally Insane?"

"That's the one," I said as I stared at the screen to take

in her picture. "But the person in that picture is not Dr. Mathers."

"That's not the same person from the picture at the asylum," Hannah said.

Which it wasn't. The photo in Dr. Mathers' file was of a woman with dark hair and a dusky complexion, also in her late forties. According to the file, Mathers started the Institute in the early 1940s, having been born in 1915.

"There's no way a woman that age is running that asylum," I said. "I doubt she's even still alive."

"According to her file she is," Artemis said. "There's no death certificate."

"Okay," I said. "Try this name instead—Krystal McQueen."

"The time traveler?" Hannah said, rolling her eyes.

"Yeah," I said as I watched Artemis input the name and stare at the screen.

"There's nothing coming up," he said. "You're sure she exists?"

"I thought she might," I said, disappointed. "It was just a hunch."

"Seriously dude?" Pan Demic said to Artemis. "How much coke have you had today? Clearly not enough." He turned to his own computer and started typing furiously. "You forget about the Black Files."

"Black Files?" I said.

"The fucking Black Files," Artemis said, rolling his eyes exaggeratedly. "Jeez…"

They were both tapping like mad on their keyboards as if racing to get to the information first.

"Does someone wanna explain what the Black Files are?" I said.

"They're just hidden files," Artemis said as he stared at the screen. "Every system has them."

"They're files no one but a select few can access," Pan

Demic said. "Buried deep in the system, usually behind layers of encryption."

"And that's if the files have even been digitized," Artemis said. "Many organizations only keep hard copies of their most important files in case, you know——"

"Assholes like us try to hack them," Pan Demic said.

"But the thing is," Artemis went on. "Even if a file is hard copy only——"

"We can still get to it," Pan Demic said.

"What? How?" I asked.

"Fucking magic, Drakester," Artemis said with a grin as blue energy went from his fingertips into the keyboard.

"We can make the code go anywhere," Pan Demic said, his keyboard lit with blue energy as well, his screen a mass of streaming code that I couldn't even comprehend, never mind understand.

"You bring the code to life?" Hannah asked, fascinated by everything that was happening.

"Angel," Artemis said. "Code is life, you feel me? When the Big Man upstairs created the universe, what do you think he was doing? Coding, that's what. Everything is code."

I looked up at Hannah and smiled. "Told you," I said. "The pleasure is all theirs."

"Anyone can hack a system," Pan Demic said. "But it takes actual *skill* to hack a *room*."

"Or a safe," Artemis said. "I found it."

"Bastard!" Pan Demic said.

"Too slow, bro," Artemis said as he continued tapping furiously. "Now all I need to do is copy the files and...done!"

"Goddamnit," Pan Demic said. "I was almost there."

Artemis smiled across at him smugly. "You just got Ctrl-Alt-Ass-Whipped, baby."

Up on Artemis' screen now were what looked like photographic representations of old documents, which he was scrolling through. A moment later, he stopped scrolling at a particular file. "And there she is. Krystal fucking McQueen. Booya!"

"Holy shit," I breathed as I stared at the screen. "So it is."

"It's the same woman," Hannah said as we looked at the picture. "It's Dr. Mathers."

"So the old lady at the asylum wasn't talking crazy," I said.

"I draw the line at Mathers being a time traveler," Hannah said, staring at the information on-screen.

"Something's still up." I leaned forward to read over Krystal McQueen's file. "According to this, McQueen is the same age as Mathers, and she's also a patient at the asylum. She was admitted in the fifties by Mathers herself."

"Look at the list of treatments this woman had," Pan Demic said. "Experimental psychoactive drugs—lucky bitch—shock therapy, and even a goddamn lobotomy. How is this woman still alive?"

"According to her notes," Artemis said, "Krystal McQueen was once a renowned physiatrist herself, with most of her patients rich and famous. It gives a list of patients here, but I don't recognize any of them. Old movie stars, maybe? Anyway, she had a nervous breakdown after becoming obsessed with, it says here, a Black Mirror, whatever that is. Any ideas?"

Both Hannah and I shook our heads. "None," I said.

"Her record only extends to the late sixties," Artemis said. "After that, it's like she died or something."

"But I can't see any death certificate here," Pan Demic said.

"That's coz she's not dead," I said.

"So she's like, over a hundred years old now?" Artemis said.

"Yeah, but I don't think she looks it," I said.

"Why not?" Pan Demic asked.

I looked at Hannah. "That's what we have to find out."

Before we left, the boys wished us good luck for the job we were going to do later on, and also told Hannah, predictably, that she was welcome to come back anytime, "even without Drakester."

"Oh, and Hannah," Pan Demic said. "If you deposit six hundred and sixty-six dollars at an automatic teller at one minute past midnight, the Devil can hear you talk to the machine. He'll make it print the answer to a question on your receipt."

Hannah stared at Pan Demic with a quizzical look on her face. "That's...good to know, I guess."

"Oh, and you two," I said, turning at the door. "Stay the fuck away from Daisy. She told me what you guys did." I pointed to my face. "This is my not fucking amused face."

"That's just your normal face, Drakester," Artemis said. "And Baby Wick called *us*, we didn't call her. She's definitely cool, though. Chip off the old block, I'd say, Drakester."

"She's not really his daughter, doofus," Pan Demic said.

"I know," Artemis said. "She still reminds me of him. Hence the name, Baby Wick."

"If she calls again," I said. "Don't answer. You got it?"

"But what if she needs our help again?" Artemis said.

"She won't."

"But what if—"

"Dude," Pan Demic said.

"Oh, right, okay. We won't answer then."

I gave them both a look and then nodded. "Good. Thanks for the info. Catch ya later."

We got back to the yard late afternoon. Daisy was busy making her latest creation in the smithy, while Haedemus hung around her, talking her to death. The Hellbastards were inside their trailer, watching TV as usual, all friends again after the stunt Cracka had pulled the other day.

When I went to see the Hellbastards, I told them to stay sharp in case I needed them later. They asked why, but I didn't tell them. If I had've, they would've badgered me into taking them along on the job. I only wanted the Hellbastards there if I really needed them. Their brand of chaos was not what I wanted to deal with on this job. I wanted it done as cleanly as possible, a concept the Hellbastards had no inkling of.

At 6.00 p.m. Hannah and I left the yard and drove to the Kennedy Subway Station, parking the Chevelle outside. As we were about to get out of the car, I felt a strange breeze blow through the interior, and then a presence in the back seat, causing a knot of anxiety to manifest in my stomach. For a terrible moment, I thought Cane had somehow found a way to get past the power of the amulet I still wore around my neck, and was now sitting in the back of the car.

Only, when I looked in the rearview mirror, I saw the ice-blue eyes of Solomon staring back at me. Looking across at Hannah, she appeared not to have noticed Solomon yet, making me think this was Cane after all, having taken the form of Solomon to torment me with.

But after a second, Hannah turned around and shook her head at the uninvited passenger, and I breathed a small sigh of relief, for she could see him as well.

"Solomon?" Hannah said.

"Hello, my lovely," he said in a voice barely above a whisper.

"What are you doing here?" I said, turning around in my seat.

"I need your partner," he said.

"Now?"

"Yes."

"Can't it wait?" I asked him. "We're about to do something here."

"I'm afraid not," Solomon said. "I need her now."

"I *am* sitting here, you know," Hannah said, sounding annoyed.

Solomon looked at her. "Did Ethan explain what I need you to do?"

"Yeah," she said. "You want me to open a portal to Hell."

"And keep it open until I have done what I need to do."

"Which is?" Hannah asked. "I hope you're not planning on bringing anyone or anything back through."

"Merely an item," Solomon said.

"What item?"

Solomon barely smiled, his face mostly hidden in shadow. "You need not concern yourself with that, my dear."

"Of course not," Hannah said, shaking her head.

"How long will this take?" I asked him.

"As long as it takes," he said. "You should have her back by tomorrow."

Hannah sighed. "I wish you would all stop talking about me like I'm some fucking object for hire."

"Tomorrow?" I said. "Shit. Can't this *wait* until tomorrow?"

"No," Solomon said. "It must be tonight."

"Of course," I said, pissed off now.

"I'm sorry, Ethan," Hannah said. "Can you do the job without me?"

"I'll still need backup."

"Is there anyone else you can ask?"

"Maybe," I said. "I'll see. Just go with him. I'll be fine." I looked at Solomon. "If anything happens to her—"

"Yes, yes," Solomon said like he expected me to say that. "You'll kill me or some such nonsense."

"It's not nonsense. I will."

Hannah leaned across and kissed me. "Be careful, okay?" she said.

"I will, don't worry. You be careful too, you hear me?"

"This is so touching," Solomon said.

I threw him a look. "What about the ritual?"

"Ritual?"

"The one that's gonna save me from Cane?"

"Ah, yes, that ritual. Preparations have already begun. We should be good to go tomorrow night."

"Glad to hear it."

"Come, my lovely," Solomon said to Hannah, stretching his hand out for her to take, which she did, reluctantly. "Enter the shadows with me, and we shall move unseen to my sanctum."

"That sounds vaguely salacious," I said. "Say hello to Stitch for me."

"Who?" Hannah asked, but before I could answer, Solomon transformed them both into pure shadow, and they slipped silently out of the car into the gray light to join the other shadows out there.

INSIDE THE SUBWAY STATION, I STOOD WAITING ON DANIKA to arrive, which she did after ten minutes.

"Where's your partner?" she asked, looking concerned as she stood inside the train.

"Unfortunately, she's not available anymore," I said.

"Why not?"

"It doesn't matter. She won't be joining us."

Danika sighed and shook her head, looking agitated now, no doubt because I had upset her carefully laid plans. "I don't think you can do this alone."

"Neither do I."

"So, what then?"

"I know two people who might be willing to help."

"Might be?"

"They will."

"Are they trustworthy?"

I nodded. "Yeah, they are."

"Okay, get in touch with them. We don't much time to waste."

HAVING MADE THE CALL, I NOW STOOD INSIDE DANIKA'S underground hideout, gearing up and going over the plan. Before leaving the yard earlier, I changed into black military fatigues and boots. Danika gave me body armor to wear, and a holster for the huge Smith and Wesson .500 Magnum, which I strapped to my right thigh. She also gave me a shotgun loaded with Dragon's Breath rounds and a sub-machine gun that I strapped around me. The plan was to use the shotgun first, setting fire to as many threats as possible to create some shock and awe. After that, I would go to town using the sub and the Magnum as I cleared a path toward the armored truck, which Danika assured me would be open, with the keys in the ignition. Her inside man would make sure of that. If he didn't, I'd have to get the keys myself somehow.

Danika also gave me a communication device that I fitted inside my ear. "I'll be in your ear the whole time," she said.

"Can't wait," I said, smiling at her.

"Could you be any more of a dirty old man?"

"Hey, less of the old."

She smiled and shook her head. "Testing, one-two. Can you hear me okay?"

"Loud and clear."

"Once you're inside, I can direct you to the truck. It's parked in the loading bay at the back of the factory."

"Wouldn't it make more sense to go in the back instead of the front?"

"This isn't just about the truck." She paused. "There are people in there as well."

"People? What people? You said nothing about any people."

"I'm saying it now."

"What the fuck, Danika?" I said exasperatedly. "I thought this was a simple robbery, not a goddamn rescue mission. What people are we talking about? And how many?"

"Maybe a dozen," she said as she stood nearby. "Most are adults, but there a few children."

Fuck's sake.

"Children? Are you serious?"

"They're victims, brought in to collect their Soul Energy and Adrenochrome. They'll probably be in terrible shape."

"And how the hell am I supposed to get them out?"

"Load them into the back of the truck and take them with you."

"Jesus," I said. "Why the hell didn't you mention this before now?"

"I'm sorry. I didn't think you'd take the job if you knew."

I shook my head at her. "You don't know me very well."

"So, you'll still do it?"

Looking at her, it seemed like rescuing the people meant more to her than the loot. "This complicates things, but yeah, I'll still do it." I stared at her for a second. "Do you know any of these people?"

She shook her head. "No. They're just victims."

"Uh-huh. This seems personal to you."

"It is."

"Why?"

Danika sighed and walked over to a computer terminal and sat down. "You'd better get going. Go through that door and take the tunnel to the exit. There's a car waiting outside for you."

"A car?"

"You want to use your own?"

"No."

"Well, then. Get going."

Still annoyed at the changes made to the plan, I gathered my weapons and left.

THE CAR OUTSIDE WAS AN OLD FORD THAT I GOT INTO AND drove off in, making it to the Industrial Zone about a half-hour later.

The district's area is divided between hundreds of businesses and facilities. In the light industry zone, you can find small workshops and garages. In the commercial zone, massive hardware outlets sell construction supplies. Derelict factories with saw-tooth roofs and filthy skylights house outdated production lines that operate with a skeleton crew, waiting for the inevitable modernization. Rows of storage units and warehouses seem to go on forever. Behind them, vast corporate production complexes and government-funded refineries stretch over miles, some covering an area greater than all the smaller zones put together and housing only god-knows-what.

The nights here reveal a well-known fact: the Industrial Zone is the city's no-man's-land. The underground scene here is thriving, with anything from delirious raves to violent pit fights. Strange gangs and secretive brotherhoods set up their makeshift headquarters around burn barrels in abandoned hangars. Above all that mayhem, the wind blows silently amid silos and cooling towers studded with bright red aircraft warning lights. From way up there, one could easily see that it's not the noisy parts of the Industrial Zone the police should be worrying about—it's the quiet ones.

It's in one of these quiet parts that the factory I was due to hit was located off to the North East of the district. I had visited the zone enough times as a cop, so I had a good idea where I was going as I made my way through the maze of buildings. To ensure I took no wrong turns, Danika gave me directions through the ear-piece until I finally arrived at the target factory.

The factory itself looked ancient and run down, but the security fence surrounding it looked new. I parked the Ford a couple hundred yards back from the front entrance gates and cut the engine.

"Let me know when you're ready to move so I can activate the EMP device," Danika said in my ear.

"I'm just waiting on the help to come," I said as I stared through the window at the factory, even though I couldn't see much in the dark. It was also sleeting outside, the icy rain covering the windshield.

"I hope they can find you in that maze. Who are they, anyway?"

"Well," I said, smiling. "One's a mouthy shark, and the other is a deadly spider."

"What?"

I laughed to myself. "Don't worry about them. They're exactly who we need."

"They better be."

In the side pocket of my combat fatigues, my phone went off, making a continuous beeping sound that I'd never heard it do before. Frowning, I took the phone out to see a message flashing on the screen saying: SECURITY ALERT.

"What the hell?" I said.

"What is it?" Danika asked.

"Nothing. Just my phone."

I tapped the alert, and the app that Daisy told me to download opened up. Another message said: SECURITY ALERT CAMERA 3.

I tapped the alert, and a window opened, showing the feed from one of the security cameras from the yard. Slightly worried that something might be happening at the yard, I squinted at the grainy black-and-white image only to see the Hellbastards all lined up in front of the camera, in a part of the yard where the crusher used to be before it was blown up. The little bastards were all standing in a line, and in perfect synchronicity, they were thrusting their hips back and forth, their oversized penises flapping up and down like meaty sausages. They each had big shit-eating grins on their faces as they did their little dance to taunt me.

"Assholes," I said.

"Who is?" Danika asked.

"My pets."

"Your pets?"

"Don't worry about it."

I contacted Scroteface straight away.

What the fuck are you idiots playing at?

What do you mean, boss?

I can see you on the damn camera…thrusting at me. Stop it. Now.

Okay, boss. We just thought it would be funny.

You thought wrong.

It's a little funny.

No, it's not.

Okay, we stop.

You're still doing it.

We stop now.

And…you still haven't stopped.

Okay, we stop now.

They finally stopped, and then Cracka started waving like a maniac.

Has Cracka been eating sugar again?

Daisy bought us sherbet. Lots of sherbet.

I could kick Daisy's ass. Go do something useful. Patrol the yard.

Yes, boss.

You're still hanging around. Cracka is mooning me now. Tell him to stop mooning me.

I did, boss. He won't stop. He says it's too funny.

I'm going now. Don't set the damn security system off again. And stay sharp in case I need you.

You got it, boss.

With Cracka still mooning the camera, I closed the app and slipped the phone back into my pocket, mumbling, "Friggin' demons."

"Did you just say demons?" Danika asked.

"Yeah, I have five of them. Little guys with big attitudes, and a massive pain in my ass."

"I can't believe you have pet demons."

"They come in useful from time to time," I said, finding my cigarettes and lighting one up, cracking the window an inch to let the smoke out. "So, while I'm sitting here waiting, why don't you tell me why this job is so personal to you. And don't tell me it isn't. I'm about to risk my life, so I think I'm entitled to an explanation."

Nothing but silence came through the ear-piece for a minute or two, and I shook my head as I thought Danika was ignoring me until she finally spoke.

"When I was nineteen, I stupidly got pregnant," she said, her husky voice low and slightly distant sounding. "I was an addict, pumping my veins with whatever I could get my hands on. The guy I was with, he left once he found out I was pregnant. Actually, he left when I said I wasn't going to get an abortion."

"Why didn't you?"

"I don't know. I thought having a child would help me turn my life around, help me get clean."

"And did it?"

"For a while, it did. I got clean and had the baby—a little girl. I called her Shona."

"Nice name."

"Yeah, she was—" She stopped, and I could almost picture her back in her hideout, struggling to contain her emotions.

"If this is too hard—"

"It is, but you asked, so I'll finish."

"Okay."

"Things were good for a while. I loved being a mom, but that feeling soon wore off, and I struggled with it all."

"It isn't easy," I said.

"It wasn't for me. I ended up back on the drugs again. I would leave Shona with strangers while I—" She paused. "Anyway, I lost all sense of responsibility. My family tried to step in a few times, but I shut them out until finally, my mother reported me to social services, and I had my baby taken off me."

"I'm sorry."

"Yeah, I wasn't. I cried, sure, but deep down, I was happy I didn't have to deal with it anymore. I was a horrible person…"

I said nothing and waited for her to go on.

"Anyway, a few years went by, and I got clean again, for good this time. I got my shit together and decided I wanted to track down Shona. If she was in the system, she wouldn't be hard to find, not for me. I found her pretty quickly. This rich couple had fostered her, and after some digging, I discovered they had fostered lots of other kids. It turns out this rich couple were part of this nationwide pedophile ring that stretched to the very top of this country's power structure. You wouldn't believe who is involved in this."

"Actually, I would," I said. "I've done my own investigating into this over the years, but I never got far before I was blocked. I know people who were taken by this ring. I lost my best friend to them when I was thirteen."

"Then you know how evil they are."

"Yeah, I do."

"I confronted this couple and asked them about Shona, and they told me they never heard of her, and that they had never fostered any kids, which was bullshit because the files said different."

"So, what did you do?"

"I hacked their home computers, and what I found was… sickening. These people had videos of kids being tortured and killed by people in the upper echelons of society—movie stars, pop stars, politicians, CEOs."

I shook my head in disgust. "People do not understand how far-reaching the evil is. If they did, they'd never sleep again."

"Yeah, well, the same evil psychopaths I'm talking about are the ones brainwashing everybody into thinking they're they good guys," Danika said.

"It's disgusting. So what about Shona?"

"I found her on a video." Her voice was only a whisper now, so deep in my ear, I could feel all of her pain as she spoke. "She was five years old by then, lying drugged on a bed as a well-known politician and her lawyer—another woman—tortured her. The politician used a knife to cut my little girl's face off, and her lawyer harvested the Adrenochrome, and...all the while, Shona...she screamed." I could hear her crying, which brought tears to my eyes. "They did horrible things to her even after that. This same politician, she wore Shona's face like a mask, and paraded in front of the camera with it on." She paused. "They're both dead now. I made sure of it."

I took a deep breath and let it out slowly. "I'm so sorry, Danika."

"So am I," she said. "My baby girl is dead because I was too fucked up, selfish, and stupid to look after her."

"You couldn't have known what would happen," I said, thinking of Callie now, despite myself.

"It was my responsibility to look after her, and I didn't. So now, all I can do is try to save other children from the same fate. I intend to shut down every Adrenochrome operation, and I intend to bring down the Cabal that runs everything, no matter how long it takes."

"You're really going after these people?"

"I've made it my life's work."

"What about the videos? Couldn't you release them into the public domain?"

"I released a few, along with other evidence, but it was all taken down straight away. One video with a well-known pop star remained on the Dark Web, but guess what? No one believed it was real."

"That doesn't surprise me. The herd is well and truly brainwashed at this point and they don't even know it."

"I have a target on my back now," she said. "I have to be careful, though I won't stop hunting these fuckers."

"Then maybe it was fate that we met."

"What do you mean?"

"I mean, I've wanted to go after these bastards for years now. Maybe we could join forces."

"These people are dangerous. You could lose everything by going after them. And this thing is so big, I'm not even sure it can be stopped."

"Well," I said, tossing the butt of my cigarette out the window. "I'm willing to try if you are."

"When this job is done, we'll talk."

"Count on it. And Danika?"

"Yeah?"

"Thanks for telling me all that. It couldn't have been easy."

"It wasn't."

I was about to say something else when something landed on the roof of the car with a heavy thud, making me jump. For a second, I thought I had been made by the Furer vampires when whatever was on the roof scuttled down onto the hood of the car and turned around to peer at me with bright red eyes, looking every inch the giant black spider that it was.

But before I could even react, something else hit the side window so hard I was surprised it didn't break. Turning my head, I was faced with a massive shark's mouth filled with row upon row of jagged teeth.

"Jesus Christ," I said, breathing out finally as I wound down the window and addressed the shark girl floating outside in the rain. "Get yourselves in the car before someone sees you."

"I take it your backup has arrived?" Danika said.

"Yeah," I said. "They're here."

Charlotte Hood scuttled down off the car and stood in the rain as she transformed herself from a monstrous spider into her normal human form, a transformation that took only a few seconds. Similarly, Delphina turned herself from a human/shark hybrid into human form in less time than it took Charlotte to transform herself. A moment later, they were sitting in the back of the car as the rain ran down their naked bodies.

"I bet you never thought there'd be two naked girls sitting in the back of your car tonight, huh, Ethan?" Delphina said as Charlotte giggled beside her. "So whatta you say, big boy? You wanna play or what?"

"What?" I said, staring at them in the rearview mirror.

Delphina burst out laughing, as did Charlotte. "Your face. Man, you're so easy."

"Shut up," I said. "I knew you were kidding. Haven't you found a way to keep your clothes on yet?"

"Ahhhh," Delphina cooed. "Are we embarrassing you, Ethan?"

"No, I'm just saying. It's cold out."

"We're used to it," Charlotte said, sounding more confident and happier within herself since I last spoke to her. Being friends with Delphina was having a positive effect on her, even if Delphina was a little crazy. But then, aren't we all? At least Delphina had fun with it, as was Charlotte now too.

"How about this?" Delphina said as she changed her skin to resemble a shark's skin, making it look like she was now wearing clothing, albeit skintight clothing. Charlotte did the same, turning her entire body obsidian to hide her nakedness. "Better? Are you less embarrassed now?"

"I was never embarrassed in the first place," I said. "That's better, though."

"So what's going on?" Delphina asked. "And why haven't you come to visit us in weeks?"

"I've been busy," I said. "I'm working for the FBI now."

"The FBI?" Delphina said, sounding surprised. "Jeez, Ethan. For someone who breaks the law a lot, you sure know how to pick your bosses."

"The job keeps me in line. Otherwise, I'd just be an outlaw like you two."

"Don't knock it," Delphina said. "We're having great fun, aren't we Charlie?"

"Doing what?" I asked.

"Taking down bad guys, just like my sister used to," Charlotte said.

"What bad guys?"

"The worst we can find," Delphina said. "Vamps, Mafia guys, cultists…whoever we damn well feel like taking out."

"Okay…" I said, unsure about this new direction the two of them seemed to have taken. "I hope you're careful, at least."

"Always, Ethan, always," Delphina said. "So are you gonna tell us why we're here? You didn't say much on the phone."

"We're gonna hit the factory over there," I said. "To steal a truck full of merchandise."

"What merchandise?" Charlotte asked, looking for all the world like a younger version of Scarlet sitting there. So much so, that I had to stop looking at her face in the mirror. Scarlet and Charlotte may not have been blood sisters, but they were still alike.

"Adrenochrome and Soul Energy."

"Shit," Delphina said with disgust. "All the Mafia guys use that Adrenochrome shit. It's disgusting. Why are you stealing it?"

"To destroy it," I said.

Delphina nodded approvingly. "And the Soul Energy?"

"Don't worry about that," I said.

"So you're selling it."

"It's out of my hands. There'll be cash. You two will get paid handsomely, don't worry."

"It's not like we need the money, but okay."

"Why not?"

"My sister had accounts," Charlotte said. "She left me a lot of money."

"Plus, we steal a lot," Delphina said. "We don't need money. We'll do the shit for free, as a favor to you, Ethan, since you helped us out."

"Nice of them," Danika said with some sarcasm, clearly not taken by either of them.

"Okay, but there's more," I said. "There are people in there, some of them kids. We need to load them into the truck with the merchandise and get them out of there."

"Our favorite kind of mission," Delphina said, looking at Charlotte.

"What do you mean?" I asked.

"We hit a lot of trafficking gangs," Charlotte explained. "We rescue the women and children and hand them over to an organization that we started."

"You started an organization?" I said in amazement. "What kind of organization?"

"Well, it was Scarlet's idea," Charlotte said. "She established it before she, you know…died. She wanted to do something good, to help the victims who couldn't help themselves. So Delphina and I, we took Scarlet's plan and finished getting everything up and running. It wasn't that hard really because Scarlet had done most of the work already. We now have people we hand over the trafficked women and children to, who then reunite the victims with their families, or relocate them as needed. We've saved dozens at this point."

"Holy shit, you guys," I said, turning in my seat to look at them both. "I'm so fucking proud right now."

Both of them dropped their cocky facades for a moment to look bashful. "Thanks, Ethan," Delphina said.

"Yeah, thanks," Charlotte said. "We couldn't have done without you."

Danika coughed in my ear. "I hate to break up this little love-fest you three have going, but can we get moving?"

"Sure," I said, turning back around.

"Sure what?" Delphina asked.

"Danika is in my ear telling me to get moving."

"Who's Danika?" Charlotte asked.

"The person running this job. I'll introduce you later."

"I'm not so sure—" Danika started to say until I cut her off.

"She can't wait to meet you both."

"Thanks," Danika drawled.

"Alright," I said, pulling on a black mask. "Let's steal some shit and rescue some people."

"Fucking-A," Delphina said.

"About friggin' time," said Danika.

The security gate wasn't much of a security gate as it was held closed only by a chain and padlock. Using a pair of bolt cutters, I cut the chain, discarding the cutters before opening the gate and hastening toward the factory, keeping to the shadows as I went, the shotgun held in my hands.

Delphina and Charlotte moved silently behind me until I held up a fist, and we stopped by the front of the rundown factory near the front doors, which according to Danika, were locked from the inside. Turning to Charlotte, I motioned for her to go up to the roof. We had already discussed the plan in the car. She was to go through the skylight once Delphina and I were inside.

Nodding, Charlotte stood, and I watched her transform into the vampire-killing human/spider hybrid that her biological father, Jonas Webb, had made her into. She grew six legs and a huge abdomen, her two arms also functioning as legs as she turned and leaped onto the brick wall, scuttling at speed up the sheer surface to the roof.

"She's somethin' ain't she?" Delphina said, smiling after her.

"I'm glad you two are getting along," I whispered. "You ready to go in?"

Delphina's smile widened as she floated off the ground, becoming horizontal to it, her body bobbing gently around as if she were floating in the rain itself. Then her entire body transformed as her legs melded into a shark's tail, and a dorsal fin grew out of her back as her skin turned a mottled gray, her underside whitening. Her head didn't elongate much, but her mouth grew huge, and her eyes enlarged themselves, becoming the eyes of a stone-cold predator. As well as the rain, she was encased in her own body of water. Almost playfully, she snapped her massive jaws at me, and I could just imagine someone inside the factory being bitten in half by those things.

Turning from her, I went to the doors and removed a small plastic explosive device from beneath my body armor. I then attached the device to the door and moved away along the front of the building.

"We're set here," I said to Danika. "Activate the EMP when ready."

"Activating EMP," she said. "In three, two, one. EMP activated."

Seconds later, the hum of machines and electricity inside stopped immediately, and all light from the windows ceased. From inside, I heard voices shout.

Reaching into my pocket, I took out a small remote detonator and held my thumb over the red button. "Breaching in three, two, one."

I pressed the button, and a loud explosion sounded as the front doors of the factory got blown open.

"Going in!" I said as I shouldered the shotgun and moved toward the doors.

Before I got there, a man came running out with a gun to see what was going on. I was about to fire on him when Delphina swooped over at incredible speed and bit the guy's head off with one bite, his body falling to the ground as his neck spurted blood. Delphina swung herself around to face me and allowed the guy's head to roll out of her mouth, where it hit the wet ground with a splash. After flashing me a bloody shark-toothed grin, she then turned and darted inside the factory.

Activating my night vision by blinking rapidly three times, I stormed inside the factory after Delphina, making my way through a short hallway before emerging into a vast space filled with old and new machinery, and thick concrete pillars.

Several men had gathered in the room, most of them armed with automatic weapons. Despite the darkness, they still fired toward the doors, albeit blindly. As bullets whizzed past my head, I rushed to take cover behind a concrete pillar, getting ready with the shotgun. If these guys were ghouls, I had to stay sharp. Thanks to the vampire blood they drank regularly, ghouls were granted supernatural speed and strength, making them more dangerous than your average human.

As Delphina went in for the kill, attacking those closest to her, I leaned around the pillar and fired the shotgun at the closest threat standing twenty yards away near a massive machine. The Dragon's Breath round lit up the darkness as it traveled through the air before the load hit its target, immediately setting the man on fire, causing him to drop his gun and scream as he reeled around in a panic.

So much for vampire blood...

Pumping the shotgun to eject the shell, I fired again at another man who was standing closer, but this fucker was fast, and darted to the side as the load from the shotgun hit a machine instead.

As I was about to fire again, Charlotte dropped from the skylight, dangling on a length of spider silk coming from her abdomen. She grabbed the ghoul with her legs, lifting him off the ground toward her waiting fangs, and then plunged her fangs into his skull, blood jetting everywhere as the ghoul screamed and kicked his legs furiously. A few seconds later, he stopped kicking, and Charlotte dropped him to the floor before ascending to the ceiling again.

Once the remaining ghouls realized there were monsters in their midst, they started firing their automatic weapons towards the ceiling almost in a panic. Thanks to the muzzle flashes of their guns, though, it made it easy to pick them off individually. I set three of them on fire with the Dragon's Breath rounds, and Charlotte and Delphina finished the others off between them.

As ghouls lay on the floor, some still burning, others in pieces, Danika told me to move toward the corridor that led to the loading bay.

"What about your inside man?" I asked her as I headed to the corridor.

"Fuck him," Danika said. "He can die with the rest if he hasn't already."

"Fair enough. What about the people we have to rescue? Where are they?"

"At the end of the corridor, take a left and then take the first door on your left. They should be inside."

Moving quickly across the floor to the corridor, I stopped when I saw a man running toward me, his eyes burning red.

Not a man, but a vampire.

I put the shotgun to my shoulder, but before I could even fire, the vampire was right in front of me, his hands on the shotgun as he ripped it out of my grip and tossed it away behind him. Then he used the palm of his hand to strike me on the chest, the incredible power of his strike sending me flying back into the room I had just come from, where I landed on the floor next to a burning body.

Before I could even get up, the vampire was on me, one knee pinning me to the concrete floor.

"Who are you?" he hissed. "What are you doing here?"

"Fuck...you," I said, hardly able to breathe thanks to the crushing pressure on my chest.

The vampire hissed and then opened his mouth, his lower jaw dislocating, his massive fangs protruding out as he got ready to bite my face off, which was the kind of savagery that Furer vampires were known for.

To save myself, I reached for the Magnum holstered to my leg, but as I pulled the heavy gun out, the vampire merely slapped it out of my hand onto the floor.

Oh shit...

"Are you okay, Ethan?" Danika said in my ear.

"Fucking peachy!" I said as the vampire's mouth continued to widen, to where it looked like my entire head might fit into that gaping maw.

But as the vampire pulled his head back in preparation to strike, something long and black suddenly pierced his chest, causing him to scream. Looking past the vampire, I saw Charlotte hanging from her silken thread, one of her thick, black legs piercing the vampire as she lifted him off of me.

Getting to my feet, I grabbed the Magnum from the floor and pointed it at the vampire, who was holding on to the leg that impaled his body as he struggled to get himself free.

"How many more of you are there?" I asked him.

"Lot's more," he said, smiling now in defiance. "You may have disabled our communications, but you forgot about one thing."

"And what's that?"

"We Furer have telepathic abilities. My kin are already on their way." He smiled as blood ran down his chin. "You'd better get moving, human."

Fuck. He wasn't lying. He was also right about one thing —I had to get moving.

Charlotte sank her long fangs into the Furer's skull, pumping him full of poison before letting him go. The vampire screamed like his insides were burning, and then just as I moved away from him, his entire body exploded like a bomb had gone off inside him, showering me and everything else within a ten-meter radius in gore.

"Goddamn," I said, wiping blood from my eyes. "A little warning would've been nice."

"Bring an umbrella next time," Charlotte hissed.

"Funny." I spat vampire blood onto the floor. "Find Delphina and clear the loading bay. I'm going to find the people we came here to rescue."

As Charlotte scuttled off, her claws clicking off the concrete floor as she went, I hurried up the corridor with the Magnum still in my hand, turning left up another hall until I came to the door Danika was talking about.

"I'm at the door," I said to her. "Going in now."

The door was unlocked, and I opened it and went inside, the room dark like the rest of the factory. But thanks to my night vision, I still saw what was inside.

Or rather, who.

I also smelled how awful it was in there, a mixture of decay and human waste hitting my nostrils, almost making me gag.

Huddled all along the back wall of the stinking room were about a dozen people, most of them adults, some of whom also cradled children in their arms. Besides the ones staring toward the door in pure terror, there were others on the floor in the center of the room, clearly dead, their corpses bloated and decomposed.

Jesus Christ…

Of those still alive, all were naked and shivering in the cold, their bodies drained and emaciated, looking like a bunch of graveyard ghouls at this point.

The kids seemed to be the worst, being barely conscious, their eyes only communicating terror and trauma.

As I moved through the doorway, bullets suddenly hit the wall beside me, causing some people inside the room to scream in fright.

Ducking my head around the door, I looked up the corridor to see who was shooting, and saw a woman armed with a submachine gun, which she fired again when she saw me.

Crouching down, I pulled back the hammer on the Magnum and took a deep breath before leaning around the door, pointing the gun at the woman and firing before she could fire back. The kick from the Magnum was massive, and it bucked in my hand as I fired. But I still hit my target, the bullet blowing a hole in the woman's chest before she dropped her sub gun and fell to the floor.

In the room, there was much screaming and crying, especially from the children. Holstering the gun, I tried to calm the people down by telling them I was there to rescue them, but most of them were so far gone, I couldn't get through to them. All they registered was terror as they clung to each other, probably thinking I was there to hurt them.

"It will not be easy getting these people out of here," I said to Danika. "They're all terrified."

"You have another problem," Danika said. "My drone footage is showing vehicles outside. Reinforcements have arrived."

"Shit. How many?"

"Four vehicles. Over a dozen men, I'd say, all armed except for a few, who I'm assuming are vamps. They're heading inside now."

I stood for a second and then bolted out of the room, sprinting down the corridor and through the door to the loading bay where I saw multiple bodies lying on the floor, and the huge armored truck.

"Delphina?" I called out as I looked around for her.

"Yeah?" Delphina swam over from a dark corner, her mouth dripping blood.

"Get Charlotte and head back to the factory floor," I told her. "Reinforcements have arrived. I need you to hold them off until I can get those people loaded into the truck. Can you do that?"

"Of course." Charlotte had now joined Delphina as she dangled from the ceiling.

"Be careful," I told them as they darted off.

When they'd gone, I checked the truck. The keys were in the ignition, I was relieved to see, and the back doors were also unlocked.

"Looks like your inside man came through," I said to Danika as I removed the keys from the ignition and put them in my pocket. "Keys are here, and the doors are unlocked. The merchandise is inside."

"Good," Danika said. "But the reinforcements are still coming."

"What?" I said as I hurried out of the room again to the corridor, just as the shooting started, and the screaming as Charlotte and Delphina attacked the newcomers. "How many more?"

"Another three carloads."

"Jesus, these guys don't fuck around."

"If you can get the people into the truck and get out of there, I can blow up the whole factory using the drone."

"I'll try," I said. "They aren't very responsive."

I ran back down the corridor to the room where the adults and children were. They were all huddled together in the corner now, fearing for their lives.

"Don't hurt us," a woman whimpered.

"I'm not here to hurt you," I said, trying to keep my voice calm, despite the gunfire and screams in the background. I also peeled back my mask so they could see my face. "I will get you out of here. Can you all move okay?"

"Some of us can't," a man said. "We're too weak."

"Okay," I said. "Everyone able, stand up now."

Most of them stood up, some barely holding the children as they did so. Two women and two men remained on the floor, having been injured by their captors. The ones who were standing, I got them to move out into the corridor. A few remained to help the four who couldn't stand on their own. One man was larger than the rest, and the small man who tried to help him up just couldn't. Telling the smaller man to join the others, I picked up the larger man myself, supporting his substantial weight as he gripped onto me, mewling in pain as he did.

Out in the corridor, I led the others to the loading bay door as I carried the injured man along with me, holding my submachine gun in my right hand as I inched along. Before we reached the door, a man darted into the corridor and was about to fire his gun before I hit him with a burst from my sub-gun. The people behind me screamed at the noise of the guns, and the children started crying.

"Keep moving!" I shouted as I continued toward the door, standing aside so the others could move through the doorway first, while I stood guard in case any of the Furer reinforcements made it through to the corridor. As it was, Delphina and Charlotte were doing an excellent job of keeping the threats at bay, especially if the death screams were anything to go by.

Once everyone had gone through the door into the loading bay, I carried my passenger through along with me and directed everyone to the truck, telling them to get inside as quickly as possible, which they did. There wasn't much room in there, but everyone was able to squash themselves in around the wooden crates filled with vials of their Soul Energy, and Adrenochrome, in the case of the kids. There was something twisted about the people being in there along with their own precious energies, packaged up and ready to hit the market, but I didn't have time to dwell on it. Better that than leave them here to die.

"Don't worry," I said as I closed the doors. "I'll get us out of here. Sit tight."

With the people now safely locked in the truck, I pulled my mask down again and headed back to get Delphina and Charlotte. The Magnum was still in my hand, which I raised as soon as I saw a man standing by a machine reloading his weapon. I stopped and raised the Magnum just as he saw me, but it was too late for him because I had already drawn a bead on his head. As he went to raise his gun, I squeezed the trigger on mine, and a split second later, the guy's head exploded like a melon.

Jesus, this gun is a beast.

"Delphina! Charlotte! Let's go!" I shouted, drawing the attention of a Furer vampire, who leaped off of a gigantic machine and landed ten yards away from me. He looked like a biker, as most of the Furer vamps did. They had their own MC, and could often be seen riding around the city on their motorcycles, causing havoc as they went.

The vampire sneered at me as I raised the Magnum. But before I could get the chance to fire, the vampire raised his hand and pulled the nearby shadows to him, which he then unleashed on me, the tendrils of shadow wrapping themselves around the long barrel of the Magnum, ripping the gun from my hands. Before I could even run the shadow tendrils were around my throat, as hard as cable wire as they constricted around my neck.

Despite the growing pressure, I grabbed the sub-gun still strapped around me, raising the gun and firing multiple bursts at the vampire, who barely flinched as the bullets hit him, still maintaining the shadow tendrils that gripped me even tighter.

"I will not kill you," the vampire snarled as he came closer. "I will keep you here and torture you for days before draining you of your soul energy. Do you even have a soul, human?"

Not that I could speak, but if I could, I would've told the vampire to go fuck himself. Not that cursing him would've done much good. With no sign of Delphina or Charlotte, I was left with no choice but to summon the Hellbastards, barely managing to subvocalize the summons.

Just as I was falling to my knees—my head light, my vision blackening around the edges—the Hellbastards, bless their little black hearts, appeared between the Furer vampire and me. The Hellbastards stood for a second as they got their bearings, and the vampire stared at them in shock.

"What the hell is this?" the fanged one said. "Have the Muppets just arrived on set?" He laughed—a laugh I knew he would soon regret.

Scroteface and the others stood facing the vampire. "Surprise, motherfucker!" Scroteface said, and then they were all on the vampire, diving at him with their claws out like a bunch of rabid dogs, clinging onto him as he started screaming.

The shadow tendrils dissipated from around my neck, and I stayed on my knees for a few seconds as I gulped in air. Ahead of me, the Hellbastards had toppled the vampire, and Snot Skull was standing over his head, spewing acid vomit over the vampire's face, which instantly melted. The other Hellbastards were going hell for leather on the vampire's body, ripping and clawing and biting, tearing the downed vampire to shreds as he continued screaming like a bitch.

Looking across the factory floor, I saw more combatants pouring in through the front doors, most of them armed, with at least half a dozen biker vampires among their number.

"Danika?" I said. "I'm seeing more of these fucks coming in."

"More just arrived," she said. "You need to get out of there."

"No shit."

I called out for Delphina and Charlotte again after shooting a ghoul with the sub-gun, and this time Delphina darted out from behind a machine and swam at speed toward me. "This shit is getting crazy," she said.

"We gotta go," I told her. "Get Charlotte and meet me at the truck. Go!"

As Delphina sped away, I whistled at the Hellbastards, who were still making a mess of the vampire on the floor. They'd filleted him like a hunk of beef, his blood everywhere, no longer able to scream because Snot Skull had melted his vocal cords.

"Let's go!" I shouted at the Hellbastards, and for once, they did as they were told and scrambled away from the vampire to join me.

"Thanks for the invite, boss," Scroteface said.

"Yeah, don't mention it," I said as I headed toward the loading bay doors. "Watch our six."

On the way to the loading bay, one of the Furer's ghouls jumped in front of me with supernatural speed. Without thinking, I kicked the guy away from me, and then a fireball hurtled past me and struck the ghoul in the chest, immediately covering him in flames. As the ghoul staggered back, Scroteface rushed past me, leaped into the air, and hit the flaming ghoul with a flying kick that knocked the ghoul to the ground.

"Scrotey like Bruce Lee!" Cracka shouted.

"Nice," I said to Scroteface as I ran past him and through the loading bay doors only to find that three Furer vampires were waiting for us.

"Where do you think you're going?" one of them said.

"You ain't getting outta here," another said.

"You picked the wrong place to rob, asshole," the third said.

As I fired at the vampires with my sub-gun, the Hellbastards attacked, doing their best to take on the three burly vampires. But the odds were different this time. It wasn't five on one, it was five on three, and it showed. The Hellbastards did their best, but they were soon flung across the room as the Furers got the better of them. Toast set one vampire on fire, but it didn't seem to slow the vamp down any, and he grabbed Toast and bit into the Hellbastard's head, causing Toast to scream in a way that I've never heard any of the Hellbastards scream before. I got that horrible feeling you get when you hear a child cry out in pain, and without thinking, I rushed toward the vampire and shoulder tackled him to the ground, forcing him to let Toast go, burning myself in the process.

Before I could get back off the vampire, I felt the back of my body armor get gripped, and then I was flung backward across the room, where I landed on an empty wooden crate, smashing it to pieces.

Inside the truck, a child screamed.

"You're dead meat!" the vampire who flung me roared as he stomped forward with his fangs out, his eyes burning red as his jaw dislocated in preparation to fucking eat me.

Fuck, I hate vampires…

As the fiend neared me, Cracka suddenly launched himself off the roof of the truck, the tiny demon landing on the Furer vampire's head. As the vamp tried to grab Cracka, the little demon scurried around the other side of him, opened his mouth wide, and then bit into the vampire's neck, biting down hard before ripping a chunk of flesh away. The vampire screamed as a massive amount of his precious blood jetted from his neck, dowsing Cracka before the Hellbastard leaped off of him to the ground.

Beside me were long shards of wood from the smashed crate. Grabbing the longest shard, I jumped up and ran toward the vampire as he struggled to stop any more of his blood from pumping out of his neck. He was so caught up in clamping his hands over his wound, he didn't react in time to me coming at him, and I plunged the wooden stake into his chest, ramming it into his black, unbeating heart.

"Fuck you," I snarled as I pushed him away, seeing the look of fear on his face as he realized he was done for, which he was, for a second later, his whole body seemed to disintegrate until there was nothing left but a pile of dust.

In front of the truck, the other two vampires—still being held at bay by the Hellbastards—shouted in rage as they witnessed their kin turn to dust. They tried to come at me, but the Hellbastards kept them busy while I rushed over to the truck and climbed into the driver's seat, locking the doors behind me.

As I did, something landed on the roof and scurried down onto the hood. Another friggin' vampire, this one a female. She jumped down and tried to pull the driver's side door open, but even with all her supernatural strength, the door held. Lucky for me.

"Have you left yet?" Danika asked urgently.

"I'm about to," I said. "I'm waiting for Delphina and Charlotte."

"You can't wait any longer. You'll be overwhelmed. You'll never make it out of there."

As if to prove her point, more combatants—mostly ghouls—came through the loading bay doors and immediately attacked the truck, punching the reinforced glass in an effort to get inside, pulling at the doors, making me glad I locked the back doors earlier.

"Ethan!" Danika pressed as the people locked in the back of the truck screamed in fear. "You need to go!"

"Shit!" I said as I took the keys from my pocket and

started the truck up, causing the vamps and ghouls to go crazy as they doubled their efforts to break in.

Outside, I saw Scroteface stamping his foot on a ghoul's face, turning the face to mush.

Scroteface.

Yeah, boss?

He stopped stamping and looked across at me.

Find Delphina and Charlotte, and tell them to get out of here now.

Who boss?

The big fucking spider and the shark. They're in the room behind us. And tell the other Hellbastards to grab onto the truck. I'm getting out of here. Do it now!

Okay, boss.

I revved the truck's engine, realizing that even if Delphina and Charlotte showed up now, I wouldn't be able to let them in. If I opened the doors, the vamps and ghouls would swarm inside, and we'd be fucked.

I just hoped Scroteface found them and got them out in time before Danika blew this place to hell.

"Moving out!" I said to Danika as I put the truck into drive and pressed down on the gas, knocking over at least two ghouls as I drove forward and down the ramp. I heard commotion on the roof, and there was still a vampire on the front of the truck, but so where the Hellbastards now, minus Scroteface who had gone off to find the girls. The remaining four Hellbastards fought with the vampire, Toast finally setting him on fire as Reggie pushed the vamp off the hood.

As I drove at speed around the back of the factory, Cracka hung onto the side mirror while the others held on to the edge of the roof like little demon stuntmen, their smiling faces looking in at me as they reveled in the exhilaration and chaos of the situation.

Driving the truck around to the front of the factory, I was greeted by a horde of ghouls who shot at the truck, which didn't worry me because the truck was bulletproof.

Two cars blocked the front gates, so I pressed down hard on the gas and accelerated toward them, the heavily armored truck smashing through the middle of the cars, sending them flying either side, so I could carry on driving onto the road and speed away from the factory.

"I'm out," I said to Danika.

"Drone is ready to fire," she said. "In three, two…one."

A second later, there was a massive explosion as a missile from the drone hit the factory, blowing it and everyone standing around it, to smithereens.

"Jesus Christ," I said as the massive impact hit the truck, causing it to sway for a second until I got it under control again.

"Make your way to the drop point," Danika said.

"Yeah," I said, thinking only about the girls at this point.

Scroteface, report.

No reply.

Scroteface? Report. Are you there?

Still nothing.

My stomach turned.

Scroteface! Answer me!

When there was still no reply, I looked out at the faces of the other Hellbastards as they stared in at me through the glass.

They were no longer smiling.

25

No one followed the truck to the drop point. Any ghoul or vampire in or around the factory had been blown to shit. As I drove the truck through the near-empty city, Danika made sure all the stoplights were clear, meaning I made it to the drop point in good time. On the brief journey, I continued to try to contact Scroteface, but he still wasn't acknowledging my telepathic calls. By the time I got to the drop point, I felt sick, convinced that Scroteface and the two girls had got blown up along with the factory.

When the steel shutter was raised, I drove the truck inside the fake garage and down the ramp to the subway station platform. Waiting in the subway was a train with a single passenger car attached. Also waiting on the platform was a blonde-haired girl about Danika's age that I'd never seen before. She barely acknowledged me as she moved around to the back of the truck and waited impatiently for me to open the back doors while she warily eyed up the Hellbastards, who I shooed to the shadows before the people in the truck saw them.

After I opened the back doors, Danika appeared on the platform and helped the other girl get the still terrified people out of the truck and loaded onto the train. As they did, I continued to assure the victims of the Furer vampires that they would be alright, and that their ordeal was over. Danika informed them that the train would take them to a private hospital—in the Underground, I assumed—where they would be taken care of. A few of the people thanked me before they got onto the train, and it wasn't long before Danika's helper was driving the train away, leaving just me, Danika and the Hellbastards standing on the platform.

"You did it," Danika said, smiling at me before staring at the four Hellbastards. "And you brought your pets."

"Yeah," I said, as glum as the Hellbastards at this point, who panicked that Scroteface was dead.

"You're worried about your friends," Danika said.

"Course I fucking am," I said with more anger than I intended. "I don't know if they even made it out of there before you blew the place to kingdom come. There was no need for that, you know."

"Yes, there was. We put a huge dent in their operation tonight, not to mention their numbers."

"And fuck the collateral damage, right?"

"I didn't say that."

"You implied it. I've heard the same shit from plenty of others over the years."

"Don't make me out to be some cold-blooded killer, Ethan. I'm not. I did what I had to do. Surely you can understand that."

"I can understand you got your merchandise."

"And *you'll* get your money," she said, walking away to the back of the truck. "Stop giving me a hard time."

As Danika climbed into the back of the truck to inspect the merchandise, I pulled out my cigarettes and lit one up, and then sat on the edge of the platform, blowing streams of smoke into the slightly fetid underground air.

Then, as I was halfway through my cigarette, I heard a

voice over by the truck say, "What the fuck, bitch? You almost blew us up!"

My eyes widened in surprise when I realized the voice belonged to Delphina. Dropping my cigarette, I jumped to my feet and ran over to the truck to see that Delphina was holding Danika against the tiled wall, her hand wrapped around Danika's throat.

Standing near Delphina was Charlotte, her naked body encased in a black skin except for her head. In her arms, she held Scroteface, who didn't appear to be moving.

"Delphina!" I said. "Let her go."

"Why?" Delphina said, turning her head to look at me. "She nearly fucking killed us."

"Ethan told you to get out of there," Danika said, boldly, I thought. Or stupidly, since she didn't know Delphina and what she was capable of.

"Just let her go, Delphina," I said, more worried about Scroteface now, who Charlotte had placed on the floor. "You're alive. That's all that matters."

"Just barely," Delphina said, finally releasing her grip on Danika's throat. "No thanks to this bitch."

"How'd you even know where to find this place?" Danika asked, seemingly more concerned about the integrity of her security than anything else.

"I tracked Ethan's scent," Delphina said. "Why? You worried about the vamps coming here and stealing back the shit you took from them?"

Danika didn't answer as she wisely moved away from Delphina, coming to stand behind me.

The Hellbastards had gathered around Scroteface by this point, who was unmoving on the floor.

"Scrotey…" Cracka said softly as he touched Scroteface's chest.

"Is he…alive?" Reggie asked no one in particular.

"The little guy wasn't as quick as us," Charlotte said. "He got caught in the blast."

"Scrotey!" Cracka wailed. "Wake up, Scrotey!"

"Stand back," I told them all as I crouched down to inspect the Hellbastard, who didn't appear to be breathing, his chest still. Leaning over him, I put my head to his chest and listened for a heartbeat. "His heart is beating…barely."

"Save him, boss," Cracka said, his little face distraught. "Save Scrotey."

"Yeah, boss," Snot Skull grunted. "Save him."

"The explosion sent him flying," Charlotte said. "He hit his head pretty bad. The back of his skull is cracked."

"Jesus…" I breathed as I now noticed the black blood pooling around Scroteface's head.

"What do we do, boss?" Toast asked, two holes in his skull from where he had been bitten by the vampire, dark, dried blood caked around his head.

"I…"

I couldn't answer his question, for I didn't know what to do, except for maybe getting Hannah to try to heal him, but she wasn't here, and was probably still tied up with Solomon.

"I have an idea," Danika said.

"What? You gonna blow him up?" Delphina said.

Danika shook her head but ignored Delphina as she spoke to me. "We could try using the Soul Energy. It has healing properties that work on humans, so why not demons?"

"Okay," I said. "Get some."

"Lucky we got a whole truck full, huh?" Delphina said, staring down Danika as she went to the truck to get the Soul Energy.

"Delphina," I said. "I'm glad you're alive, but maybe give the attitude a rest for a minute, huh?"

Delphina stared at me for a second and then shook her

head. "You owe us after this, I hope you know that."

"Sure," I said, staring down at Scroteface. "Whatever."

A few minutes later, Danika returned with a small glass vial filled with cobalt energy, making me think for a second of the God Machine I secured for Knightsbridge years ago. The machine had been full of the stuff, and I wondered then as I did now, who the energy used to belong to. Not that it mattered. Now, the energy was just a commodity like everything else in this world.

Danika handed me the vial. "You wanna give it to him?"

I took the vial and kneeled by the side of Scroteface's small body, removing the rubber bung from the top of the glass container.

"I don't want Scrotey to die," Cracka suddenly wailed. "I sorry for torturing you, Scrotey. I never do it again if you don't die, I promise."

Reggie put an arm around Cracka's small shoulders and held him. "Calm down, little guy," he said. "The boss has got this. Right boss?"

I nodded. "Sure, Reggie."

With everyone watching, I gripped Scroteface's jaw and opened his mouth so I could pour in the Soul Energy. It was a strange substance, not quite liquid and not quite gas, but something in-between, a consistency all of its own. When I poured it out, the Soul Energy disappeared down Scroteface's throat as if it knew precisely where to go in his body. It never occurred to me to wonder before if the Hellbastards even had a soul, given that they weren't made by God, but by other demons. Would the Soul Energy even have an effect on a soulless being?

"It not working," Cracka said after a minute, beginning to panic again. "It not working!"

"Give it a minute," Reggie said, not sounding too hopeful himself.

"Come on, little guy," Charlotte whispered. "You can do

this."

As if hearing what she said, Scroteface moved suddenly, his body stretching and his back arching as though the Soul Energy was doing something unseen to him. Then his enormous eyes flung open, and he sat bolt upright as he took a huge breath.

"Scrotey!" Cracka shouted as he threw his tiny arms around Scroteface. "You alive!"

Scroteface sat blinking. "What the fuck happened?" he asked.

"You almost got blew to shit, little guy, that's what happened," Delphina said, throwing Danika another scornful look at the same time.

"Blew up?" Scroteface said. "Oh yeah, now I remember. Big explosion."

"Lucky you got a thick skin, brother," Reggie said, helping Scroteface to his feet.

"I got big balls too," Scroteface said, grabbing his crotch and laughing, the other Hellbastards soon laughing along with him.

"Hysterical," Delphina said, shaking her head. "Well, now that everyone's alright—no thanks to some—we should blow this party. Let's go, Charlie."

"Hey," I said, walking over to the two of them. "Before you go."

"What?" Delphina said.

I grabbed them both and hugged them for a moment. "Stay safe, you two. Alright?"

"Yeah, we will," Delphina said. "Long as we don't hang around you."

"Delphina," Charlotte said. "It wasn't Ethan's fault what happened."

"Yeah," Delphina said, looking at Danika. "I know it."

"You should come out to the woods," Charlotte said to me. "To visit Scarlet. She probably misses you."

I smiled and swallowed as I thought of Scarlet and how much I missed her. "I will," I said.

When the two girls left, I turned around to find Danika sitting on the edge of the platform. After lighting a cigarette, I joined her.

"I'm sorry," she said after a moment. "I may have jumped the gun with the explosion."

Exhaling a stream of smoke, I shook my head. "We all do what we think is right, and we all knew the risks. Making decisions under that kind of pressure isn't easy."

"I'm not sure your friends would agree with you."

"They'll get over it, although something tells me you aren't too worried if they do or not."

"You think I'm callous?"

"I just think you're focused on the job. That can make you callous."

Danika reached across and took the cigarette from my hand, putting it to her lips and taking a drag. "I don't smoke before you ask. I used to, though. Stressful night."

"Yeah, it was fucking stressful, alright. I think I'm getting too old for this shit."

She smiled. "Okay, Murtaugh."

"I never pegged you as a *Lethal Weapon* fan."

"What can I say? I have hidden depths."

"I'm still too old for this shit. My body feels like it got hit by a truck."

"You pulled it off, though. You saved all those people."

"Where did your friend take them?"

"They'll stay here in the Underground until they are well enough to leave. They'll be looked after, don't worry."

I didn't doubt her sincerity. "And the merchandise?"

"The Adrenochrome will be destroyed, as planned."

"And the Soul Energy?"

"I'm giving it to the Underground hospital."

"Giving it? I thought you were selling it on?"

"I changed my mind."

"Good for you then."

"There's enough cash in that truck to save your business."

"You're not taking your cut?"

"I got what I wanted. I'll wire the money to your account once it's been cleaned. It shouldn't take long."

"I won't ask if you need my account number."

She smiled. "No need."

"What about the truck over there?"

"It will be repurposed at some stage."

"For what?"

"Future jobs. As I said, I intend to bring down the evil Cabal in this town. Can I count on your help with that?"

I nodded. "Sure, once I deal with the evil in my own life."

"Well," she said, extending her hand, which I shook. "If you need any help, let me know. I'm here if you need me."

Upon leaving the subway station, I told Danika I would take the old Ford back to the yard and stash it there. Once I got the new machines, I would have the Ford crushed.

All seemed to be well as I drove back to the yard with the Hellbastards in the back until I was halfway there and realized the amulet Solomon had given me was no longer around my neck.

"Fuck," I said in a panic. "I must've lost it at the factory."

And then to top it off, I got a phone call from Hannah.

"Ethan," she said, sounding distressed.

"What's up?" I asked her, surprised to hear from her so soon.

"Something went wrong at Solomon's."

"What? What do you mean something went wrong?"

"Solomon never made it out of Hell," she said. "He's gone."

26

Back at the yard, I got the full story from Hannah as we sat in my trailer drinking whiskey and smoking cigarettes, Hannah visibly shaken by the entire experience as she recounted what happened.

"I gave control to Xaglath as planned," she said. "Mostly anyway. I was still in the background, ready to suppress her if need be, though she seemed different this time."

"Different how?" I asked.

"Just...not as arrogant, maybe? Like she knew she couldn't get away with stuff like she did before, and that I was in control this time, and could banish her anytime I wanted to."

"So you—or Xaglath—opened the portal to Hell. Then what?"

"Solomon went through."

"Did he say what he was after in that place?"

"He said something about wanting to see a demon about a dog," she said. "I think he thought he was being funny when he said that."

"Solomon is like the least funny person I know."

"Yeah, Stitch is okay, though. I liked him."

"Stitch is probably more human than his master, which isn't hard. Anyway, what happened next?"

"We waited, Xaglath and I. We talked."

"About what?"

She shrugged and shook her head. "She tried to argue for her freedom, finding a way to release her from me."

"Yeah, right," I said. "As if."

"I told her I'd think about it."

"What? You'd let Xaglath loose as her own entity? Are you mad?"

"She tried to escape, anyway."

"What do you mean? How?"

"When Solomon tried to come back through the portal."

"I thought you said he didn't come back."

"He didn't. As he was about to come through again, something grabbed him from the other side and pulled him back. He screamed for help."

The fact that Solomon of all people would scream for help meant things must've been bad. "So, what did you do?"

"Xaglath tried to go through the portal at that point, but I stopped her. She said she wanted to save Solomon, but I think she was trying to make a run for it back to Hell. She knew if she could drag me into that place, she'd have a better chance of regaining control over this body again."

"Sneaky bitch."

"Yeah. I put her back in her box again."

"Good. Keep her there."

Hannah lifted the whiskey bottle and refilled our glasses. "So what do we do then?" she asked.

"About what?"

"About Solomon."

I shrugged. "There's not much we can do, is there? I'm

sure as shit not going to Hell to save him, I'll tell you that much. I'm not going to Hell *at all*. It's bad enough here."

"He won't be able to save you now either," Hannah pointed out.

"There's that." I shook my head at the inconvenience. "I don't even have the amulet now. I'm just waiting for that bastard Cane to make another appearance. It's just a matter of time." My guts twisted up at the thought.

"Unless we get to him first."

"What do you mean? Go after him?"

"Why not? It seems to me you have little choice now."

I sat and thought about it as I sipped on my whiskey. She was right. I *didn't* have much choice. It was either go after Cane myself, or sit around waiting for him to drive me insane, or worse, kill me...or those close to me. The latter wasn't an option.

"Solomon said I'd be no match for a Spreak like Cane," I said.

"Maybe not," Hannah said. "But I would."

I stared at her, knowing she might be right, but I wasn't in love with the idea of Hannah risking her life for me. "And what if you're not? What if he kills you, or sends you back to Hell somehow?"

"He won't."

"You don't know that."

"I could turn Xaglath on him. He can't be more powerful than her."

"She's your attack dog now?"

Hannah shrugged. "Seems to me, she'd be ideally suited to kill a warlock like Cane. She'd relish the chance. I can feel her in me now, her eagerness, her excitement."

"Jesus, is she making you wet too?"

Hannah laughed. "Not quite. You, on the other hand—"

"Forget it," I said as she reached across and rubbed my

inner thigh. "I'm beat. We don't all have your celestial energy, you know."

"Does my 'ittle baby just wanna go to sleep?" she said in a pouty voice.

"Yeah, I do," I said, standing up. "We'll discuss this again later."

"Alright, old man," Hannah said, standing now. "Let's get you to bed before you fall off your feet."

"Will you be like this when I really am old? You don't exactly age, do you?"

"You can be my sugar daddy."

"I'm serious. You'll have to watch me die someday."

"Don't be morbid. We'll figure something out."

"Like what? I don't want to live forever, anyway."

She put her arms around my waist. "You don't want to spend eternity with me?"

"Maybe my soul could live on inside you after I die."

"You'd become a part of me then." She smiled. "Who says romance is dead?"

"I'm not sure if I could share your space with Xaglath, though."

"You'd just have to get along."

I shook my head. "I can't believe we're even talking about this. Come on, let's lie down for a while. You can watch me sleep."

"I'd like nothing better," she said, smiling as she took my hand and we went to the bedroom where I fell asleep five minutes later and dreamed about Callie.

A FEW HOURS LATER, I WOKE UP TO THE SMELL OF SIZZLING bacon and hot coffee. Hannah was in the kitchen, making breakfast. Groggily, my body aching from the night before, I padded into the living room and sat down, lighting up a cigarette to have with the coffee that Hannah handed me. She also handed me my phone.

"Bradley's been ringing," she said. "You might wanna call him back."

"You didn't answer?" I croaked, my voice hoarse.

"He didn't call me. He called you."

Holding the phone, I hit Bradley's number and put him on speaker.

"Ethan," he said, sounding a little rough himself, as if he'd been up all night. "Your search warrant has come through. I want you and Hannah to take a team and go to the asylum. I've already made the arrangements. The team will meet you there when you're ready."

"Okay," I said, looking at Hannah, who was standing chewing a piece of bacon. "You okay, sir? You don't sound too good."

"I'm fine," Bradley said, sounding far from it. "One more thing. I've also arranged an arrest warrant for Evelyn Mathers."

"On what grounds?"

"On whatever grounds you like. Just arrest her and bring her here. I'll deal with her after that."

"Mathers isn't who she says she is," I informed him. "She's a woman called Krystal McQueen. I think she might've killed Mathers and took over the asylum."

"There you go then," Bradley said. "Arrest her for murder."

"Will do," I said. "Maybe you'd like to arrest yourself, sir?"

"I would, but I'm tied up right now trying to save this department."

"I hope you do, sir."

"So do I, Ethan."

When he hung up, Hannah asked me what he was talking about.

"Wendell Knightsbridge," I said.

"What about him?"

"He's trying to get the President to close down Special Affairs."

"What? Why?"

"So Blackstar can take over."

"What an asshole," Hannah said, her face reflecting her anger. "I knew there was something going on lately."

"I hate to say it, but I think our jobs are done for."

"How could the President let someone like Knightsbridge take over the security of the country?"

"Probably because Knightsbridge didn't give him a choice," I said. "I know how Knightsbridge works. He has dirt on everyone, which he uses to blackmail people."

"That's disgusting."

"It's how the world works, I'm afraid. This is how the elite do business."

"Are we just going to allow this to happen?" Hannah said as she handed me a plate of bacon and eggs.

"I'm not sure there's anything we can do to stop it," I said, before shoveling forkfuls of scrambled eggs into my mouth, surprised by hungry I was.

Hannah stood in the kitchen and stared over at me as she held her coffee. "Then maybe we should stop him."

I stopped eating for a second. "You want to go after Knightsbridge?"

"Don't you?"

I said nothing as I started eating again.

AFTER I WAS DONE WITH BREAKFAST AND HAD GOTTEN myself ready, Hannah and I took the Chevelle and drove straight to Danver's Asylum. Turning the radio on, we heard on the news that a vaccination for the virus afflicting the city had been found, and that it was already being given to people who had the virus.

"Good news, right?" Hannah said. "Maybe things will get back to normal around here."

"I kinda like the lockdown. The streets are clearer."

Hannah shook her head. "You are so antisocial."

"You say that like it's a bad thing."

"Just shut up and drive."

As we came through Bricktown, we soon became aware that the streets weren't so clear as they had been. People were out now, some in groups, some alone, but all with a strange look on their face, a dark look somewhere between despair and hatred. The way some people glared at us—and at each other—you'd think they promised murder.

"Weird," I said as we drove past a group of people in the midst of an argument that looked like it would soon devolve into violence. "Why is everyone acting so strange?"

"I don't know," Hannah said as she gazed out the window. "It's like they've just found out the world will end."

"Well, let's hope not," I said. "It could just be the lock-down having weird effects on people."

Giving it no more thought, I sped on toward the asylum.

A team of Special Agents awaited us at Danvers Asylum. I say a team, but there were only three agents to conduct the search, and two SWAT guys in case there was any trouble, which I didn't expect there to be.

"All right guys," I said after explaining everything to them. "Let's do this."

The agents mostly grunted in response. Like most of the other agents in the department, they hadn't taken too kindly to Hannah and I coming in and taking over their cases, as they saw it, even getting a cushy office next to the boss's office. Never one for office politics, I ignored the hard stares and snide remarks, even the ones directed at me now from the three agents, who had, like everyone else, been aware of my reputation before I started with Special Affairs. Hannah got the same treatment, not because she was Fallen, for no one but Bradley knew about that, but because she came in with me, and nothing more. Not that any of that mattered now, for soon, there wouldn't be any Special Affairs, and everyone would be out of a job, anyway.

After we were buzzed in, we went through to the receptionist's office, the receptionist even less pleased to see us than she was last time, not even trying to hide her disdain for me and the rest of the team as she stood scowling at us.

"You're back," she said scornfully.

"We are," I said, the other agents already heading into the file room to begin their search. I took out the paperwork one agent had handed to me earlier. "And we have a warrant to search the place this time. I also have a warrant to arrest Dr. Mathers."

The receptionist's face crumpled slightly. "What? What for?"

"Murder for starters," Hannah said, enjoying seeing the receptionist squirm. "Of the *real* Dr. Mathers."

The receptionist shook her head like she didn't know what we were talking about. "Nonsense," she said dismissively.

"If it's nonsense, the good doctor can tell us herself that it is," I said. "Where is she? And don't tell us she's not here, or you'll find yourself getting arrested along with her."

"On what grounds?"

I stared into her hard, dark eyes, knowing she was up to her neck in whatever went on inside the asylum. She knew a lot more than she was letting on. "We'll think of something."

"We don't need a reason to arrest anyone these days,"

Hannah said. "Especially when they're suspected of terrorism."

"Terrorism?" the receptionist balked. "I've never heard such nonsense."

"I'd say what Dr. McQueen has been doing counts as terrorism, wouldn't you, Special Agent Drake?"

"Absolutely, Special Agent Walker," I said, enjoying seeing the receptionist squirm in her tight uniform, especially upon the mention of McQueen's name.

"There is no Dr. McQueen here," she said.

"We think there is," Hannah said. "And you will tell us where she is or—" Hannah produced her handcuffs. "I'm gonna cuff you and take you downtown myself, in which case you'll be thrown in a cell with no legal representation until we decide to let you out."

"*If* we let you out," I added gleefully.

"Dr. McQueen won't stand for this," the receptionist said.

"Ah, so you admit Dr. McQueen exists then?"

"Where is she?" Hannah demanded. "Tell us, or I swear you'll spend the rest of your days at an off-shore black site with all the other terrorists."

"And let me tell you," I said. "The guards at those places are worse than the prisoners. They'll break you down in ways you could never imagine until there's nothing of you left. You think this place is bad to be locked up in? Lady, you ain't seen nothing."

The receptionist stood for a moment, clenching her jaw before saying, "Alright, fine. Dr. McQueen is in the North Wing."

"Thanks, bitch," Hannah said, already walking away.

"Don't go anywhere," I told the receptionist. "You'll be coming with us for further questioning after we arrest your boss."

"You're disgusting, you know that?" the receptionist said as I walked away.

"This place is disgusting."

HANNAH AND I WALKED TO THE NORTH WING OF THE asylum, ignoring the nurses, most of whom had the same look of scorn on their faces as the receptionist, though one or two seemed pleased to see us as if we there to rescue them. The guard we spoke to last time was standing by the locked door that led to the North Wing. He folded his arms across his broad chest when he saw us coming, as though he had no intention of letting us go any further.

"I can't let you—" he began, but I cut him off.

"Save it, big guy," I said. "We have a warrant this time, and unless you want to get yourself arrested, I suggest you take your keycard and open this door."

The guard stared at me for a second as he debated what to do before sighing and using his keycard to open the door, which swished across, releasing an unpleasant smell as it did so.

"Jesus," I said, reeling back slightly. "Did someone shit themselves?"

The guard smiled as if it was funny. "Some of them do."

Shaking my head, I went through the entry and into the North Wing, but as I did, the door immediately closed behind me, leaving Hannah and the guard on the other side. Hannah ordered the guard to open the door again, but when the guard tried to use his keycard, it didn't work. After a minute of trying, Hannah shook her head and held up her hands.

"You go on," she shouted through the glass. "I'll see about getting this door open."

Thinking it strange that the door should suddenly close

like that, I turned around and made my way into the North Wing, the place where all the experimental therapies are carried out, apparently. As I moved down a dimly lit corridor with grubby walls and rows of iron doors on either side, I was reminded of the solitary wing of a prison, except for the Perspex windows in some of the walls that allowed me to see inside a few of the locked rooms.

The first room I came across held a wretchedly under-nourished man wearing nothing but a pair of grubby white underpants. With his wild eyes and erratic movements, you'd swear he was tripping on something. His eyes widened to where they almost bulged from their sockets when he saw me standing looking through the window at him. Running to the window, he put his face against the thick Perspex and started licking it like some dog who hadn't had water in days. When his hand went down his underpants, I thought it was time to move along.

Lights flickered overhead, adding to the creepy atmosphere of the place. It was also freezing, and on some parts of the ceiling, icicles hung. On the walls, the damp had turned to frost.

"Hello?" I called out, my freezing breath pluming out in front of me. "Krystal McQueen? This is FBI Special Agent Ethan Drake. If you're here, I need to ask you some questions."

My announcement got no reply as I carried on walking, stopping to stare through one of the windows at an adolescent girl strapped to a table in the center of her small cell. Directly above her, attached to the ceiling, was a TV screen, but because of the angle, I couldn't see what was being shown on the screen. Through the glass, I could hear faint screams of anguish, so fuck knows what the girl was being forced to watch.

Shaking my head, I turned away from the window and then froze when I spotted someone standing just outside a room at the very end of the corridor. A tall nurse in a white uniform, though it was difficult to make out her face in the dim light. I sensed she was smiling, though, as she turned and walked into the room beside her before I could even say anything.

Creepy bitch.

I took out my sidearm and made my way to the room the nurse had gone into.

"Hello?" I called out as I approached.

The nurse didn't answer.

Holding my gun out, I stepped quickly in front of the doorway and pointed my gun into the room. The nurse was in there with her back to me, staring at something hanging on the wall. A mirror, the glass of which appeared to be black, though there seemed to be images swirling around in it.

"Who are you?" I asked the nurse as I stepped inside the room, which was even colder than out in the corridor. Ice and frost covered every surface, and in the center of the compact room was an old bed with filthy, bloodstained sheets.

Well, this isn't creepy or anything. Not at all.

The nurse turned around slowly and stared at me. Despite her grubby, bloodstained uniform, I couldn't deny her striking beauty. Her blonde, almost white hair framed a delicately featured face with the brightest blue eyes I'd ever seen. Her pale skin seemed to glow, covered as it was with tiny ice crystals, and when she smiled, there was no warmth in it. Her smile was one of the most chilling I'd ever seen.

"Hello, Ethan," she said in a deep, throaty voice that sounded highly educated and upper class, from another era, almost. "I've been expecting you."

As I stared at the woman, I realized she was no nurse. It was Krystal McQueen, the woman I was looking for. The woman I had come to arrest.

I kept my gun trained on her as I said, "Krystal McQueen, I presume?"

"How do you like my asylum?" she said.

"It's not your asylum, though, is it? It's Dr. Mathers' asylum. You just took it over when you killed her years ago."

"I see you've done your homework," she said just as small snowflakes fell all around her, appearing from nowhere. "Yes, I killed Evelyn a long time ago. She deserved it after everything she did to me. In this very room, in fact. Would you like to see?"

I shook my head. "Not really."

The Snow Queen stood aside anyway so I could look upon the Black Mirror, which was oval-shaped and held in a gilded frame. Why it was hanging in the room in the first place, I didn't know. But as soon as I stared into it, I found myself unable to take my eyes off of it.

"Look," McQueen said in an almost soothing voice that made me want to lower my gun, but I resisted and continued to point it at her. "Look into the mirror, Ethan. Look at what they did to me."

As I gazed into the Black Mirror, I was soon treated to a series of moving images that showed a young Krystal McQueen in the room we were now in. For the most part, she was strapped down on a table, surrounded by doctors and nurses that appeared to do indescribably horrible things to her—filling her full of drugs, screaming at her, lobotomizing her, electrocuting her, even making her take part in demonic rituals, summoning demons that came to fornicate with her, all to the delight of a dark-haired woman in a white doctor's coat that I recognized as Evelyn Mathers.

"They tortured me for years," McQueen said. "All in the name of therapy."

"How...how did you survive?" I asked her as the horror continued to unfold within the mirror.

"Sheer will. After that, my Affliction kept me from dying

and from aging. I was one of the first to be afflicted, you know."

It took all of my will to stop looking at the Black Mirror. When I finally wrestled my gaze from it, I turned to the side so I could no longer see it.

"What is this mirror?" I asked her. "Why do you have it in here?"

"It's a Black Mirror," she said, looking upon it with some ambivalence, as if the mirror was both a source of strength and monumental pain. "It does many things, but most of all, it shows us who we really are."

"So who are you then?"

"I am one of the Afflicted, and the one who will soon show everyone else in this city who they really are."

"What are you talking about?"

"Why don't you lower your gun and I'll tell you."

"I'm good, thanks." But as I said it, the gun suddenly became so cold that I could no longer hold it. As it fell from my hands, it shattered into pieces on the stone floor. "What the hell?"

"I told you to lower it."

Feeling somewhat powerless now without my gun, I moved a few steps away from her, knowing she could probably freeze me solid in seconds if she wanted to.

"What's your game?" I asked her. "What do you have against the so-called Afflicted that would make you start an organization just to eradicate them, to make them feel so low that they end up trying to kill themselves?"

"The answer to that is more complicated than you will ever know, but I will give you the short answer," she said, catching a large snowflake in her palm. "The world is full of hate. It is hate that drives us all, and our self-loathing that keeps us from seeing the truth."

"Which is?" I asked, wondering when Hannah would get here.

McQueen stared at me with her cold blue eyes, a stare that almost froze me on the inside. "That none of us deserve to live."

"Well, that's bullshit."

"Is it? I've seen you in my mirror, Ethan. I know what kind of man you are. I know the pain that you've endured. After your daughter was taken from you, so was your will to live. You hold the deep-seated belief that you don't deserve to live any longer, don't you?"

I stared back at her, saying nothing, uncomfortable under her hard stare that appeared to see right through me.

"It's okay," she went on as the snowflake in her hand inexplicably turned black. "Eventually, you will admit the truth to yourself, just like everyone else, and then you can take the appropriate action."

"Kill myself, you mean? Why haven't you?"

"It's my purpose to get everyone else to admit the truth first."

"Everyone?"

"Starting with the people in this city."

"What are you talking about?"

"I'm talking about a plan that has already been set in motion. A plan that cannot be stopped."

The frown on my face deepened. "What plan?"

"The virus," she said, coming closer, the cold coming off of her making me shiver.

"What about it?" I asked, still not understanding.

"I created the virus right here in this institution, which over half the city has in their bloodstream now."

"But why? It just makes people sick. It does nothing else."

"Not yet. But when all those people are vaccinated, as is happening right now as we speak, the vaccine will react with the virus, and the people shall finally see the truth. They shall see the depth of their own hatred and self-loathing, and they won't be able to stand it. They will turn on each other, and then they will eventually turn on themselves."

I shook my head at her. "You're fucking insane."

Anger flashed across her face as she suddenly came forward and planted her hand on my chest, instantly transferring her supernatural coldness into me. "I...am not...*insane*," she snarled as she kept her hand on me, and I somehow could not move away from her. "Everyone else is!"

"Stop—" I said as I tried to move her arm away, but I was so weak with cold that I could hardly move.

"Don't worry," she said as she finally took her hand from my chest. "I won't kill you, Ethan. I want you to see the truth for yourself."

"Get away from him!"

Hannah stood in the doorway now, her gun aimed at McQueen. Behind Hannah, the two SWAT guys pushed past her and pointed their automatic weapons at McQueen, who merely stepped back with her hands up.

"I'll come quietly," McQueen said. "I have seen my plan through now, anyway."

"Cuff her," Hannah told the SWAT guys, who moved toward McQueen.

"Be careful," I told them. "She has powers."

Even though she could have probably frozen the two SWAT guys in an instant, McQueen allowed herself to be handcuffed and taken out of the room, smiling to herself as they moved her along. "The truth is coming for you, Ethan," she said before they pushed her out the door. "Are you ready for it?"

"What the hell is she talking about?" Hannah asked me.

"She..created the...virus," I said, still shivering violently.

Hannah put her gun away and then wrapped her arms around me, and as quickly as McQueen had filled me with coldness, Hannah radiated her warmth into me, slowly thawing my insides. "Is that better?"

"Yeah," I said. "Thanks."

"What did she do to you?"

"It doesn't matter," I said, taking out my phone. "I need to talk to Bradley so I can get him to stop the vaccination program before people start killing each other."

"Oh. I think it might be too late for that."

I paused with the phone halfway to my ear. "What?"

"The other agents said there are reports coming in over the radio about mass violent attacks on the streets."

"It has started."

"What has started?"

"The killings," I said, looking at her. "Killings we're too late to stop."

"Let's get out of this place," Hannah said. "We can go back to the office, and you can explain what's happening on the way."

"Okay. We need to take the mirror, though."

Hannah frowned. "What mirror?"

"The mirror that's—" I turned and looked at the wall, but the mirror was gone.

"Ethan? Are you okay?"

"Not really," I said, shaking my head in confusion. "Let's just get the fuck out of this place before we go as insane as everyone else in here."

27

"At least now we know why everyone was acting so strangely earlier," Hannah said when we were inside the car. The other agents had already left, taking Krystal McQueen with them as they headed back to the SAD building.

"Yeah," I said, lighting up a cigarette. "That crazy bitch planned and executed this whole pandemic just so everyone ended up as hateful as she is. What the fuck is wrong with some people? They can't just kill themselves, can they? No, they have to make everyone else's life a fucking misery instead."

"Sound like anyone you know?"

At first, I thought it was Hannah who said it, but after a second, I realized she hadn't spoken. The voice came from the back.

Turning around, I saw Angela sitting there in the back seat.

"Oh, for fuck's sake," I breathed.

"Miss me, Ethan?" Angela said, smiling.

"Ethan?" Hannah said, staring at me before looking toward the back. "Is he—"

"She," I said, turning back around. "Angela is sitting back there."

"You don't sound pleased to see me, Ethan," Angela said.

"I'm not," I said, continuing to smoke my cigarette.

"What's she saying?" Hannah asked.

"Nothing worth repeating."

Angela leaned forward to look at me. "That was unsporting of Solomon to give you that amulet," she said. "And to think we used to work together."

"I know who you are, Cane, so you might as well just stop pretending to be Angela."

"Solomon filled you in then, did he? Nice of him. Not that I expected any loyalty from him, anyway."

"No honor among Spreaks, eh?"

"I wish you wouldn't use such derogatory terms as Spreak. I hated it at Blackstar, and I still hate it."

"Okay, how about I just call you asshole instead? Would that suit better?"

"Call me whatever you want," Cane said, having dropped the facade. No longer looking like Angela, he was back to being the tall, shadowy figure he was when he messed with my head in the European Borough. Despite the daylight inside the car, his entire face was a mass of shifting shadow, which freaked me out more than when he looked like my dead ex-wife. "It hardly matters."

"Asshole it is then. So what do you want, asshole? I got shit to do, so I hope you haven't come just to taunt me again."

"Not exactly. I'm here to arrange a proper meeting with you—face to face."

"What for? You're sitting here now, aren't you?"

"Not really. I'm just in your head at this moment. I would like a physical meeting with you."

"Why? So you can kill me?"

"I've never had any intention of killing you, Ethan. If I was going to kill you, I'd've done it by now. No, what I'd like is for us to come face to face properly. It's the only way I can show you what I have to show you."

"Show me what?"

Even among all the shadows, I sensed his smile. "I don't want to spoil the surprise."

I shook my head as I glanced at Hannah. "He says he has a surprise for me."

"Doesn't sound good," she said, glancing toward the back as if she could see Cane for herself.

"Meet me at midnight at your former home in Crown Point. It's still empty, I believe. No one wants to live in a house in which two people were so brutally murdered, do they?"

I spun around and glared at his eyeless face. "You son of a bitch. Why there?"

"I just think it's appropriate, considering the surprise I have for you."

"Fuck you. I'm not playing your games any longer, Cane. I'll hunt you down, and then I'll kill you."

"Will you now? I'm not easy to kill, you know. Didn't Solomon tell you that? Where is Solomon, by the way? A little birdie told me he met with an unfortunate accident in Hell of all places." He chuckled to himself.

"Are you saying you had something to do with what happened to Solomon?"

"He shouldn't have tried to help you."

"What did you do?"

"I infiltrated his sanctum and found out he was planning to go to Hell to steal an artifact. I merely informed the demon he was going to steal from."

"You set him up."

"Precisely."

"Jesus."

"What?" Hannah asked.

"He set Solomon up. It's his fault Solomon got nabbed."

"Solomon is a big boy," Cane said. "He can look after himself."

"In Hell? I doubt it."

"You loathe him. What do you care?"

I said nothing as I sighed and turned away from him.

"Is he still here?" Hannah asked.

"Yeah."

"Meet me tonight," Cane said. "And afterward, you will never have to see me again. If you don't meet me, then I promise to haunt you for the rest of your life, until you inevitably *take* your own life. It's up to you, though I think we both know what your decision will be."

When he vanished from the car, I sat for a moment staring out the window before lighting up another cigarette.

"He wants me to meet him tonight at Crown Point," I said to Hannah.

"Your old house?"

"Yeah. He says he has a surprise for me. Fuck knows what it is."

"Are you going?"

I nodded. "I have to. If I don't, he'll never leave me alone."

"I thought we were going to kill him."

"You mean *try* to kill him? At least this way, we don't have to take the risk."

"It's a risk I don't mind taking if it gets you free of this asshole."

Reaching across, I took her hand. "I know, and I appreciate it, but this way is better. We have no real idea what this guy is capable of. He made sure Solomon never made it out of Hell, for Christ's sake."

"I can't believe he did that."

"I'll meet with him tonight and go along with his little game, whatever it is, and then it'll all be over."

Hannah didn't seem convinced. "And what about finding out why he's doing this? And who he's doing it for?"

"I'll try to get it out of him tonight," I said. "If he doesn't tell me anything, I'll find out myself one way or another." I paused as I took a drag of my cigarette. "Maybe you were right."

"About what?"

"About Knightsbridge. Maybe it's time to think about bringing him down."

"So you believe he's behind this, what Cane is doing?"

"I don't know, but I know he's behind a heap of other shit, including fucking up our employment prospects, not to mention infiltrating the government at the highest level, putting this country in god knows what kind of danger. Somebody has to stop him."

"You mean, you do."

"I mean us," I said, squeezing her hand. "There's no one I trust more."

Hannah smiled as her eyes teared up a little. "Partners?"

I nodded. "Partners."

THE DRIVE BACK TO THE SAD BUILDING TOOK A LOT longer than it should have because the city had now fallen into complete chaos. Those who had the virus had rushed out to get vaccinated against it, amounting to thousands of people, and now all those people had become infected once more by Krystal McQueen's cold hatred, turning their minds dark, and their uncontrollable urges violent.

Every street we drove down had people scattered all over, most of whom were lashing out violently at whoever was nearest them. Often, the person nearest to them was themselves, and as Hannah and I watched in horror, people set about hurting themselves in the most gruesome of ways as they wailed in despair.

Driving past, we saw a woman slit her own throat with a shard of glass from a broken window and then drop to her knees, crying as blood jetted from her opened throat. We saw a man dive off the roof of a car and impale himself on a spiked iron fence. We saw kids fight each other to the death, and those left standing turn on the adults afterward. All around, people were committing suicide by jumping off of buildings, their bodies smashing on parked cars, sometimes landing on other people. It was total carnage, and the streets were quickly filling up with blood.

"I've seen nothing like this," I said as I struggled to navigate the hellish streets, sometimes having to knock people out of the way when they dived in front of the car.

"I have," Hannah said. "In Hell. The damned souls often turn on each other like this."

"What the fuck are we supposed to do about this?" I asked as I swerved around a group of people busy tearing each other apart in the middle of the street, while beside them, an old lady murdered her cat with a kitchen knife.

Hannah shook her head. "I'm not sure there's anything we can do."

"The entire city will burn at this rate."

And speaking of burning, people were running around on fire, having doused themselves with gasoline so they could set themselves ablaze. Running and screaming, the burning people crashed through shop windows before collapsing, the flames spreading into the properties, setting the buildings on fire.

As I continued to drive, people threw things at the car, smashing the side windows. Others dived onto the hood and tried to smash the windshield with their fists until I could shake them off. Those that refused to let go soon did when I held my gun out the window and fired past them, which was enough to scare the joyriders off.

Soon, the sound of gunfire echoed off the surrounding buildings as bullets inevitably flew. As one guy stepped out into the street and sprayed the car with an AK-47, Hannah and I quickly lowered our heads as I hit the gas pedal and run the gunman over, somersaulting him over the roof of the car.

"Jesus," I said, none too happy about what I had to do. "It's like fucking Mad Max here. Not to mention the car. It's destroyed. We'll be lucky to make it to where we're going," I added as smoke streamed from the engine.

Luckily, we weren't far away from where we were going, and the car held out until we made it to Special Affairs. Once I cut the engine, I knew the car would never start again. One more thing of Cal's I'd managed to get destroyed.

The SAD building had been put on full lockdown, with all ground floor doors and windows covered by steel shutters. We had to wait a few minutes as the chorus of chaos rose in pitch all around us, with constant screaming and intermittent explosions the norm now. Those were innocent people out there, and their screams of pain and fear didn't sit well with me. The population had been touched by evil on a mass scale, on my watch, and I wasn't happy about that. Not at all.

"Hurry!" Bradley shouted when he came to open the door. An angry mob had rounded the corner and were charging down the street toward us, but we made it inside just in time, and Bradley slammed the door shut, bringing down the steel shutters a second later by pressing a button inside. Outside, the mob banged on the shutters with their fists as they roared their rage and hatred.

"Fucking hell," I said, glad to be inside so I didn't have

to listen to the city destroying itself any longer. "It's bad out there."

Bradley looked like he was beyond caring. No longer the impeccably dressed man he usually was, he stood in a sweat-stained shirt open to the chest, with a growth of beard on his haggard face. He also stank of whiskey, making me realize I needed a drink.

"No offense, sir," Hannah said, taking him in. "But you look like shit."

Bradley shook his head as he walked over to the reception desk, where a bottle of Jim Beam sat. "Thank you, Agent Walker. I'm well aware."

"Where are the other agents?" I asked him. "The ones with us at the asylum?"

"I don't know," Bradley said before swigging Jim Beam from the bottle.

"What do you mean, you don't know?" I said, a trace of anger in my voice now, pissed off that Bradley didn't have his shit together. "This is your department. You *should* fucking know."

"Well, I don't, alright!" he snapped. "They haven't radioed in, and they haven't showed up here either."

"So they're still out there with McQueen?"

"I would say so. It doesn't matter, anyway."

"The fuck it doesn't matter," I said, stomping over and snatching the bottle from him. "That crazy bitch is responsible for what's going on out there. You do know that, right?"

Bradley glared at me and snatched the bottle back. "I didn't know that. Not that it matters."

"Of course it fucking matters."

"No, it doesn't," he said. "It's all out of my hands now."

"What do you mean?"

"I mean, I'm no longer in charge here. No one is.

Special Affairs is no more. Disbanded. Broken up. Flushed down the fucking toilet like a piece of shit."

"If that's the case," Hannah said. "Who is going to stop what's happening out there?"

"I believe it's Blackstar's responsibility now. The great savior of humanity."

"Fucking Blackstar," I snarled. "What are *they* gonna do?"

"You would have a better idea than I would, Ethan. You used to work for them."

"So Knightsbridge is running the show now?"

"Yes, Ethan," Bradley said bitterly. "Fucking Knightsbridge is running the goddamn show now. You might as well go home and let them take care of this."

"Take care of it how?"

"I believe they are rallying troops at this moment."

"To do what? Fucking kill everybody?"

"Please, Ethan," he said. "Stop asking me questions I don't know the answer to. If anyone should know their modus operandi, it's you."

Shaking my head, I snatched the bottle from him again, about to take a drink when someone outside banged on the shutters, screaming to be let in. Checking the CCTV screens behind the reception desk, I saw it was the two SWAT guys who were with us at the asylum earlier, and they still had Krystal McQueen with them.

"I'll be damned," I said, then shouted to Hannah to open the shutters, allowing the two SWAT guys inside along with the still cuffed Krystal McQueen.

"Where are the others?" I asked the SWAT guys, ignoring McQueen for the moment.

"Dead," the taller of the two SWAT guys said. "Our car got attacked on the way here. We had to take the last two blocks on foot."

Glancing at Bradley, I saw him close his eyes and shake his head when he heard three agents had died.

"It's quite the show out there," McQueen said, smiling coldly. "Better than I could've hoped."

Bradley stomped over to her. "You're responsible for all this chaos?" he asked.

"Indeed I am," McQueen said before Bradley slapped her hard across the face, causing everyone else to freeze in surprise for a second.

Bradley then took his sidearm out and aimed it at McQueen's head.

"Wait, sir," I said. "Don't."

"Why not?" Bradley said. "This woman has caused untold death and destruction. She deserves to be executed like a dog."

"Go ahead," McQueen said, showing no fear whatsoever. "You might be surprised at the result when you pull that trigger."

"The result will be your brains blowing out the back of your head," Bradley said.

"Sir, we may still need her," I said. "She might know how to stop what's happening."

McQueen balked at the idea. "There is no stopping what I've put in motion. It will only stop when all the infected are dead."

"You evil bitch," Bradley said through gritted teeth, and then to everyone's surprise, he squeezed the trigger on the gun and shot McQueen in the head.

But the bullet didn't penetrate. Instead, it ricocheted off of her and hit Bradley in the face, putting a groove in his right cheek. Screaming, Bradley dropped the gun and clamped his hands over his face as blood seeped through his fingers.

McQueen laughed like a maniac. "I said you wouldn't

like the result, didn't I? A property of ice is that it deflects bullets."

Hannah ran to Bradley to make sure he was alright. Despite all the blood, it appeared to be just a flesh wound on his face.

"Come on, sir," Hannah said. "Let's get you cleaned up."

"Lock that bitch up!" Bradley bawled. "Now!"

"Yes, sir," the SWAT guys said.

"What's your game here?" I asked McQueen before they took away her. "You could've escaped by now. Why haven't you?"

McQueen smiled like I was too dumb to see what was going on. "The game is not over yet."

"What fucking game?" I said.

Her smile widened. "You'll see."

28

With something as big and as widespread as mass chaos on the streets of the city, the mainstream media could hardly ignore what was going on. Inside Bradley's office, we switched between the various TV news channels, all of which were reporting on riots in the streets, beaming out footage taken from helicopters that hovered above the heads of the throngs of violent citizens below. The media were already putting out that the people who received the vaccine had had an unforeseen reaction to it that turned them violent. The government was telling those not afflicted to stay indoors, which most were, even though many were being attacked in their own homes. The death toll was already sky-high.

But not to worry because the government's new specially equipped action force, created just to handle such dire circumstances, had now been deployed, and the government promised everyone that this highly trained force—dubbed the Blackstars—would soon bring the city under control by whatever means necessary.

"Jesus Christ," I said. "The fucking Blackstars. You've got to be kidding me."

"Knightsbridge is in control now," Bradley said as he sat at his desk while Hannah prepared to heal the wound on his cheek by placing her hand over it. "This is just the start. How long will it be before Knightsbridge's goons take over law enforcement entirely?"

"I doubt it will go that far," I said. "They'll stick to dealing with the Occult Underground and leave the ordinary crime to the existing authorities."

Bradley zoned out for a moment as white light glowed under Hannah's hand. It was like he was experiencing a minor orgasm that made him half-close his eyes, causing me to smile slightly. When Hannah took her hand away, saying she was done, Bradley looked almost disappointed. But surprise and gratitude registered on his face when he felt his cheek and realized his bullet wound was gone.

"Amazing," he said. "Thank you, Hannah."

"You're welcome," Hannah said, smiling.

Bradley turned to me again. "You don't see the conspiracy here?"

"What conspiracy?"

"Knightsbridge is clearly making a play for control of the shadow government," he said. "He's used their own tactic of the Hegelian Dialectic against them—create a problem, in this case the virus and a faulty vaccine; have the public react to it as they call for a solution; and then step in with a solution to the problem he created in the first place. The solution being the Blackstars and the new vaccine. Problem-Reaction-Solution. It's classic manipulation."

"To what end?"

"That's the million-dollar question, isn't it?" Bradley said.

It was disturbing to think Knightsbridge could end up with control over the shadow government, though I always assumed he had influence over it anyway, just from a distance. Was he not content with subtle influence anymore? Did he now want to dominate the global elite and take control of, not just the Occult Underground, but the entire world?

I wouldn't have put it past him, but it seemed like a bold move even for Knightsbridge. There were those in the global elite who wouldn't take kindly to someone like Knightsbridge taking control of the ship, and they would no doubt try to stop him. Though, stop him how I didn't know. I mean, he'd got this far, hadn't he? And I of all people knew just what kind of power Knightsbridge had at his fingertips. Enough to overthrow anyone who stood in his way.

Excusing myself, I left the room, stepping out into the hallway, where I phoned Eric Pike. If anyone knew what was happening, it would be him. Though maybe not, given that he was just a grunt, albeit a higher-up one.

"Yeah?" Pike said when he answered, sounding like he was in the middle of something. I had no doubt he was out in the streets, leading the charge at Knightsbridge's behest.

"Pike, it's Drake," I said. "What the fuck is going on?"

"Ethan, I can't really talk right now. We got violent citizens to take care of."

"Take care of how?"

"You know I can't tell you that. We have it under control, though, don't worry. This shit'll be sorted out in a couple days."

"Are you in charge of this bullshit action force, the Blackstars?"

Pike laughed like he knew it was all a joke. "You know it, brother."

"What the fuck is Knightsbridge up to, Pike? Why is he doing this?"

"Doing what?"

"Taking over like this."

"Hold on." Gunfire sounded, followed by screaming, and then more sustained gunfire.

"Pike?"

"I gotta go, Ethan. Shit is going down here. You might want to stay indoors for a while. Later, bro."

"Pike? Pike? Fuck."

Putting my phone away, I lit up a cigarette, and then took the phone out of my pocket again, just as a security alert flashed on the screen. Tapping into the relevant camera, I soon saw that Haedemus had triggered the security system at the back of the yard. My eyes widened as I saw him busily having sex with a much smaller mare that he must've lured to the yard. As he bucked the poor mare wildly, he also bit down on the horse's neck, drawing much blood.

"Jesus fucking Christ," I said, shaking my head. "I can't watch this shit. 'Yeah, Ethan, I've changed, I promise.' Fucking bullshit."

I exited from the app and called Daisy, who answered straight away.

"Ethan, are you alright?" she asked, sounding worried. "Shit is crazy out there."

"I know," I said. "I'm fine. Is everything okay there?"

"Yeah, we're all locked up here."

"No one's tried to get in?"

"A few crazies have. The Hellbastards scared them off."

"How did Haedemus get a mare into the yard? Did you know about it?"

"A mare? No, I didn't know. What's he doing with a mare?"

"Don't ask."

"Eww."

"Yeah. Listen, just stay vigilant, and if there are any problems, call me. Alright?"

"Sure, I will. Be careful, Ethan."

"You too, Daisy."

With little else to do until I had to meet with Cane, I headed to the holding room to have a little chat with Krystal McQueen. As she was the cause of the chaos outside on the streets, I figured it wouldn't be a leap to say that she was in league with Knightsbridge. Knightsbridge had a habit of conscripting powered individuals like McQueen into his schemes. They were just another resource to be used to him, so maybe McQueen was one of those resources.

When I got to the holding cell, the two SWAT guys were sitting outside in the hallway smoking cigarettes, their guns leaning against the wall beside them. They made no move to get up when they saw me coming, and directed my attention to the holding cell door, which was covered in a thick layer of ice. The reinforced window was also frosted over.

"The bitch has sealed herself in," one SWAT guy said.

"She's a cold motherfucker," said the other.

"Literally."

They both smiled and continued to smoke their cigarettes, probably glad they were safe inside the building instead of stuck outside among all the chaos.

Shaking my head at the SWAT guys, I went to the door and banged on it with my fist.

"McQueen?" I shouted. "It's Agent Drake. You mind letting me in? I wanna talk to you."

Nothing happened for a moment, and then the layer of ice sealing the door receded in a way that it shouldn't have been able to. The control she had over the ice was amazing, and under different circumstances, I might've been impressed. For now, I was just impatient to get inside as I turned the handle and pushed on the door, which opened and allowed me to enter the room.

The holding room was freezing. A layer of frost covered everything, including McQueen herself as she sat on a chair by the table, her hands no longer cuffed. She stared at me as I walked into the room and said nothing as I tried not to be too affected by the subzero temperature in the room. When I sat down, I casually took out my cigarettes and lit one up, blowing out smoke that was thick in the frigid air. I sat for a moment, making no move to talk to her yet, acting like I was in no hurry, which I wasn't.

"One thing I don't get," I said eventually, trying not to shiver in the cold. "Why do you wear a nurse's uniform if you're a doctor?"

McQueen smiled as she sat with her hands clasped on the table, a picture of calm. "Because I like it," she said. "It turns me on. Does it turn you on, Ethan?"

I shook my head like she was being ridiculous. "The bloodstains are a little off-putting if you ask me. It makes you look like a maniac, which we both know you are, anyway."

Her eyes narrowed for a second as if she was going to jump to anger, but she didn't. Instead, she maintained her composure. "I suppose it takes one to know one. You exhibit many maniacal traits as well, you know. Or doesn't your blinding insight extend toward yourself?"

"I don't make people kill each other."

"No, you just do the killing yourself. You like to get your hands bloody, don't you, Ethan?" Her head tilted to the side for a second. "Why do you think that is? Was it all the violence you witnessed as a child?"

I toked on my cigarette, keeping my expression blank. "You seem to know a lot about me. You wanna tell me why that is?"

McQueen smiled as snowflakes drifted languidly around her. Once again, I got the distinct impression that she was waiting for something, and that she was merely here to kill time. Realistically, she could probably escape any time she wanted to. She could've easily resisted arrest back at the asylum and fled. But she didn't, and instead, she was sitting here talking to me. Why was that?

"I have counseled many patients who experienced violent trauma in childhood," she said, ignoring my question as she kept her icy eyes on me. "Most grow up to become adults who struggle with feelings of low self-worth and challenges with emotional regulation. Are you plagued by flashbacks and nightmares, Ethan? I can tell you are persistently hypervigilant, irritable, and aggressive. You also engage in risky or destructive behaviors much of the time, don't you? Is that why you became a soldier who hunted beings greater than yourself? Is that why you then went into law enforcement?"

Shifting uncomfortably in my seat, I dropped the rest of my cigarette on the icy floor and ground it underfoot. "I didn't come in here so you could head shrink me."

"You've never been to therapy before, have you?"

"Nope, and I don't plan on starting."

"Perhaps you should." She paused. "You lost your wife and daughter not too long ago. How has that affected you? I imagine your mania has become exacerbated, often to the extreme. Have you ever considered suicide, Ethan? Of course you have." She stared hard at me, her eyes searching. "I wonder why you haven't done it yet. Is it because you seek justice for your wife and daughter? Will you avenge their deaths and then blow your brains out after?"

I wanted to scream at her to shut the fuck up, but that would've played right into her cold hands. So instead, I took a deep breath and did my best to remain composed, reminding myself of what a crazy bitch she really was, doctor or not.

"Have *you* ever considered suicide?" I asked her. "If you have so much hate in you, for yourself and for the world, then why have you stuck around all these years? Why go to the trouble of organizing the Mirrorists, and brainwashing other therapists into spreading your hatred?" I paused to let her answer, but she merely stared back at me. "You must get some perverse pleasure from what you do."

"And you'd know all about that, wouldn't you, Ethan?" she said, smiling coldly.

"Maybe it's your only pleasure, knowing you helped some poor soul kill themselves," I said, as if she never spoke. "Most of the Afflicted, as you call them, are good people. They didn't ask to be changed in the way that they have. You of all people should understand that, as you're one yourself."

"I understand, alright," she said, a note of bitterness in her voice now. "I understand that I'm nothing but a blight on society, a worthless being who can't even call themselves human anymore. The only worth I have left is in making others like me see for themselves that there is no place for them in this world. Surely you don't believe the Afflicted have any worth? If you did, you wouldn't be helping to apprehend them and lock them up."

"We only lock away the ones who can't control themselves, so they don't hurt others. What else are we supposed to do with them?"

She stared at me for a second, then said, "And what about little Daisy?"

"What?"

McQueen smiled. "You're surprised I know about her? I know what she is. The mirror showed me."

"Your mirror was wrong."

"I don't think so. The spirit of Joan of Arc has been awakened in her, just as the spirit of the infamous Snow Queen has been awakened in me. It's only a matter of time before she hurts innocent people, you know. What will you do then? Will you have her locked up with all the others? I doubt you will. You see her as your daughter, don't you, Ethan? But let's be honest here. We both know she's just a means for you to ease your guilt over the death of your real daughter. Isn't that right?"

"You're wrong."

"Am I?" She shook her head her cynically. "You know, Ethan, therapy doesn't work if you aren't willing to be honest with yourself."

"We're not in therapy," I said, glaring at her.

"Then why did you come in here?"

"I want to know what your connection to Wendell Knightsbridge is."

"Wendell who?"

"Don't play dumb with me. You know who I'm talking about. You expect me to believe it's a coincidence that Blackstar is out there dealing with the mess that you created? That they just happened to be waiting in the wings in case something like this happened?"

"I only roll the snowballs," she said. "What happens after I throw them is out of my hands."

"That's cute," I said. "What about what you said earlier? That the game wasn't over yet. What game were you referring to?"

"If I told you, it wouldn't be a game anymore, would it? Let's just say that this particular game has reinvigorated my desire to go on living."

I looked away from her as she was making little sense, and if she *was* working with Knightsbridge in some capacity, she wasn't saying. With no interest in talking to her any longer, I stood up as if to go.

"You're leaving so soon?" she said, smiling like she didn't care. "I was hoping we could get further into your past, Ethan. We haven't even mentioned the little boy you accidentally shot in the head."

My nostrils flared as I glared at her, balling my fist as if I wanted to punch her in the face. It was tempting to do so, but I held back, partly because I didn't want to give her the satisfaction, and partly because I was afraid of what she might do if I did hit her.

"Whatever path you think you're on, it will come to an abrupt end soon enough. You'll either destroy yourself, or Knightsbridge will destroy you. Either way, your game is up."

As I walked away, she said, "I could say the same about you, Ethan. You have no idea of what lies ahead for you."

I stopped and turned around. "And you do?"

"I just know you'll find out soon."

"Stay here in your freezer," I said as I opened the door. "It's where you belong."

29

With little else to do, I spent the next several hours inside the SAD building—former SAD now—with Hannah and Bradley as we watched the chaos unfold on TV, and through the windows as we looked out onto the street below. The mainstream media were showing continuous footage of the city as buildings burned, explosions went off, bullets flew, and people did their best to kill each other. The look on their faces was one of pure hate, and frequently, the news footage had to cut away because the violence was too extreme. One or two channels kept their cameras rolling, however, showing people as they literally ripped each other apart in a violent rage, or battered each other to near-death with their fists. All over the city, people were committing suicide, taking swan dives off buildings, shooting themselves in the head, cutting their own throats, even hanging themselves from street lamps.

"Is this what Hell looks like?" Bradley asked Hannah wearily.

"Parts of it," she said like she didn't want to talk about it. "You want me to show you?"

"No, thanks."

Around 10 p.m., the Blackstars rolled into the street below in their heavily armored trucks, some of which had devices attached to the roof. I'd seen these devices before. They were Directed Energy Weapons that fired concentrated radio and microwaves. As we had already seen on the news, the Blackstars were using the DEWs to subdue the crowd. Outside, the armored trucks blocked off each end of the street, sealing in the demented citizens. If any of the crowd tried to attack the Blackstars, the Blackstars would shoot them with rubber bullets that were enough to stop most. Tear gas was also used to slow the crazy citizens down even more. Anyone who persisted with their attacks after that was shot with real bullets. Watching through the window, it seemed like many people *wanted* to be shot dead as they ran at the Blackstars with looks of pure rage on their faces, not afraid of dying, welcoming death with open arms.

Once the Blackstars had sealed the street and subdued the crowd, they turned on the DEWs. After the weapon had been switched on, it was like watching dominos fall as the previously violent crowd fell to the ground and stopped moving, fully incapacitated by the energy weapons. There was no doubt the DEWs were effective, rendering most people unconscious.

With the crowd down, the Blackstars then went around administering a counter-vaccine to everyone, which would return the once violent citizens back to normal, apparently.

An anchorman on TV commented, "I know I speak for us all when I say that we are very grateful for the Blackstars in this unprecedented situation. All those guys deserve medals."

Bradley shook his head as he stared out the window to the street below, half-drunk at this stage. "And of course, they just happened to have the vaccine ready to go, didn't they?"

"Knightsbridge is putting himself across as the savior," I

said. "The President and the country will realize how much they need Blackstar now. You can fully expect other false flag operations like this to happen across the country, even the world."

"And Blackstar will always be there to save everybody," Bradley said, walking away from the window and sitting down again.

"What will you do now?" I asked him.

"Retire, as I'll be forced to do, no doubt."

"You don't seem happy about it."

"Of course I'm not happy about it. Would you be?"

"No, sir."

"It's not like I have much else to do. This job was my life."

"Maybe we can all start our own agency," Hannah said. "Like a private investigation company?"

Bradley raised his eyebrows for a second as he thought about it. "I suppose there are worse options."

"Well, you could always just drink yourself to death, sir," Hannah said dryly, making me smile.

"I suppose you have a point." He looked at me. "Ethan, is this idea something you'd be on board with?"

My mind was on Cane, so I just nodded. "Sure. Why not?"

"We *do* work well together, don't we?" Bradley said, his mood seeming to improve at the prospect of having a future now.

"Think on it, sir," Hannah said.

"I will," Bradley said. "But only if you stop calling me sir. I'm not your boss anymore. Raymond will do just fine."

"Okay, Raymond," Hannah said, smiling, seeming happy herself that this suggested partnership might come to fruition. It's what she always wanted anyway, deep down, for me and her to work together in a private capacity with no superiors to answer to. It seems she didn't mind adding

Bradley into the equation now as well. Neither did I. Bradley was a good man, and he knew how to organize things. If we were to set up on our own, we would definitely need someone like Bradley to steer the ship and take care of the business side of things. If it was left to just me, the ship would no doubt run aground in no time, or sink beneath the waves.

"What name would we use?" Bradley mused as he poured himself another whiskey. "Bradley, Drake and Walker Investigations, perhaps?"

"All-Seeing Eye Investigations?" Hannah said.

"Nice." Bradley looked at me. "Ethan? Any suggestions?"

I shook my head, too distracted to think about it. "I don't know. Damage Inc.?"

Bradley stared at me. "It doesn't exactly put across the right tone, does it?"

"I tell you what," I said, moving away from the window. "You two keep spitballing. I have to go."

"Oh, right," Bradley said. I'd already filled him in on what was happening with Cane. He couldn't believe I'd been dealing with it all this time when I told him. "Be careful, Ethan. Don't do anything foolish."

I nodded and walked out of the room, with Hannah walking beside me.

"I still think I should go with you," she said. "It's too dangerous."

Stopping, I put my hands on her shoulders. "I'm going to do this Cane's way. Anything else is too risky."

"And what if he's lying just to get you there, so he can… kill you?" Her eyes seemed wet. "I can't lose you, Ethan."

I kissed her on the forehead. "You won't, I promise."

She did her best to smile. "If you need me, just call. I can fly straight there. In fact, maybe I should stay nearby, just in case—"

"No. I have to do this alone. This is between me and Cane. No one else."

"That's stupid."

"It is what it is. Stay with Bradley. I'll come back here when I'm done."

As I walked away, Hannah said, "Ethan?"

"Yeah?" I said, turning around.

She stared at me for a second, her eyes still wet. "I love you," she said.

I stared back at her. "And you."

I KNEW IT WOULD BE A JOB TRYING TO DRIVE A CAR THROUGH the city, given everything that was going on, so a while ago, I contacted Scroteface and told him to tell Haedemus to meet me outside the SAD building. When I went outside, Haedemus was already there waiting. The street had been cleared by this point, the Blackstars having moved on to another area, though some people were still wandering around as if they'd just woken up from a dream. A very bloody dream.

"Ethan," Haedemus said excitedly. "What is all this craziness? There is food lying everywhere."

"You mean bodies?" I said, hoisting myself up onto him.

"Food, yes. I couldn't help myself on the way here. I stole a few tasty morsels. In fact—" He stopped and let out a loud fart, the stink of which nearly made me gag.

"Jesus, Haedemus. That's fucking gross."

"It's the liver I ate. It always makes me stink. Here, have some more." He swished his tail up and down to waft the stench further around me and then laughed at my reaction.

"Get moving, you filthy beast," I said, banging my legs into his side as I held the reins, forcing him to gallop away.

"And speaking of filth, I saw you fucking that mare earlier today."

"What?" He sounded surprised. "How?"

"The security cameras."

"You dirty bugger. Were you spying on me? Indulging in a spot of voyeurism, were you?"

"No, you just tripped the alert system."

"Actually," he said as I steered him around a corner. "You may have just given me a brilliant idea, Ethan."

"I don't wanna hear it."

"Why not? It's a magnificent idea. Where are we going, by the way?"

"Crown Point."

"Oh. Anyway, my idea…"

I sighed. "What is it?"

"Porn."

"Porn?"

"Porn. I could star in my own porn films."

"Most people can't see you. Have you thought of that?"

"Damn. That's okay. We can market to all the others who can see me."

"We?"

"Yes, well, I'll need help in filming the footage, and then distributing it. Perhaps your friends could help with that side of things. Artemis and the other one."

"Pan Demic."

"Yes, that's the one. The one who smells like semen all the time."

"Semen? I never noticed."

"He does. But anyway, we need to think of my porn star name. Any suggestions?"

"Filthy Beast?" I offered as we rode past a group of people who were busy beating each other to death with their fists.

"No, Ethan, not that. Too crude. I was thinking more along the lines of Wild Stallion or Haedemus Hell Cock."

"Your real name already makes you sound like a pornstar."

"Haedemus Sassoon? You think so?"

"Definitely."

The next street we turned into was full of burning cars, which Haedemus leaped over without hardly breaking stride before we came across the Blackstars, who were busy sealing off the next street, so I steered away from them, breaking east before heading back north again.

"I would have to write a wonderful script," Haedemus said when we were back on course again, still taken with the idea of being the first ever Hellicorn pornstar. "Something meaty with lots of drama and excitement. Even a touch of poignancy. What do you think, Ethan?"

"I think you'd be making a damn porn movie, not trying to win an Oscar."

"Nonsense. We still need a good script. In Hell, people used to talk about their favorite porno movies, and their favorites were always the ones that were proper films, with storylines and everything."

"Okay," I said, happy to indulge him for now as it was taking my mind off the fact that I might be heading to my doom. "What story did you have in mind?"

"Picture this," he said as we galloped through suburban North Elmview toward Crown Point, even the 'burbs a hothouse of frenzied violence and bloodshed, with houses burning and people screaming, and all the while the news helicopters hovered overhead, broadcasting every second of it from a safe distance. "We open in a gorgeous meadow, the wind causing the long grass and wildflowers to sway ever so gently. You know, like that scene in *Gladiator*."

"Where did you see *Gladiator*?"

"I watch TV with the Hellbastards sometimes. Anyway,

the camera moves through the field toward a majestic oak tree in the center, and underneath it stands Haedemus Sassoon in all his decadent glory as he looks out over the meadow at the stunning mares in the next field. We sense his sadness and pent up frustration, and we soon see that this great steed has been tethered to the tree by some cruel person or other. As Haedemus gazes longingly at the mares, the mares gaze longingly back, their pretty eyes full of lust, for they want nothing else but to have Haedemus' majestic cock deep inside their dripping wet cunts."

"Dripping wet?"

"It's porn, Ethan. Anyway, the camera zooms in on our hero's mesmerizing ruby eyes, and we follow his gaze to somewhere else, to a man who has entered the field. Haedemus' nemesis, the one who has cruelly tethered him to the tree, and who looks a lot like you, Ethan, with his cold, dark eyes, and his air of menace—"

"I do not have cold, dark eyes," I said as we neared Crown Point, riding alongside the river now.

"Yes, you do, Ethan."

"Whatever. Don't expect me to be in your stupid movie."

"It's not stupid, and who else will play my nemesis, the one I must overcome in order to win my freedom so I can finally make it to the field of patiently waiting mares?"

"Wise up."

"You're so selfish, Ethan," Haedemus said. "This could be my one true calling, and you're already fucking it up for me. Honestly, Ethan, it's like you don't care about my well-being at all."

I shook my head, wondering what I ever did to deserve a talking Hellicorn. "Alright, you big baby, I'll be in your stupid film."

"Awesome. I'll give you some good lines, Ethan, though not as good as mine obviously. You could say lines like,

'You're never getting outta this damn field, you filthy beast.' That would elicit sympathy from the audience because they will clearly see what a magnificent beast I really am, and obviously not the filthy beast that you say I am. And I could say lines like, 'You can tether me, but you'll never break me.' Or how about, 'This field is only big enough for one of us, and it ain't you.' Or even, 'There's only one animal in this field, and it's not me.'"

I couldn't help but laugh. "You're insane, you know that?"

"A fucking genius is what I am, Ethan, and as you said that with love, I won't take offense." He let out an energetic whinny. "Damn, I'm excited. This is better than coke. It makes me hard just thinking about it."

"I hope not."

"Maybe just a little."

Soon, we reached Crown Point and the house I used to share with Angela and Callie. The street was empty and eerily quiet compared to everywhere else we had passed on the way. The sounds of frenzied violence still reigned in the background, but the street seemed oblivious to it, as if it existed in its own bubble of reality, making me wonder if Cane had made it that way.

"Where are we?" Haedemus asked as I drew him to a stop.

"Somewhere I used to live," I said.

"Very nice. I can't really picture you living around here, Ethan. It's very…upmarket for you."

"It was. This is where my wife and daughter died, in that house right there."

"Oh, I'm sorry, Ethan."

"So am I," I said, getting down off him. "Wait here for me, alright?"

"Of course. What are you going to do in there?"

"It doesn't matter." I came around the front and looked

him in the eyes. "If I don't come back out again, tell Hannah and Daisy that I love them."

"What? Ethan, what is this? You're not going to die, are you? What about our film?"

I patted his snout, rubbing his coarse black hair. "You're a good buddy, Haedemus."

As I walked away, Haedemus called after me. But I didn't answer him as I opened the already unlocked front door of the house and walked inside.

3 0

A s ever when I walked inside the house, the familiar surroundings and lingering smells elicited a burst of memories that hit me all at once, overwhelming me to the point where I had to lean one hand against the wall for a moment until the memories receded, and the accompanying emotions along with them. Right then, I vowed that if I ever walked out of this place again, I would never return to it. It was just too damn painful, and every time I came back, it was like reliving the night that Callie and Angela died all over again.

Taking a few deep breaths to compose myself, I walked down the hallway and into the living room, my gaze, as usual, automatically falling on the bloodstained floor, my mind showing me unwanted images of Angela, bleeding out and mewling like a wounded animal.

Looking around, I saw no sign of Heinrick Cane. Perhaps he was upstairs, or maybe he was invisibly watching me from somewhere like the creepy Spreak that he was.

"Cane?" I called out, my voice loud in the house's silence.

If Cane was here, he didn't answer. As the front door

had been unlocked, I figured he had to be here somewhere, unless he had just popped out for something. Down the shop for a candy bar, maybe? Or a pack of cigarettes?

I shook my head at the absurdity.

"Cane?" I called again. "You here?"

Still no reply.

"Fuck you then," I mumbled as I went into the kitchen, reaching up to the top of one cupboard and feeling around until I found what I was looking for.

A hunting knife.

When I lived here with Angela, I had weapons stashed all over the house. As a cop, I figured I couldn't be too careful, and if anyone ever broke into the house, I would rather have had the weapons to hand if I needed them rather than trying to find one. Looking back, I could see my paranoia got the better of me. Too many drugs, I guess.

In coming here, I hadn't intended to try anything against Cane. I figured there would be no point since thanks to the bastard's carefully cultivated power, he could resist any attempts on his life. That's the impression Solomon gave me, anyway. Slipping the unsheathed hunting knife into the inside pocket of my trench, I decided to test that theory if I got a chance. I had my gun, of course, but I knew from experience that for a Spreak, stopping bullets wasn't too big of a stretch for their power.

"I see you made it."

Startled, I spun around to see a man standing in the doorway. A tall man in a strangely cut black suit, with a waistcoat underneath and an old-fashioned cravat around his neck. Black leather gloves covered his hands, and on his face was a mask that appeared to be made of metal, depicting a skull. The mask only covered his face, leaving his short, steel gray hair exposed. The air of menace coming off of him was palpable, and the dark power he radiated was undeniable. Through the holes in his metal mask—a mask that seemed to be bolted to his forehead—a pair of dark eyes shone with malevolence.

"Jesus," I said. "And I thought Solomon was creepy. You take it to a whole new level, don't you?"

"My appearance unsettles you?" His voice was deep and partially muffled by the mask he wore.

I shook my head as I casually took out my cigarettes and lit one up. "Hope you don't mind if I smoke in my own house. I'd offer you one, but I don't see any holes in that mask. Do you ever take that thing off? Probably not. I mean, it's bolted to your face. Are you disfigured or something? Is that why you cover your face? Or do you just not like people to see what you really look like? Maybe you just think you look cool." I was aware I was rambling, as I tend to do when I'm unnerved. It was difficult, though, not to be unnerved next to Cane as he stood there, more intimidating in the flesh than he was even as a projection in my head. Spreaks have always freaked me out, more so than most other MURKs. There's just something about them that deeply disturbs me. I didn't believe a human should have that much power at their fingertips.

"You are stronger than I gave you credit for," Cane said. Looking at his mask was like looking at some soulless entity, which I guess he was when all was said and done. Despite all of their power, that's all people like Cane and Knightsbridge were—soulless beings with a void inside them filled with nothing but darkness. "Most would have broken by now. Many have, in fact."

"Maybe you've noticed, I'm not your average bear," I said, smoking my cigarette, unconsciously tapping the ash into the palm of my hand, still reluctant to disrespect the house—and Angela—by flicking the ash onto the floor.

"We'll see how much of that strength you maintain after we're done here."

The son of a bitch had me rattled, I'll give him that.

"What are we doing here? You said you had some surprise for me. Is it going to be sick and twisted? If so, I've seen it all at this point. If what you're doing here is trying to rattle me again, you might as well forget it. Nothing about you is real. Everything you do is no more than a game. A game I can't be fucked playing anymore."

"No games," he said. "Not this time."

Turning around, Cane walked into the living room. With his back to me, my hand reached for the knife inside my trench, but for some reason, I paused, suddenly unwilling to take the chance. Or perhaps I just wanted to see what he would do first. Either way, I withdrew my hand from my coat and followed Cane into the living room.

"So, what are we doing here?" I asked him, wishing he would just get on with it now.

Cane started slowly walking around in a circle as I stood near the spot where Angela was killed, still hearing her last breaths inside my head like a creepy background ambiance, as if this whole situation wasn't harrowing enough. "Your wife died in here, yes?"

My jaw clenched. "You know she did. You fucking arranged it. Why?"

"I was acting on behalf of another. Care to guess who?"

My eyes followed him as he walked. "Knightsbridge?"

"Yes," he said. "But you've known that all along, haven't you, Ethan?"

Screwing my eyes shut, my jaw tightened as I exhaled forcefully through my nose.

There it is. The truth. Out in the open at last.

My eyes snapped open as I stared straight ahead, so much anger flowing through me now, I didn't know what to do with it except to stand there and seethe.

"Wendell came to me and asked me to do what I did," Cane said, still strolling around the room, his voice coming from behind me. "As I was in his debt over something, I couldn't say no. He wanted you a broken man, and he said the best way to accomplish that would be to have your wife and daughter killed. You coped with their deaths better than expected, so I was asked to up the ante and get a little more hands-on. By haunting you with the ghosts of your past, I thought I could break your resolve. But as I've already stated, you proved to be stronger than expected."

"Why did Knightsbridge do it?" I demanded, turning to face him. "Why did he have them killed? They were innocent!"

"Precisely," Cane said. "They were both innocent, which was all the more reason to kill them."

"You sick fucking—" I made to go at him, wanting to choke the life from the fucking bastard, but he made some quick and complicated movement with his fingers, and the next thing I knew, I was on my knees, screaming in pain as my head filled up with molten lava. That's how it felt, anyway.

But despite the searing pain, it wasn't enough to keep me down. My boiling rage countered the pain enough that I could suddenly jump up and grab the knife from inside my coat. With a roar, I lunged at Cane and stuck the hunting knife in his chest, burying it to the hilt as I held onto it and glared into his eyes set behind the mask, seeing only my own rage reflected back at me.

"Fucking die, you cunt!" I shouted through gritted teeth, but I knew even as I had plunged the knife in that Cane wouldn't die that easily.

When he punched me on the chest—a small, almost imperceptible movement—I went flying back and landed on the floor, my head cracking on the spot where Angela had died, my blood now adding to the stain already there.

A second or two later, Cane was standing over me, the bloody knife now in his hand. "You obviously didn't listen when I told you I don't die that easily. Do you think I've spent decades collecting power only to let a mere knife wound take it all away from me? For a smart man, that was a dumb move."

I said nothing as I lay on the floor, having used up the one move I had, my head still burning from the inside, my skull leaking blood.

Now I had nothing.

Now I was at Cane's mercy, and he didn't strike me as the merciful type.

"As you refuse to behave," he said, standing over me. "I'll have to make you."

After making another movement with his hands, it wasn't long before a strange sensation came over me, a numbness almost, and then I found myself unable to move a muscle. In seconds, I was flattened out on the floor like a paraplegic who'd just fallen out of bed.

"Don't try to talk," Cane said. "You won't be able to. Keep staring at the ceiling, however. I have such sights to show you."

Okay Pinhead. Fuck you.

As I lay staring upward, the surface of the white ceiling soon changed, shifting almost as if it was now made of water, until gradually, images formed. It was like looking through a shimmering window that gave a first-person view of something flying over a dark and hazy landscape, zooming over great cities and barren, mountainous regions in between.

"I'm sure you are aware of the Void," Cane said, his deep, muffled voice now full of relish. "The Void is where all departed souls go to now in the absence of any Heaven. You may have heard that the Light Bringer closed the gates of the Celestial City, dumping all souls into the Void before He did so. Nice of him, yes?" He chuckled to himself, a deep rumble behind his mask. "No one knows why the Light Bringer betrayed his flock in such a cruel way. After all, the

Void is nothing. He didn't even do people the courtesy of taking away their consciousness. The souls floating aimlessly in the Void are trapped in their own minds, forced to live with their memories, however good or bad, held there as prisoners. There is talk that the Light Bringer is creating an alternative universe for the departed souls to live on in, but such rumors are unreliable, especially when you consider that Hell's gates are still open for business, and souls continue to flood into it."

Through the window on the ceiling, the images continued to race by, and I soon realized that the world on display was not Earth.

It was Hell.

"One thing about the Void," Cane went on, his voice almost hypnotic in tone, "is that it makes the souls there easy pickings for those who know how to grab them. I'll spare you the details on how we did it—no doubt Wendell will explain everything when he gets here—but we were successful in grabbing the souls of your wife and daughter from the Void. Like plucking fruit from a tree, really. It wasn't hard."

Upon hearing that Knightsbridge was coming, I struggled against my paralysis. Hearing that the souls of Angela and Callie had been taken from the Void, I screamed internally.

"Do you care to hazard a guess as to where the souls of your wife and daughter are now, Ethan?" Cane said. "I'm sure you know, just as I'm sure you know the place you are looking at now. Speaking of which, I believe we have arrived. Watch closely, Ethan."

The window on the ceiling now offered a view of some terrible room full of hanging chains and walls adorned with all manner of torture implements, most of which I had never even seen before, and which could only have been designed by a mind so dark and nasty that it beggared belief.

But that wasn't even the worst of it.

Also in the room bathed in blood-red light was a stone slab, and on the slab was a person, hands and feet tied to each corner of the slab. As the "camera" hovered above the terrified person, I saw with utter horror that it was Angela. Despite having seen her image multiple times of late thanks to Cane, this was different. Before, I knew it wasn't really her; it was just someone else pretending to be her. But now, there was no doubt that it was really her, right down to the rose tattoo on her left thigh, and the birthmark under her right breast.

And the screaming.

Oh my god, the screaming.

I'd heard that scream before when Angela was in labor with Callie. Only now it was worse as a hooded figure cut into her abdomen with a multi-pointed blade, eviscerating her in seconds before pulling out her entrails and dumping them on the floor like so much unwanted meat.

ANGELA! NO!

"Look upon your poor wife, Ethan," Cane said. "You did this to her."

NO!

"It's your fault she's on that slab, getting cut to pieces."

NO!

"Can you feel her pain, Ethan? Her utter terror? Just think, Ethan. Right now, she's probably blaming you for this, knowing that she died because of you, knowing that all of her pain and torment are down to you."

NO. STOP THIS...STOP THIS...PLEASE.

"But keep watching, for all is not lost. You are about to see your dear wife get snuffed from existence. It's for the best, I'd say. At least she won't have to think any more about how her husband betrayed her."

A million negative emotions erupted in me as I was forced to watch Angela endure her torture, all that emotion combining into a giant ball of agony that I'd never felt the like of before.

Unable to even blink, I stared up as I watched the hooded figure next to Angela plunge his hands inside her, causing her to scream even more. The figure seemed to root around for a moment before pulling his hands out again, holding in them a sphere of cobalt energy that I knew represented Angela's soul.

The figure then pulled back their hood, revealing a face that I can't even describe because it was so monstrous. An enormous mouth opened, and Angela's soul was dropped inside and swallowed whole.

Angela's body stopped moving on the slab.

"Now poor Angela is truly dead," Cane said with almost mocking sympathy. "That demon just ate her soul. There's no coming back from that, I'm afraid."

Despite my paralysis, a scream could somehow erupt from my mouth, a scream that curdled even my blood.

"Harrowing, I know," Cane said. "But the show isn't over yet. Keep watching."

The view above me switched to something like the inside of a cave, and my blood ran even colder because I knew what was coming next.

"You remember that demon who took your daughter?" Cane said. "That was no illusion. The demon was real, and so was your daughter."

"No..." I managed to say.

"Oh, yes. Your pretty little daughter has been getting ripped apart over and over for quite a while now, as you can see for yourself."

The window into Hell was now focused in on the same demon that had appeared in the European Borough. The demon I thought was an illusion, but wasn't. Hanging from a rope next to him was Callie, the rope bound around her wrists as she hung naked, already covered in blood. As the demon went to work on her, I had no choice but to watch. Tears ran from my eyes. I wanted to be sick, but my body wouldn't let me. Moments later, Callie lay on the cave floor in pieces, only to reassemble again in a spinning dervish of blood and flesh and bone. As she screamed, the demon grabbed her and suspended her once more using the rope.

"Who knows how many times your daughter has 'died,'" Cane said. "Hundreds probably. Rest assured, she feels the agony of her death anew every…single…time."

"Please…stop."

"I'm afraid it isn't up to me," Cane said, now crouched over me, his death mask looking down. "This is between you and Wendell now. I've done my part, paid off my debt." He paused. "It's been fun, Ethan. Perhaps our paths will cross again, but I doubt it. In the meantime, Wendell will be along soon. Don't go anywhere, will you?"

As the window to Hell closed on the ceiling, Cane stood up and walked away without saying another word, leaving me to lie there on the floor, paralyzed, feeling like my insides had been torn out the way that demon had torn out Angela's insides.

Powerless, all I could think about was my little girl, trapped in Hell, and having to die over and over because of me.

For the next while, I lay on the floor, staring at the blank ceiling, my mind still projecting the harrowing images I had seen earlier. Cane was gone, and apparently, Knightsbridge was on his way. For what reason, I didn't know. Probably to gloat and kick me while I was down. Maybe even to finish me. Either way, it seemed pointless to resist anymore. The forces I was up against were just too powerful. I thought I'd been making progress, when really, I was being played this whole time.

By Knightsbridge.

Long runs the fox, Ethan.

"Fuck you, Knightsbridge."

I could speak again, for all the good words would do me. At least when Knightsbridge got here, I could tell him to go fuck himself.

But that won't help Callie, will it?

No, it wouldn't.

Maybe I could strike a deal with Knightsbridge. My life in exchange for returning Callie's soul to the Void. The Void was a nightmare unto itself, but at least it wasn't Hell.

After a moment, I remembered that Haedemus was

probably still outside, waiting for me to come out. I thought about shouting his name, but didn't see the point. He would leave once he saw the cavalry arriving, anyway.

Son of a bitch, I thought. *I shoulda listened to you Cal when you tried to tell me not to get involved with Blackstar. I wouldn't be lying here now waiting to die if I'd listened to you.*

Fuck, I want a cigarette bad.

I was just wondering if Knightsbridge would allow me a smoke before he did whatever he was going to do to me when a noise came from my pocket.

An alert sound on my phone.

A security alert.

I ignored the sound at first, but it kept beeping incessantly until I got annoyed by it, to the point where I started forcing my arm to move just so I could reach the phone and turn the damn thing off. With much willpower and great physical effort, I fought against my paralysis and moved my arm by degrees until I could get my fingers into my pocket and get a light grip on the phone, clasping it just enough to take it out of my pocket and throw it up onto my chest as it continued to beep.

Exhausted by the effort, I lay there for a minute before going to work again, forcing my arm to move and my index finger to tap on the phone. I only wanted the stupid sound to stop, but after tapping the phone and lying there for another moment, I decided I wouldn't be content until I saw what the security alert was about. It was probably the damn Hellbastards fucking around again, but at least I would get a laugh before the death squad arrived.

Again, with great physical exertion, I lifted my head off the floor inch by agonizing inch, and then my shoulders. It was like trying to move after you've been frozen solid for decades. I'd imagine so, anyway. It wasn't easy, but eventually, I could hold the phone up, and my head a little, so I could see what was on the screen.

And when I saw, I gasped with shock and horror.

"No…" I breathed once I saw what was on the phone.

It was the feed from the camera on top of my trailer. It showed Daisy outside the trailer, and she was being held by someone who had a sword to her throat. Someone wearing full samurai battle armor, including a helmet with horns on it.

Not just someone.

Fucking Susumu Yagami.

"What the fuck?" I said, thinking I would never see Yagami again because, you know, I shot the fucker in the chest with a high-powered sniper rifle. I saw him go down and not get back up again. How could he have survived?

It didn't matter how he had survived. The fact was, Yagami was alive and breathing, and he was standing with a sword held to Daisy's throat as he stared directly at the camera, his gaze focused and intense, all but telling me what he would do if I didn't show up at the yard.

Daisy seemed dazed, her eyes pleading for me to save her as she too stared at the camera.

Then, almost as if he knew I was watching, Susumu reached down to his side and took something from his armor, which he held up in his right hand, his left hand still holding the sword to Daisy's throat. Under the yellow glow of the security lights, I saw what it was—a *shuriken*, which Yagami threw at the camera, causing the screen on my phone to gray out.

"Yagami, you motherfucker, if you hurt her…" I said.

There was no way I would allow Yagami to kill Daisy, which he would inevitably do if I didn't show up at the yard. That's what the bastard wanted. He wanted me there so he could kill me, probably in a duel. Otherwise, why go to the trouble of wearing all that armor?

Dropping my head back on the floor, I considered contacting Scroteface to tell him and the others to move on

Yagami. But I decided against that idea when I realized it would be too risky. Not only would Yagami likely slice the Hellbastards to bits, but he might end up doing the same to Daisy, and I couldn't take that chance. Wherever the Hellbastards were, I hoped they stayed away.

It was me Yagami wanted, so it was me he would get.

But I had to get off the damn floor first, preferably before Knightsbridge and his team got here. I'd been lying here for quite a while now, so I didn't expect the Blackstar boss to be too far away. No doubt, the bastard couldn't wait to get here just to gloat.

Filled with a new resolve, I forced myself to move, fighting against the paralysis as I willed my muscles to respond to my demands, which they did after much effort, albeit sluggishly. My limbs felt like they were made of lead, and I screamed with effort as I forced my legs to move, and then my torso and shoulders until I could flip myself over onto my belly, so I was now faced down on the floor. From there, I continued to scream and grunt as I used my arms to push my body up off the floor, cursing the fact that I was so damn big and heavy, all the while keeping Daisy's pleading face in my mind, knowing that if I didn't get to the yard soon that I wouldn't be able to save her.

No way was I going to allow her to die for my mistake.

After what felt like an eternity, I finally forced myself up to my knees. With sweat dripping from my face, I sat for a moment while I prepared myself for the next phase of agonizing effort, which would comprise me getting to my feet and standing up straight.

My legs were still as heavy as lead weights, and my feet might as well have been encased in concrete, so hard were they to move.

But move them I did, roaring with effort as I finally struggled to my feet. Just remaining upright was a job unto itself. My body was so heavy and unresponsive that it wanted to hit the deck again, but I'd be fucked if I would let it.

"Don't dare fail me now, you old bastard," I grunted, lifting one heavy foot at a time as I trudged toward the front door. It took an agonizingly long time, but I finally reached the front door and opened it, maneuvering my heavy ass outside, the cold night air like a slap to the face, which helped to clear my head and invigorate my body a little.

The first thing I did when I stepped outside was to look for Haedemus as I called his name, but he was nowhere to be seen. The street was still quiet, and in the background, the rest of the city still sounded like it was waging war.

"Haedemus?" I called as I moved down the driveway like Frankenstein's Monster. "Where the fuck are you? Haedemus!"

No answer.

Haedemus was gone, that much was obvious. Gone where, I had no idea. Nor did I have time to think about it. I needed transportation, so I headed toward the first car I saw, which was a BMW parked in the next-door neighbor's drive. When I reached the car, the alarm went off when I tried to open the door, and a moment later, a man in his early forties wearing jeans and a T-shirt came out of the house holding a shotgun.

"Get away from my car!" he shouted, pointing the shotgun at me.

"Lower your gun, John," I said. "It's Ethan Drake, your former neighbor."

"What?" John said, seeming relieved that it was me and not some crazy person. Despite being a realtor and a bit of a douche, John and I got on as neighbors when I lived here. "Ethan? What are you doing here?"

"I don't have time to explain. I just need your car."

"My car?" We both knew the car was his pride and joy. "Why?"

"Lives are at stake, John. Just toss me the fucking keys, will ya?"

"Is this a cop thing?"

"It's an FBI thing. Now throw me the keys before I arrest you for obstruction."

"You wouldn't."

"Try me."

John sighed as he held the shotgun in one hand. "You promise not to scratch it?"

Jesus Christ.

"Yeah, John, I promise. The keys. Hurry the fuck up."

"Alright, alright. Gimme a sec." He went inside the house and came out again a few seconds later, walking over and reluctantly handing me the keys. "You look like shit these days, Ethan."

"Thanks, John," I said, awkwardly snatching the keys from him. "You still look the same."

"I still work out every day," he said, patting his flat stomach.

"That's great. Gotta go, John."

"Why are you moving like that? Is something wrong?"

"Go back inside, John. It's dangerous out here. I'll get the car back to you."

"Don't drive her too hard, will you?"

Inside the car now, I said, "I promise I'll be gentle," and then slammed the door closed before starting the engine. Partly because I was in a hurry and partly to annoy John, I spun the wheels on the BMW as I sped out of the drive, almost losing control as I went to turn up the street, my limbs still not responding properly. In the rearview, I saw John still standing in the driveway, his face a picture of worry as if I'd just driven away with his only child.

∼

Driving as fast as I was able to, given my lingering paralysis, I tried to stick to the back streets, staying off the main streets where I knew most people would be. Despite this, many of the backstreets were a hive of chaos and violence, and several times I was forced to slam on the brakes and reverse out of a street because it was blocked by people or burning cars.

As journeys went, it was the most frustrating one I'd ever been on. The whole time, I could only think about Daisy and what Yagami might be doing to her. It occurred to me to call Hannah and let her know what was going on until I realized I'd left my phone back at the house, which perhaps was for the best. The fewer people involved in this, the less chance the situation had of going south. Who knows what Yagami might do to Daisy if I didn't arrive at the yard alone? If it was just me there, Yagami might be more inclined to let Daisy go. Though I remembered his warning that he would kill everybody I knew if I fucked with him. Still, I had a feeling it was just me he wanted for now. At the very least, I could distract him, giving Daisy a chance to escape.

When I got to within a few miles of the yard, the streets seemed to be clearer as if the Blackstars had been through this sector, for which I was glad. It meant I could speed up and gain some ground. The more I drove, the more my body seemed to return to normal, my limbs becoming less heavy and more responsive. Despite this gradual improvement in mobility, I still wasn't anywhere near limber enough to take on Yagami. What I needed was a boost of some sort, a thought which prompted me to remember that my old neighbor John liked to embrace his inner Charlie Sheen every chance he got. He always had a gram or two on hand back when I used to attend his barbecues.

Flipping open the glove compartment, I rummaged

around inside for a moment until I came up trumps, finding a small plastic bag half-filled with white powder.

"Good man yourself, John," I said as I fumbled to open the little plastic bag, pouring the contents onto the back of my hand as I held the steering wheel, and then hoovering the whole lot up my nose in one go.

The huge blast of coke hit me immediately, clearing my head, pumping my body full of much-needed energy, flushing out the residual effects of Cane's working until I felt like myself again.

By the time I reached the yard, my mind and body were pumped, if not exactly ready for action, as I prayed Yagami hadn't done anything to hurt Daisy.

D riving into the yard, I pulled the BMW up outside my trailer, wondering before I even got out why there was no sign of Yagami or Daisy. As I exited the car and looked around me, the yard deathly quiet in the small hours, I couldn't help but doubt myself. In my paralyzed state earlier, was it possible that I had imagined what I saw on the phone? After the mental stress of watching Angela's soul get eaten and Callie get ripped apart, did I end up hallucinating Yagami? He should be dead, after all.

"Daisy?" I shouted, running toward her trailer and opening the door. "Daisy, are you in here?"

But she wasn't. The trailer was empty.

I checked the smithy next, but even as I did, I knew she wouldn't be in there, which she wasn't. Becoming more and more frantic, I began to think that maybe I hadn't been hallucinating. Something was up. I could feel it in the air. Yagami was here somewhere, feeling the need to play hide and seek with me for some reason.

Before I left the smithy, I spotted a Katana lying on top of a long table surrounded by sharpening stones and metal polish. Daisy had obviously made the sword, though it didn't seem to be finished yet. Testing the blade with my finger, though, it felt sharp enough, so I took the sword with me as I walked out of the smithy and stood outside for a minute.

"Yagami?" I shouted. "Enough with the games. Show yourself!"

I waited for a moment, but there was no reply.

Fucker.

I moved back to where my trailer sat, and when I got there, Yagami was standing in the middle of the empty space by the front of the trailer. He had Daisy with him as he held her with one arm firmly around her throat.

"Ethan!" Daisy shouted, or tried to, as Yagami was holding her tight.

Despite knowing he was here, it was still something of a shock to see Yagami standing there, seemingly none the worse for wear after getting shot in the chest just days ago. As I saw in the camera footage, he was dressed in full battle armor, his entire body covered by iron and leather plating that looked both ancient and new at the same time. In the center of his helmet was a gold disc that caught the light of the full moon overhead, a light that also reflected off his dark eyes, which were full of vengeance.

"Let her go, Yagami," I said. "This is between you and me. Let the girl go."

"She fought well," Yagami said. "But she is no match for me. Neither will you be, Drake."

"Let her go, and we'll soon find out," I said, twirling the sword in my hand. "Come on. It's me you want. Let's do this."

With a grunt, Yagami flung Daisy away from him with such force that she slammed into the side of the trailer and banged her head, falling to the ground a second later, unconscious.

"Daisy!" I shouted, then glared at Yagami. "You son of a bitch, you didn't have to hurt her."

"I'll do much more than that after I'm done with you," he said, holding his sword straight out to the side as if he was about to attack me, which he did, running straight at me with great speed despite the heavy armor he wore. With my body still somewhat sluggish, it was all I could do to avoid his attack as I jumped to the side and spun around to face him again, my sword held out now as we circled each other.

"How are you still alive?" I asked him, really wanting to know. "No one could've survived a shot like that."

"I tried to tell you," he said. "You do not understand the power you are dealing with."

"So tell me then."

"Gladly."

He charged at me again, this time bringing his larger sword down toward my head, forcing me to raise my own sword to block his attack, at which point he kicked me in the chest, sending me reeling back until I landed on my ass. Quickly, I scrambled to my feet again as Yagami resumed his circling like a predator stalking his prey.

Going by his kick, he was immensely strong. Putting a guy of my size and strength on my ass that easily was no mean feat. Yagami had gotten a boost from somewhere.

"Let me guess," I said as I circled, my sword held in both hands now. "You woke up one day to find that a strange unknown power had come over you."

Yagami seemed surprised when I said that, so I took advantage and attacked him with a downward cut that he easily avoided, his counter attack drawing his sword across the top of my right arm. It was done so swiftly, I barely realized I'd been cut until I felt the blood run down my arm, making me glad I'd taken all that coke earlier, which did a grand job of numbing the pain.

"Not just any power," Yagami said as we circled again, and my blood dripped from his sword. "None other than the legendary Miyamoto Musashi has awakened in me, the greatest swordsman who ever lived. In this hour of vengeance, he has come to me to give me the strength to defeat my enemies, starting with you, Drake. You do not stand a chance against me. Musashi was undefeated for a reason, as you are about to find out."

When he came at me again, I was ready for him, ducking underneath his downward cut, slashing my sword across his abdomen. But when I faced him again, I saw that my cut had done little damage, and barely put a mark in his heavy armor.

"Submit now, Drake, and I might make your death painless," he said.

"I'm not ready to die yet," I said, thinking of Callie and how much she needed me, or her poor soul at least.

"You don't have a choice!"

He charged this time with the intention of impaling me in the chest, but I jumped back and swiped his sword away with my own. He didn't stop there, though, coming at me again with blow after blow that I only just managed to defend against before his sword penetrated my right shoulder and stayed there as he delighted in twisting the blade before pulling it out with a spray of blood that splattered his armor.

My sword was on the ground at this point, and he could've ended me right then and there with a killing blow if he chose to, but he didn't. Clearly, he didn't want to kill me too quickly, and instead, he stepped back, giving me a chance to grab my sword from off the ground. As I bent to pick it up, I glanced over at where Daisy lay, but saw that she was gone.

Good girl, I thought. *At least you got away.*

The puncture wound in my shoulder was bleeding profusely, but again, the cocaine numbed most of the pain and allowed me to hold the sword up again as I prepared to continue with the fight.

"You know," I said as we circled each other once more. "In all the conversations I had with your father, he never once mentioned you. Why do you think that is, Susumu, eh? You'd think you being his number one son and everything, he'd've at least mentioned you in passing. But no, not a dickie-bird. In fact, I didn't see one single picture of you in his office. Could it be that daddy-dearest was ashamed of number one son? Why would that be? Tell me, Susumu, I'd like to know."

I could see his face darkening, his eyes filling up with anger as he glared at me, which is what I wanted. The more anger he felt, the more inclined he would be to make a mistake. "You have no idea what you are talking about, you ignorant fool," he said. "My father was a great man, and you took his life!"

"He still didn't have much time for you, though, did he? Hannah told me as much."

"What would that bitch know? She was nothing but a junkie whore."

"Yeah, but it was *her* that Daddy Yagami wanted by his side, not you. He would rather have had a demon beside him than his own son. Jeez, Susumu. What does that say about little old you?"

With a roar of rage, Yagami charged at me, his blows sloppier and more frantic than they were before as he let his anger fuel his attack. It was my intention to throw him off balance, which my taunting of him did, allowing me to strike him several times with my sword. If he hadn't have had armor on, my blows would've left him in pieces. But he did have armor on, fortunately for him. Unfortunately for me, however, the armor prevented my sword from doing him any damage. Once I realized this, I drew my sidearm and tried to shoot him in the face where he wasn't protected, but the one shot I got off missed before Yagami used his sword to knock the gun from my hand. As I tried to counter with a downward cut, he blocked the blow and then moved his sword in a circular motion, which had the effect of twisting my sword out of my hand.

Now weaponless, I had the point of Yagami's sword pressing into my chest as I backed away from him. I was at his mercy now, and it would only take a quick thrust to impale and kill me.

"This dance is over now, Drake," Yagami said. "It's time to die like the filthy *gaijin* you are."

"No need to get racist," I said, grabbing the blade of his sword suddenly and angling my body away from its point. At the same time, Yagami drew the sword back, and the blade cut deep into both my hands, eliciting a cry of pain from me.

With my blood running down his sword, Yagami raised it and prepared to bring it down on my neck, but before he could, his own cry of pain left his mouth, and he staggered back away from me to reveal Daisy now standing next to him. She must've snuck up on him in the darkness, for I never even seen her coming either. She had just stabbed Yagami in his armpit with a knife that she left sticking in him.

Once I got over my surprise at seeing her, I thought, *Clever girl. She knows the weaknesses in his armor.*

Daisy had come armed with her own Katana, and she circled around to stand next to me as I quickly picked up my sword from the ground.

"I thought you had left," I said to her. "You *should've* left."

"And leave you to die?" she said, her eyes focused on Yagami. "No way."

With another cry that was more anger than pain,

Yagami ripped the knife from out of his armpit and threw it away.

"I should've cut your throat, you little bitch," Yagami said to Daisy. "Now I'll make sure you suffer along with him."

With admirable boldness, he came at both of us, quickly alternating his blows from me to Daisy, back and forth at blinding speed, making it difficult for the two of us to do anything but defend ourselves.

At some point, Daisy grabbed a handful of dirt from the ground, and the next time Yagami turned to face her, she threw the dirt at him, temporarily blinding him. Taking advantage of this, I struck down on Yagami's sword arm, striking at his wrist to try to get him to drop his sword.

Meanwhile, Daisy scurried around behind him and slashed the back of his knees, a place where his armor didn't quite reach. Yagami cried out as he lost his balance and fell to his knees, slashing blindly at me with his sword, which was enough to keep me at a distance, but did nothing to stop Daisy from grabbing the knife that lay on the ground and using it to cut the straps on Yagami's helmet. He tried to grab her while she was doing it, but she stabbed him in the throat. To prevent him from using his sword from stabbing her back, I continued to chop at his arm, my blade bouncing off his armor, but the blows were enough to keep him distracted, which is all I wanted.

Seconds later, Daisy ripped off Yagami's helmet, exposing his head and neck as blood ran from the stab wound in his throat. Knowing he was now vulnerable, Yagami rolled to the side away from us, coming up onto his feet as he brandished his sword at us once more. He was full of rage by this point, but I could also sense the fear in him. Clearly, he wasn't expecting things to be this hard.

Daisy had regained her sword and ran at Yagami with it, her skill with the Katana taking him by surprise as he moved back defending against her blows, many of which landed on his armor to little effect.

Unwilling to give him a chance to come back at us, I rushed in, only able to hold my sword with one hand now thanks to the immobility in my right shoulder where Yagami had stabbed me.

As Daisy continued to drive Yagami back, I came at him from the side, aiming for his exposed neck.

But Yagami still had some fight left in him, and he quickly turned the tables on us, coming at us with attacks so fierce, it was all we could do to defend ourselves, and I panicked that Daisy would get overwhelmed and fatally cut, which almost happened when Yagami swung his sword at her neck.

But Daisy was fast and light on her feet, and she ducked under the blow just in time before diving and rolling past Yagami, coming up behind him and slashing the back of his knees with her sword once more.

Whatever damage she inflicted on Yagami was enough to bring him down, and he fell forward, forced onto his knees.

Seeing my chance, I went for him.

Running toward him, I dropped to one knee and did a full 360-degree turn to gain momentum before my sword cut into the side of Yagami's neck, slicing right through until his head came away from his body and dropped to the ground. His headless body remained upright for a moment as blood spurted from the stump of his neck, and then fell forward like so much dead meat.

Daisy stood behind the now dead Yakuza, breathing hard.

"Are you alright?" I asked her.

"Are you?" she said, staring at my blood-soaked trench.

Despite the pain, I nodded. "I'll be fine. You did good, Daisy. You probably saved my life."

"Probably?" she said, smiling.

"You did."

"Do you think he'll stay dead this time?"

"He doesn't have a head, so I imagine so."

"We should incinerate his body, just to be sure."

I shook my head at her. "You've nothing to learn, have you?"

"Cal once told me if you wanna make sure someone stays dead, burn the body."

"Sounds like Cal alright."

"We should check that wound of yours before you bleed to death," Daisy said as she came toward me.

I stared up at her. "I can't believe you're the same little girl who used to sit outside her apartment reading books."

"That little girl is dead."

"Yeah," I said. "Sometimes, I wish she wasn't."

Daisy said nothing, and then a noise from behind us made us both turn around. It was Haedemus galloping toward us, with Hannah riding him. As they pulled up, I stood to greet them.

"Ethan," Haedemus said. "I got worried about you being in that house for so long, so I went to get Hannah. When we got back, you weren't there, obviously because you were here, killing someone." He glanced down at Yagami's head. "Is anyone going to eat that?"

"What happened here?" Hannah asked after she got down off Haedemus.

"Yagami wasn't dead, that's what happened," I said.

"We took care of him," Daisy said, a note of pride in her voice as she looked at me.

Hannah shook her head and then threw her arms around me, hugging me tight. "I thought something bad had happened to you," she whispered.

"Something bad *did* happen," I said. "You're hurting my shoulder."

"Sorry. Do you want me to heal it for you?"

"That would be great."

As I stripped off my trench and my shirt, wincing at the pain in my shoulder, I asked if anyone had seen the Hell-bastards.

"I haven't seen them now that you mention it," Daisy said. "Not since earlier when they were messing around out here."

"They're probably out reveling in the chaos," I said.

Hannah placed her hand over my stab wound, and a second later, I felt her soothing celestial energy envelop my wound, healing it instantly. "You said something bad happened," she said. "What happened?"

Not that I wanted to answer her question, but before I could, the sound of multiple vehicles entering the yard filled the night air.

"What the hell is that?" Daisy asked, grabbing her sword once more.

My heart sank as the noisy vehicles got closer. "They're here for me," I said, putting my bloody trench over my naked torso.

"Who is?" Hannah asked, naturally concerned.

"Blackstar," I said as the first of five black SUVs came rolling into the yard. "Or rather, Knightsbridge."

The armored vehicles drove around us, throwing up dust before coming to a halt, closing us into the middle of them. Almost immediately, black-clad soldiers with automatic weapons spilled from each of the vehicles and pointed their guns at us.

"Ethan, what is this?" Hannah asked.

"Everybody relax and don't do anything," I said. "They're here for me. Stand down, and no one will get hurt."

"I will not let them take you, Ethan," Hannah said.

I cradled her shoulders as I looked into her eyes. "It has

to be this way. Take care of Daisy and yourself."

Tears welled up in Hannah's eyes. "What are they going to do to you, Ethan?"

"I don't know yet. They have Callie. They trapped her in Hell. If I go with them, they might free her."

"No, Ethan, you can't trust them."

"I don't have a choice."

From the circle of armed men, a familiar face emerged. "Sorry about this, buddy," Eric Pike said. "I have orders to take you."

I nodded. "I'll come quietly."

"I know you will, brother. And hey, I'm sorry. I'm just doing my job here."

I stared at him, wanting to tell him to go fuck himself, but he was right. He was just doing his job. "Where's Knightsbridge?"

"Right here, Ethan."

Everyone spun around to stare at the man in the three-piece suit and horn-rimmed glasses standing by one of the vehicles. It took everything I had not to run at Knightsbridge so I could wrap my hands around his scrawny neck and throttle the life out of him. But if I did that, everyone here would suffer, me especially. And then there was Callie, though it was difficult to imagine her situation being made any worse than it already was.

"All this because I left your fucking company?" I said, stepping away from Hannah and Daisy.

"Yes," Knightsbridge said. "Although there is a little more to it than that."

"You murdered my fucking family!" I roared at him, unable to help myself as I went to walk toward him, but immediately found myself surrounded by a dozen heavily armed men.

"This is neither the time nor the place to talk about it,"

Knightsbridge said, showing no remorse. "Surrender yourself, Ethan. Now."

It was difficult to contain my rage, but I knew I had to. If I resisted them, Knightsbridge wouldn't hesitate to kill Daisy. And Hannah may have been immortal in the sense that she couldn't die naturally, but she could still be killed, and god knows what killing technology Blackstar had at their disposal nowadays.

"I want your word that this ends with me," I said. "You leave Hannah and Daisy alone."

"Your new family will not be harmed if you come with us now," Knightsbridge said. "But don't test my patience, Ethan. You know how I don't like to have my patience tested. Bad things can happen."

As I went to walk forward, Hannah jumped in front of me. "You're not taking him. I won't let you. I'll kill you all."

"As powerful as you are, Ms. Walker, I very much doubt that," Knightsbridge said. As he stared hard at her, Hannah suddenly clasped her hands to her head and screamed.

"What are you doing to her?" I shouted. "Stop it!"

Knightsbridge smiled as he stopped his psychic attack on Hannah. "I'm merely showing her she's not the most powerful one here. Now, surrender yourself, Ethan. I won't ask again."

The bastard was trying to humiliate me on top of everything else, but I had to comply. After helping Hannah to her feet, I went down on my knees and put my hands behind my head.

"Take him," Knightsbridge ordered, and within seconds, his men proceeded to beat the shit out of me, punching and kicking me before someone shoved the butt of their gun into my face.

The last thing I remember before blacking out was Daisy crying, and Hannah screaming my name.

"Wakey-wakey."

I awoke in a familiar-looking room, strapped to a hardback chair. My wrists were secured to the chair's arms and my head to the chair's back, thanks to a leather strap going around my forehead. My body ached immediately from the beating I had taken earlier, my head especially thanks to the gun butt that had slammed into it.

In front of me, still dressed in her nurse's uniform, was Krystal McQueen. She stood smiling down at me like I was one of her unfortunate patients.

"Hello, Ethan," McQueen said. "It's nice to see you again."

"Where the hell am I?" I groaned.

"Danvers Asylum. The North Wing."

"What? What the hell am I doing here? And why am I strapped to this fucking chair?"

"We like to keep our patients secure here," she said. "So they don't hurt themselves."

"Let me out of here."

"Sorry, Ethan, but it's not my decision, I'm afraid."

"Then whose is it? Knightsbridge's?"

"Yes. I'm sure he'll be along soon. In the meantime, why don't I give you something to keep you awake." She held up a syringe and pressed the plunger with her thumb, ejecting liquid from the needle. "We wouldn't want you nodding off now, would we?"

"Whatever that is, I don't want it."

"You don't get a choice in the matter," she said, sticking the needle in my bare arm and emptying its contents into my veins. Whatever it was, it hit me immediately, like a rush of adrenaline going through my system. "That should keep you going for a while."

"I don't understand," I said. "What's going on here?"

"You'll soon find out." She paused to smile at me. "I should really thank you, Ethan. Working with Wendell has helped me move on, leaving my old life behind. None of it would've been possible without you." She leaned down then and planted her frigid lips on mine, staring into my eyes as she held the kiss for long seconds. When she stopped kissing me, she said, "Perhaps we could get to know each other a little more intimately when the time is right. What do you think, Ethan?"

"I think the time will be right when Hell freezes over, bitch."

McQueen's face filled with anger as she raised her hand to slap me, but before she could, the door opened and in walked Wendell Knightsbridge. "Will you excuse us, Dr. McQueen?" he said.

"Of course," McQueen said, throwing me a last look of contempt. When she moved out of the room, I noticed for the first time, the Black Mirror on the wall in front of me.

"Well, Ethan," Knightsbridge said as he closed the door after McQueen had left. "It's been a long time, hasn't it?"

"Fuck you, Wendell," I said, refusing to look at him.

"You can be angry with me, Ethan. That's fine. But you shouldn't be surprised that any of this has happened.

Everyone who joins Blackstar knows it's a lifetime deal. You knew that more than most, and yet you still came to me and asked to leave. Not only that, you dared to blackmail me." He came to stand in front of me, leaving me no choice but to look at him. "Of course, I knew you were bluffing."

"Why did you let me go then?" I said, my voice sounding deadened to my ears.

"To punish you."

"Punish me?"

"Yes, Ethan. You thought you could get one over on me, despite knowing that no one gets one over me. No one. I was also disappointed. I always made sure you were looked after, Ethan. You were given more privileges than most. Heck, I considered you to be my very best operative, which you were, until you came to me that day and threw it all back in my face."

"I'd had enough," I said. "I wanted a different life. Why can't you understand that?"

"That had nothing to do with it. You signed a contract, and business is business."

"That's what you call killing my wife and daughter? Just business?"

"Of course," he said, staring at me. "Everything is business, Ethan. You never grasped that fact, which is what led to your downfall."

"But you waited so long. You waited until I had a family…"

"Yes, well, I wanted to leave retribution until you had the most to lose, so I waited for a time I could hurt you the most. You remember what I said to you before you left?"

"Long runs the fox."

"Exactly. Plus, it's not all about you, Ethan. I had a lot of other business to attend to over the years." He leaned down, so his eyes were level with mine. "But really, I wanted to maximize your suffering, Ethan. You will now learn all over again that I am not a man to be trifled with, and that I and I alone sit at the top of the pyramid. When you're at the top of the pyramid, you have to stamp hard on anyone who tries to undermine your position. Otherwise, you won't last long up there. No one plays the game like me, Ethan. That's why I've lasted all these years, and why I get more powerful every day."

"So trapping my daughter's soul in Hell, that's just a game to you?" I said, seething now with anger. "Having some fucking demon eat my wife's soul, that's just a fucking game to you?"

"Everything is part of the game," Knightsbridge said. "Another concept you failed to grasp, Ethan, which is why you now find yourself a pawn in a much larger game."

"What are you talking about?"

"I have no intention of explaining everything to you right now, Ethan, except to say that there is a reason I trapped your daughter's soul in Hell."

"What fucking reason?"

"Because I want you to go there, that's why."

I frowned in disbelief, thinking this shit-show couldn't get any worse. "To Hell?"

"Yes."

"What for?"

"To find Lucifer and bring him to me."

I laughed like he was crazy, which he was. "That's insane, even for you, Wendell."

"To you, maybe. But not to me."

"Why the fuck would you want Lucifer brought to you, anyway? More to the point, what makes you think Lucifer would even allow himself to be taken *anywhere*?"

"I have no wish to explain everything now," he said. "The only thing you need to know is, if you don't do as I ask, your little daughter will remain in Hell forever, as will you, Ethan. Complete the mission, however, and I will free your daughter. I'll even let you walk, Ethan. Scot-free."

"You're a fucking devious bastard, Wendell," I said. "I can't believe I used to admire you."

"You know," he said, smiling now. "It's funny you should say that. I am actually much more than I used to be, Ethan."

"More of a dick, you mean?"

A searing pain in my head made me regret calling him that.

"Don't be rude, Ethan. You know how I hate rudeness. Anyway, as I was saying, I have recently evolved into someone…different, but yet the same."

"You look the same to me." *Same dick as always.*

"Do I?" As he stood in front of me, Knightsbridge suddenly transformed in the blink of an eye into something resembling a demon, with red skin and wild dark hair, his eyes a glowing yellow, his hands clawed and leathery.

"What the fuck?" I said, wanting to draw back in horror, but unable to.

"I am Mephistopheles," he said, smiling with pointed teeth. "But you can call me Mephisto."

"Your…a Mytholite?"

"Indeed." He transformed back to his normal self in an instant. "I suppose it was inevitable. Destiny even. I had much in common with Mephisto anyway, even before the Fallen energy transformed me. We have a way of forcing the transformation now. With our method, we can use the Fallen energy to transform almost anyone."

I could only sit and stare dumbly at him, my capacity for further talk having abandoned me. It was all too much, and my brain shut down in the face of it, despite the drugs still raging in my system.

"Anyway," Knightsbridge said. "I'm going to go now. We'll discuss this further in a few days, probably, depending on my timeline. It could be a week. Who knows? In the meantime, why don't you relax and enjoy the show that Dr. McQueen has prepared for you?" He leaned down, so he was level with my face, and smiled. "It was good seeing you again, Ethan. I look forward to us working together once more. Just like old times, eh?"

As I remained silent, Knightsbridge left the room, closing the door behind him. A second later, I heard someone lock it.

The silence in the chilly room was palpable, and my eyes inevitably drifted toward the Black Mirror, which soon shimmered until moving images formed.

A sickening and all too familiar scene.

The Black Mirror was now a window into Hell, and through the window, I saw Callie in that cavernous room along with her tormentor, the demon.

"No," I said. "Please, God, no, not again."

Within the mirror, the demon turned and looked right at me, and then it smiled as if it knew I was watching. It walked toward Callie, who was once again bound with rope and suspended from the ceiling.

As the demon went to work on her, she screamed.

And so did I, like I'd never screamed before.

MAKE A DIFFERENCE

For an indie author like myself, reviews are the most powerful tool I have to bring attention to my books. I don't have the financial muscle of the big traditional publishers, but I can build a group of committed and loyal readers...readers' just like you!

Honest reviews of my books help bring them to the attention of other readers.

If you've enjoyed this book, I would be very grateful if you could spend just five minutes leaving a review (which can be as short as you like) on my book's Amazon page by clicking below.

And if you're still not motivated to leave a review, please also bear in mind that this is how I feed my family. Without reviews, without sales, I don't get to support my wife and darling daughters.

So now that I've shamelessly tugged on your heart strings, here's the link to leave the review:

Review Infernal Justice

Thank you in advance.

TEASER: BLOOD MAGIC (WIZARD'S CREED # 1)

When the magic hit, I was knocked to the floor like I'd taken a hard-right hook to the jaw. The spell was so powerful, it blew through my every defense. For all my wards and the good they did me, I might as well have been a Sleepwalker with no protection at all.

The faint smell of decayed flesh mixed with sulfur hung thick in the air, a sure sign that dark magic had just been used, which in my experience, was never good. Coming across dark magic is a bit like turning up at a children's party to find Beelzebub in attendance, a shit-eating grin on his face as he tied balloon animals for the terrified kids. It's highly disturbing.

I sat dazed on the floor, blinking around me for a moment. My mind was fuzzy and partially frozen, as though I'd awakened from a nightmare. I was inside an abandoned office space, the expansive rectangular room lined with grimy, broken windows that let cold air in to draw me out of my daze. Darkness coated the room, the only real light coming from the moon outside as it beamed its pale, silvery light through the smashed skylights.

I struggled back to my feet and blindly reached for the

pistol inside my dark green trench coat, frowning when I realized the gun wasn't there. Then I remembered it had gone flying out of my hand when the spell had hit. Looking around, I soon located the pistol lying on the floor several feet away, and I lurched over and grabbed it, slightly more secure now that the gun's reassuring weight was back in my hand.

There were disturbing holes in my memory. I recalled confronting someone after tracking them here. But who? I couldn't get a clear image. The person was no more than a shadow figure in my mind. I had no clue as to why I was following this person unknown in the first place. Obviously, they had done something to get on my radar. The question was what, though?

The answer came a few seconds later when my eyes fell upon the dark shape in the middle of the room, and a deep sense of dread filled me; a dread that was both familiar and sickening at the same time, for I knew what I was about to find. Swallowing, I stared hard through the gloom at the human shape lying lifelessly on the debris-covered floor. Over the sharp scent of rats piss and pigeon shit, the heavy, festering stench of blood hit my nostrils without mercy.

When I crossed to the center of the room, my initial fears were confirmed when I saw that it was a dead body lying on the floor. A young woman with her throat slit. Glyphs were carved into the naked flesh of her spread-eagled body, with ropes leading from her wrists and ankles to rusty metal spikes hammered into the floor. I marveled at the force required to drive the nails into the concrete, knowing full well that a hammer had nothing to do with it.

Along the circumference of a magic circle painted around the victim was what looked like blood-drawn glyphs. The sheer detail of them unnerved me as I observed in them a certain quality that could only have come from a well-practiced hand.

I breathed out as I reluctantly took in the callous butchery on display. The dead woman looked to be in her early thirties, though it was difficult to tell because both her eyes were missing; cut out with the knife used to slice her throat, no doubt. I shook my head as I looked around in a vain effort to locate the dead woman's eyeballs.

The woman looked underweight for her size. She was around the same height as me at six feet, but there was very little meat on her bones, as if she was a stranger to regular meals. I also noted the needle marks on her feet, and the bruises around her thighs. This, coupled with how she had been dressed—in a leather mini skirt and short top, both items discarded on the floor nearby—made me almost certain the woman had been a prostitute. A convenient, easy victim for whoever had killed her.

If the symbols carved into her pale flesh were anything to go by, it would seem the woman had been ritually sacrificed. At a guess, I would have said she was an offering to one of the Dimension Lords, which the glyphs seemed to point to. The glyphs themselves weren't only complex, but also carved with surgical precision. The clarity of the symbols against the woman's pale flesh made it possible for me to make out certain ones that I recognized as being signifiers to alternate dimensions, though which dimension exactly, I couldn't be sure, at least not until I had studied the glyphs further. Glyphs such as the ones I was looking at were always uniquely different in some way. No two people drew glyphs the same, with each person etching their own personality into every one, which can often make it hard to work out their precise meanings. One thing I could be certain of was that the glyphs carved into the woman's body resonated only evil intent; an intent so strong, I felt it in my gut, gnawing at me like a parasite seeking access to my insides, as if drawn to my magic power. Not a pleasant feeling, but I was used to it, having been exposed to enough dark magic in my time.

After taking in the scene, I soon came to the conclusion that the woman wasn't the killer's first victim; not by a long stretch, given the precision and clear competency of the work on display.

"Son of a bitch," I said, annoyed. I couldn't recall any details about the case I had so obviously been working on. It was no coincidence that I had ended up where I was, a place that happened to reek of dark magic, and which housed a murder that had occult written all over it. I'd been on the hunt, and I had gotten close to the killer, which was the likeliest reason for the dark magic booby trap I happened to carelessly spring like some bloody rookie.

Whoever the killer was, they wielded powerful magic. A spell that managed to wipe all my memories of the person in question wouldn't have been an easy one to create. And given the depth of power to their magic, it also felt to me like they had channeled it from some other source, most likely from whatever Dimension Lord they were sacrificing people to.

Whatever the case, the killer's spell had worked. Getting back the memories they had stolen from me wouldn't be easy, and that's if I could get them back at all, which I feared might just be the case.

After shaking my head at how messed up the situation was, I froze upon hearing a commanding voice booming in the room like thunder.

"Don't move, motherfucker!"

～

Get your copy of BLOOD MAGIC online today!

～

TEASER: SERPENT SON (GODS AND MONSTERS TRILOGY BOOK 1)

They knew I was back, for someone had been tailing me for the last half hour. As I walked along Lower Ormond Quay with the River Liffey flowing to the right of me, I pretended not to notice my stalker. I'd only just arrived back in Dublin after a stay in London, and I was in no mood for confrontation.

I was picking up on goblin vibes, but I couldn't be sure until I laid eyes on the cretin. The wiry little bastards were sneaky and good at blending in unseen.

As I moved down a deserted side street, hoping my pursuer would follow me, I weighed my options. There were several spells I could use: I could create a doorway in one of the walls next to me and disappear into the building; or I could turn myself into vapor and disappear; or I could even levitate up to the roof of one of the nearby buildings and escape.

Truthfully though, I didn't like using magic in broad daylight, even if there was no one around. Hell, I hardly used magic at all, despite being gifted with a connection to the Void—the source of all magic—just like every other Touched being in the world.

Despite my abilities, though, I was no wizard. I was just a musician who preferred to make magic through playing the guitar; real magic that touched the soul of the listener. Not the often destructive magic generated by the Void.

Still, Void magic could come in handy sometimes, like now as I spun around suddenly and said the word, "*Impedio!*" I felt the power of the Void flow through me as I spoke. But looking down the street, there appeared to be no one there.

Only I knew there was.

I hurried back down the street and then stopped by a dumpster on the side of the road. Crouching behind the dumpster was a small, wiry individual with dark hair and pinched features. He appeared frozen as he glared up at me, thanks to the spell I had used to stop him in his tracks, preventing him from even moving a muscle until I released him.

"Let me guess," I said. "Iolas got wind I was coming back, so he sent you to what...follow me? Maybe kill me, like he had my mother killed?"

Anger threatened to rise in me as blue magic sparked across my hand. Eight words, that's all it would take to kill the frozen goblin in front of me, to shut down his life support system and render him dead in an instant. It would've been so easy to do, but I wasn't a killer...at least not yet.

The goblin strained against the spell I still held him in, hardly able to move a muscle. To an ordinary eye, the goblin appeared mundane, just a small, rakish man in his thirties with thinning hair and dark eyes that appeared to be too big for his face. To my Touched eye, however, I could see the goblin creature for what he was underneath the glamor he used to conceal his true form, which to be honest, wasn't that far away from the mundane form he presented to the world. His eyes were bigger and darker, his mouth wider and full of thin pointed teeth that jutted out at all angles, barely concealed by lips like two strips of thick rubber. His skin was also paler, and his ears large and pointed.

"I don't know what you're talking about," the goblin said when I released him from the spell. He stood up straight, his head barely level with my chest. "I'm just out for a stroll on this fine summer evening, or at least I was before you accosted me like you did..."

I shook my head in disgust. What did I expect anyway, a full rundown of his orders from Iolas? Of course he was going to play dumb because he *was* dumb. He knew nothing, except that he had to follow me and report on my whereabouts. Iolas being the paranoid wanker that he was, would want eyes on me the whole time now that I was back in town. Or at least until he could decide what to do with me.

"All right, asshole," I said as magic crackled in my hand, making the cocky goblin rather nervous, his huge eyes constantly flitting from my face to the magic in my hand. "Before you fuck off out of it, make sure Iolas gets this message, will you? Tell that stuck up elf...tell him..."

The goblin frowned, his dark eyes staring into me. "Go on, tell Iolas what?" He was goading me, the sneaky little shit. "That you're coming for him? That you will kill him for supposedly snuffing out your witch-bitch mother——"

Rage erupted in me, and before the goblin could say another filthy word, I conjured my magic, thrusting my light-filled hand toward him while shouting the words, "*Ignem exquiris!*"

In an instant, a fireball about the size of a baseball exploded from my hand and hit the goblin square in the chest, the force of it slamming him back against the wall, the flames setting his clothes alight.

"*Dholec maach!*" the goblin screamed as he frantically slapped at his clothes to put the flames out.

"What were you saying again?" I cocked my head mockingly at him as if waiting for an answer.

"*Dhon ogaach!*" The goblin tore off his burning jacket and tossed it to the ground, then put out the remaining flames still licking at his linen shirt. The smell of burned fabric and roasted goblin skin now permeated the balmy air surrounding us.

"Yeah? You go fuck yourself as well after you've apologized for insulting my mother."

The goblin snarled at me as he stood quivering with rage and shock. "You won't last a day here, wizard! Iolas will have you fed to the vamps!"

I shot forward and grabbed the goblin by the throat, thrusting him against the wall. "First, I'm a musician, not a wizard, and secondly—" I had to turn my head away for a second, my nostrils assaulted by the atrocious stench of burnt goblin flesh. "Second, I'm not afraid of your elfin boss, or his vamp mates."

Struggling to speak with my hand still around his throat, the goblin said in a strangled voice, "Is that why...you ran away...like a...little bitch?"

I glared at the goblin for another second and then let him go, taking a step back as he slid down the wall. His black eyes were still full of defiance, and I almost admired his tenacity.

"I've listened to enough of your shit, goblin," I said, forcing my anger down. "Turn on your heels and get the hell out of here, before I incinerate you altogether." I held my hand up to show him the flames that danced in my palm, eliciting a fearful look from him. "Go!"

The goblin didn't need to be told twice. He pushed off the wall and scurried down the street, stopping after ten yards to turn around.

"You've signed your own death warrant coming back

here, Chance," he shouted. "Iolas will have your head mounted above his fireplace!" His lips peeled back as he formed a rictus grin, then he turned around and ran, disappearing around the corner a moment later.

"Son of a bitch," I muttered as I stood shaking my head.

Maybe it was a mistake coming back here, I thought.

I should've stayed in London, played gigs every night, maybe headed to Europe or the States, Japan even. Instead, I came back to Ireland to tear open old wounds…and unavoidably, to make new ones.

Shaking my head once more at the way things were going already, I grabbed my guitar and luggage bag and headed toward where I used to live before my life was turned upside down two months ago.

As I walked up the Quay alongside the turgid river, I took a moment to take in my surroundings. It was a balmy summer evening, and the city appeared to be in a laid-back mood as people walked around in their flimsy summer clothes, enjoying the weather, knowing it could revert to dull and overcast at any time, as the Irish weather is apt to do. Despite my earlier reservations, it felt good to be back. While I enjoyed London (as much as I could while mourning the death of my mother), Dublin was my home and always had been. I felt a connection to the land here that I felt nowhere else, and I'd been to plenty of other places around the world.

Still, I hadn't expected Iolas to be on me so soon. He had all but banished me from the city when I accused him of orchestrating my mother's murder. He was no doubt pissed when he heard I was coming back.

Fuck him, I thought as I neared my destination. *If he thinks I will allow him to get away with murder, he's mistaken.*

Just ahead of me was *Chance's Bookstore*—the shop my

mother opened over three decades ago, and which now belonged to me, along with the apartment above it. It was a medium-sized store with dark green wood paneling and a quaint feel to it. It was also one of the oldest remaining independent bookstores in the city, and the only one that dealt with rare occult books. Because of this, the store attracted a lot of Untouched with an interest in all things occult and magical. It also attracted its fair share of Touched, who knew the store as a place to go acquire hard to find books on magic or some aspect of the occult. My mother, before she was killed, had formed contacts all over the world, and there was hardly a book she wasn't able to get her hands on if someone requested it, for a price, of course.

As I stood a moment in front of the shop, my mind awash with painful memories, I glanced at my reflection in the window, seeing a disheveled imposter standing there in need of a shave and a haircut, and probably also a change of clothes, my favorite dark jeans and waistcoat having hardly been off me in two months.

Looking away from my reflection, I opened the door to the shop and stepped inside, locking it behind me again. The smell of old paper and leather surrounded me immediately, soliciting more painful memories as images of my mother flashed through my mind. After closing my eyes for a second, I moved into the shop, every square inch of the place deeply familiar to me, connected to memories that threatened to come at me all at once.

Until they were interrupted that is, by a mass of swirling darkness near the back of the shop, out of which an equally dark figure emerged, two slightly glowing eyes glaring at me.

Then, before I could muster any magic or even say a word of surprise, the darkness surrounding the figure lashed out, hitting me so hard across the face I thought my jaw had broken, and I went reeling back, cursing the gods for having it in for me today.

Welcome home, Corvin, I thought as I stood seeing stars. *Welcome bloody home…*

~

Get your copy of SERPENT SON online today!

BOOKS BY N. P. MARTIN

Ethan Drake Series

INFERNAL JUSTICE
BLOOD SUMMONED
DEATH DEALERS

Gods And Monsters Trilogy

SERPENT SON
DARK SON
RISING SON

Wizard's Creed Series

CRIMSON CROW
BLOOD MAGIC
BLOOD DEBT
BLOOD CULT
BLOOD DEMON

Nephilim Rising Series

BOOKS BY N. P. MARTIN

HUNTER'S LEGACY
DEMON'S LEGACY
HELL'S LEGACY
DEVIL'S LEGACY

ABOUT THE AUTHOR

I'm Neal Martin and I'm a lover of dark fantasy and horror. Writing stories about magic, the occult, monsters and kickass characters has always been my idea of a dream job, and these days, I get to live that dream. I have tried many things in my life (professional martial arts instructor, bouncer, plasterer, salesman…to name a few), but only the writing hat seems to fit. When I'm not writing, I'm spending time with my wife and daughters at our home in Northern Ireland.

Be sure to sign up to my mailing list:
readerlinks.com/l/663790/nl
And say hi on social media…

Printed in Great Britain
by Amazon